Stella

——LILIAN——
ROBERTS FINLAY

Stella

POOLBEG

All characters and events in this novel are entirely fictitious and bear no relation to any real person or actual happening. Any resemblance to real characters or to actual events is entirely accidental.

A Paperback Original
First published 1992 by
Poolbeg,
A Division of Poolbeg Enterprises Ltd
Knocksedan House,
Swords, Co Dublin, Ireland
Reprinted 1993

A catalogue record for this book is available from the British Library.

ISBN 1 85371 194 2

10 9 8 7 6 5 4 3 2

Cover painting by Tom Roche
Set by Richard Parfrey in ITC Stone Serif 10/15
Printed by Cox & Wyman Ltd, Reading, Berks.

For Finola Finlay
who lives in the House by the Lake
in token of love and gratitude

STELLA

Thou Stella wert no longer young
   When first for thee my harp was strung...
In all the habitudes of life
   The friend, the mistress, and the wife...
Variety we still pursue
   In pleasure seek for something new...
But his pursuits are at an end
   Whom Stella chooses for a friend.

Jonathan Swift
Dean of St Patrick's Cathedral
Dublin 1692

CHAPTER ONE

"Congratulations, Sybil!" Her daughter was given to sudden intentions suddenly revealed and Stella tried to put enthusiasm and warmth into her voice as she put down the newspaper and looked up at her. Sybil was tall and slim and boyishly handsome. "Congratulations, darling!"

"I tell my mother that I have become engaged to be married, and she says 'Congratulations' as if I were seven years old and had just won the egg-and-spoon race. You don't even ask to whom I am announcing my engagement."

Stella was afraid to smile and equally afraid not to. She had often thought as Sybil approached thirty that she had all the makings of an eccentric old maid. "Of course I want to know! Of course I want to be the first to share your happiness!" Stella was a maternal and very caring woman; her warmth now was natural.

"You won't be the first," Sybil said shortly. "Daddy knows."

"Oh," Stella continued to smile, "I wondered at the two of you yesterday, incarcerated for hours in the study. So who is the lucky man?" Some fellow-lawyer in Sybil's world, Stella supposed.

"Do you always have to talk in clichés?" Sybil would claim, for herself, that she never minced words. And isn't that another cliché, Stella thought. "I am going to marry Alec," Sybil said, and she watched the effect on her mother.

"Alec!" Stella could not conceal her amazement. For over twenty years, Alec had been part of the family. "I thought Alec was a confirmed...I mean a settled...I thought he was a born bachelor. I mean to say I never thought of..." But Stella had thought of Alec as her special friend. She had come to depend on him, and he was only nine years younger than she was. He had come to their house as a graduate of Dave's. Dave was very proud of his prizewinning graduates. There had been many of them through the years. Alec was one who had never lost touch. In fact, he was Hazel's godfather, and Hazel was twenty-six. Alec must be on the wrong side of forty five by a year or two.

"A born bachelor!" echoed Sybil tartly. "He never said so!"

Yes he did, Stella thought. He often told me that he would steer clear of marriage. He used to laugh and say the single life was the only one for him, provided the supply of pretty girls did not run out. So

Alec had fallen in love at last! And with Sybil? Stella smiled again at Sybil. "Alec is a charming man, darling. But isn't he a good deal older than you?"

"You know our ages, Mother. You can figure it." Sybil had a way of closing the door on any conversation with her mother. She did not bang that door; yet it had the effect of a slap on the face.

Stella avoided confrontation. Questions disturbed the peace. Years ago, she had let go her hold on this daughter who recognised only one parent, her father. It was ironic, since Sybil had become a successful lawyer, that as a little girl she had set up her own court of law in which her daddy was advocate, counsel, and judge. Stella had, long since, coped with being left outside the courtroom which Dave's study had become for Sybil.

Later that evening, Stella sought out Dave in his study. His desk was loaded with papers. He looked up at her a little impatiently, "Yes, my dear?"

"You didn't tell me that we have an engagement in the family?"

"Naturally," he answered, "I told my daughter that she must tell her mother. Naturally." His pen was poised. The subject of who told whom was not important enough to interrupt his work for more than a moment.

"I know you are very busy with end-of-term stuff.

But please, Dave, let's talk a little."

"What is there to say?" But he laid down the pen.

"Are you quite happy about this? About this engagement?"

"Of course!" he answered robustly. "We know Alec. He has known Sybil all her life. He can support her. He will allow her pursue her career—very important to her. I am not over-influenced by his wealth but it has to be a factor."

"But his age, Dave? He is twenty years older than she."

"That might be important if she were a teenager. Sybil is twenty-eight. She knows her own mind."

"She may know her own mind," Stella said slowly, "but she doesn't know many men. She has never knocked around."

"Well, thank the Lord for that." Dave was becoming impatient. "She needs an older man. Indeed, she is accustomed to older men in her peripheral life."

Older men like yourself, Stella thought. She has modelled herself on you. Alec Mackay is an older man but he is not like you in anything. Not like you at all. Though she had become unable to voice her ideas to Dave, Stella made an effort to defend her opinion. "I think the difference in age is very important."

"Not in this case." Dave was decisive. "She will

have a protector. With her nature, that is much more important than a few years of age difference. Sybil is vulnerable. She has come to depend on me a great deal. I shall be passing on my charge to Alec, who was in his time a charge of mine also. A rewarding charge, I must say, one of my most brilliant students. I may say, possibly the most brilliant, judging by his financial successes. One of the top entrepreneurs in the country. I may take a serious pride..."

Stella dared to interrupt the heavily professorial voice. "But, Dave, is that what marriage is about?" Stella wanted to ask about romance and tenderness, and love most of all. Surely those feelings were essential in the beginning, even if they were to fade in the middle years?

Dave took up his pen. "Marriage today may be looked at from a different angle. If you will excuse me, my dear?"

The previous night, Sybil was in his study for hours. What had they talked about?

Stella went out into the garden and took the path into the woods and up to the ruined castle. Here there was an ancient abbey. It was favourite place of Stella's at all times of the year, especially in spring when the chestnut trees were in bloom. It was a haven of contentment. Today, Stella's thoughts were restless. It seemed to be years since she and Dave had had a real conversation. Years and years. Then quickly she defended Dave. This was, after all, the very worst time of the year for a college professor who had a department to run. Dave always needed the long vacation to restore his verve and good humour. Next year he would be retiring. Stella was looking forward to Dave's retirement. She was sure they would enjoy doing things together at last. Maybe walk here in the chestnut woods. Maybe go sailing as they used to before there were too many children. Stella loved sailing. Perhaps even a holiday together to celebrate retirement. Once, when there were only the two little boys, Philip and Ross, Stella's mother had taken them for a month. She and Dave had gone on a walking holiday in Austria. Stella remembered every moment of that holiday. Dave was a real friend then. And their renewed passionate love affair had lasted almost until she told him she was pregnant. Pregnant with Sybil. It was a strange thing to remember now how greatly Dave had resented the pregnancy and the addition to the family. The two boys were enough. And yet, how that so-resented baby had grown to dominate his life! Hazel, the daughter who came afterwards, was a mere accident of nature. By then the once-unwanted Sybil kept all others at bay.

That baby, that little queen of Dave's life, is now about to leave Dave's care at last. Stella could not but wonder would she herself come back into her own, take her rightful place, be needed by Dave, be necessary once more. There will be only the two of us, Stella mused: Philip married to his pleasant Mída, Ross in New York, Hazel with her own flat for several years now. Only the two of us. Will Dave need me as he used to long ago? Is it not more likely that I shall be a golf-widow? A club-widow? Dave won't change. Stella pulled down the shutter of her imagination. Grow up, she told herself, and grow old. You have a good life. You are better off than most women of fifty-five.

From Easter on to the end of June, the preparations for Sybil's wedding took up every moment of Stella's days. When Philip was married to his Mída, the Shanes had none of the hassle. A daughter's wedding is altogether different from a son's wedding, when his future mother-in-law looks after everything. Dave was insistent that the wedding reception would be held in their own home, and it would be a full-dress affair with six bridesmaids and six groomsmen, not to mention flower girls and singers. Stella's family had owned this old house for generations but Dave had never offered to spend big money on renovation. Now a firm of contractors came in to paint all the reception rooms. New covers and curtains were ordered and fitted. The carpets were still of superb quality and they were expertly cleaned. The hedges were trimmed and the garden was tidied. The gravel drive was re-laid. The front gates were re-hung and painted white. For months, the house and garden were full of workers. The phone never stopped ringing. Stella was seldom alone. Alec Mackay, who had always been a tower of strength in emergencies, never came now to the house. There had been an engagement party and then he stopped calling. Sybil and he quite evidently met somewhere else. Stella missed him. On an impulse she rang his apartment.

"Stella!" There was relief in his exclamation.

"Alec, I have missed you. Do you think we could meet and have a little talk?"

"Of course. Where and when?"

"I mean, just the two of us," Stella said, very surprised at her daring. She had not known how much she missed him until that moment. He must have felt the same; he was quick to take up the invitation. "If you could get the country bus into town, I will meet you at Busáras and we will drive out to the Coast Guard Inn for dinner. Would you do that, Stella? I would drop you home afterwards."

She knew Dave would be away overnight on Thursday and Sybil was on country circuit. "Sure," she said. "Would Thursday be a good day for you?"

They had never made arrangements to go off to

dinner on their own. The Coast Guard Inn had been a popular place years ago for family celebrations. Stella had not known it still existed.

"What made you choose this place?" she asked Alec when they were drinking sherry and consulting the menu.

"Oh, I had a reason," he smiled. "What made you ring me?"

"I missed you," Stella answered. "Always, on all those big occasions you have been around to lend a hand."

"I will be there on the day." Alec was not smiling and his voice was serious.

Stella chose to ignore the seriousness, almost the sadness, in his tone. She put out her hand to him. He took it and held it warmly.

"I want to wish you all the happiness in the world," she said. "I want to welcome you into a family where you have always had a special place."

"Thank you, Stella. You know I have always appreciated everything you have done for me since the first day Dave brought me out to the house."

"His top-of-the-class prize-winning graduate!" Stella teased, laughing. Then she added very sincerely, "Dave has always been so proud of your successes." She longed to ask him if he himself were happy now. It was a dicey question for Stella, the mother of his prospective bride. After all, he was not a man in his first youth and he had always been resolute. But was he in love with Sybil? Stella would like to be assured.

"I think I shall have some more sherry," she said. Dave was always telling her to keep off the wine—she was apt to lose the run of herself, he said. Dave felt free to make comical remarks at Stella's expense as if, in his eyes, she had not quite grown up.

She made an effort to chat to Alec very factually, informing him of all the changes in the house in preparation for the wedding. He listened in an agreeable silence. In between the colourful sentences about magnolia paint and drapes of rose velvet, they chose from the menu and were escorted to a table overlooking the harbour.

"This is grand," Stella said. "Isn't this the very table with that very view, where we all celebrated your thirty-fifth birthday? Or was it your first million?" She was teasing to make him laugh.

"We came here long before that," Alec told her. "It was when Dave sold the rights of his book on George Bernard Shaw. Do you remember? The book about the Prefaces?"

Stella remembered. Dave had drunk far too much, plied by his agent and the publisher and the sales people, all of whose names she had forgotten. When they got home, Alec had helped Dave into bed. Then he and Stella had sat in the garden. It was a perfect summer night. "Yes, I remember that night."

"Then let's talk about it," Alec said. "Please let's talk about it. We have never referred to that night but you cannot have forgotten. After June, when I am married to your daughter, we will never be able to talk. The final door will be shut."

Stella was puzzled. "But, Alec, a door was always shut."

"I do not mean to be brutal, Stella, but at the rate Dave drinks, a door has been ajar. Ajar for your escape. If not to me, then at least to escape. But I hoped…to me."

All in his own mind, thought Stella, and never in mine. How to tell a man you are fond of that he was never more than a good companion? Not, long ago when I was in my twenties and certainly not now when we are getting old. "Alec," she said, "I am not very good with the words and my experience is limited, but since we never—what do people say nowadays—since we never went to bed together, surely I never gave you the hope you are talking of?"

"That night, you gave me hope. That night was the night we sat in the garden until the dawn chorus began and we listened to the birds with wonder, don't you remember? You allowed me to make love to you as far as our ethics and our religion would allow us.

A lot of things have changed since then."

What did I allow? Stella wondered how many glasses of wine she'd had that night. Dave was right: she had no head for wine. She had a recollection of talking her heart out, but what about? And now she remembered Alec's spirited response and his warm embrace, although it could be any memory of any night. Surely that close communion of their friendship happened a hundred times in their long and close relationship?

"Didn't we always have long talks and didn't we always hug and kiss?" She hoped he was not offended by her hazy memory.

"Yes, always, but that night was different. You know it was, Stella. You must remember. To do those things with a married woman was an overwhelming happening in my life, and I am sure it was in yours— thirty years ago! I stayed away from the house for weeks, don't you remember? Then I met Dave in the United Service Club and I drove him home. Someone had to; he was way over the top. But I wanted to because I had missed you so much. Our coming back together again was wonderful, you said. You were so excited to see me again, you said. Surely you haven't forgotten?"

Was that what I said, Stella asked herself. I was blind to the effect on him. Best be careful now.

"So long ago, Alec. Now your life has taken on a whole new meaning. I did not even know you and Sybil were seeing each other...seriously, I mean."

"This marriage in June will have grown out of Sybil's need for me. Similar to your need, Stella. In these latter years, I have had to divide myself."

Was Alec always so sententious? Divide himself? And I never even noticed.

"You did it very well," Stella said teasingly. "I have not observed myself being put in second place to anyone!"

Now Alec smiled in the old familiar way. "Until June, your place will still be first. In fact (but don't take this too seriously) if I had to marry one of your daughters, I would prefer it had been Hazel. She is you all over again. When I see her, I see you in the garden with Philip and Ross the first day Dave brought me home from College. Philip was three or four, and Ross was toddling. You were giving them their tea under the trees. You were about twenty-plus then, and I was nineteen."

Stella could easily imagine herself looking up and thinking: Oh God, another undergraduate. There had been scores of them through the years. Graduates, young professors, visiting academics. Many of them housed for weeks on end. Alec Mackay had gone through all those stages and had ended up by being a special friend, often the only friend when Dave had awkward young geniuses who overstayed their welcome, and Dave retreated to his study, leaving Alec to chauffeur the unwanted guest back to town.

"I shall always think of you as my dearest friend, Alec." Stella gave it her best effort at a tender tone.

"I know." He said it so dismally that they both laughed. Then he said, "Stella, I have always wanted to give you pleasure and spare you pain."

"And you have always succeeded. More than that was not destined to be." She hoped that covered her desire to move the conversation on to less personal ground. They finished the dinner amiably but in the car going home Alec came back to the question of his early hopes.

"Stella, even now, tonight, this moment, if I were not engaged to marry Sybil, could you...?"

"Could I what?" She wondered at him. He must have proposed to Sybil. He could have gone on being a tame bachelor, if that was what he wanted.

He stopped the car, pulling over on the country road to let other cars pass. His courage seemed to have ebbed.

"Could I what?" Stella asked again.

"What's the use?" he said. "The very fact that you have to ask the question is a measure of the distance between us. Let it be. I should never have thought that you would remember that night. I staked my life on what happened that night. I waited year after year. I persuaded myself that some miracle would happen. I accumulated wealth to be ready when you would drop into my arms. No, I know you never gave me grounds for hope but I hoped against hope. What happened to the years! Soon Dave will retire, I know he is ten or eleven years older than you, and you will see him as an old man, and knowing you—you will not leave him then, old and finished. Oh, Stella..."

To cover her amazement, and afraid her voice would betray her hurtful incredulity, Stella turned and took him in her arms. She murmured words about the future being all before him and a new world opening up, and how greatly she had always valued and cherished his wonderful friendship. Then she found the car-door lever and she extricated herself from his detaining hands.

"Don't come any further, Alec; it is only a few yards to the gate. Goodnight, my dear one, and take care of yourself."

When Stella was out of the car into the cool air, her instinct was to fly up the road as if from a fiery furnace. She controlled her feet, stepping out purposefully. Closing the hall door, the unbidden thought came to her that for Alec Mackay her main attraction must have been that she was safely married to Dave. He had rested on that fact for years and she had always assumed that he was born to be a simple bachelor. How had Sybil swung him round? And why? Did Dave advise both of them? All three were close. But wouldn't Dave have talked to his wife about such advice? Or would he? Stella wandered into Dave's study en route for bed. She often sat at his desk and read his literature notes. It was the only way she knew of getting close to him, of knowing a little of his mind. Now she remembered a note in the margin of a book:

Any idealization of sexual love, in a society where marriage is purely utilitarian, must begin by being an idealization of adultery.

She pondered on the possible truth of the words. Alec Mackay had left the discipline of English literature for the hard-headed world of commerce; yet he could quite easily have perceived, and believed, that her marriage had become utilitarian, a background to a useful ordinary life. Had he waited in the wings for the last shred of respectability to drop away and his dear Stella to fly into adultery with him?

Stella sat in Dave's chair, her fingers idly turning over the papers on his desk. Alec was wrong if he had such thoughts. Her marriage was her fortress. Even in the bare essentials that remained, it was her fortress. Breaching those walls had not happened with a tipsy groping in the back garden. No matter how cool Dave's ardour had become, she had been his. Simply and matter-of-factly his.

Alec Mackay had a problem: he was about to enter a fortress which also belonged to Dave. Dave's influence over Sybil would be long lasting. Only to her father had Sybil ever been open, responsive, malleable. What sudden change was this? Whose decision was it that Sybil could leave her beloved father and enter into a union with a man almost as old as her mother? Alec had revealed his unwillingness. And Sybil's insistence. And Dave had expressed his overwhelming acceptance. Why would Dave be so willing to give Sybil to Alec...Sybil who had given him love and companionship more and more as the years went on? More and more to the exclusion of everyone else.

Stella assured herself that often during her lifetime she had heard the expressions: "Daddy's girl"; "her mother's daughter"; "his father's son" and others like that. It was natural. Such children could not all have problems in their marriages. Or could they? She would try to talk to Dave again. On the other hand, Sybil would get married some time, she supposed. But not to Alec—somehow that did not seem right. Surely

Dave would agree with her about this.

Dave was never available for long discussions. The marriage went ahead.

CHAPTER TWO

The year-long honeymoon spent travelling in the Far East was over. The married couple had resumed their busy careers and settled in their luxurious home on the far side of the city. Dave was now retired. Because of all the work done on the house and garden for the wedding, there were now no small jobs waiting for a retired man. He felt free to devote himself to his favourite pursuits: active golf, the camaraderie of the golf club, and the armchair perusal of all sport on his new television set. His latest extravagance had been a very expensive aerial overtopping the tall trees. Tennis, cricket, snooker, golf, rugby, were all available on the Box in season. His study was seldom entered; the ideas for another book on Shaw had been shelved. When he went to his club, frequently enough, he usually took dinner there with other retired cronies who, unlike him, had no one at home waiting. As he said to Hazel one day, "I fill my life."

"So long as you leave me at the bus, Dad." Hazel laughed at his important voice. "I want to leave my car here while I am in the West."

"Whenever you are ready, Hazel," was Dave's courteous answer.

"You may not realise it, Dave," Stella's voice was not quarrelsome, "but this is the fifth day in this week that you are going to play golf."

Stella caught Hazel's eyes signalling: Mum, don't start the golf-widow bit again. He could decide to hit the roof and I need that lift to the bus—please!

Dave had his own way of dealing with challenges to his freedom. "Oh, come, my dear, I will merely drop into the club when I have left Hazel to the bus. Fifth day! Not at all. You are mistaken. That was a delicious lunch, my dear!"

Stella knew it was the fifth day in this week and last week and every other week. She opened her mouth to argue. She had promised herself so many things they would do together the very moment he retired. That was nearly six months ago. Why argue? The man was golf-crazy. Had been for years. What use now to make a row. And that meaningless "my dear." She wished he would speak her name once in a while. "My dear" was cold and distancing.

Hazel stood up and took hold of the knapsack for her field trip. There was relief in her eyes that her mother had stayed serene. "I will ring you, Mum, about the car. Hardly before this day week. After the actual trip—the—er—debate goes on a few days—

you know how it is!"

Now Dave stood up. "You dedicated young professors have to compare notes," he jeered.

"You should know, Dad," she jeered back. "You did these junkets with your students in your day." She hugged her mum as she headed out to her dad's car.

At the door, Dave turned to Stella. "That was a lovely meal, my dear. You must be the best cook in the world! See you later—oh, by the way, if Sybil phones, be sure to write down their new phone number."

Stella watched the car disappear down the tree-lined drive. The partings-with-kisses never happened now. Stella missed the kisses. She missed a lot of the things other couples seemed to share. Dave, she knew, was of the generation that believed a woman was truly, and totally, fulfilled by the domestic scene of children, cooking and cleaning. He had not noticed that the scene had shifted into a non-laborious duet. A man's life, in Dave's philosophy, was his career: at first the building of it and then the colleagues who entered the completed edifice.

Stella longed for the day when that edifice would collapse like a house of cards and Dave would be given back to her. He would return to their private world after an absence of thirty years, years of belonging to other people. The companionship she yearned for, and had never known, would be their day-to-day living: long walks in the woodland trails under the autumn trees; long talks beside the fire in wintertime; long sunny days in the garden planning for spring. Did Dave ever have dreams like those dreams?

Stella finished in the kitchen. She went out to the garden. It was best to make a start somewhere. Soon spring would come when the grass would need constant cutting and weeds would appear hourly to choke the herbaceous plants now struggling to survive. There is a therapy in gardening which banishes worry. As when you are under the shower, Stella thought, or soaking in a hot tub. Those are the times it is impossible to keep on worrying. Once or twice she thought she heard the phone ringing but it had stopped by the time she got up from kneeling and had taken off the gardening gloves. Gardening, especially weeding, leads on-and-on from one patch of earth to another. Stella was surprised to hear the bell from the local village church ring out the Angelus. Six o'clock! Walking down the garden back to the house, admiring the results of her afternoon's work, she was amused to find her good humour fully restored. She was glad now she had not attacked Dave at lunch time about the endless golf, or the whiskey, come to think of it!

The garden gate creaked open and Stella's neighbour, Beth Moore from down the road, came around the side of the house. "Stella! Stella! I have been trying to get you on the phone for the last hour. I thought you were out or I would have come over."

Beth's gentle face was distressed, and anxious.

"What's wrong, Beth? Can I help? Is it your poor mother? Just give me a second to take off these muddy shoes."

Stella bent to unlace the shoes. Beth bent down also and put her arm around Stella's shoulders.

"No! No! It is not me, not my mother. The hospital has been ringing for you to come. They tried your phone several times and then they tried mine."

Stella straightened up. It could be Hazel, a bus accident? But she knew the accident was Dave's. The instinctive shock went into a part of her, a part never before known to be there, a deep inner core, a shock of such rigidity she felt paralysed.

"It is Dave, isn't it?" Her voice was almost strangled.

"Yes, yes, they want you at the hospital. I'll drive you." Beth was equally distressed.

"Was it a car—was it in the car?" Stella began. The thought of a car accident when Dave drank whiskey was a constant fear.

"I don't think so," Beth answered very carefully.

She was always gentle.

On the half-hour journey to the hospital neither woman spoke. One because she knew the worst, the other because she was hoping against hope for the best and struggling to release the inner core of shock that gripped her despite her hope.

When they entered the hospital hall, a nun advanced graciously with extended hand.

"Poor woman!" she murmured.

"Mrs Shane," a young doctor came forward, "we may have to ask your permission for a post-mortem."

"We will, of course, wait for your husband's own doctor," said the nun in a tone that reprimanded the young doctor.

In a stunned way, Stella remembered that Dave had his blood pressure checked as a normal routine by the doctor in the health clinic in the college. Dave considered himself to be in perfect physical condition. He asserted this undoubted fact every Sunday morning or every Saturday night or every time he took a third glass of wine or a double Jameson. "I'll certainly make the three score and ten! Look at that! Not a bald patch on my head! Sixty-eight! And not a sign of age!" And Stella had looked, and admired, and believed.

The nun put the two women into a waiting-room. She advised against a request to see the dead man.

She must wait for the doctor. He had been phoned and informed. Waiting simply took over. Beth Moore was soft-spoken as always, and kind. Stella found no voice for gratitude. Waiting was an eternity.

Very late in the evening the doctor from Dave's college came. There would be no post-mortem. Dave's death, he told Stella, was expected. This word "expected" took on a strange significance. It joined and reinforced the rigid shock deep within Stella's sub-conscious. Expected by whom? To ask the question would be to reveal the utter lack of Dave's confidence in his wife.

The word, the loaded word "expected" was pushed far back in the days that followed Dave's death on the golf course. Practical necessity with its multiple considerations, can oust grief, can oust questioning, can postpone reckoning.

CHAPTER THREE

The funeral was over. Dave was now sharing the grave of Stella's parents in the local parish churchyard. This cemetery was at the far end of the garden, and Stella, in a stupor of shock, awoke many times in the night to hear her voice imploring. "Dave, Dave, Dave." It puzzled her that he was near enough to hear her and too far away to answer. It was very strange and frightening to find herself alone now in a house of creaking noises. The sons and daughters, called out suddenly from their separate lives, had to return to their places. She was slow to realise that she was not a part of their existence. That was over, just the same as the funeral. For a while, it had seemed that the funeral was a solemn rite to bring Dave back. Even the kindly mourning neighbours held that hope for the time they lingered. Then they, too, were gone. The very tidiness of the empty house was a final verification. Life was over.

From day to day, Stella ignored the ringing of the phone. She could not summon up the energy to welcome commiseration. She wondered at herself, she who had loved the chance cup of coffee with a guest. She supposed she had been changed by her husband's going; all feeling gone, deadened by death. Trailing through the woods to the abbey to pass the long hours of the afternoon, she pondered on the word "widow," the total unexpectedness, the unpreparedness, the being taken by force and made to face loneliness. She had never before known a lonely day. Since she was eighteen years of age, Dave was there fixed and certain. Wasn't this the time to count her blessings? She had her two sons and her two daughters. Now there was a son-in-law, a daughter-in-law, the grandchildren. Should not her widowhood be a full, useful, even pleasant time? Any part of her life that was not perfection (as for instance Sybil's uncaring attitude and her peculiar actions at Dave's funeral) could now be taken for granted. No need for jealous comparisons. That thought surprised Stella. There had to be a way of dealing with loneliness. Cooking, polishing, cutting flowers, all household tasks were useless if no one came home in the evening to enjoy the food, admire the flower-arrangement.

Stella began to question herself. Why am I being punished? Where did I go wrong? She remembered the many evenings when Dave had not come home to the evening meal so carefully prepared and which tasted like sawdust when eaten alone. Why did I reproach him bitterly? It was only food. I should have greeted him with a happy smile at midnight, glad to have him safely home. Why did she realise now, and not then, that her part was to reassure, to put on a show of wifely love no matter what? She knew very well, she had always known, just exactly what Dave's expectations of a wife were during his working life. She had become so careless. She had become selfish in expecting him to give up his pursuits which he had looked forward to in all the years that he had toiled to keep his family in comfort. She had taken all. She had given nothing. The punishment was his death, sudden and untimely. Perhaps he had been a little bit weak at times. Was it asking too much of her to be forbearing? To overlook. Why did she not overlook?

Stella's grief became cloaked in guilt. She longed to weep until her face was blotched and her eyes swollen. No tears came to lift the remorse for love not given, not even recognised.

Somehow weeks had passed. Stella was going through the motions of getting by, never surfacing. It was enough to turn over the bills, shuffle them together and turn them over again. The bills: for the undertaker, the grave-digger, the requiem Masses celebrated by all Dave's cousins in holy orders, the whiskey, the Guinness, the gin, the vodka, the food, the lettering on the headstone. She found bills connected with Sybil's wedding, the bills for car-repairs long overdue.

Stunned and shocked, Stella was ill-prepared for the necessary visit to the bank manager. She had never met the bank manager, only the desk clerks. The bank was Dave's department. He handled the money expertly—Stella remembered how often he had boasted of his prowess in high finance.

The visit started equably. He seemed a nice man, the bank manager. In a gentle way, he enquired if she had private means. He had assumed so, in his conversations with her husband. Maybe stocks and shares to dispose of? A little property to sell—to tide her over, as it were?

"I thought," Stella had asked, "if you could transfer Dave's account into my name and give me a cheque book, so I can have ready money?"

The bank manager gazed into the computer on his big desk.

"You see," Stella was determined to give him the idea that in household payments, she had always been the cherished lap-dog, "Dave just signed the cheques and dealt with all those things like car tax and house insurance. I just wouldn't have a clue!" Her voice tried unsuccessfully for a flippant note. The flippant note was always in Dave's dealing with bills. She was aware that the manager's eyes were resting admiringly on her well-groomed appearance, her black suit, her matching accessories. It was then he enquired about her private means and it was then she realised what he hesitated to say.

"I thought," Stella tried again, with no bravery now but a deal of diffidence, "I thought the gratuity, the, er, golden handshake that Dave took instead of a pension, I thought..." She had no idea how to continue because she had never thought at all.

Now the bank manager lowered his eyes. The respect had gone out of them to be replaced by an apprehensive pity. She was a woman he had admired for her smart appearance. Her status was about to be sadly reduced. He knew this would have happened eventually and he had spoken to Dave on several occasions. Now she would have to bear it on her own. Of course, she had a family. Surely they would help?

"I had hoped you had other resources, Mrs Shane. Dave's gratuity went to pay off his overdraft."

"Is there nothing left?" Stella asked faintly.

The man looked again at his desk computer. "A little less than nine hundred pounds, Mrs Shane. Dave was a man who loved life, wasn't he?"

Stella gripped her hands tightly together. Wasn't he just! Dave's infatuation with life, with his career,

with whiskey, with sport, and with his male companions had been a matter for her resignation long since.
There was no bitterness left, no reply to all the friends
down the years who had said that very same thing,
Dave is so in love with life. Perhaps only she knew
that the life so loved was life in the broad arena of
the work place, in the conviviality of his golf club,
with his male friends, never the life of the domestic
fireside.

The couple of years of his retirement before his
sudden death had been disastrous. His gallant need
to cope with the end of his career and his income,
coupled with the loss of his colleagues, had told
heavily on him. The blustering defiance of time, the
showy bravado, had ebbed sadly, but the deceptive
appearance was maintained.

Stella wondered now what had Sybil's wedding
cost? Something catastrophic. All that style and
elegance and now this. "Is that all there is?" she asked.

"Of course you will qualify for a widow's pension,
and there is an extra allowance for living alone. Will
it be contributory or non-contributory?"

Stella looked bewildered. Dave had never discussed
the eventuality of his death nor had she dared to
bring up the subject. Dave could be touchy if
questioned; it was always best to humour him.
Adopting his flippant stance had become second

nature, until now.

The bank manager felt it his duty to be helpful. The interest on Dave's long drawn overdraft had been enormous. With the end of his earning power, the overdraft had to be called in. Out of the residue of the gratuity he had continued to draw a monthly income not less than he had been earning before retirement. The end was inevitable.

"Mrs Shane," he said, "I think, with your permission, I will phone Dave's late employers. They have a welfare division. I feel fairly confident they could suggest some alleviation of your situation."

So Stella waited at home for the welfare man. Every time the phone rang she thought: and there will be a phone bill. Every time she made a cup of tea, she thought: and there will be an electricity bill. There had been biscuits and cake but they were gone. She wondered if the welfare man would accept a bottle of beer—there were a few bottles left.

The welfare man was young, brisk, probably efficient. He expressed sympathy in a few suitable clichés, finding it necessary to add, "Of course I did not know your husband personally." Did that make a difference, Stella wondered. Dave had known how to be a popular man, a man among men.

Stella offered tea, coffee, a bottle of beer but the young man declined. He had other calls to make;

they would get down to business.

"Your age, Mrs Shane?"

Into the fifties, or heading for sixty? Stella said, "I am not a senior citizen yet." Let that answer do, despite the hesitation of his biro, and his raised eyebrows.

"Your means, Mrs Shane?"

"Nil," Stella answered calmly.

"Perhaps we could be a little more specific?" the young man suggested.

"Nil is mighty specific," Stella said.

"You have resident family? Family support?"

"Neither." Her answer surprised Stella. She usually gave loyal praising responses to enquiries about her sons and daughters. The young man consulted his welfare notes.

"Did your husband invest his gratuity?"

"No," Stella answered, "he paid his debts with it."

"Rather considerable debts, Mrs Shane?" There was an edge of disbelief in the question. Stella smiled serenely, and very proudly she replied, "When you have put a family right through third level education, you don't have much savings, Mr—er—Welfare."

"The name is Ryan," he said.

"Mr Ryan," Stella agreed politely.

"Did your husband qualify for contributory—there is no means test for contributory."

As Stella had no means anyway, she saw no point in trying to answer this question, so she shrugged indifferently.

The young man's voice became slightly nettled. "What were you expecting Mr Shane's late employers to do for you?" he enquired.

Now Stella's humiliation descended on her. She felt like a small animal cornered, trapped. Oh, Dave, how could you let this happen to me? You used to say what a proud little person I was, how independent. You never prepared me to fend for myself. I am a fool in front of this condescending youth, a half-wit in front of the bank manager. When I have paid for your funeral, there will be nothing left. Oh, Dave, did you ever stop to think of how it would be for me?

The young man was talking. "I am empowered to take away some of your outstanding bills. The college trustees will look into the matter of a small monthly payment, perhaps to cover your rent. It may be a temporary measure; that will be decided."

Stella made an effort to look grateful and murmur words of gratitude. It would have been easier if the young man were a little bit friendlier.

"I gather you own the house, but is there ground rent? Is it high? Are you carrying a mortgage?"

Stella had no idea. A mortgage? Maybe I do not have a roof over my head if Dave raised a mortgage to pay for that wedding? All that paint and drapes and finery. Mr Welfare has noticed the splendour. No wonder he is suspicious.

"You are a long way from a village or a shop of any kind? That means you must run the car. How will you afford that, Mrs Shane?"

"I just don't know, Mr Ryan." Nor how I will pay for electricity or the phone or petrol for the car, if I can keep it. Maybe I will use candles and boil the kettle on sticks and have coddle for Sunday dinner. People survived that way. Oh, Dave, where are you now? Do they serve whiskeys and chasers in Heaven? And are you surrounded by friends as always?

"Mrs Shane, I said we will be in touch."

"Oh, I am sorry, Mr Ryan, my mind must have been wandering. Are you sure we could not share a cup of tea?"

When he had taken his final disapproving look away with him, Stella sat down to read the day's newspaper. She was very conscious of the space around her, the emptiness, the quietness. Unable to concentrate on the paper, she sat staring at the window, watching the shadows of the garden trees moving in a breeze. In a vague way, her mind was accepting the ending of life and seeing the good things: no more worry about money; no more remorse for the hard time she gave poor old Dave when he came home drunk. He did not like that word. "A little obfuscated, my dear," that was all he would allow when he was practically footless.

"Oh, Dave, I'm sorry," Stella murmured. "I just was never able to persuade myself that there is meaning in that word 'alcoholic.' I just thought you lacked the will-power. Oh, forgive me for the aggressive way I used that word 'drunk.' I never stopped to think how that must have hurt. Sorry, sorry, sorry, Dave. In this room, I am going to spend the rest of my life being sorry, because there is nowhere else to go now; a penniless widow, growing old rapidly, probably starving to death, dying alone and unloved, no new clothes, no make-up, no perfume, probably never washing. Stinking. A smelly decayed ancient female."

Suddenly Stella sat up straight. She would hate not to wash; she would hate not to wear this year's fashion. Designer labels are deeply comforting! She would hate her hair unstyled. She was not particularly vain but she adored being groomed—and hygienic. Money? There was plenty of it out there, somewhere beyond that window. She would go out into the world and get a job. She could not type, nor book-keep; she knew nothing of the mystery of computers and word-processors! But she was useful; she was clean; she could cook; she had reared a family; she liked small kids and dogs and kittens. I'm sorry, Dave, you know I am. I'll come back here when I am really old and I'll visit the grave every day. I promise I will. And I'll get Masses said for the repose of your soul when I earn enough money. You were always a great one for getting Masses said for your dead family and friends. We used to say you would have made a good priest. Yes, Masses. You enjoyed going to Mass. I promise faithfully, just as soon as there is money I will give it to the parish priest for Masses. Only, I will have to get a job to earn the money. Yes, I know you didn't approve of women taking jobs, but Dave..."You can't hear me," she was saying it out loud. "You left me for a better place. You don't have to worry any more. You are gone and I can get a job if I want to. I have to get a job, no matter what you might have said if you..."

Stella was a little frightened by the vehemence of her thought. Dave was gone, weeks and weeks now, he could not stop her doing anything she wanted. It was a frightening thought. Aloneness was scary. Terrifyingly, she imagined him standing by the window in his muddy grave-clothes, his sad face reproaching her. If she had really loved him, he was saying, she would be the loneliest widow in the world. She would stay there near him and mourn his death with him. Mourn Dave's death, the sad face insisted;

mourn your husband's death; mourn for Dave who was so in love with life. If you ever loved me...

Of course, I loved you. Way back when I was young, I was crazy about you and I cared for you in a loving way. You know I did. Why am I to feel guilty? I did no wrong. We just grew old, that was all. But I was a good wife. I meant to be, honestly, and there were times when love was marvellous. The holiday in Austria. The sailing holiday. Please, Dave...Stella stood up and moved further from the window. She could almost smell the rank odour of the withering hands. The yellow face, coming closer, had an indescribably fetid breath.

Stella was racing out of the house, soundlessly screaming, every muscle clenched. Half a mile up the country road, she came to her senses. She walked for a while, taking deep breaths, making her body regain its flexibility. She turned and went back into the house, carefully, hesitantly, half-praying. There was nothing here. An empty, tidy, pleasant room. No offensive stench. ‑

She made some strong coffee, added a spot of whiskey to it and then picked up the *Irish Times* again. She found the Positions Vacant column. The first three ads were obviously aimed at young au pairs. Then suddenly, there it was, ordained by fate. The very exact job to suit a penniless widow.

*Required for wealthy household in Philadelphia a
plain settled older woman to care for one male
baby. Non smoker. Licensed car-driver. Reply to
phone number for address to send genuine references.
All data checked.*

Stifling the nightmarish imagination (probably—
Stella assured herself—brought on by worry over
money, lack of sleep, forgetting to eat) and all the
time being careful not to glance towards the window
for fear of shadows drifting into the garden from the
graveyard, Stella took a sheet of paper from Dave's
bureau. She wrote down the phone number, then her
own name, address and phone number. Then the
address of the local parish priest, the guards and two
eminent people who would surely give her good
character references. She checked the time on her
watch. It should be around midday in Philadelphia,
she calculated, as it was now seven pm in Ireland.
Her second eldest, Ross, was a lecturer in a university
in New York and it was not long since she had to
phone him when Dave died, so she knew the
procedure for phoning the States.

She dialled, she heard the long smooth beat, and
a woman's voice answered immediately. She was
passed from one secretary to another. Then she heard
herself, quite confidently, answering the questions

put to her in a lawyer-like way by a man who had a deep and pleasant voice.

Stella agreed to give away a year of her life in one short phone call. She had set the measure in motion and the idea pleased her. She would emigrate to the United States of America to get work. Twenty-eight thousand Irish citizens had emigrated in the year 1990. She had heard it deplored on all sides. Draining the country, people said. And they could not all be young, Stella was thinking. For me, it will be just the year. A year is nothing.

CHAPTER FOUR

Trying to act in a single-minded way, Stella went about the collection of her references. "Just in case she needed to find a job in a while," she told her son Philip, who did not take her seriously. The phone calls to and from Philadelphia proceeded. The family name was Nathan, the little child was Carlo. The parents, in their early thirties, were a very busy couple: she an architect, he in furniture manufacture. Her mother and step-father lived with them part of the time, as also did his uncle, most of the time. They accepted Stella's references and checked them. They would like her to come as soon as possible. They would pay her air fare and, at the end of a year her return fare. Stella's passport was in order and she obtained a multiple entries visa from the American embassy. She stated blandly that she was going to visit her son Ross who was lecturing in history at a University in New York. Mr Nathan had sent her two air tickets, one Shannon to New York, the other New York to Philadelphia. At times, Stella wondered at herself. She had never in all her thirty-eight years of married life had to make arrangements of any sort outside the home. It was quietly exhilarating to feel the reins in her own hands. She did not allow her mind to dwell on the idea that once across the Atlantic she would no longer be her own mistress, merely another woman's home-help. The idea was there, and it was defeating, but Stella had much use for concentration, and concentration kept the dreaded return of the grave-clad Dave from taking over in her loneliness. Sometimes, at the head of the stairs, she imagined a greenish shadow. This sickly fear would surely end when the plane lifted off from Shannon. Meanwhile she redoubled her efforts to think calmly of all the necessary details. When at last, the day of the flight had been fixed, she announced her departure to the family.

Her eldest son, Philip, held a very responsible position and he had the reputation of being sage and serious. He thought she was a bit touched. "Emigrate! People of your age do not emigrate! Mother, you are acting in a state of shock." His voice was sad for her. "There is absolutely no need for you to emigrate for a menial job. You couldn't face that, Mother. Please be sensible. Do not do this. It's money, isn't it? I could help you."

Stella had thought he might offer this, so she was ready with her answer. "It's not just money, not just

loneliness, I want to get away. Have an adventure!"
Unfortunately, her voice broke on the last word.

"Some adventure!" Now his voice was sharper.
"They'll work you to death for a few miserable dollars!
This poor Irish emigrant stuff is not for you—you
couldn't take that kind of hardship! Forget it! I'll help
you! Emigrate! The idea! You can come and live with
us, maybe help out a little?"

Stella noticed that Philip's wife said nothing. Wise
girl, Stella thought. A young couple putting up with
a mother, his or hers, were at a disadvantage with
each other. A young couple needed the freedom to
fight and shout at each other if they felt like it.

"Thank you, Philip," and Stella smiled very
affectionately at Philip's wife. "And thank you, Mída.
You are wonderful people, but my mind is quite made
up. I am going to Philadelphia."

"I don't know what's got into you, Mother," Philip
grumbled. "Father's sudden death was a terrible shock.
He was never sick! I realise that. But this isn't the
answer. If money is what this is all about, I am sure
the bank...I mean, I know that Dad took home a
decent gratuity when he retired, and I..."

"No, no, no," Stella said quickly, "that is all taken
care of. And, Philip, it is only for a year—I'll be given
the return ticket at the end of the year."

"It may not last a year, Mother. You know, of

course, that it is illegal to take up a job in the States unless you have a proper visa to do so? You could be deported in handcuffs! There was a case in the paper only last week. In handcuffs!"

Which would upset Philip, no doubt, in his important position. Stella was not about to go into details as to how Mr Nathan had asked her, on the phone, to say nothing about employment. Mr Nathan said they would regard her as a friend come to help, temporarily, with baby Carlo. Mr Nathan, on the phone, seemed a very capable person. He was a practising lawyer, he told her, so Stella was happy to let him take charge. The visa issued to Stella was a holiday visa, no more than that. She had given Ross's address for the holiday.

"Philip, you worry too much!"

"Maybe you should consider what you are doing, Mother. Have you thought of, perhaps, a visit to your doctor, a tonic, maybe Valium? You are shaking your head but this is serious. Have you told the family? Ross? What does Hazel say?"

"Oh, Hazel understands me. Ross—I am not sure about Ross but I will see him in New York if I stay overnight. He is to phone me to-morrow. Hazel is full of excitement for my trip but she is into the last lap of her doctorate. She will worry when she finds time to worry. That's Hazel!"

"And Sybil? And her rich husband. Isn't Alec a very old friend?"

Stella took a deep breath. She had never found favour with Sybil. She had stopped trying years ago. Philip knew that very well. "Sybil was her Daddy's girl—always. With Dave gone, she will cut adrift from family ties."

"But the rich husband, Mother? He is nearer your age than Sybil's. He might choose to be generous. He is very wealthy."

Stella found this slightly insulting, but when Philip meant well he saw no need to be subtle. She said nothing more of her impending departure. Until she was getting into her car to return home, they talked of other things. At the last moment, Philip uncharacteristically hugged her. "Take good care of yourself, Mother," he whispered. "I wish you had come to me for advice. But take care—maybe you'll be back soon!"

When a young man has lived in New York and Boston for five years, the idea of a runaway mother is no great matter for comment. Stranger things than that happen every hour of every day in those cities. That, Stella felt, was Ross's attitude. He was more affectionate than Philip and also more sophisticated. He uttered neither recriminations nor commiserations but slipped a wad of dollars into her purse.

"You know my phone number, Mother. If there is

any bother, give me a buzz and I'll come galloping on the nearest express train. But take it easy. The US ain't Ireland and the Yanks ain't soft!"

He really is nice, Stella thought. His casual clothes hung very well on his tall, slim body. He looked more handsome than she had remembered. She had been in a state of shock in the days after Dave's death and at the funeral. The family were there. Their faces stood out clearly. Each one different. Each one feeling grief in an individual way. She could not detach her own mind to think of them. She analysed, instead, the blinding relief of being on the last stage of the journey away from Dave's death. His ghost would not appear on sleepless nights in Philadelphia as he had been appearing in her own bed at home. She had begun to dread the nights: the sudden waking to feel a presence hovering at her pillow, and to hear the sound of a sorrowful sighing like the wind in the trees outside the window, only so much closer that she felt the breath on her brow. She would surely know in Philadelphia that it was her fevered imagination that conjured up the accusing face. She must remember that her own dwindling interest in married life, so guilt-ridden in her hidden self, had never seemed to matter to Dave. Dave was an extrovert, a man for the outside world; or so she had thought. Was there another Dave who also had a hidden self and now needed to meet in darkness with the hidden Stella? In Philadelphia she would be a totally different person. An indifferent person, immune to these horrible night vapours. She hoped so.

Stella trained her eyes on the landscape beneath the plane's wings. Already, New York's endless street sprawl had been swallowed into the clouds, and a green tree-filled land now came into view. Pennsylvania seemed a paradisal country, unspoiled, truly sylvan, watered by wide rivers. The hour's journey took less time, she thought, than an hour.

Stella's new employers, Mr and Mrs Bart Nathan, would (they had so arranged by phone) be at the airport to meet her. They would be holding their little baby Carlo, in their arms. That, they said, would be a sure way of knowing them, quite apart from the photographs they had exchanged in the previous weeks. Stella stood beside her two heavy suitcases (enough plain clothes for the changing seasons of a servant's year) watching out for a glamorous young couple with a baby.

There were many people. It was a busy airport. They must have been delayed. There could even have been an accident. That would be an ominous start, really bad luck. She was beginning to feel like a poor Irish emigrant without the return fare, when a man approached her. "You are Mrs Shane from Ireland?"

he enquired.

He was a large, opulent-seeming man, and Stella felt apprehensive. It took courage to answer politely, "And who are you?"

Now the man smiled, not unattractively.

"I am Gil Nathan, Bart's uncle, and little Carlo's grand-uncle. May I call a porter to get your bags out to my car?"

Stella hesitated. Was she about to come to a disastrous end, as Philip had warned? The large man took an identity card from an inside pocket. "You see," he said, "here is my name, and as you will notice, you will be sharing the same address as mine in Larch Hill."

Stella hesitated. "They said they would be here to meet me," she said. "Shouldn't I wait?"

"With that pair," he answered lightly, "one should ask for everything in writing. All I got was a phone call, asking me to pick you up. You will get used to them, Mrs Shane. You will have met more reliable people in Ireland, I am sure."

Well, Stella was thinking, I hardly look suitable for the white slave traffic people talked about when I was a teenager! What else can I do now, unless I use Ross's dollars to go back to New York? And after that, what?

"I shall just have to trust you, Mr Nathan."

Soon they were moving into avenues of traffic. It's like the Wicklow road on a Sunday in summer, Stella thought, only all these cars are twice as big. She was too apprehensive to start chatting. Mr Nathan did not chat either. Moving in that traffic took skill. Stella suddenly remembered that "licensed car-driver" was one of her necessary qualifications for this job, and driving on the right side of the road would be hazardous. For the first time, she suspected that the job would entail more than child-minding. Car driving was a daunting thought.

After several junctions that seemed like a tangle of coiled snakes when the crush of traffic split in many directions, they were out on a tree-lined road. Mr Nathan relaxed and smiled at her.

"That traffic was terrifying," Stella told him. "I do not think I could cope with traffic like that."

He reassured her. "You will not be asked to drive within the city limits. Out in Larch Hill, the roads are easy, like country roads."

"Oh, that's a relief," Stella smiled.

"You know, Mrs Shane, there is one way in which you do not, so to speak, fit the bill. I it was who drafted the advertisement which brought you here. I was very specific, for reasons which will be clear to you, no doubt, quite soon."

Stella faltered a little. "I don't understand. I thought

I answered all Mrs Nathan's questions very specific-
ally."

"The advertisement asked for a plain, settled, older
woman. You are not plain, Mrs Shane."

Stella was pleased by the compliment but it was
too early in their acquaintanceship to take it seriously.
"No beauty!" she responded lightly.

"No make-up, a little bit jet-lagged, but very appealing. I watched you standing by your suitcases. I have
not known an Irish woman for many, many years.
Appealing is the word."

"Thank you, Mr Nathan." He is into the sixties
himself, Stella thought, slightly paunchy, hair on the
way out, heavy eyebrows, a very aggressive jaw-line,
but there's something nice about him all the same.
She stole a sideways look at him. Sort of kind. Or is
it sort of strong? She liked the timbre of his voice.

"Larch Hill is reckoned to be a classy suburb," he
told her in a very friendly voice. "Velva and Bart are
living in it for four years now. It is hard to know the
neighbours because each house is set on its own acre."

"Sounds like a lot of garden or do they keep a
horse?"

He laughed delightedly at this. "We are pretty well-
off," he chuckled, "but not yet into the equestrian
circles. That is really top-of-the-market! In the suburbs,
gardening is contracted out. Men and boys come

around once a month, or whenever, in a jeep. They bring all the equipment and keep the yard (as we call it) in good shape. Cut the grass, trim the bushes, whatever. It's one of the Italian types of occupation; they have cornered that market in Philly, anyway."

"We seem to be going a long way away from the city?" Stella suggested.

"It is fifty minutes by car."

"Shall I never see the city again then?" Stella asked, a little wistfully. "I like cities, although at home in Ireland I live in the country."

"You will see the city every Sunday if you wish," Mr Nathan said. "You'll have Sundays off. That is agreed." He said that as if he were the one who had agreed it. "There is a train from Ambler station and it is a twenty-five minute journey. Someone will run you over to Ambler, ten minutes is all to the station."

Stella wondered what use would Sunday be for shopping. On the other hand, since she intended to save every cent, while letting the widow's pension mount up at home, why should she worry about shopping? She supposed museums and art galleries were open on Sundays. It was years since she had been in either such place at home. She would be re-educated although she would prefer to look in fashion shops.

"That's nice; that sounds grand," she said. "I have

been admiring how wonderfully wooded the countryside is, trees of lovely colours."

"Does the maple grow freely in your Irish country-side? One hears the phrase 'the Irish oak.' This hill beginning now is Larch Hill. The larch looks good in springtime, the bark seems to shimmer. It has given its name to this suburb. I often wonder if the trees were growing when the Indians were here, or if William Penn propagated them, giving his name and the trees to the state. A bit of both, maybe?"

"I love finding out things like that," Stella said. "I know a little about William Penn. He lived with the Quakers in Dublin before he came here."

"You will see his statue sitting up, or is it standing up, on the council chambers in Philly. No one is supposed to build higher than the top of William's hat!"

They were turning into the short wide avenue of a house set in a park of dissimilar houses, each well distant from the next. Many types of architecture were represented, colonial, Italian, Spanish, stately, even Gothic castle style.

"At home in Ireland," Stella told him, "in a park like this, all the houses would normally be identical—only curtains and gardens would be different."

Mr Nathan was opening the car door for her. She almost forgot she must now assume the role of the hired help. She was to learn in time that the American dream of house and home consisted not merely in separate architectural identities but in a supposition of neighbourly equality that was wholly fictitious to an Irish woman. In Ireland there is equality among equals, and you don't get notions above your station. Stella stepped over the Nathan threshold into a very different world.

"There is no one at home," Mr Nathan said in an apologetic way. "I expect Velva is out chasing-up Bart."

"And the baby?" enquired Stella.

"Oh, she has probably rammed him into the back of the car in his crib, or whatever."

Stella was trying to take in the space and magnificence of the house. The kitchen area ran the width of the back. To Stella it looked as big as a ballroom. There was a long sun-deck beyond sliding glass doors.

"Come," Mr Nathan said, "I will take you upstairs with these cases. You must be tired."

The house was in three tiers, served by a wide circling staircase. The effect was theatrical: the parterre, the dress-circle, the upper circle. Stella's room was in the upper circle. It had an en suite shower and toilet. The bed was large, and looked comfortably festooned with cushions. There was a television and a telephone. Also an apparatus high up in a corner which emitted a regular "click."

"A television in my bedroom," Stella exclaimed, "and a telephone!"

Mr Nathan shrugged his shoulders helplessly. "Velva has a fetish about the absolute necessity of telephones! Every room must have one, is her idea!"

"And what is that, Mr Nathan?" Stella asked, pointing to the clicking corner.

"Also in every room, a camera! Some time tonight, Velva will run the photography of the day through the television, and the sound also will be picked up— we are now on TV," he added.

Stella thought this was funny but she could see Mr Nathan found the entire idea irksome.

"I think you should have a rest, Mrs Shane. I will make some coffee. I doubt if there is tea. Don't Irish people always ask for a cup of tea?"

He is nice, Stella thought; there is humour in him.

"Thank you, Mr Nathan." She took off her coat and her shoes. When Gil Nathan came back with the coffee, she was curled up in an armchair, fast asleep. He put the coffee on the bedside table and, shutting the door gently, he went away to his study.

CHAPTER FIVE

The sound of a baby's fretful crying woke Stella. Quickly she splashed her face and washed her hands, marvelling at the abundance of soaps and towels and toilet accessories in her shower-room. Then she found the baby, close by her room, in a gaily decorated nursery. The little thing looked as if he had been dropped hurriedly into his cot: he was still dressed in woolly outdoor garments. Stella picked him up, he was very wet. His response to her gentle hands was instant. His little mouth still open, he stopped crying.

"Carlo, Carlo," Stella said softly, cuddling him, and kissing the top of his head. He nestled against her in a natural way that surprised her.

"So Carlo does not make strange?" she murmured. "Carlo and Stella going to be friends."

In the well-stocked nursery, she found all she needed. There was a table to put Carlo down on while she undressed him and made him clean and dry. There were so many sets of little garments folded on shelves that the nursery was almost like a baby store.

Dozens of boxes of disposable nappies were piled in one corner and an electric chute took away all used things.

"Wealthy household is right," she murmured to Carlo, who followed her every movement with his huge solemn black eyes. "I wonder, now, do I go all the way downstairs to find out what you are going to eat. Are you on to semi-solids or some magic American formula?" She took him up in her arms, and again he lay easily against her. Out on the circular landing, or upper circle, Stella noticed half a dozen doors. Again on the lower circle, more doors. Now she became aware of voices from the kitchen area raised in argument—the angry voice of a man and the shrill voice of a woman. She sat on the stairs, holding the baby fondly, her lips against the fine black fuzz on his head. Her ears were not yet tuned in to the accents of the two fighters; nevertheless she knew the language was coarse and violent. She felt the baby trembling as he too heard the voices. She held him closer and his soft mouth found the softness of her throat for comfort. "Poor little Carlo," she murmured over and over, "there, there, poor little fellow."

Stella became aware of someone coming down the stairs and pausing as if to examine her where she sat cuddling the baby. Stella looked up expectantly. She almost gasped. The most beautiful woman she had ever seen was standing a few steps above her. The woman smiled an enchanting, spellbinding smile. Stella realised instantly this must be the grandmother of Carlo. She was not in her thirties but beyond early forties she was ageless. Her wavy auburn hair framed a face without a trace of a line. Her eyes were large and lustrous and her eyelashes were separate dark spikes like the points of stars. If a smile is held, it becomes a grin. Not so with this lady: her smile became more deeply sensuous, more persuasive, exciting, coaxing.

"No, no," she said in a voice little above a tender whisper, "do not get up. I will see that my daughter comes to make you welcome. Velva is upset to-day—a little upset!"

The lady continued down the stairs to the entrance hall, turning in a stately manner into the kitchen area. There was an immediate silence, followed closely by the banging of a door. Stella was to learn that the entrance hall was used only for guests. The side door of the kitchen laundry area led directly into a big garage, and since everyone in the household used a car, that was the way they came and went.

Now Stella heard a flood of lamenting tears. The same shrill voice became a teenager's voice looking for consolation, a thin voice full of self-pity. The soft whispering voice of the beautiful woman could be heard counselling calm. After a time the two women, mother and daughter, came into the hall. Stella descended the last few steps; baby Carlo had fallen fast asleep in her arms.

"Oh," said Velva of the shrill twanging voice. "You are younger than I expected!"

Much older, Stella thought, and I'd be too old to travel. She smiled, and waited.

"Uncle Gil brought you from the airport? Wasn't that kind! You have changed Carlo? I will feed him."

If Stella had been expecting any sort of a gracious apology, she would learn soon to expect nothing.

The moment his mother took Carlo into her grasp, he woke and began to whinge.

"Oh, what's the matter with you?" His mother sounded very irritable. "We will go into the den." She led the way into a room off the hall. She switched on the television set, and seated herself opposite it. Carlo was now wailing loudly and his mother was telling him to shut up. The beautiful woman had stolen quietly away. Stella perched on a nearby chair.

"Shit! I hate this business!" Velva was now bare-breasted and turning the baby's head towards a nipple. He continued to cry loudly, so his little mouth could not close over the offered milk—if indeed there was any milk to offer. From her angle, and trying not to be curious, Stella could not see the usual creamy droplet that comes on at feeding time.

Velva continued to struggle with the baby while not missing a flicker on the TV, and talking loudly to Nanny, as she immediately christened Stella.

"This is a bold bad boy, Nanny! Did you breast-feed your children, Nanny? You had dozens, hadn't you?" Velva asked a lot of questions but never bothered to look for answers. "My friend, Lana, she breast-feeds for years. She says it gives her a sexy sensation; she says it is good for your love life; she says all women love it. She says a husband loves to watch because he knows it gives the woman the urge for him. Did that happen to you, Nanny? Or is it so long ago you have forgotten? I have news for Lana. It doesn't give me any vibes, and Bart hates seeing it. Oh, shut up, kid, why can't you just shut up! Have you got this series on the TV? Have they TV in Ireland? I have been following *The Love Worshippers* since I was fifteen. Bart says Ireland is in the Third World. Is it?"

Carlo was now screaming his head off, and obstinately refusing the proffered breast. Suddenly Velva struck him. "You hate me, kid, don't you? Here, Nanny, take the little monkey-face. He stinks anyway. There's stuff to feed him in the fridge. I'll show you, when this episode is over!"

Stella took the baby. His exertions had caused him

to dirty his disposable. She went back up the circular stairs to the nursery, her heart wrung with pity for the little thing.

"Wouldn't it be lovely," she murmured to him, as she changed him, "just lovely if all mothers had milk on tap all the time, not just after having a baby, and I could feed you now. I know you are hungry, and I do remember how it was feeding a new baby. How could any woman forget that very special sensation? But, you see, little fella, I am just the nanny. I will get a bottle for you in the kitchen and we will see if that helps. Ah, look at you! You are trying to smile at me! Do I see a little tooth peeping up?"

Velva Nathan was in the kitchen when Stella brought the baby down. She had placed bottles and formulas on the long table-top. She made no attempt to read the directions or fill mixture into the bottles. That was Nanny's job, and Velva was no more concerned on that first day than she would be on a last day. That Nanny might be jet-lagged or need a bit of help was of no concern. Velva's attitude would always be that she hired the help, not vice versa. Life with Velva began on Stella's first day exactly as it would go on. So far as Velva was concerned, Nanny was just another technical device. You could not ask the washing machine to say sir or madam, neither could you expect a nanny from the Third World to understand the complex mental gyrations of a twentieth-century, highly civilised, madly sophisticated, hugely educated, young American architect. No, sir. In the same way you switched off the cooker, you switched off a nanny. Velva never revealed to Stella that it was a status symbol in Philadelphia to have a well-set-up, English-style nanny devoted to your child. Stella often overheard herself so described and listened smilingly to the responding oohs and aahs. Two black women, Debby and Leola, came in on alternate days to keep the house in good order, to launder and iron and polish the various bathrooms and Jacuzzis. They were, in Velva's estimation, technical devices on a lower scale. Their language concerning Velva was probably on the lowest scale of all.

Stella was told to occupy herself solely with little Carlo. They went into each other's hearts from the first touch. Each needed love, and loving each other was a mutual response. Carlo made Stella see for the first time how a child's psyche slowly, but surely, develops. She had been in her twenties when she and Dave had their children. She had doted on them and she assumed Dave did, too. They got all the love in me, she thought now. I never noticed they had need of it because I just gave it anyway—all I had. But was there a special need in Sybil? Was her disposition such that enough was never enough? Did she think

Hazel got just that bit more? And *did* she, being the baby? And did Dave take Sybil over from me for that reason? Her mind shied away from these questions but they returned. Bathing and changing and feeding Carlo, and holding his attention, had made him an integral part of her life's experience. She came to love him so much that she had to remind herself constantly that he was not hers and she must not allow herself to fall into the trap of resenting his mother, no matter how chilling Velva's attitude to the little boy.

Carlo's father, Bart, was the direct opposite in character to Velva. His ability to charm was apparent when Velva was not around. He would make a delightful friend, Stella thought. He had inherited a chain of furniture manufactories from his maternal grandfather. He was deeply interested in his work and very successful. He was also a gifted musician. He enjoyed playing the piano for Carlo's entertainment, and the baby would move in rhythm with the music's beat. When they had these little piano sessions, Stella would pray fervently that Velva would stay away, wherever she was.

"He likes southern blues, and jazz, doesn't he, Mrs Shane? Do you?"

"I did not know I did," Stella answered, "until I listened to your playing. It is fantastic the way you make the piano syncopate—if that is the word?" She thought he looked surprised, so she hastened to add, "Of course, I am the merest amateur but I think this small chap will play, also."

"Why do you think that?"

"I notice that his ear detects the separate sound of your car on the drive and he is able to urge me over to the piano to be ready for your arrival."

Bart beamed at this. "As accurate an ear as that, eh? You are going to sit up here with me, Carlo, and get your little fingers on the notes?"

"Look at him, Mr Bart, he knows just what you mean." And there was no mistaking the look on Carlo's vivid little face. His dark eyes were shining brilliantly.

"Is there some Irish music you would like me to play for you, Mrs Shane?" Bart asked often. "Jigs and reels?"

"Oh, no, no, no, Mr Bart! I am still much too close to leaving home to listen to Irish music of the dithery-idle sort. And as for 'Danny Boy'—please, not on any account!"

Bart smiled with sympathy when Stella said things like that. "We don't want to make you lonely. We want you to be happy here with us, don't we, Carlo?"

Stella wondered at him. Was he so completely immune to the devastating rows created by his wife that he thought anyone could be safely happy in this household? Living on the edge of Vesuvius would be safer than in the vicinity of Velva. Her hysterical screeching made Stella's blood run cold.

When the sound of the up-and-over garage door announced her arrival home, Bart was up the stairs in a single movement, under the shower, into fresh clothes, down, into the car, gone through the same up-and-over door. His fast escape had a touch of the Houdini, Stella always thought, as she watched the twinkle fade out of Carlo's eyes. Then Stella would sit on the piano-stool with Carlo and let him run his fingers along the keyboard. That did not last long. Velva, once in, banished Nanny and Carlo to the nursery. Stella soon developed ways of getting the little boy over his disappointment and he responded easily to her loving distractions.

There were times when Velva was not there, and, as the months passed Carlo began to pull himself up by the piano-seat to reach for the notes. Bart would hold him firmly against his chest and Carlo, his tiny fingers resting on the keyboard, would gaze in awe-struck admiration up into Bart's face and down to the fingers racing up and down. He would catch Nanny's eye and chuckle in response to her approval, his whole body alive to the rhythm.

Stella supposed that Bart was a man accustomed

to the admiration of women, a man accustomed to
charming women. She often watched his handsome
face and thought what a popular man he must have
been at parties in his college days. Everyone admired
the guy who could make music. Probably he was still
a very popular man. As time familiarised Stella with
Velva and Bart, she learned from their endless quarrels
that Bart was tired of marriage and of coping with
Velva. There was no way to avoid listening: they
seemed to need an audience. Velva wanted her
beautiful mother to hear how Bart ill-treated her by
his refusals of every request she made. He wanted his
Uncle Gil to show sympathy for a divorce. It appeared
that Uncle Gil discouraged the idea of a divorce.
Neither did Velva want a divorce, rather did she want
to possess her husband jealously and to the exclusion
of everyone else. She had not the beauty of her mother
to whom divorce had come easily, almost as one
would return unwanted goods only slightly damaged.
The beautiful mother was now married to the man
who had been her first husband; there had been five
divorces in between. Velva was the daughter of the
third husband. There was a good-looking son by the
second. He came occasionally to visit, always
accompanied by a handsome blonde girlfriend. Velva
hated this half-brother Serl. She said his girlfriends
were young men and, constantly airing her views on

sexual perversions, told her beautiful mother that her darling son, Serl, was a double transvestite. Velva's voice carried through the house. It was a sound which gave Stella creepy shivers and from which she always sought to escape.

The beautiful Mrs Rosen, and her husband, had their suite on what Stella thought of as the dress-circle. Also on that level were the rooms of Cousin Ambert and his wife Alice, a secretive sort of a pair in their late sixties. Stella had the impression that their role in the house was one of watch-dog. They specialised in appearing out of their rooms onto the stairs when least expected. The entire household, apart from Stella-Nanny and little Carlo, went out to breakfast, returned in the afternoon and disappeared again for dinner, all in their separate ways and seemingly not with each other. The telephones were busy in the afternoons, the television sets were perpetually switched on and the cameras clicked away merrily.

To Stella from the countryside of Ireland, all of these arrangements were difficult to fathom. It took many weeks to sort out the complicated lifestyles of this Larch Hill mansion. Uncle Gil alone seemed nearer than the others to Stella's idea of normal.

Much as she loved Carlo and took to him from the start, Stella began to look forward to her days off. On the Sunday morning, Velva would hand over the eighty dollars, a week's pay. Stella never took more than forty with her for train fare and a meal and maybe postcards and stamps. Uncle Gil took her to the station at Ambler for the 10.15 train down to the city. They brought little Carlo in his baby-seat in the back of the car. His huge black eyes always looked downcast when Stella got out of the car and waved good-bye. She always wondered, a little sadly, what sort of a day he would have without her?

As soon as the car had driven off, for the first time, Stella felt at ease to think her own thoughts. She shook herself free of the imposed Nanny image. She came back into her own body. She smiled at herself: the Irish emigrant, illegal, poorly paid, glad of the free food, the free electricity, humbly bowing the knee for six days of the week; and on the seventh day the city of Philadelphia was hers, all hers, to enjoy in solitary freedom. So many wonders there were in this beautiful city that it never occurred to her to be lonely.

The first thing was to go to Mass in the cathedral. Mass on Sunday was a life long habit. Stella could not get back more easily into her own tradition than by going to hear Cardinal Kroll saying his old-fashioned Mass. It was the proper kick-off for the day, in Stella's mind, and it kept her in good conscience.

The discovery of Philadelphia was exciting.

Although she was alone, and warned by Gil Nathan never to get into conversation with anyone of any colour or either sex, Stella was never lonely on Sundays. After Mass, she went to the tourist centre. She was able to buy a tourist ticket for the old-fashioned open trolley to take her to Fairmount Park along the Benjamin Franklin parkway. The ticket could be used for the round trip which took over an hour and a half, or it could be used as a stop-and-start-again ticket. Fairmount Park, the trolley guide told the tourists, was the biggest park in the world. Stella could not but observe that black people made exclusive use of this wonderful park. As the trolley toured around, there was no mistaking the fact that the barbecues, the horse-riding, the ball-games, the tennis courts, the loud radio music, the children playing, the hundreds of cars and campmobiles, gave Stella a picture of the Deep South as she imagined it, rather than a modern cosmopolitan city a mere ninety miles south of New York. When the trolley stopped for the tourists to visit in one or other of the historical mansions in the park, there seemed to be only white people interested. These mansions, now museums, represented history in Philadelphia, having been the elegant homes of early statesmen. Stella gathered all the leaflets and brochures. She had a genuine feeling for folk history. As the weeks went on, her Sundays

became more and more enjoyable the more she
learned of Philadelphia and the more she became
acquainted with its history and culture. Other things
being equal (which meant having social class and
lots of money) this would be a wonderful city in
which to have been born. Stella knew that "belonging"
is the most important part of "being," and Stella
belonged elsewhere. So she viewed Philadelphia as a
place to discover by weekly instalments: the new and
vigorous commercial city which arose in serene
contrast to the older, humanitarian city, now three
hundred years of age. Stella read in the guide book:
"Those who came later had superimposed a very
gracious, spacious, living area over the squares where
Liberty was born." Coloniser's language, thought the
rebel in Stella. What about the Red Indians' liberty?
She determined to look for a history book.

One Sunday, she went into the massive Free
Library. She would need a card signed by a citizen to
be a member and take away a history book. She was
free to walk about and read, and every Sunday she
spent an hour doing that. She debated the idea of
asking Velva to sign a library card for her. She could
easily imagine Velva's reply. At last she plucked up
the courage to mention the matter to Uncle Gil. In
Nanny-Stella's mind, he was Uncle Gil because that
was how she addressed him for Carlo: "Say morning

to Uncle Gil, Carlo; big kiss for Uncle Gil." And clever little Carlo was learning to blow a kiss from his fingertips as Uncle Gil turned at the door after his statutory five minutes' daily visit.

"Of course, Mrs Shane. I will be pleased to assist you in getting a borrower's card for the Free Library." Stella handed him the card and he signed it.

That night, he knocked on the nursery door. Stella had thought everyone in the house had gone out, as happened most nights. In fact, Stella had got quite used to being alone until midnight.

"May I come in?" Gil Nathan asked. "I am not disturbing you? You will have no difficulty now in the library. I am glad you are here so early in the year. Summer Sundays in Philly are quite amusing for visitors. They put on ethnic shows for the tourists; dressing in their national costume and playing their national music, very showy."

The punctilious way he talks, thought Stella. A bit full of his own importance! Or is he a bit shy? Surely not?

He paused at the door. "Have you been to the Rodin Gallery? No? The Norman Rockwell Museum? Ah—all in good time."

Still he paused. He seemed reluctant to go. "Would you like me to tell you a little bit about the history of Pennsylvania?" he asked.

Stella was very pleased. "I would be delighted if you would. Won't you come in and sit down?" He took the chair inside the door and Stella sat in the rocker. Stella had read somewhere that lawyers have to be good actors, and certainly Mr Nathan knew how to make his voice interesting. It was a nice voice anyway, she decided.

"I think you know that William Penn was the founder of Philadelphia. I remember we talked a little about him on your very first night in this city. He it was who coined the name because he thought it possible to found a city of brotherly love. But it was William's father who founded Pennsylvania, he was William also. The province was given to Admiral Sir William Penn by Charles II in 1681 in payment for services rendered. The English king was determined that this middle-Atlantic region must be settled by loyal Englishmen. I believe that the trees were here always, hence the name '-sylvania' but there are many trees not native to the region, so who knows? William who was influenced by the Quakers (as you know, I remember) was full of noble ideals. He wished each man to have his own green plot for his dwelling-place. He envisaged a land of peace and tranquillity. His special dream was an impossible one, a place of religious tolerance for all. A hundred years after William's death Philadelphia had become a city of immense wealth, the major centre of the early industrial revolution in the States. The Declaration of Independence was signed here in Philadelphia and in 1787 the Federal Constitution was framed here."

"Was Philadelphia the biggest city in the United States?"

"It was the capital until 1800; then other cities outstripped it. Washington was eventually created to be the capital."

"You say his dream of religious tolerance is an impossible dream? Aren't all religions tolerated in Philadelphia?"

"It is a city of warring cultures. All religions bring with them their own intolerance of other religions. Of its very nature, religion breeds fanaticism and bigotry."

"I do not feel such strong emotions about my religion," Stella told him seriously and slowly, "I just like the tradition of it, sort of eased and gentled down the centuries."

His luminous smile seemed to tell her that he liked her saying that. Too late, she remembered that he was probably a very learned man with whom ordinary mortals did not trade opinions. He stood up to go. "Mrs Shane, you are a credit to your tradition. Thank you for listening so nicely."

"Thank *you*," Stella said. "I know so much now. It

would have taken me weeks and weeks to read all that."

"Good night," he said but not with any finality, as if he were still reluctant to go.

"Good night, Mr Nathan. And thank you again."

Still he did not go. "I often think," he said, "that if I had lived in Philadelphia two hundred years ago, I would have been a follower of William Penn. Talking of him to you brings back to me my early admiration for his ideals. He deserves to stand on City Hall and survey the city he created. Do you know how high he stands, Stella?"

"From the ground he seems about life-size but he must be bigger if one can see him so clearly."

"He is thirty-six feet tall with his old-fashioned hat on!" He was smiling at Stella. "And you can go up in a lift and view for yourself."

"I know," Stella said, "but the lift is not open to the public on Sundays."

"Well, well," Gil's smile beamed, "here I have lived all my life, and I did not know that William's lift was closed on Sundays."

He was still smiling when he closed the door and Stella was thinking, "Three smiles in three minutes!"

CHAPTER SIX

Carlo woke up at 6 am, so that was Stella's time to rise. It was a long day because, at eleven months, he did not sleep during the day and he was active, ready to be amused, demanding to be played with. Now Stella felt all of her fifty-six years. Carlo needs a young, spirited mummy, she thought, not a granny. She learned that there had been a couple of young *au pairs* before her. Bart had managed to get them into his bed or himself into theirs. One of them, a Swiss girl, was still "seeing" him. "Seeing" implied a continuation of her bed and this was one cause of the many upsurges of Velva's rage. The Swiss girl often rang Bart, usually around midnight when he was in bed with Velva. Bart, apparently, always took the call in lover-like fashion, fending off his wife's attempts to snatch the receiver from him. The ensuing rows echoed to the upper circle, occasionally wakening little Carlo into a kind of peevish whingeing that was hard to endure. Those were bad sleepless nights for Stella but next day no one referred to the disturbance. There were other sleepless nights when

Bart and Velva were reunited, celebrating their new-found ecstasy in their Jacuzzi, drinking champagne and demanding that baby Carlo in his swim trunks join them. Naturally Nanny demurred at disturbing the little fellow's sleep. Sometimes Velva brushed past her objections and carried him from his cot to the Jacuzzi. They never found it necessary to clothe themselves on these occasions. Stella, very much an emigrant from a countryside where partial nudity for sunbathing was permitted in a heatwave and having no previous experience of high-life (if that is what it was) had to suppose that wealthy Americans were weird. Velva's display of her bony, hipless, breastless figure in the Jacuzzi, her crazy eyes, her graceless gestures, her fawning on her husband's body, all struck Stella as the height of stupidity. They had everything, Stella thought; why don't they sleep happily in their beds! She puzzled how such a person as Velva could have achieved the elevated status of being a well-known architect, seemingly a clever one, seemingly a very well-paid one. Maybe not so educated, if she insisted that Ireland was part of the Third World, but no one ever contradicted Velva; not even Bart contradicted her: he merely walked away from her when it suited his purpose.

Not every night was fraught with horrific disruption. There were nights when Stella was peacefully at ease with Carlo cosily sleeping in his nursery. Then she got out paper and pen and set about keeping in touch with the family. She was always hopeful they would reply with block-busters of letters but they never did. She wrote a lot about the city of Philadelphia and she sent picture postcards. She wrote a lot about little Carlo, what a darling he was, what a handsome little boy, how clever. She could not find suitable things to say about the Nathans. She did not like to say they were all weird. She could not moan about the insulting, patronising remarks Velva made about her and her country of origin in the Third World, for the simple reason that she, Stella, scarcely listened any more to either Mrs Rosen or Velva. Who would you want to be, Stella asked herself, to merit praise from either of them.

As the spring days grew warmer and Carlo became ever more alert, Nanny was allowed take him for little walks in his stroller. She must never go outside the confines of Larch Hill. To do so, Velva said, would be to risk Carlo's being kidnapped. The kidnapping was another of Velva's fixations and one of the reasons for the camera in every room. Stella always remembered to keep out of the camera's eye while getting undressed at night. She did not fancy having that picture run through Velva's video.

It took one hour to walk slowly on the footpath

up one side of the park, passing each of the ten houses set on its own acre and each one different. Another hour to walk down the other side, with another ten houses to view. The acreage was mostly at the back of the houses: swimming pools, sun terraces, tennis courts, flower gardens. Stella never saw any vegetables growing; she supposed that, as in Velva's house, everyone ate pre-packaged meals that took a few minutes in the microwave. Stella had grown very tired of this food. It was not appetising. After a few months she noticed (not without some pleasure) that she had shed about twelve pounds. The couple of hours walking every day with Carlo's stroller was also doing her good and she tanned very easily. She chatted away to Carlo as she walked along. She described the houses and her own reaction to them. She never met any people since only cars ever emerged from the driveways. She wondered sometimes if people looked from their windows at this strange walking lady. In Ireland, she reflected, even in big suburban houses, lace curtains would stir with curiosity. In her home place, the woman of the house would come to the door to see whose footfalls were heard, a greeting would be shouted—some remark about the weather probably. She told these thoughts to Carlo but not with sadness. With Carlo, she always smiled, and patted his fuzzy black head, and every now and then, kissed his little hands and cheeks. Carlo's big black eyes followed every movement. He was utterly responsive to her affection, learning to kiss back and touch her hands as he twisted around in the stroller, tugging at the firm harness. Stella was aware that this little American baby was filling her own need for love. He was the substitute for the family back in Ireland but he was also so very lovable for his own sake. Every day the same thought came to her as she attended to the tiny boy: never was there such a clever, attractive, adorable baby in all her experience of children. How will I ever leave him, was the constant cry in her heart, but I must: I am here for only a year. And I could not live for ever with Velva's appalling rows.

One day early in June, when Uncle Gil came into the nursery to visit Carlo, he had an announcement to make. He was more urbane than usual, not so stiff. He actually smiled so nicely that Stella saw at once how handsome he had been in earlier life.

"The family are going to Florida for a week. They usually spend the winter there, spring and summer here. So only a week."

"All of them, Mr Nathan? Carlo too?"

"Yes. Do you wish to go with them, Mrs Shane?"

Stella hesitated. It would be nice to see Florida. She wondered why Velva had said nothing? Gil

Nathan read her thoughts.

"For you, Mrs Shane, it would be from one nursery to another. There would be no sightseeing. I have suggested you be given a week's break—if that would seem all right with you?"

"My life is not so hard," Stella protested. "My little charge is a delight to care for."

"Nevertheless," he said, "you will not take offence if I note the undoubted fact that you have lost some weight and also a lot of sleep. In six months, that can add up."

"But who would look after Carlo?" Stella asked.

"The house in Boca Raton is fully staffed. And perhaps his mother would give a hand." There was a certain edge in his voice on these words. Stella hesitated.

"I feel responsible for you, Mrs Shane. It was I, for the baby's sake, who insisted on an Irish nanny."

"I did not know that," Stella told him. "Why an Irish nanny?"

Now it was his turn to hesitate. He leaned over Carlo's play-pen and gently set a hanging mobile in motion. Little Carlo chuckled in his funny little voice. Gil Nathan turned to look at Stella. "Well, you may smile," he said. "I had an Irish nanny until I was six years of age, and I have never forgotten her in more than fifty years."

"Were there Irish nannies in those days?" Stella asked in wonder.

"That is when there *were* Irish nannies in Philadelphia. Now we have to advertise for them in Irish newspapers in Ireland. No one like them. Their status should be legal."

"I am sure that is a kind compliment," Stella said. "There is still one thing though."

"And that is?" he said.

"I should be terrified to stay alone in this big house."

"I will be here," Gil Nathan said. "I cannot spare the time to go to Florida. There will be a car, Mrs Shane. You have a driver's licence. You took the test when you came."

"Yes, but I am terrified to drive here," Stella said, almost quaking at the thought of the traffic.

"The rest from work will do you good." His tone was brisk. He had resumed his very correct demeanour; the smile had vanished. He clicked shut the door very smartly. Back to being full of himself again, Stella thought. How come he does all the ordering around here?

In due course, Velva gave *her* orders about the packing of Carlo's garments—as many as if he were to be away for a month. She ordered Nanny to iron and fold innumerable outfits for Velva herself.

Although this was not part of Stella's work, it helped to pass the time. Little Carlo amused himself by crawling around his mother's bedroom, an area totally unfamiliar to him. Soon he had shoes scattered all over the floor, which caused Velva to start screaming abuse at him until he took refuge under the ironing-board near Nanny's legs.

"You have succeeded in spoiling my baby, Nanny," shrilled Velva. "It is a good thing to get him out of your clutches for a few days, and bring him back to what he was. Your influence is not progressive. Why don't we strap him into his high chair in front of the television?" There was no need to answer. It wasn't expected. Stella was not afraid that Velva would bother to put her clutches on Carlo. Velva would find someone, anyone, to take the baby off her hands. Stella could only hope it would be someone nice, and young.

When the three big cars had moved down the drive, *en route* for Florida, Stella had to fight off a crying jag. She walked around and around in the back acreage. Distressfully, she questioned herself. Is it only my little boy's sudden departure? Or is it the thought that he is now face to face with his irritable, impatient mother? Or do the tears want to fall for Dave? I never cried for you, Dave. I am always so busy being practical. I am so far from my familiar

home away across the Atlantic. What was it James
Joyce said of the Atlantic...that bowl of bitter tears.
Oh, hell, I am not going to cry. It does terrible things
to my eyes but each thought of Dave is a stab of
remorse.

Maybe I drove him to drink...if only I had been
more understanding, more tolerant. Why wasn't I
compassionate? He was a king compared with the
husband in this house. Bart should save Carlo from
Velva's screaming tongue. Oh, Carlo baby, will you
be all right? Will you understand that they took you
with them? Not that I stopped wanting to mind you—
please, Carlo, don't think it was my fault.

The thought of baby Carlo's bewilderment when
Nanny was not there first thing in the morning
threatened a deluge of tears. Stella sat in a garden
room and gave herself up to sadness. A widow, she
was thinking, that's all I am, a lone widow. I read
that somewhere—a lone widow. It is only now I realise
that. I have been living all the time since I came here
in a pretend world, the nanny in an old movie. My
real world is in Ireland, and Dave is coming home
each evening from college and I have his dinner ready.
And he is not inebriated. He is his old cheery self, like
long ago.

But this is the real world. Dave is not at home, not
at the golf club, Dave is gone. The house is empty,

locked up, the garden overgrown. There is no one there. Even if I went home tomorrow, I am a lone widow.

It was evening when Stella wandered back into the house. She caught sight of her heavy eyelids in the hall mirror. You never knew you were capable of so much self-pity. Being sorry for yourself doesn't suit you at all.

Stella made coffee and took it up to her room. She had all the time in the world without her little Carlo. She lay down on the day bed in the nursery. She left a damp face-cloth folded across her eyes. She drifted off to sleep, subconsciously waiting for Carlo's funny little croaking voice to wake her.

"Mrs Shane! Mrs Shane! Are you all right? Mrs Shane! Stella!"

Stella sat up suddenly. The cloth fell from her eyes.

"What happened to you? You look as if you ran into a wall! Your eyes!"

Gil Nathan was standing beside her. She knew his bulky outline although her eyes would not focus. Far, far away she had heard a voice calling Stella. She must have been dreaming.

"Oh, sorry, sorry, Mr Nathan. Did you ask me something?"

"What happened to you? Your face?"

She turned her face into the pillow. He sat on the side of her bed and put his two hands under her shoulders, lifting her up. "Have you been crying? Poor Stella, why?"

"Don't say anything," she whispered, "or I'll start off again. I'm a sucker for sympathy."

He held her against him, smiling his nice smile. "There's a good manly chest to cry on!" he invited.

For a few moments Stella enjoyed this comfort. When had she last been held in a man's arms? It was almost like being young again.

"Thank you, Mr Nathan," she said, softly disengaging herself. "I fell asleep, I guess. I must bathe my eyes properly."

"Do that," he said, brisk and imperious again, "and we will get something to eat."

She had never been asked to cook a meal, only to look after herself and Carlo. "It is all microwave packages," she said tentatively.

"Which I know," he snapped, "and that is what you have been living on since you came."

"It is fine," she asserted, but weakly.

"Probably the cause of these weary eyes," he said. "We are going out to eat food."

Now Stella was standing up. Going out with Uncle Gil? She would be sacked. Sent home in disgrace. But Velva was in Florida. "I look too awful to be seen in public," she said. "You go on your own, Mr Nathan."

"While you are my guest, call me Gil. May I say Stella? No, no objections. We will both have showers. Be ready in twenty minutes and wear your sun glasses if you are worried about appearances." He stalked out of the room without waiting for a reply. Stella wondered if she should feel affronted and bang the door. Should she? She headed for the shower.

When he came back, he examined her eyes. "I would have preferred to take you out with your ordinary eyes, Stella," he said, "but you are still very appealing." Very gently, he kissed her eyes. What next, Stella wondered in astonishment.

"I know a nice place out on the Valley Forge Road," he told her. "You will like it."

"Just one thing, Mr Nathan, I mean Gil, would Mrs Velva allow me to go out to dinner with you? She employs me."

"I am your employer. You are here because I arranged it. But you are not quite according to specifications. Let's go."

CHAPTER SEVEN

S tella's mind was full of questions. Gil Nathan was a very gracious host; she had to push the questions aside and accept all his attentions with an equal grace. In his comfortable car, he gave her a commentary on the countryside through which they were driving. Valley Forge was an area rich in history.

"George Washington was only a name to me," Stella told him, "as perhaps Brian Boru is to you. But I am reading American history now every Sunday in the Free Library. I can take a couple of books home every week."

"Do you get time to read with little Carlo to be cared for and played with?"

"Not really," Stella confessed, "but I keep the books on my bedside table, and maybe by osmosis I will learn."

"Osmosis!" he echoed, and he was smiling hugely. "Osmosis indeed! You should remember that the hired help uses common one-syllable words and does not read history!"

"Oh, dear," Stella smiled also, "please don't think

too badly of me."

Now Gil laughed, but very gently. "Velva thinks you may be an adventuress! She worried a lot in the beginning that you might very well be an agent of an international kidnap gang!"

"Good heavens!" Stella exclaimed. "So that is why she is always going on and on about people coming to kidnap Carlo! An adventuress?"

"Well," Gil said, "she discovered that you are able to speak French, and Italian."

"No more than a head waiter," Stella smiled, "things I re-learned with the children growing up and helping them with their homework. No television in those days in our house."

"And a good thing too! Tell me about your children."

Stella touched his arm. "Don't you know mothers go all soppy when they start reminiscing about their children's childhood? Please, you tell me instead about George Washington and the battles his men fought to free themselves from English rule."

He glanced around at her. "Is it the Irish in you that rebels against England, that great coloniser of the world? Colonisers always founder. Remember Spain?"

"But the tail-end of the colonisers linger in isolated spots, and even then, it takes a couple of centuries to recover from them." Stella's voice told him that she felt quite deeply about her country's history.

"No more history, Stella. It makes you sad, and I have no feeling for it at all—not even for Spanish history, despite my ancestry. History is embittering. Tonight, our lives are in limbo."

Stella was content to let a companionable silence fall. Being driven along in such a comfortable car and being taken out to dinner (albeit by a man who could abruptly dictate the course of conversation) were pleasurable sensations which were unlikely to come her way very often in Philadelphia. Earlier that day she had filled with tears for the first time in her widowhood. The unshed tears must have been for the loss of Dave, for the loneliness of the world in the absence of her little Carlo. She thought now, as the car moved smoothly through the twilit countryside, that she had come to depend on Carlo's need of her. He was full of trusting and loving and giving. To have all that warmth withdrawn even for a week was a threat to her self-control, and self-control had almost gone down under the threat.

"I am sorry about my eyes looking so red," Stella said to Gil Nathan. "I did not realise that I had been holding back since I came here. I am all right now."

He took his hand from the steering-wheel, and covered her hand. "I understand," he said. "I've been there. When my wife, Elaine, died of inoperable cancer—six years ago—I thought I was a man of cold unfeeling discipline. Eventually, I broke—after a year."

"You loved your wife very much, I am sure," Stella said softly.

For a moment he did not speak. "I had loved her. Yes, I had loved her," he replied.

"And your children?" asked Stella, very quietly.

"We did not have any family. Elaine was absorbed in her career. As I was, also, of course. Maybe we would not have had a family, anyway."

"I am sorry for asking," Stella said. He was still touching her hand, and now he pressed it.

"No," he said, "no family. Which is a large part of my concern for Carlo. He is the present generation. And he is the only one."

"I thought Mister Bart has two brothers. They may have children, and Carlo will have cousins, or maybe he will have brothers and sisters."

"Stella, you will hear in time that Velva had a hysterectomy directly after Carlo's birth. Some complication, nothing could be done. As for Bart's twin brothers: brilliant brains, charming fellows, both homosexuals."

Stella was rather overwhelmed by all this rush of confidential information. There had been plenty of time in five months for her to have been told something. On the other hand, what business was it of hers? She would be gone home to Ireland in another six or seven months. The thought of leaving Carlo was not an easy thought, but neither was the thought of staying away from Ireland and her own family.

"Here we are, Stella. This is one of my favourite little places for food."

"The Place" had been a farmhouse long before. There were several big wooden barns with rounded roofs. The original farmhouse had wide decks off the main building. There were white painted palisades. The effect achieved was of ranch house hospitality. Gil Nathan was well known to the manager. They were escorted to a corner table. Stella was very impressed with the lighting, the linen, the size of the menu. It crossed her mind to wonder why she was being given this special rags-to-riches treatment. She had no illusions that overnight she had turned into a *femme fatale*, irresistible to the rich lawyer. Might as well enjoy it, she supposed, put on the social smile despite the red eyes. The lighting at their table was so subtle that maybe she did not look too bad.

"Were you considered very beautiful when you were a young girl?" enquired her host as he studied the menu.

Stella laughed. "You are not even looking at me!" she teased. "You could just as easily have asked me was I the ugly duckling of the family!"

Now he looked. "The first time I saw you in the airport, I told you I found you very appealing. Tonight, even more so. And now answer the question, please."

"I have no idea," Stella answered pleasantly. "I just don't know. I was eighteen, and pregnant, when Dave married me. Neither my Mum nor my Dad ever got effusive about my looks, and I never remember Dave using the word beautiful. An Irishman's extreme compliment is to tell you you're not the worst."

"Was Dave older than you?" Nathan asked.

"Yes, he was," Stella answered quickly, "twelve years."

Dave, Stella thought, had not quite made it to the three score and ten.

"Were you just out of school then?" Nathan seemed to want to pursue the subject.

"Yes," Stella answered, "I was in my first, and last, term in college. Dave was my tutor." She almost heard the lawyer in Nathan adding his own words, "her tutor and her seducer." Stella added bravely, "Dave was desperately good looking. I was head over heels in love with him."

Gil Nathan has the manner of a prime minister, Stella was thinking as she watched him ordering from the menu: he is quite dogmatic about the appropriate sequence of dishes. He presumes he knows my taste in food and wine. And sure maybe he is right; and I like the quizzical way he smiles after each choice; it assumes my ignorance of Pennsylvania country-style eating.

"Are you hungry?" he enquired.

Stella smiled back at him. "I have been hungry for weeks!"

"Since you left Ireland, I suppose?"

"Since I left home," Stella said lightly.

"Have you heard about the rich miser and the down-and-out during the Depression? The down-and-out was looking for a hand-out; the poor old fellow was starving. 'I am that hungry, I could eat a man!' he pleaded, to which the rich miser replied, 'Do not spare him on my account!'"

Stella was highly amused at this story, which pleased Gil greatly. He joined his deep chuckles in her subdued recurring giggles, relishing the impression he had made on her. Shared laughter drew them into an unexpected friendship as their meal proceeded. Stella let him hold the floor, contributing only a smiling response to his many anecdotes and lawyer-like quips. The few opening questions were all he asked of her personally, and Stella was glad of that. Instinctively she felt there was not yet a sufficient interval since Dave's death for her to chat easily about her life with her husband, and even the thought of her far-distant family threatened tears.

Gil was generous, and knowledgeable, in his appreciation.

"I have seldom enjoyed a meal so much," he told her as he escorted her to his car, his arm linking hers companionably. "You are a very sympathetic listener."

"And you, Mr Nathan, are an entertaining host. Thank you very much, very very much."

In the car, they were silent, at ease with each other, Stella hoped. The journey outward had taken an hour. Stella was always bemused by the enormous amount of traffic on these six-lane highways. She knew the speed limit to be less than sixty miles an hour but the cars seemed to streak up and past as if they were doing ninety. All those cars, all those people, all over this vast land; and at midnight they were all as much on the move as they had been at midday. She suddenly realised that she had been dozing off to sleep when she felt the car pulling over into a lay-by.

Stella clenched her fists into her jacket pockets. Was this what it was all about? In the lay-by, she was going to pay for her candle-lit dinner! Was that expected? She sat rigidly back into the car seat, aware of the bulky figure beside her, aware also that the car door could be opened only by the driver. Where could she run to if she got out? The city of Philadelphia in broad daylight was one thing; the woody open countryside was filled with desperadoes like movies of the Wild West.

But Gil did not touch her. For a long moment there was no sound but the drumming of passing traffic. Then he said in an ordinary voice, neither urgent nor gentle, "Is this a heightened moment for you, Mrs Shane?"

If he meant was she terrified, then yes it was! She did not answer. Her body drew into itself in defence.

"Then this is the moment for me to ask you a question..."(Stella could almost hear the lawyer's voice echoing in a courtroom) "Why are you here in Philadelphia?"

Stella exhaled slowly but her body remained tightly opposed to this inquisition. What the hell were these Nathans on about? Did they think she was a secret agent to be wined and dined to reveal secrets?

"This is ridiculous," she breathed.

"Take your time," advised the lawyer. "Take your time."

Stella was getting angry. "What was the purpose of taking me out to dinner?"

"You surprise me," he said. "Perhaps our minds are on different tracks."

"It was unnecessary to give me wine to make me give a different answer to the one I have already given to Carlo's mother and his maternal grandmother—

more than once. I am here because I answered an advertisement in an Irish newspaper: "plain settled woman etcetera."

"Let us take this easy," said Gil. "You may know I investigated your credentials very thoroughly. Your husband was in a well-paid job all his life. He took a considerable sum of money in lieu of a pension only a couple of years back. Your family have successful careers; they could undoubtedly help you. You have a house—a roof over your head. At home in your own place you could have a good life. Why exactly did you come halfway across the world, lonely, missing your family?"

"Is it not enough that I came in good faith?" Stella felt almost like venting anger just as, earlier that day, her tears had almost vented themselves. "Is it not enough that I am a proper nanny to my charge? What do I have to go on proving? And why? And to whom?"

"You are the best nanny that little boy could have—completely, lovingly trustworthy. So good that I fear ever to lose you for—for him. But you know, and I know, that there is more to you than that. Please, please, give me one reason why you left home so hurriedly. Please, Stella."

So, we are back to Stella again, she thought. What's the matter with him? I'm damned if I'm going to tell him that I have no idea what Dave did with the money. I'm damned if I'll tell him what happened when I went to the bank to ask for a cheque-book.

"Was it shock, Stella? The death was unexpected?"

Stella had been expecting Dave's sudden death for several years. No one had ever said alcoholism. The relief was that Dave had not died in an accident while under the influence. Nor killed an innocent person on the road while he was in that state. It could so easily have happened. His sudden death on the seventeenth green of his golf course was truly a glorious way to go, just what he would have most wanted: no lingering painful, humiliating disease. Dave would not have liked that. That kind of death was for other people.

"Not his death," she muttered.

"Was it money, then?"

"Oh, there's always a problem with money but it was not merely money." Stella's voice was sad now. The anger had given way to poignant remorse.

"Tell me, Stella. I want to know. I must know."

Stella wondered why he must know and what point there was in telling him. She began to speak, at first hesitantly, then plunging on.

"Please don't laugh at me when I tell you why I thought I could not get away from home quickly enough. Please don't. I know I'm an old woman and should have more sense. It does not happen here. By the time I fall into bed here I sleep like a top until Carlo's little chirrup wakes me at six. I know it's all imagination but back at home it was something else. You see—and please don't jeer at me—I could not get away from Dave. He was waiting at the turn of the stairs; he was in the garden lurking behind trees...in his grave-clothes, that awful brown habit of a dead monk—all torn and muddy—and his face was only a cobweb, only a dusty cobweb and Dave had such a handsome face when...when...whe..."

Gil pushed the seat back and took her in his arms. "There, there, no more, no more." Stella was scarcely aware of the comfort offered. Her words stumbled on: "...and one night, the last night I slept there in my home, he was in my bed. The stench was unbearable. And he said, and he said, and he said, 'I can always come, the grave is at the end of the garden.'" Stella was shuddering, reliving her fear.

"And is it," Gil asked, "at the end of the garden?"

"Yes," Stella whispered, "the graveyard begins where the garden ends."

"You should not have had the fear of being haunted, Stella. You were the pure faithful wife of forty years. Few men could have that boast."

Now Stella became aware of Gil's comforting warmth, his chin resting lightly against her head. His last words echoed around her ears. Now was not the time to tell him, and there would never be a time to tell him or tell anyone else either, that the pure and faithful wife had ceased to love her husband, had lost interest in his loving. Never admitted. Never confessed. Dave had never accused her. His silence had judged her. That was when the heavy drinking began in earnest. That was the cause of his death and in death he would continue to demand remorse and retribution.

"So it was fear that made you decide to leave Ireland. To put time and distance in place of grief. Fear can be a terrible thing."

His arms were holding her and his kindness was very welcome.

Stella allowed herself to lie in his arms for a little while. She was not about to start an affair of small comforts with him. She was a woman now in her own rights, no longer an uncaring wife to an uncaring man. Marriage had ceased to be a rewarding state for her, no longer a state of grace. She did not think that a sleazy affair between the nanny and the uncle would be any better. She withdrew to her side of the car. Very gently she patted his coat sleeve and said, "Time to go back to Larch Hill, I guess."

Alone in her room, undressing slowly, pretending to herself that she had been taken to dinner by a nice (and very rich) man for the value of her bright conversation, Stella was aware of a vague bewilderment. He had not made a pass at her but he had wanted something. Why the insistence on finding out her motive in becoming nanny to little Carlo? It should be very plain and obvious to a learned lawyer that behind her endurance of Velva's cruel ignorant patronage lay the motivation of money. But why was this old guy making up to the poor emigrant nanny? A poor emigrant who was in America to save a few dollars, an emigrant from the Third World no less. For consolation Stella took out her savings book. Counting the weeks that the widow's welfare pension was accumulating in the bank afforded her a kind of joyless satisfaction. At least she would have a bit of spending money when she went home at the end of this year.

CHAPTER EIGHT

Stella had the following days to herself. She heard Mr Nathan's footsteps on the stairs at night, no more than that. She caught up with her letter-writing to the family, noticing how many questions were in the letters as to their health and events and how little she had to tell of herself. She longed for letters in return. She longed for news of Ireland; any sort of news, even of the weather, would do. She had bought, several times, a bulky newspaper on her day off but there was never a mention of Ireland. Indeed the newspaper contained no news outside of Pennsylvania and was ninety per cent advertising.

The family were due to return home on Sunday. On Friday morning, Gil Nathan joined her in the kitchen for breakfast.

"You look very well," he said, "rested. Do you care for opera?" The usual imperious manner, thought Stella.

"I have not often been to the opera in Dublin, Mr Nathan, because we always lived in the country. But yes, I love the music."

"Operas only in Dublin, the capital city?" he queried.

"Perhaps in Cork also. Belfast too, I'm sure. But yes, every year in Dublin." She had often thought it was a duty for her to introduce her youngsters to opera and theatre, but Dave saw better recreational uses for his hard-earned money. They were getting an education, weren't they?

"Your eyes can go moody, Mrs Shane. I was saying I have tickets for *Madame Butterfly* for Saturday. The Metropolitan!"

The buttering-up process again? Stella was not sure how to look. Wide-eyed acceptance? Or withdraw haughtily? Oh, what the hell! The week was nearly over.

"You are taking a party to the opera, Mr Nathan?" She hoped her tone was cool, detached.

"No," he said abruptly, "I am taking you. You, Stella. To see *Madame Butterfly*. Tomorrow night."

"Thank you. I have always wanted to see that very opera. Thank you, Gil."

Within seconds, she heard the up-and-over garage door, and his car moving out. Did he have to be so two-faced? A beautiful invitation, and then not even the usual "Have a good day!" Come to think of it, he never used hackneyed phrases.

Late that night, when she was reading in bed, he

came in with barely a tap on the door.

"I saw your light, Stella."

Stella felt she wanted to clutch up the bedclothes but being coy seemed silly with this man. She half-closed the book of American history, holding her fingers on the page she had been reading.

"May I?" he said, sitting on the edge of her bed, his eyes fully on her. Stella was apprehensive but to let apprehension show would be offensive. She held her breath.

"We dress for the opera," he said.

"Good Lord!" Stella was relieved. "If you had told me this morning, I would have told you I have no evening wear. Remember what you said about the hired help getting above her station?"

"Did I say that?" His smile was amused, indulgent. Stella knew any woman would fall for him when he smiled that tender smile. Watch it, Stella, she warned herself: he is playing games.

"You will have to take someone who has a better class of wardrobe." Stella, feeling safely in charge, gave him her best smile. No point in telling him she had lovely clothes at home. Home was far away. "No evening dress, I'm sorry."

"Did I not see you in a long full skirt the night of Velva's Trivial Pursuit party, when you filled in for Bart?"

"But that is only a summer skirt," Stella said.

"A dark colour with vivid flowers?"

"Black with red flowers like poppies. Is that the one?"

"Wear that," he said, standing to go, "with the black blouse you wore at the airport."

He closed the door firmly as he departed. His action plainly said: If you had any ideas, Mrs Shane, you can forget them! Or so Stella thought. She went over to the mirror. The nightdress was pretty. She looked as ordinary as ever, middle-aged, pink-cheeked, a little plump. She was puzzled by the feeling of being let down, lightly and politely.

The Metropolitan Opera House was overwhelmingly splendid. The foyer and the stairs were thronged with elegant people, each lady more glamorous than the next. Stella was inclined to stay in Mr Nathan's bulky shadow, hoping no one would notice her lack of designer label. Gil, on the other hand, kept on drawing her forward to be introduced to the many acquaintances who accosted him. "Ah, Charles! Ah, Anita! Meet a friend of mine, Lady Shane on a visit from Europe!" His friends quickly took in the title and seemed very impressed.

When they were seated, he was smiling at her the amused tender smile to which she could easily become addicted. "You are mischievous," she told him.

"Yes, Nanny." He was still smiling and pressing her hand.

"But I felt so ill-dressed beside all those gorgeous women. So unfashionable!"

"You look perfect," he said. "Those dames will be all down Fifth Avenue tomorrow, looking for full skirts with bright flowers! What was it your Irish playwright said, 'Fashion is what one wears oneself; dowdy are the clothes of other people.'"

Stella thought it sounded like Oscar Wilde but not quite correctly quoted.

"You are quite amazing," she said to him.

"And you are very appealing." She felt the warmth of his hand on her thigh as he smoothed the skirt of bright flowers.

Did Gil Nathan know, Stella mused, that of all the operas, *Madame Butterfly* was the one most guaranteed to open the heart? When Butterfly breathed out the last note of her passionate hope for the return of her lover-husband, Stella's tears were running down her cheeks and she had sought the comfort of Gil's hand. When the packed audience rose to its feet in a thunderous ovation, she tried apologetically to withdraw her hand; Gil held on. Bending his head low to hers against the storm of clapping, he said, "That was the best part of the opera!" His hand comforting hers, or the aria, "One Fine Day?"

Outside the Metropolitan, a cab drew up to receive them as if Gil had ordered its magic appearance. They had made the six o'clock flight up to New York and they would make the eleven o'clock back to Philadelphia. Gil was full of apologies. "This is no way to treat a guest, first time in New York. We should be going to supper. Can you hold off from fainting until we hit Philly?" In this genial, bantering tone he was very attractive. I should be steeling my heart and all my senses against this man, Stella thought. He is up to something, and here I am, eating out of his hand.

In the airport, Gil surprised her by taking her to the bar for a drink. "This is a celebration, Stella, and you do not remember? You always raise the left eyebrow when you want to ask a question."

"I did not know I could raise one eyebrow on its own!" Stella smiled at him. "A celebration of what?"

"Six months to the day since I met you in this airport!"

Stella wished she were safely home in bed in Larch Hill. All this flattery could have an effect on her. She had begun to have an instinctive feeling that there was more in Gil Nathan's intentions than a bit of a one-night stand. In fact, despite his tender smile, he was building up to a request of quite another sort. As she was to discover.

"We will have a bite of supper before we go home. I hate talking important stuff in the car."

He was fussy over the supper. He actually consulted her likes and dislikes. Stella was watching him from under her eyelashes. He was even, for the wily lawyer which she was sure he was, a little nervous.

At the coffee stage, he began to talk about Carlo. Now the attentive host disappeared and Stella felt they were in a courtroom, with him arguing a case.

"As I have explained to you, Carlo is likely to be the last of the line from my great-grandfather. No, not likely, certain. At eighteen he will come into his inheritance from my father and my grandfather. My brother and I at eighteen, Bart and his two brothers at eighteen and then Carlo." Stella waited, pretending to sip the coffee. Quite evidently there was a purpose in all this preamble.

"To the Nathans money is important," he said. "It is more important than people, most of the time. When Carlo inherits, it will be a vast fortune. It has been accumulating for many years, and there are many years to go before he will be eighteen. Do you understand, Mrs Shane, that when I say vast, I really mean vast?"

Stella nodded, and successfully stifled a yawn. He had put her neatly back in her Nanny role with his "Mrs Shane." Oh, well, the association of ideas, she supposed. Irish emigrant nannies and vast fortunes were very unrelated.

"Yes," he continued, "it is inevitable that Velva will sue for divorce—eventually. You will excuse my bluntness when I say that she got Bart into her bed when she was fourteen and now he is very tired of her. He is an impossible character where women are concerned but I doubt if he has ever cared seriously for a woman, no matter how beautiful—and there have been some such. Perhaps he felt a mistaken sympathy for Velva. That surprises you? When I was young, I read a very moving book. It was by Stefan Zweig. The name of it was *Beware of Pity*. A gallant young man marries a cripple. In marriage, pity has not a long duration."

Gil Nathan ordered more coffee and Stella took the occasion to glance at her watch. Two in the morning!

"You know, and no doubt admire, Velva's ageless mother. She is a lady who has no need of money. She has reefed and skinned five rich husbands, and the present incumbent is extremely wealthy. She is the one who is encouraging the divorce. She resides in the house for that purpose. Velva will not be able to hold out against her mother. You will have observed that she becomes an hysterical twelve-year-old when her mother is angry. When there is a divorce, Velva will get custody of Carlo. A junior attorney could shop Bart: he is notorious in Philly—call girls, night clubs, bawdy houses, the whole lot."

"I like him," Stella said.

He did not appear surprised. "Yes," he said. "Away from Velva, well away from her, he could amount to something."

He glanced at Stella. "Will we continue this conversation at another time? You are tired."

"There may not be another chance," Stella answered. "I think you were about to make a point?"

"Very well," he said abruptly. "If there is a divorce, I intend to use my influence, considerable influence, to obtain split custody. In effect, neither Velva nor Bart will get the child."

Stella stared at him. He had all the appearance of an angry man. He drained his coffee cup and rose as if ready to go. Stella detained him with a hand on his sleeve.

"And what would become of Carlo?" Stella asked most fearfully. "I love that little boy as if he were my own."

Now he subsided back on his chair and gave Stella the full spread of his attractive smile. "Then *you* will have custody of him and the parents will have equal visiting rights."

He saw the look on her face. "Dumbfounded"

described it for him. Stella could see that. "Mrs Shane, I think you are very tired. Do not say a word. No, please. As they say, sleep on it."

Without seeming haste, he ushered her out of the restaurant and into his car. He said nothing on the drive back to Larch Hill and each time she opened her mouth to voice an objection to his assumption that he could order her life, she had a vision of little Carlo's big black eyes filled with tears as they sometimes were when Velva took no notice of him. Stella could feel his soft, baby lips against her throat, as so often they were, seeking her reassurance to his need for pity. Now he was only a baby, trying his first hand-grip on a chair, trying out his first words. Must he go on all on his own, becoming a little boy without a friendly shoulder to lean on? Stop it, Stella, she cautioned herself. Stop it. Stop it. You are here for a year, remember? A year to get together a bit of cash. A year, and six months has gone already.

He did not accompany her up the stairs, and she was uncertain if a speech of thanks for the evening in New York was seemly, after his outburst. Although sleep did not come easily, she was too tired to think coherently. Next morning there was no sign of Gil Nathan.

In the afternoon, the family returned home. If Stella had a fear that Carlo would have forgotten her, the fear was completely banished when Bart lifted the little fellow out of his car seat. The baby's black, expressive eyes sought Stella immediately and once in her arms he settled in against her, his lips on her throat, his fingers curled around her upper arm. Her heart swelled with love for him; then almost immediately her heart contracted. She seemed to hear Gil Nathan's voice telling her that money is more important than people. She hugged the little boy gently, whispering against his ear so he would remember what had become her constant cuddle-word for him: "Dotey little lamb, Nanny's dotey little lamb." He remembered, he knew, his little body pressed closer.

"Don't stand there ogling, Nanny," was Velva's greeting. "Take the kid up to his own quarters. He's awake since six o'clock this morning and peevish as hell. Oh, Nanny, what's the matter with you! Get moving!"

Upstairs in the nursery, it was a repeat of Stella's first day. Carlo needed badly to be changed. Stella lowered him into his bath-tub, encouraging him with gentle splashes. His eyes never left her face and they were questioning eyes. Stella kept answering the questions: you are back with Nanny. Nanny loves you. There's a big kiss on your shoulder to prove it. Yes, I missed you—most awfully I missed you. Yes, I worried about you—all the time. There's another big kiss on the other shoulder. You love me? Sure, I know you do, you dotey lamb. And who loves you? Nanny does.

Wrapping him in a fleecy towel, Stella carried him back into the nursery and seated in the rocking chair she dried him most carefully. "Now, the little toes, have to be careful to dry between the little toes. And what about the little ears? These little cotton-buds for the ears. There now, there now. No need to keep looking up at me. I'm not going away. Nanny loves you."

Zippered into his cosy sleeper, she held him against her shoulder, gently rocking the chair with one foot, singing to him in a low murmur any old Irish songs that came into her head from the long-ago nights when she rocked her own little babies to sleep. So many old Irish songs seemed sad and lullaby-like, so many songs of exile and lost love. She closed her own eyes as she saw his lids drooping, her voice growing softer and slower. She loved to hold him like that. It brought back the long ago joy of holding her own children, of holding Dave in the first years of their marriage, when the romance of young love was in the air day and night. When at last she stood up to put Carlo down in his cot, she became conscious of a figure standing in the doorway.

"That was beautiful," Gil Nathan said. "You restored my early childhood. You are my nostalgia."

Stella turned to face him, to defy him if the ready words would come. "I..."

"No!" he said abruptly, "not now. You are still thinking, considering. There will be an occasion." Then he was gone. The door of his suite was clicked shut.

He infuriates me, Stella thought, he really does infuriate me. Who the hell does he think he is? God Almighty? Then she smiled at her vehemence. The likes of him probably wouldn't acknowledge such a person as a God almighty!

The days resumed their course as before the break. The turbulent rows between Velva and Bart had been reduced in the summer temperatures to a hateful snarling bickering, endlessly flaring and smouldering. To an Irish person, accustomed to the summer weather of an island, some sun, some rain, always a balmy breeze, the weather of a Philadelphian July was spectacular. The days of brilliant heat, blue skies, red sunsets, hot nights, all came one after the other, as if summer had been declared not a season but an eternity. The many varieties of blossoming trees in Larch Hill were a delight during the walks taken by Stella with her little charge in the stroller. These were the times she should have spent in mulling over the confidences of Gil Nathan; in speculating and debating with herself what was best to do; best to do for Carlo and for her own future. Instead she spent the time talking baby-talk to little Carlo, and anyway, the weather was too hot for serious cogitation. Time enough when the summer ended. Carlo would be that little bit older, that little bit less dependent. Just sometimes, she was afraid. Carlo had begun to call her by a little name he had invented: mum mum mum.

CHAPTER NINE

The week in Florida had had a dual purpose, Stella learned in time. Property had been sold and different property had been bought. The family always spent the winter months in Florida, and the previous house had not been big enough or grand enough or sufficiently well placed by the ocean. The newly purchased house would be ready for occupation at the end of September.

Any information Velva wished to convey to Stella, she directed to Mrs Rosen. As the three women were scarcely ever in the same vicinity, such conversations were few and brief. Stella was a mere cypher in these exchanges.

"Nanny will travel with Carlo and Uncle Ambert in the last week, and Aunt Alice, of course. She can drive."

"Is Aunt Alice a reliable driver?" asked the beautiful Mrs Rosen.

Aunt Alice and Uncle Ambert were the silent couple who lived on the "dress-circle." They were retired from teaching in Bryn Mawr, a university for women.

Stella thought of them as the "scuttle-butts." It was her impression of their hurried ascent of the stairs. She had come to suppose they occupied some kind of watch-dog presence in the house. It was disturbing in the beginning to see the glint of an ancient eye in a door jamb but Stella had got used to that along with the endless phone/camera/television presence. Stella could not imagine that Aunt Alice would be very entertaining company on a two-day drive but she would have Carlo to take care of. She and Carlo would be sufficient company for each other in two months' time.

Mrs Rosen directed her enchanting smile in Stella's direction and her words to her daughter. "So that you are sure that Carlo will be in safe hands?"

"I am more worried about you than I am about Carlo, Momma." Stella drifted insufficiently out of ear-shot. Apparently, during the week away, Mrs Rosen had had consultations with a cosmetic surgeon of international repute. She would spend part of the winter months in Florida in having the size of her bust reduced. Now she and Velva were talking of his estimated bill and nursing expenses which had arrived that morning. It was clear to Stella that the whole idea of surgery on her Mother's bosom gave Velva the shivers. Velva's fourteen-year-old tearful whine took over from her normal demanding voice. Stella always hurried away from either of these sounds, as she did now, up the stairs to the nursery.

With relief she heard the shrill-voiced Velva making plans with her mother to go out shopping to their favourite mall. There never seemed an end to their need for more and ever more shopping. Stella sometimes wished they would buy food that was not always the deep-frozen variety. But even so, she thought, even with the ghastly microwave packets, I am glad I ran away from home. I was truly terrified of Dave getting up out of the grave in that awful brown ragged shroud and trailing down through the trees to get into my bed. This place may be peculiar, and the people very weird, but I am not afraid. I can handle it. I think I can handle it.

The door of Gil Nathan's suite was ajar. He called her name as she reached the nursery door. "Mrs Shane!"

Stella wondered if she were going to be Nanny or Stella. She stood at the door.

"Come in," he said impatiently, "and shut the door."

Nanny, Stella thought, but she was wrong. He was watching something from his window. Then he turned, and his voice softened.

"They have all gone out," he said, "and Carlo is having a wonderful nap. Sit down for a moment, please."

They sat facing each other across his big desk which was littered with documents.

"You have been thinking over, considering, what I said to you?" His question was more of an assumption.

"No, Mr Nathan," Stella said in a very business-like way.

"Do you mean, no, you will not comply with my suggestion? Or no, you have not given your mind to the matter?"

Stella looked at him for a long moment. He was a big man, putting on weight, going bald. He had dark eyes, compressed lips. What was there to be afraid of? He was nothing to her. Why had she been thinking of him? His attractive smile had been a lure to trap her into a kind of compliance.

"I meant two things by no, Mr Nathan. Firstly I have no clue as to what all your talk was leading to. No understanding of it. And also, I hate the idea that I should be forced into some sort of collusion."

"Forced?" he repeated. "Surely your love for Carlo would lead you into the path of what is best for him? Your very natural love. If you knew what that little boy had gone through in the months before you came! A succession of French and Swiss girls. Cheap whores! Forgive the expression. You are the answer, the perfect answer. In your care he is blossoming. Carlo snapped back after the week in Florida (in *her* care or lack of it). I feared for him but he snapped back. You had laid the foundation. Stella, think! He..."

"Mr Nathan." Stella could not take any more. "Please let me speak for myself, please, for once. Surely, humble as my position is, I am entitled to a voice?"

"Speak then," he said. He placed his palms together as one who grants a prayer.

"All right," Stella swallowed her pride. "No one asked me to come here. I am a free agent. But I came for a year only. When the year is up, I am free to go home."

"You are not a free agent," he said. "You are illegal. You could be deported tomorrow."

"And you could be heavily fined for bringing me here," Stella answered but not impertinently. The year was important to her. Only by staying a year could she hope to have saved enough at home to pay off the debts and make a fresh start. And have the Nathans pay the return fare.

"So we have a fair equation, Mrs Shane." Stella could see he was angry because she was not immediately bending to his will. She had to make a point.

"Mr Nathan, I will admit I love little Carlo. I pity him. I want to be his friend. But I am firmly convinced that his mum and dad are the best people for him.

No, wait, Mr Nathan. I know they are going through a bad patch just now..."

He laughed harshly. "It has been like that for ten years, since the first day. They went into a marriage counselling course—well, she did anyway. They were advised to have a child to solve their difficulties, to bring them together in united love for their child. Bart did not want a child by her; he wanted a divorce." Now he hesitated, then he said, slowly and carefully, "But a child was begotten. Mistakenly, perhaps. You can see the results."

Stella said carefully, "I think Bart loves little Carlo and feels akin to him."

"Yes, Carlo is a Nathan," he snapped shortly.

Stella rose to go. "Don't go!" he said. "Don't go yet!" He stared at her in a kind of hungry way, so Stella had to lower her eyes. "I think maybe you are right. If I could be sure that Bart would get custody of the child, I would let the divorce get under way."

Stella voiced her important question very gently, "So it comes down to this: the Nathans must not lose Carlo because his vast fortune would go to Velva and her mother? It is money, isn't it, Mr Nathan?"

For a while he did not speak, his head lowered into his hands. Then he looked at her, pleading, supplicating: "Money?" he muttered. "Money? I could buy Velva out tomorrow without a thought. No, it is not money." His voice broke on a tragic sob. "Carlo is my son."

Stella got out of the room as fast as a flash. She closed the nursery door and collapsed onto the rocking-chair. Her mind was blanked-out. She could scarcely take in what he had said. She could not believe it, but she made herself think. Was it some sort of blackmail to make her tune-in to his plan to outwit Velva and Bart of the custody of their child? But that was ridiculous. Velva had to know the father of her child. But did Bart know? Would such knowledge enable Bart to rid himself of Velva? Stella suddenly recalled the warm relationship between Bart and Uncle Gil. Little as she saw of the assembled family, that friendship between those two men had stood out. Had, indeed, been a source of some of Velva's unending jealously: "You think more of your Uncle Gil than you do of my mother or of me!"

Stella was glad when Carlo woke from his nap. Busying herself with the baby, making him comfortable, talking to him, reading to him all the little animal and fairy-story books on his packed shelves, kissing him, loving him, and answering the need for reassurance which was always, like a question, in his great black eyes. "You are a handsome fellow," she told him. "Any girl would give an arm and a leg for those long, black eyelashes. Oh, Carlo baby, if only we lived in Ireland, you and I. This America is such a queer, unwieldy place. If you and I were together in my little country house, you could have a dog for a pet. You'd like that? You could even have a donkey and ride on his back. In Ireland it is easy to get a donkey. And you could have a big black furry cat. And the cat could have kittens. You'd just adore little kittens, Carlo. When they are a week old and the mother cat is feeding them, maybe six of them, they are just so sweet. You could see them every day, Carlo baby. They get every day a little bit bigger and fluffier. You'd like that, wouldn't you? And we would give each kitten a name. Not silly names like Wishy and Pussy but real legendary names. Did I tell you about the monk hundreds of years ago who shared his cell with his cat called Pangur Bán? It must have been a big cat because it caught mice for its breakfast, dinner and supper, and white because 'bán' is the Irish word for 'white.' I will teach you the little verses when you are bigger.

Me and Pangur Bán, my cat,
Each has its inspiration:
Pangur's mind is set on mice
And mine on education.

More than any fame, I love
My books, pursuing learning;
Nor does my friend envy me—
Mice are Pangur's yearning.

And there are more verses, Carlo baby, for you to learn when you are bigger. When you are bigger! When you are bigger! But I won't be here then, Carlo. You will be a little American boy, eating hot-dogs and going to baseball games."

Stella kept thoughts of Gil Nathan, the unbelievable thoughts, at bay all day and every day, while she devoted all her energies to her little charge. She endured the nerve-wracking rows that flared up daily between Velva and Bart. She noted the deadly silence in the house when only the phones and the television worked and Bart had taken off with his latest love. There were nights when Velva took out her car and searched the clubs for Bart, returning with him in the small hours, celebrating the reunion with champagne in the Jacuzzi. The Jacuzzi made a noise like a launch at Cape Canaveral and no one at all could sleep on those nights.

There were quiet nights when no one stirred, nights when Stella tried to face the fact that Carlo was the son of Gil Nathan by Velva, wife of Bart. How can I believe it, Stella wondered. I cannot believe it of Gil

Nathan. He hates Velva even though he says she is the mother of his son. When did he begin to hate her? I hated myself for hurting Dave. One wild foolish stupid night when the best friend put a very drunk Dave to bed. The best friend was a very good best friend: kind, lovable, understanding. I was the wicked one. Tempting. Flirting. Suggestive. Lying on the grass. Flaunting. Provocative. Did I see all that as retribution on a drunk husband? How idiotic can one be at twenty-six! Dave saw some of that stupidity at five o'clock in the morning. He was flamingly angry because I had stayed out in the garden all night. He was still drunk when I sashayed into the bedroom, half-undressed. He exercised his rights—that was his own untender term for his action. And out of that encounter came Sybil whom he wanted to deny. Even at birth she was the image of Dave and grew more like him with every passing year. I remember the night of Hazel's conception. Oh, how well I remember! I was longing for Dave to love me again as he used to in the beginning.

But Gil Nathan wasn't a mere thirty-odd years of age when Carlo was conceived. He was near sixty and Velva was thirty-three. Yes, Carlo was a Nathan. He is as like Bart as he is like Gil. And Velva is crazy about Bart, crazy, possessive, jealous. And Gil hates Velva. And Gil brought me here, a strange woman, to replace

Velva in the baby's affection. But on the other hand Velva displaced herself. Would she have cared for any baby, no matter who the father was? Another question. Was Velva play-acting with both her husband and his uncle, and so is unsure who is the father? How can Gil Nathan make out that he is the father? Does Velva know? Oh, Velva knew everything. She had a line of talk about perversions that always came out in the screaming rows. No, it was all a lie. Gil Nathan was trying to blackmail me into staying, by playing on my affection for the little boy. If I were to be assured that the child was Gil's then I would have to be his ally in a custody contest.

When loneliness descended on her Stella longed poignantly for Ireland and her own dear house among the trees. Somehow she would make up for the past even though Dave was not there any more. She would be a model grandmother. Ireland began to seem a safe and easy place to live in. She forgot all the years of making-do: all the years of resenting the genteel poverty, the keeping-up of appearances, the interviews with Reverend Mothers and Reverend school principals when school fees were due and long overdue. All the years when formal demand notices for everything were the order of the day. All of those things were natural, Stella thought, but the events in this house were confusing, mystifying, unnatural by her standards. Here were people who had money to burn, luxury in abundance, every possible blessing of education and culture, and yet there was no prospect of happiness for them. Their lives had become a battleground.

Back home in Ireland the prospect of spending the winter in Florida would have seemed an exciting prospect to Stella. Now, she began to fear that August and September would prove too much to endure. The only way out would be to appeal to Gil Nathan for the return fare when the ten months were up. Gil Nathan? He would turn on that attractive smile, his voice would soften charmingly, he would tell her again she was his nostalgia.

Yes, Stella thought, and underneath all that plámás he is a double-dyed villain. I must not trust him. Maybe he was in Velva's bed (although that is hard to put a picture on) and maybe he is just a liar. Remember what he said: money is more important than people. The funny thing is, added Stella to herself, that if I stay here long enough, I might find money the most important thing too. After all money fluctuates only in the market-place. Emotion is not so easy to control. But she was damned if she was going to dig into her savings for the return fare. Being an Irish emigrant had probably never been easy. Longing for home and the old familiar ways was a universal longing. Just a year; just a year. She put the thought firmly to the forefront of her mind that Carlo was her charge, not her child. Loving him was another matter—nothing to do with her mind.

Every morning when Gil Nathan came to visit, Stella repeated the formula: "Say morning to Uncle Gil, Carlo! Good boy, you nearly have it. Now blow a big kiss to Uncle Gil, pet. Oh, you are a lamb!" And Stella kept her eyes on Carlo's vivid little face.

CHAPTER TEN

V elva was never in a hurry to hand over letters from Ireland. She left them unsorted with her own letters in her desk. Pride would not allow Stella to ask "Any post for me?" The contempt in Velva's negative voice could upset a day. So a letter became a rare occasion. One morning, a letter in Alec Mackay's handwriting was easily distinguishable, so Stella held out her hand. Velva's voice was malicious. "It is to be hoped, Nanny, that you read all these letters in your free time on Sundays, and not in my time." There was not the slightest point in answering back to Velva. Stella put the letter in her apron pocket and continued to coax Carlo to eat his cereal. Eventually, when Velva had gone out, and Carlo was playing with his toys, Stella opened the letter from Alec.

Dear Stella,
I have made a hundred attempts to write this letter,
unsure if I should be writing to you at all, not
wanting to ask anyone for your address, and finally
getting it in Philip's phone book under pretence of

making a phone call in his house. They had us o
ver, a dinner party for the newly-weds. I cannot get
used to the idea that you are my mother-in-law, a
kind of forbidden species, and I miss you out of my
life more than I could ever express. I want to say
please help me but I do not want to place a burden
of responsibility on you. The fact is I am not making
a success of Sybil's happiness. I think she is unable
to recover from her father's death. I miss Dave too,
greatly.

A couple of hours have gone in since I wrote
that last sentence. Stella, maybe a few lines from
you to your daughter would help her. After all, you
too must be grief-stricken. In some way, which is
impossible to understand, she resents your going
away. She is full of distrust. It is pitiable.

Always your friend,
Alec

Sybil's happiness? Stella could swear an oath that
her happiness had never relevance to anyone but her
father. With the usual feeling of having failed, of
having gone wrong somewhere, a feeling always
associated in Stella's mind with Sybil, she remembered
watching Dave and the bride walking up the centre
aisle of the village church. She remembered the glad
feeling of relief that this reign was almost over, that

the rightful wife would at last take her rightful place. Twenty-eight years of usurpation. Now the thought came into Stella's mind that perhaps Dave had not been able to face the future with Stella and without his little queen, his princess, his *Altezza*, and even at times, Your Royal Highness. No, that was childish, just a game they played. It had ceased to make Stella jealous years and years before. Now she remembered Sybil's choir-boy face as Dave handed the bride to Alec at the altar steps. She had not gone fully, radiantly, onto Alec's outstretched arm. Rather she had clung to her father, kissing his lips in a sort of lingering farewell. And she had kissed him on the lips when he lay dead in his coffin, passionately, slowly, as if to prolong the kiss into eternity.

Stella read the letter again. She felt a great sympathy for Alec, but "grief-stricken" was not a word she could apply to herself. She knew, and hoped her instincts were correct, that a letter from her to Sybil would only exacerbate whatever emotion was being portrayed. Sybil had never outgrown her need for attention. There had been times when Dave was away at conferences, when Daddy was not safely lodged in his study, so to speak, and Sybil had made the entire household suffer her fault-finding. As they grew older, the others had put distance between themselves and her. Sunday lunch had become a ritual family event for getting together and this had always included Alec. Up to the day she got married, Sybil had lived at home. There was never a question of her taking a little apartment in town. Would Dave have permitted that? Would he, Stella wondered, have preferred that? I'll never know now, Stella thought, we just drifted farther and farther apart. Seldom any time for me but for his princess he had all the time in the world. Guilty, remorseful, regretful, puzzled? Yes, all of those feelings. But grief-stricken? No, not since the day I had the interview with the bank manager. And yet, when Gil Nathan questions me I long for home, for my own place, my own people, my own country.

Perhaps I *will* write to Sybil. Maybe I will write to Alec, or will I? Some day when—when what? I should, I suppose. Poor Alec. Poor old Alec. He deserves better than that. He was my friend.

In August the tremendous heat died down. Stella and little Carlo were able to resume their walks with the stroller up and down the avenue. Carlo was now a very sturdy little fellow. "You'll be making bits of this stroller, boyo," she smiled at him, "the way you are jumping up and down! A proper pram you should have had! One of those with a dip in the middle so you could sit facing either way and not have to turn around twistiways to see my face." Carlo had a string of words which babbled along in harmony with her talk. He had learned to raise his voice in an interrogative way at the end of each babble, so a reply was called for. This gave him the great pleasure of being answered and his little face beamed with delight. There were times when Stella knew that Gil Nathan was in his study, and she suspected he was watching the antics of Carlo and Nanny when they came within his range. She often saw the gimlet eye of Uncle Ambert at another window. She knew the police, the fire brigade, the ambulance and even the lifeguards would all be called out if she and the stroller left the environs of the avenue. Uncle Ambert had perfected his plan for foiling the Gang of International Kidnappers. Stella often thought he must be hard-up for something to do.

He left his updated plan on large sheets of drawing paper outside the door of her room regularly. She never bothered to leave the avenue because at each end of its curve there was a main road with endless streams of heavy traffic and no footpaths. Wasn't it a wonder that a retired university professor had not twigged these circumstances? A sense of humour, so much in evidence in everyday life in Ireland, was never in evidence in the Larch Hill house. But here is where you would need a sense of humour, Stella often thought, wistfully.

In the middle of September, Velva announced that

she and her friends Lana and Zoe were taking their children, four in all, to a lakeside resort in the Poconos Mountains, for a long weekend.

"We were to have gone in August," Velva said to her mother, "but Lana was still feeding Julianna. At three, disgusting! I couldn't stand to see that big lump guzzling Lana. She has stopped and Lana is pregnant again. She is thinking of an abortion. Momma, do you think she should?"

"She should have aborted after one," answered the beautiful Mrs Rosen smoothly, directing her enchanting smile in a circle. Velva directed her attention at Stella. "I have a plan to help you fill your empty weekend, Nanny. You can make a start on packing for Florida. Packing for four months should give you something to do. You will be at a loss otherwise." Then she swung around and her voice was venomous. "Mr Bart's Uncle Gil wishes to see you in his study."

Stella tapped on the door of Mr Nathan's suite. "Come in," he called out. "Do not close the door. I have an idea we have an auditor. So we will go public."

"Yes, Mr Nathan?" Stella said politely. What a household, she added inwardly. "You sent for me?"

His manner was abrupt, almost abrasive. "While the long weekend is taking place in the Poconos, you should take the opportunity of going up to the Amish country. You have heard of the Amish people?"

"Yes, Mr Nathan, but I could not afford it."

"Here is the all-in ticket, bus and accommodation. Get the bus at the Tourist Centre."

Stella looked at the ticket. It had cost quite a bit. "Thank you, Mr Nathan, but I have been told to start packing for Florida."

"Take this ticket down to Velva, show it to her. Ask her if Aunt Alice could drive you to the tourist centre. Friday 6.30 pm. Put that skirt with the flowers in your travel bag. They have a folk evening when all the tourists dance barn dances. Otherwise, sensible gear—warm."

Stella went back down the stairs. She could get used to being ordered around when it meant jolly week-ends. He was thoughtful, after all. It would be a nice break to get off on her own. She had read all the brochures for the Amish country, in the tourist centre. It was a two-and-a-half hour coach run from Philadelphia. They gave you supper on your arrival. You had a chalet—bedroom, shower, toilet all to yourself. Saturday was spent showing the tourists around the farms and potteries and weaving sheds. All your meals. The dance on Saturday night. Lunch and tea on Sunday, and back to Philadelphia in the coach. The Amish lived an unspoiled life. They did everything in the old-fashioned way and were known for their crafts.

Velva looked at the ticket as if she would like to shred it. Stella wanted to tell Velva how glad she was that Carlo was going to spend a whole weekend with his Mum. She almost opened her mouth to give Velva a few instructions about Carlo but she thought better of it. She remembered, in time, that nannies were mere technical devices that only by chance happened to breathe like humans.

"Make sure you pack correctly for Carlo's weekend," Velva barked. "Four swim trunks, not two. And please inflate his wrist pads and rings. Why should I have to blow up those things? Four, do you hear me! See to Carlo's packing in good time."

Mister Bart was at a two-week-long conference in Paris, which accounted for a lot of Velva's waspish remarks. Although, thought Stella, what's new?

Velva, her friends, their little children and a mountain of baggage departed on the Friday in a chauffeur-driven luxurious mini-bus. Zoe had brought a younger sister who would, no doubt, fill in as a baby-sitter. Carlo clung to his nanny for a while but he was by nature a sociable little fellow. When he saw the other little kids he wanted to be one of the party. He was not yet walking on his own but he was well able to scramble up, kneel up, and get about in his own way from hold to hold. Stella thought him the handsomest little boy she had ever seen. The fuzzy black hair had become a mass of tight black curls which clung close to his head. Stella longed to warn Velva to be careful with the hairbrush: the curls were tangly in the morning, especially in hot weather.

Back in the nursery, she picked up each little discarded toy and tidied them away. He is only gone for a weekend; how will I feel when I am going away for ever? Back to Ireland but never to see Carlo again? Stella had to push this thought aside constantly. Carlo had crept into her heart in such a very special way because she was so completely alone after so many years of a home full of family and then of a home alone with a husband whose love she had always hoped to win back.

Stella told herself sternly to stop mooning about. After all, she too was getting a weekend. A note left outside her door had informed her to be ready on the dot of five-thirty pm. Aunt Alice would drive her to the tourist centre for six-thirty. It took an hour at that time of the evening to drive from Larch Hill to Philadelphia. Stella wished she could go to the Larch Hill Superdome and have her hair styled but she had never taken out Velva's car and she was afraid to do so now. She washed and set her hair, and made a great effort to look less like a nanny and more like an attractive middle-aged lady. She packed the skirt with the flowers. A barn dance would be nice. Someone would surely ask her up. Or were barn dances danced in a big ring?

Aunt Alice was prohibitively silent on the drive to the tourist centre. She made it very clear that she was being used to drive an uninvited passenger. Any polite remark of Stella's was greeted with a disapproving sniff. It was a great relief when she drove away and Stella sat down in the thronged reception area of the tourist centre to begin her weekend. Looking around, she saw that of the tourists waiting for the coach most were Japanese. She wondered if they spoke enough English to allow her to get into an interesting conversation. It would be something new to hear all about life in Japan.

"Is this all your luggage?" asked a familiar voice. "Come, the car is outside."

In a dream, Stella followed Gil Nathan out of the centre and into his car.

"What's gone wrong?" Stella asked. "Has there been an accident? Is Carlo all right?"

"No accident," he answered, cutting smoothly through the heavy evening traffic. "Just keep the talk until I get out of this mess."

Ko-Ko, Stella thought, the Lord High Executioner. God, how I hate this man. So damned full of himself he can't even be polite. So he has changed his mind!

Back to Larch Hill! If he thinks he is going to talk out his psychological problems for one whole empty weekend…well, he isn't. I'll lock myself in my room. Who the heck does he think he is, anyway! I came to do a job and I'm doing it, and I am going home at the end of the year. Yes, I am. Money or no money. And nothing is going to stop me. If they don't give me the return fare, I'll get it out of what I have saved.

They were out now on a six-lane highway. Since one road looked much the same as another to Stella, and since she went only by train to Philadelphia on her Sundays off, she assumed they were returning to Larch Hill. Her rebellious spirits subsided into a drowsy disappointment.

"Well?" he said at last. The car had settled into a steady fifty miles an hour. It was a comfortable silent car. The interrogative "well?" was almost an intrusion on Stella's quietness.

"Well?" he repeated.

"Not too well," Stella said, "disappointed. I was looking forward to seeing the Amish country."

"You'll see it," he said. And at that moment, Stella saw the white coach full of Japanese tourists passing on the inner lane. She looked at the ticket which she was still holding in her hand.

"You could get a rebate on that!" he said in that odd mischievous, youthful voice he used occasionally.

"Are we really going to the Amish country?" Stella asked. "And if so, why? I mean, why are you going?"

"Yes, and because I want to. It is years since I have been up there. It is interesting but changing with today's technology. Once it was a way of life; now it is tourist country."

Stella stared out at the modern "technology" highway stretching away into infinity. The vastness of this country was overwhelming, terrifying. She did not dare to say the words that came to her lips. Let me out. Put me down. Go on without me. I won't be part of your scheming. You are trying to make me part of a life that could never be my life. Let me out! Put me down!

Stella took a firm grip on her feelings. She had seen a film once which was set in a wilderness part of America. She could not remember the name. It was about three men who took a couple of paddling canoes on to a river where there were rapids. This river was about to be overflooded for an electricity scheme. Even now, Stella's imagination backed away from the story of those men's disastrous adventures. Oh, no, Stella would not ask to be put down on this highway. Just beyond those straggling forests at the side of this highway were settlements of hobo Americans who had not moved into the twentieth century, castaways who had only recently replaced the Wild West Indian tribes.

"We will stop for dinner in an hour, Stella," and now he had restored her to his good graces, signalled by his suave voice, his use of her name. What is he up to, Stella puzzled.

"Will that be in a town?" she asked, and the fear of strange places was in her voice.

"Of course," he answered. "Not much of a town, more what would be called a stop-over! But I know a decent restaurant. Trust me."

I suppose I have to, Stella thought. Not much option. I suppose he means trust him to recognise a good menu!

"It is on the brochure-ticket that they give supper when you arrive," Stella told him.

"Ah, yes," he said in that mischievous voice again, "but we are not going by the ticket, Stella, are we? We don't really want to share our supper with the Japanese, do we?"

"I wouldn't mind," Stella said.

His manner sharpened in his reply. "I have booked a double chalet. There is a sitting-room. We will eat there."

"Because," Stella said almost boldly, "you have a lot to say?"

"Quite so!" he answered genially, and half-turning to smile at her. "I have. And in private." He was swinging the car into another lane, and then another, uphill and over a bridge and down. The place announced itself as Jonusburg. Soon they were comfortably seated and he was snapping his fingers for the waitress.

"We will have two courses only," he told the pretty coloured girl, "whatever you best recommend. We are travelling. No wine. Plenty of coffee."

He turned to Stella. "I noticed the ladies' room by the door, Stella."

"Thank you, Gil!" Stella had come to the reluctant conclusion that she might as well go along with this game for the moment. She kept remembering she hadn't much option.

CHAPTER ELEVEN

In the last hour of the journey to the Amish country, night had fallen. Stella was silent, scarcely able to think ahead. During the meal in the restaurant, Gil had become more open, more friendly than previously. Stella had become more demure. She was careful to remember that for whatever purpose she was in his company, she was still the hired help, he her employer.

"Are you tired?" he asked courteously.

"Perhaps a little," she answered, sinking more deeply into the comfortable car seat.

"Aren't you afraid I might fall asleep?" There was a smile in his voice. "An old man like me and all this driving! Shouldn't you talk to me and make sure I stay awake?"

"I do not think of you as old," Stella used her gentlest tone, "not at all."

"So how do you think of me, Stella?"

"As ageless and very powerful," Stella answered truthfully. "But you know," she added, "I was always told not to keep on nattering to a driver. A driver, especially at night and in constant traffic, needs to concentrate."

"Nattering!" he repeated delightedly, "nattering!" Please natter to me, Stella!"

"You always make me laugh, Gil Nathan, when you put on that mischievous, small-boy voice. That is your legal, breaking-down-resistance voice, isn't it?"

Now he laughed with her. "Who told you that a driver had to concentrate on driving? In these lanes, it is mechanical. What are Irish roads like? Tell me, Stella."

He is getting very keen on the sound of my name, Stella thought. The nice silky swish he gives it! I like his voice though.

"Ah, now," she said, "I keep my mind well away from the thought of Irish roads. You wouldn't want me to start weeping?"

"Is your loneliness for Ireland as bad as that?" he asked.

"Sometimes," Stella said. "Sometimes my own road in summertime swims into my mind, the chestnut trees all laden with their pink candle-stick blooms. And the ancient tree beside the gate. It is an evergreen that screens the house. And a laburnum planted when my grandfather was a young man. It sheds its golden blossom on the grass in summer-time."

"No, I am sorry," he said. "Don't go all sad on me. I would like to ask questions about Ireland but not if it makes you sad. I thought, in one way at least, that you were glad to be far away from your home?"

He is thinking, thought Stella, of the time I told him of my fear of being so near to Dave's grave. The sheer terror of that. I will not tell him that sometimes the fear wakes me in the night. Sometimes, but only sometimes.

"You are right," she said. "In one way, I am happier in this big, uncaring, unknown, unknowable country. You are thoughtful, thank you."

The chalet which he had booked for them was surprisingly commodious and not uncomfortable, in a simple, puritanical, pinewood way. Stella was relieved to see two bedrooms, each with its own toilet and shower. The beds were double beds as to indicate that the chalet was designed to suit four people.

Gil had collected the keys at reception. Now he must go and sign their names. Stella, a little shy at all this sharing, decided to have a quick shower while he was away and be in bed with her bedroom door securely closed when he came back. She heard him return, heard the shower noises from his side of the chalet and, a little while later, his tap on her door.

"Come in, Gil," she called out. She was sitting up in bed, the same book of American history open and her fingers marking her reading place. It is up to him, Stella thought. I never meant to be trapped, but I am.

"May I?" he said as before, and he sat on the side of her bed. He must have been quite handsome in his day, Stella could see, but in his dressing-gown, out of the magnificent suit, his white hair all tousled, he looked a bit out of character. And, strangely, he reminded Stella of her darling little Carlo.

"I got coffee and tea and biscuits at reception," Gil said. "I have put the kettle on. Tea or coffee? No, stay where you are. I shall bring it in. Tea or coffee, Stella?"

"What are you having, Gil?" Stella was bent on being demurely polite, and uninviting.

"Well, actually," Gil answered, "I brought some bourbon (absolutely forbidden in Amish country!) and I am going to have a dram or two."

The self-conscious "dram" made Stella nervous. Am I in for an orgy, she wondered, all alone in the middle of nowhere? Get a grip on yourself; he would never be so stupid.

"Well now," Stella answered, "that's a good idea. I shall have tea, with sugar, and a little whiskey. Bourbon is whiskey, isn't it?"

"Sure is," he told her, "and mighty strong!"

She followed him out to the living area. "I think the Amish manufacture the coffee themselves," he informed her as he held up the packet. "No brand name that I can see."

"During the war, in the 1940s, we used to make coffee out of dandelion roots. Desperate stuff," said Stella.

"The tea is called Earl Grey," Gil said. "Will you chance it? I guess the whiskey will help."

"And the sugar," Stella said.

They settled down companionably at the table. Gil was quite at his ease. They might as well have been sharing supper for years. He chatted away about the Amish country, and their own plans for Saturday. If Stella liked, they would eat a communal meal to sample Amish cooking, but also if she liked, they would drive for dinner to a town not too far away.

"We will decide tomorrow," Stella said, and she hoped he did not notice the quiver in her voice when she spoke. She had an apprehensive fear of what demands might be made on her in the next quarter of an hour. Her fears were groundless. At the door of her bedroom, Gil patted her shoulder very lightly, very lightly indeed. "I hope you sleep well in that very flat-looking bed, Stella. Good night."

"Good night, Gil," she answered.

The bed was as hard as a wooden table but Stella fell asleep immediately, and did not dream. When she woke next morning, it was to find Gil standing with a tray of tea and biscuits. Stella was covered with confusion wondering what she must look like as she struggled to sit up, and run her fingers through her hair. He was smiling, and it was the special smile he seemed to keep for special occasions.

"You could undermine my confidence," Stella scolded him. "You are a meany! You are all showered and shaved."

"Am I a meany?" He sat on the side of the bed, and watched Stella drinking the tea. His eyes were admiring as if he would like to pay compliments but he contented himself with watching.

"We are going to go for a long walk around the farms. There is a pathway so that tourists can view the whole work of the farm. It is now eight-thirty: the Amish have been working since dawn and the Japanese cameras have been taking it all in."

"Were you out already?" Stella asked.

"No," he looked down at her, "I was window-gazing. And contemplating. And rehearsing what I want to say to you."

Stella groaned inside. She knew that tone: it was his courtroom voice, the one that brooked no opposition. The way I am made to dither by this man! One minute I am afraid he is going to hop on me and I will be fighting for my virtue. The next minute I am in the dock and on my solemn oath to be part of some nefarious scheme to rescue the Nathan millions from falling into the hands of the big-bosomed but fantastically beautiful Mrs Rosen. One minute I am in fear of having to pay in kind for a candle-lit dinner and the next minute I am going to sign away years of my life (such as it is) in exchange for a happy weekend in the Amish country. Well, I'm not, Gil Nathan. So put that in your pipe and smoke it!

Nevertheless, Stella was entranced by his interesting voice. Slowly, humorously, they toured around the luxuriant fields and into the farm buildings. Gil being knowledgeable, entered into conversation with some workers in their quaint attire, smocks and stove-pipe hats. They spoke in an obsolete way. It was difficult to know if their speech were artificial or unchanged for a century. Gil thought they knew both ways since they understood both ways.

"How will they continue like this in our modern world? They seem poor, somehow." Stella found them extraordinary. They seemed worse off than the peasants of Connemara, long ago .

"They are not poor," Gil told her. "They will change their ways when and if it suits them. Their young people nowadays prefer the bright lights to the tilled fields. They leave, not always to their betterment."

"It is like that in Ireland, too," Stella said. "For

centuries there was emigration and now there is more than ever."

He smiled at her. "Let us sit here in the sun on this bench and talk about one Irish emigrant I know."

Here it comes, Stella thought, the reason we are here. She waited, cautioning herself not to interrupt.

"My big concern, Stella, is to have you made a legal immigrant. That is not easy under the present quota. Apparently there are many hundreds in your situation, in positions in the like of which American citizens could be similarly employed. Apparently it is easy enough to track down illegal immigrants in factories and hotels where they enter the system, as it were. They can be deported. Not so easy to track them in private households where they become part of the family."

Stella sighed. "I think we have been over this ground before," she said drily.

"But for me," he persisted, "it is necessary to get you the legal visa because I want to be ready to set you up in an apartment with the custody of Carlo. They will divorce, I am sure; it is only a question of time."

Stella moved further down the bench. "Let me get this straight," she said. "Without any prior consultation with me, you are going to use my presence to defraud the parents of their child. No, wait. What makes you think I would agree to that?"

"Your love for the little boy—especially now you know he is my son."

"Well now, Mr Nathan, I don't know that, because you see, I don't believe that. And—no, wait—even if I believed it, legally Velva and Bart are the parents of Carlo. I have see the birth certificate in the bureau in the nursery where she keeps the bills for everything relating to Carlo."

"Yes, I know," he said harshly, "for everything. Carlo is her investment!"

"Most people pile up bills," Stella said mildly.

"Let us come back to the point, please." And now he was unyielding. "When Velva and Bart separate, I want you on my side. I will get Carlo made a ward of court, rather than let him go to Velva and her mother."

"Another thing, Mr Nathan. I have the impression that Velva will not divorce Bart. Actually, I believe she is quite madly in love with him. His Casanova life is not new, I gather. So why did she not divorce him years ago?"

"She will divorce him because her mother will force her to. Years ago, her mother did not give a curse what Velva did. Mrs Rosen was in and out of several divorces in the last ten years (and several before that) and what Velva was doing with her life did not worry her. That was before Carlo was born. Since Carlo's birth, Mrs Rosen has kept her apartment in the house."

"Are we back to talking about Carlo's inheritance? What I hear people here calling big money—the megabucks?"

"Stella, I want you to be very serious. Yes, to Mrs Rosen, the money is almost within her grasp. Velva will succumb to her mother's greed. She will not be allowed to go on refusing Bart's request for divorce. Please, understand, it is the boy who concerns me. Surely I am not asking more than you would give out of love for that little fellow."

"What exactly are you asking?"

"I want you to stay—indefinitely. I want to get you out of Larch Hill and into a downtown apartment in a block which I happen to own. I shall move into another apartment in the same block."

Stella was bemused. "Why downtown?" she questioned.

"Better life for you," he said, "the city to your hand. Close to shops. Fashion, cinema, theatre. Your favourite, the Free Library. Easier to get help with the apartment and with the boy. You will admit Philadelphia is a very beautiful city. You might as well be living on the moon as in Larch Hill."

Stella looked out across the rolling plains of the

Amish country and the distant vista of mountains. She looked up at the immense dome of the sky. This is not my country, she thought. I am always a midget in an immense space in America. In Ireland I am part of the landscape; I fit in with the people and the fields among the sheltering trees. This continent is primeval, not yet used to the humanity of today; it should still be peopled with Indians. It is the wonderful New World. I want my old world, that is seamed with thousands of years of people who look like me, who look like my forebears and my family.

"Stella, I am offering you a lot."

"You are offering me nothing, Mr Nathan; you are prepared to sacrifice me on some sort of altar for some sort of personal gain the reasons for which I do not comprehend."

"It is for the child. I must not lose the child," his voice was still strong, still imperious.

"When you talk in that way, like an actor acting Napoleon," Stella said to him, "I could almost imagine you taking Bart's wife. Almost—but not quite. I do not believe you would do that. I think you are telling a lie for some purpose of your own."

"Suppose I did go to bed with Velva a year ago; suppose I did make love to her; suppose I did get her with child. Why could that not happen? How could you not believe it? How?" His voice was his lawyer's voice.

"Instinct, Mr Nathan," Stella said very steadily. "Instinct tells me that you are not a man for such. But instinct tells me that you could tell a lie and convince yourself it was all legal."

He turned to face her. "Sometimes I wonder why you were afraid of your dead husband coming back to haunt you. Before I sent for you to come here, Stella, I had your history investigated. There was never any finger pointed at you in your home place. You were a devoted wife, a perfect mother. And since you have lived in Larch Hill, instinct tells me that you are a pure and lovely woman. Instinct, Stella? Yet, I know that you were afraid. Instinct or legal training?" If there was an implication there, she chose to ignore it. Stella had very little worldly experience with which to judge this man. Yet instinct was strong. Gil Nathan would not commit himself to an act in which he had no pride.

They had stood up, and were walking to the chalet. Suddenly, Gil put his arm around her shoulders.

"Why don't we go and get ourselves a really good dinner and then come back to the barn-dance? You will have another night to sleep on it, Stella."

"You are a bit irresistible, Gil Nathan!" Stella said.

"You think so?" he smiled at her.

"A bit, I said!"

For a big, heavily built man, Gil was as light on his feet in the barn dance as Stella was. They whirled around and around, he letting her go to arm's length and drawing her back into a close embrace. The tunes were old, and long-forgotten words came back to be hummed. Gil was singing words of his own for her amusement: we must come back again; see you here next week; pity it is such a long drive; we could come in the coach the next time but we both prefer the car.

When they were walking, arm-in-arm back to the chalet, Gil asked playfully, "Tea or coffee to-night, Stella?"

"Oh, I think I'll have some bourbon. I need a pick-me-up after all that mad dancing. My dancing days were over long ago."

"We were the best dancers in the barn," asserted Gil. "Those Japanese hadn't a clue!"

They lingered over the whiskey, they were reluctant to end the night.

"I wish I could make love to you, Stella."

I wonder what's stopping him, Stella thought. It must have been in his mind, surely? She smiled what she hoped was a slow, moody smile. She could see his response.

"I think I'll shower and go to bed now, Gil."

"I guess you are right, Stella. Me too."

When Stella was in bed, with her fingers marking

the place in her history book, Gil came to her door. He stood gazing at her.

"Gil Nathan," Stella said, "do you remember telling me that the au pairs who came before me were all cheap whores?"

"They were," he said, "for Bart and for his friends."

"And do you remember telling me that money for a Nathan is more important than people are?"

"I remember," he said. "I should have said more important than some people, maybe even than most people."

"Gil Nathan," Stella said, "less than a year ago I did not know you. I can only know you now from the impressions I have formed in the last six months. Some of those things you said raise important questions in my mind—not in your favour. Other things about you, some actions, are in your favour. Your sometime courtesy, your sometime generosity. Your talk of making love is the talk of a man who would take advantage. I am quite defenceless but I would appreciate a quiet goodnight. Perhaps we could wind up our talk tomorrow."

"I am sorry, Stella."

"Do not be," she answered serenely. "It would be an attractive proposition under completely different circumstances."

Which will never arise, said Stella to herself, as Gil

Nathan closed her door and she settled to a short read of the history book. It was not easy to get off to sleep. She read for a long time.

CHAPTER TWELVE

On Sunday, Gil decided they would attend the Amish hall of worship. They walked across the path by the fields, not exactly hand-in-hand, but they were joking and amiable with each other.

"All we need are hats to make us a sedate couple!" he said.

"It used to be a mortal sin for a Catholic to go into a place of worship for a service, if it wasn't a Catholic church," Stella told him.

"Isn't it still a mortal sin?" he asked.

"I don't think so," Stella said. "A lot of things have changed in the past twenty years."

"I thought the Pope never changes his mind?" Gil asked in his mischievous voice.

"What about you? Do you worship?" Stella had wondered about this.

"I am not orthodox," Gil answered. "Not anything. I have too many doubts about all religions. I used to read that stuff intensely, not so much any more."

"I like tradition," Stella said, "whatever about religion."

He smiled at her. "Yes, you would, wouldn't you!"

After the service they sat in the sunshine until the Amish lunch. They talked of nothing in particular. Then they went to the chalet to gather up their things. Gil went to reception to pay. Stella watched him from the window as he walked across the pathway. Hard to say what impression he makes on me, Stella thought. Maybe I could really like him a lot but I keep on being afraid he will ask me to do something I don't want to do. I really do want to go home at the end of the year. This could never be my country. Lines from a poem she had always loved often came back to her in this new world:

> This is a song a robin sang
> This morning on a broken tree,
> It was about the little fields
> That call across the world to me.

And suddenly she was struck by the thought of leaving Carlo, and lines from another poem of the same beloved poet murmured in her mind:

> He will not come, and still I wait
> He whistles at another gate…
> The world is calling, I must go
> How shall I know he did not pass
> Barefooted in the shining grass?

"Stella!" Gil looked closely into her face. "There are tears in your eyes. What were you thinking of?"

Stella dried her eyes. "Sometimes when I think of Carlo or of home or of both together, I go all poetical. Don't mind me. I'm getting old."

"I phoned the house when I was over at reception. Aunt Alice said the Poconos Mountain people will not be home until Tuesday, midday."

Stella was disappointed. "I was hoping we would all be home together to-night."

"And you would be able to put Carlo to bed with your own two hands, Stella!"

"Something like that," Stella admitted.

"Instead you are going to have to put up with me for yet another dinner when we get back to Philly. Look, I got a flask of coffee and some of their famous biscuits, for the road."

He was all out to please her. Stella wished she had the nerve to make provisos—no problems, no urgent decisions. He was not the kind of man with whom one could make free, by telling him to knock it off. Although, come to think of it, she had done just that when he asked to make love. Or was that a try-out? Would he have run a mile if she invited him into the bed? We'll never know, thought Stella.

On the road, they drove along like old friends. He did most of the talking, and none of it was personal.

He knew a great deal of the late nineteenth- and early twentieth-century development of the United States: railways, roads, hydro schemes, architecture. He related it in an anecdotal way which held Stella's interest. His father and his grandfather had been big investors in many of the major plans.

Halfway through the journey, Gil pulled over into a lay-by.

"We'll have a half-hour break for coffee," he said. "My neck is beginning to stiffen-up."

"Would you like me to massage your neck?" Stella asked. "That used happen to Dave, my husband, when we drove long distances. His neck used get stiff, too."

She had spoken impulsively but he took up the suggestion immediately.

"That would be real generous of you, ma'am," he said, slyly affecting a cowboy brogue, "real perlite!"

They got out and into the back seat of the car. For ten minutes, Stella kneaded the muscles across his shoulder and the top of his spine. His back was toward her but she had the impression his eyes were closed.

"Did you enjoy that, Gil?" she asked.

"It ranks with another experience you gave me," he said, turning to smile at her, "when you put your hand in mine at the opera."

"That calls for a coffee." Stella felt a little confused by the intimacy of his smile.

When they were drinking the coffee, he said in the manner of a lawyer building up an argument, "There could have been a third experience or should I say a second?"

"Unfortunately," Stella smiled at him, "I am unable to testify to that, sir."

"Do you have any regrets for refusing the plaintiff?" the lawyer Gil queried.

"None at all, sir."

"May I presume the proposition was repulsive?"

"No indeed, sir! Quite the contrary." Stella's voice was steady and decisive. With this man, one could not play coy and flirty as one could with an Irishman at a cocktail party.

Now Gil's voice was interested. "So the court may presume that the witness had quite other reasons for refusing the plaintiff's suit?"

"The court may so presume," Stella answered.

Gil took her hand in his. "Would it be pushing my luck to ask why I was refused?"

"You amaze me," Stella said. "Does every woman give in to your every desire?"

"That is another question, not an answer. But, yes. It is assumed that women need the total experience equally as men need it."

"To round off the night, as it were?" And Stella was jeering him, if only a little.

"Stella, we are friends. Tell me your reasons."

Stella withdrew her hand from his. His question opened up years of her recent past. Well, let him have it. Let him make what he would of it.

"Would you accept lack of experience, total or otherwise? Would you accept the phrase 'out of practice'? Would you accept that because a woman has been married for many years is not a guarantee that she has all the tricks of a courtesan? And more, much more than that, I am foremost a lover of tradition."

Stella preferred being truthful but now she felt a guilty pang for refusing him. He had given her a really lovely few days. After all she was a free agent now, wasn't she? Who would care if she stepped out of line for once? But then, suppose she were asked to do things she had never done before? Oh no, better to be sure than sorry.

Gil was silent for a moment. "Would it have been a mortal sin, Stella? Like going to a non-Catholic church?"

"Theology did not come into it, Gil. I think I have answered sufficiently." And that is all you are going to hear on that subject, Gil Nathan.

"Stella, you have given me a lot to think about." They resumed the journey in what Stella took to be a companionable silence. She was aware of her own conflicting thoughts: he didn't get much out of the weekend, after all. Funny but I think I could get addicted to his way of smiling, his way of speaking, the comfortable bulk of him. Watch it, Stella. All he wants (apart from a bit on the side—where did I get that phrase?) all he wants is for you to commit yourself to being a nanny for years to come. Maybe you should tell him your savings book is your hold on life in this awesome country. Your savings book—just that. Then she remembered Carlo and the way his soft lips pressed against her throat when Velva and Bart started their screaming matches. When she had to hurry upstairs to the nursery holding his little body close to hers. His little clinging body trembled piteously when his parents' rows erupted, as if they were wild animals and he was a tiny bird trying for a higher branch in a tree, trying to escape from their grinding, lashing fury. The household to which this car was bearing them back was not a comfortable place.

"I should like to thank you, Gil Nathan, for a very pleasant week-end."

"Why do I like it when you say 'Gil Nathan'?"

"It is an Irishism," Stella told him. "Give a man his full title and you put him in his proper place. This time it was an honourable place."

"Yes," Gil said, "I rather suspected it would work both ways!"

They laughed together as friends do when the accord is struck happily and simultaneously.

Dinner was an enjoyable ending to their weekend. This time Gil made her a partner in the choice of dishes. She felt quite enveloped in the warmth of his special smile. She almost forgot to be on her guard against the possible implications of all this delightful, candid ambience which he so easily created around the two of them.

At the end of the meal, Stella was instructed to phone Aunt Alice to pick her up at the tourist centre.

"It is later than Alice would expect," Gil said, "so you will tell her that you were hungry and waited to buy some dinner. I apologise for this, as I do for many things. Our association is best kept to ourselves."

That figures, Stella said to herself.

"By the time I put you down at the tourist centre, you will not have so long to wait. Alice is not an adventurous driver."

But a mighty resentful one, Stella thought. Alice stares with a hooded beady eye like a toad. But she smiled at Gil graciously. It would have been nice to be driven home in his big comfortable car but in some obscure way she seemed to have consented to any devious plan, without quibbling. Stella hated arguments. To revert to being the hired help proved easy enough.

Apart from Aunt Alice and Uncle Ambert, who dealt with their own suite, the house on Monday was given over to Leola, the coloured girl who drove up in her own little jalopy promptly at nine to take over the laundry and the cleaning. This would all be done again on Thursday by another coloured girl, Debby. Stella was friendly with Leola and Debby. She, too, was a hired help, and she had no feelings of racism. She had never encountered any coloured people in Ireland. Velva had forbidden her to talk freely with the "niggers" but Velva was not always there to monitor her thousand-and-one injunctions. The gimlet-eyed Aunt Alice would report, so Stella had learned to be careful. On this Monday morning, Alice and Ambert drove off shortly before Leola arrived. Gil Nathan always breakfasted downtown on his way to his office.

"Good morning, Leola!" Stella called from the stairs.

Leola rolled her eyes upward in an encompassing circle, a silent plea for Stella to beware of who might be listening.

"It's all right, Leola, we have the place all to ourselves. No family. No baby. I could help by turning out the nursery and my own room. Would that be okay with you? That would leave us time to have a bit of lunch together?"

Leola seemed cautious as if some civil rights were being infringed here.

"I get fifty dollars, Miss Ma'am," she said uncertainly, "fifty dollars for my day."

Nearly as much as I get for a week, Stella thought, but then there's my bed and board. "Of course, Leola," Stella said, "fifty dollars!"

Leola brightened considerably. "An' kin I play my transistor?" Another of Velva's injunctions. Stella smiled down at Leola. "See you twelve-thirty," and she went back up the stairs. If she shut her door firmly on her "upper circle," she would not have to hear Leola's loud reggae music. It gave Leola the right beat for working, the louder the better to drown out the other mechanical noises necessary for her work. All it gave Stella was a headache.

At twelve-thirty, they sat in the kitchen to eat their lunch. Velva never left any food ready for the hired help, so Leola was accustomed to bringing her own food in a plastic box with a flask of coffee.

"Wouldn't you share with me?" Stella asked but Leola refused.

"When I first came to work here five years ago, the missus put out tuna salad every time," Leola told Stella. "I suspect it was the same tuna salad the week after what I didn't eat the time before. So I bring my box, like you see."

Stella could believe anything of Velva, so she did not protest loyally. Velva's stinginess was well known to her; she was often the victim of it.

"Do you have a family, Leola?"

"Kids, you mean? Yes, I've two—both boys. But no family. No husband. He left."

"Oh!" Stella said. "I'm sorry."

"I'm not!" Leola said, eating and drinking busily. "That bastard was no good. Where's your kid today?"

"Carlo? They are having a weekend in the Poconos."

Leola almost dropped the flask. "Him and her and the kid!" Her brown eyes were huge with incredulous astonishment. "A weekend!"

"Yes," Stella said. "A weekend. But not Mister Bart. He is in Paris. Just Mrs Nathan and Carlo, and her friends and their children."

"I nearly choked," said Leola. "They never got on, even before the kid. She was bloody lucky to have one, all the miscarriages she brought on!"

"Can a woman do that?" asked Stella, who was not averse to hearing bad things about Velva.

"If she can get the stuff. You have to know someone. Missus got it easy through her friend, Lana Something. Her husband is in the university."

"Lana?" Stella repeated. "But her husband is a doctor of mathematics, a professor in economics. He is not a doctor of medicine."

"What's the difference?" Leola was scornful. "It's the university, isn't it—and that's where she was getting the stuff." But Stella was not convinced. Where would Velva get abortifacients? Didn't Bart and Velva want to have a baby to untangle all their marital problems? Hadn't they been advised by the marriage counsellor that a baby was the wonderful solution? The baby would bring them together.

"I used to come the two days before I got laid with Junior," Leola said. "You learn a lot when you spend *two* days in their houses every week. You could write their history by the end of five years. I know what I saw. She spent more time down in that back toilet than anywhere else. I know. I had to clean up her mess."

"But Mrs Nathan did have Carlo," Stella said faintly.

"She did when they fertilized her egg for her. Don't they have that in where you come from? Where is it? Holland?"

"No, Ireland. I don't know," Stella said. "What happens? Have some more coffee, Leola."

Now Leola was in her element. Imparting brand new information, on such an important subject to someone from some backward place, was a duty she relished.

"It was the big man who found out what was going on. She swore she was trying to get herself pregnant. That was a bleedin' lie. The husband swore that all he wanted was a divorce; the big man would not have it—divorce I mean. He said there has to be no more divorce in the family. I suppose someone convinced him that a child would settle the fights. A child! Don't make me laugh! A child is only a worser complication."

"Leola, have another biscuit. Let me pour out that coffee and make some fresh."

"I have to get finished by three o'clock." Leola liked to be pressed to stay, so she half stood up to go.

"Oh, you will, easily," Stella said. "You need not go near the top floor at all; it is all done."

"Vacuumed?" asked the perfect hired help primly, as she settled down to the fresh coffee.

"Tell me about this strange new thing," asked Stella.

"It is not all that new over here," began Leola with great assurance. "When the big man found out what was going on, there was a row I'll never forget. Missus was bawling and crying and screaming and roaring."

"But how did the big man find out?" asked Stella, who could not picture Gil finding Velva in the throes of a miscarriage in the back toilet.

"She had to be rushed to hospital. I was the one

who found her. I was the one who made the phone calls. I had to try all the numbers beside the phone, and I got the big man in his office. He gave me a number to ring and a private ambulance came and I went with her in the ambulance and the big man was there in the clinic, in the hall. He took charge." Leola described the incident with great verve, as if she were the heroine of the hour in a movie. Her actions were graphic: leafing over the numbers, dialling the phone, rushing to lift Velva and stuff towels around her, bathing Velva's face, dashing upstairs for Velva's dressing-gown.

"And Mister Bart, was he in the clinic?"

"No," said Leola with great importance, "he couldn't be found! The big man drove me back here to clean up and I heard the phone calls. That dude had gone to Washington with his latest. The big man was ringing all the hotels. The big man had moved in with them temporary after his wife died. It was to be for a month while he got an apartment or sold a house or whatever. It was three or four years. When she got pregnant the right way, the big man stayed."

"The right way?" asked Stella, not at all sure if she wanted to hear any more.

"Yes," and now Leola herself poured out the coffee for herself. "Yes. That's the way it is done here nowadays. They take out the woman's eggs and they fertilise it with the husband's seed, and they implant it in her womb. That was what they did to her."

"And there were no more miscarriages?" Stella wondered if Leola knew what she was talking about.

"They made damn sure there were no more miscarriages!" asserted Leola. "They kept her in the clinic for three months to make sure it took. She was as big as a house when next I saw her—and she didn't like that—losing her figure. The rows over that!"

Stella gazed at Leola's triumphant face. She felt faint and unsure and somehow guilty to be listening to a servant's gossip. She wished with all her soul that she was at home in Ireland, in her own house, mistress of her own destiny.

"My sister is a nursing aide in the hospital of the university and she told me how the nurses get the seed. It is easy, they..."

"Wait a minute, Leola. I do not think I want to know. This is all so strange."

"Holland must be very old-fashioned" was Leola's disdainful comment as she headed off to attend to the rest of her work.

CHAPTER THIRTEEN

Carlo simply flew into Stella's arms the moment Velva lifted him out of the car.

"Mummuum," he cried in a croaky little voice, "mummuum!" His little body was wet and trembling when he clung to her. She could feel he had lost weight.

"You have that kid thoroughly spoiled, Nanny," Velva shrilled in a scolding voice the very sound of which made Carlo press closer to Stella. "He never stopped whingeing and whining. I cannot understand why Uncle Gil insisted on your having a weekend off. Your place is here. A nanny. That's what you are here for. Why is that kid not potty trained by now? Why? Zoe said her children were potty trained by eight months. He is more than eight months, isn't he? He is a monster for wetting. I used dozens of boxes of disposables—dozens, and still he got sore. Take him out of my sight!"

Stella hurried upstairs. The beautiful Mrs Rosen and her silent husband had returned earlier from their week away at race-meetings. She would emerge on the "grand circle" to see what all the shouting was about, and somehow the absent Bart would get blamed for Carlo's wetness, as he was blamed for everything. It had long been obvious to Stella that Velva's mother encouraged, and often initiated, Velva's raging tantrums. Stella's feet had wings and she reached the safety of the nursery, closing the door firmly behind her.

How can I ever leave Carlo, Stella was thinking. God, that woman! She has no heart. Her own child. No matter what way it was conceived, she bore this little fellow in her body for nine months. All the time, Stella was kissing Carlo and undressing him, noting how he had become docile and sweet under her hands, his eyes fixed on her face, his little mouth with his six little teeth, trying to smile.

His poor tail was raw and sore. Dozens of boxes indeed, thought Stella savagely. She left you lying in your one disposable for hours. Then Stella noticed the purplish marks on his shoulders and upper arms, and one very blue mark on his thigh. Stella looked at them closely. Surely Velva would not strike him? But why? For what? For crying? But that would only make him cry more. Stella bathed him very gently. She knew his little bottom must be hurting immersed in warm water but he did not make a sound, only watching her, only trying to give her his toothy smile.

Stella found some calamine lotion and she anointed all the blue marks, wondering again at them. It was not a rash. She spread a nappy-rash cream on the sore parts and placed cotton wool between his skin and the disposable. "Perhaps a little sleep before you have your dinner, pet," she whispered. She held him against her shoulder and rocked him gently. She felt his lips against her neck, and his croaky voice murmuring, "mmmummuum." In five minutes he was fast asleep.

Next day, life resumed its accustomed ritual. Mister Bart was away. Mrs Rosen and Velva were forever in deep conclave, Mrs Rosen's deep southern voice contrasting with Velva's shrill teenage squeal. The subject of their conversation, which they made no effort to cloak with lower tones, was still the same: Velva's divorce from Bart, Mrs Rosen's insistence on it, Velva's compromises and excuses.

And Uncle Gil resumed his daily call to see Carlo:

"Say good morning to Uncle Gil, Carlo?"

"What is that mark on his leg, Nanny?" Stella lifted Carlo up and opened the neck of the little boy's tee shirt. Gil bent down closer. "Is it a skin rash? Should we call a doctor?"

"Perhaps Velva knows what it is," Stella said.

He went down the flight to the "dress circle." His voice ripped across the stairs, "Velva."

Stella watched from the upper banisters.

Velva had been resting, she stumbled, half-clad, dishevelled. Mrs Rosen walked out from her own suite, immaculate as always. "My dear Gil!" she intoned, quite beautifully. He ignored her in a polite way.

"Velva, what are the marks on Carlo's body?"

"Oh, they're nothing. You fuss too much."

"What are they?" His voice was glacial.

"Just little pinches and maybe bites," and Velva tittered nervously.

There was a second of absolute silence when the perpetual humming of the televisions and the cameras seemed to hold breath, then his voice came out like a thunderclap, "Explain yourself!"

"Zoe's little Heidi, she's three, a bit spoiled. She didn't like Carlo; so she bit him, maybe pinched him."

Gil stepped back, almost as if he would strike Velva. "I am not hearing this," he said.

"He was whining so much. He got on everyone's nerves."

"Did that child's mother punish her for biting Carlo?"

"Oh no, Uncle Gil," Velva was prepared to gush out explanations. "Zoe is a practising psychiatrist: she would not punish a child of three. Do you mean slap her? That would give the child a complex, Uncle Gil. Zoe said Carlo will learn to bite back. It is called self-justification, and all children are best prepared for future encounters by..."

He interrupted with a harsh sound of his voice and he stepped further back to descend the stairs. In a deliberately insulting voice, he said, "Only for the fact that it would be distasteful to me, I would bite you, Velva Nathan."

Stella drew back into the nursery. Carlo was playing on the floor quite happily. He gave her a brave little smile when she sat down beside him. Kissing the top of his head, she whispered, "Whose child are you, anyway? What gives Uncle Gil the right to question your mother, even on your behalf? Why does she cower in front of him? Why didn't her mother step in and tell Uncle Gil to mind his own business? From what Leola said, if anyone could believe her, you are really and truly Velva's child, and Bart's. But oh boy, did I shake when I heard that icy voice. He really cares about you, baby, he really does!" But the lurking fear persisted in Stella's mind that Gil Nathan cared also about Carlo's prospective fortune.

The last few weeks of the hot weather slipped by without further incident. Carlo healed quickly. He was progressing very rapidly now. Bart returned and with him came the piano playing in which the little boy delighted. Bart was in wonderful form. He had distinguished himself at the Paris conference, and

quite obviously Paris had supplied all his other needs,
including his need to be free of his wife's endless
possessiveness. For him, Carlo took his first few steps.
Bart showed great enthusiasm. He knelt down on the
floor to be level with Carlo. The little boy chuckled
with enjoyment.

"Always provided he can see you, Nanny, out of
the corner of his eye and not too far away, he has
great confidence," Bart said.

"He lives for that little session on the piano, Mr
Bart," Stella told him. "You know, he can recognise
the sound of your car." She did not add: and the
disappointment on the evenings you don't come
home.

"He can?" Bart was very handsome when he
smiled.

"You have an ear, little fellow." They had had this
conversation several times. He turned to Stella. "It is
a God-given gift, an ear. But like all God-given gifts,
it has accursed drawbacks, when there are voices you
don't want to hear—ear-splitting!" Then he smiled
again, a smile Stella recognised as the smile prefatory
to departing. "You are doing a wonderful job with
Carlo, Nanny. He is a lucky little boy." Then Mr Bart
was gone. He never had any more time than a few
minutes for the lucky little boy.

In a way, Stella was reminded of Dave. He, too,

belonged to a world in which his family had no part. His friends, all male of course, were friends unknown to his own sons. All those men at Dave's funeral, from his college and his various clubs, had had to introduce themselves to Philip and Ross.

The sons could not tell one from the other at the end of that day. Did they even know that Sybil and Hazel were Dave's daughters? Stella sometimes reflected on the day of Dave's funeral as if she were running a film through a mental camera. Only now, at this distance in time (was it almost a year?) and at this distance in space, could she remember the details. There were so many necessary arrangements, so many phone calls. The members of her family were scattered abroad. Even Philip, who resided in Dublin, was in America on business that day. She had not cried then. Would she ever? Was there a monstrous grief stored up, a tension held in? Stella was perpetually amazed at the lack of discipline in Velva, whose constant outbursts shattered the globe. Was that way of letting go maybe a better way? Afterwards Velva could shower, put on her eyelashes, make up her face, flick her reddish hair into a gamine style, and sally forth to dinner ready to charm all around her.

Stella picked up little Carlo for attention. Maybe devoting herself to him had been a salvation of sorts, a necessary expression of emotion, of loving emotion, that had kept her sane in this strange house. This prison, she thought in sudden alarm. Because of you, baby, am I condemned to exile? But Stella could banish these thoughts quickly by assuring herself that home was only a few hours' flying-time away and that by now she could spare the fare if the Nathans would not give it. The nuts and bolts of having to get the money and the air ticket, and make her way to the airport—all apart from leaving the house under her own steam—could be dealt with when the time came, she hoped, but she was never sure. She had to steer her mind firmly into the ways and means of looking after Carlo, now a very energetic little boy, stretching out in all directions for experiences and attentions. He had become a whole-time job.

The packing was completed; the weather had changed; it was almost the end of September. The winter in Florida lay just ahead. There was a mountain of baggage. Mr and Mrs Rosen would travel down in their own car with their own things. They would be visiting in Atlanta her son by an earlier marriage. Alice and Ambert would take the main baggage in their car. They would leave a day early, open up the new house and engage a couple of staff. It was easier, Velva said, to get cheap staff in Florida than in Philadelphia: Hispanics, Mexicans, Filipinos. Bart and Velva with Carlo and Nanny would make the third car. Velva had taken a year away from her work to devote herself to her baby (Stella heard this repeated many times and she always found it ironic) and these few months would be the end of her year. In January she would resume her work in Mr Rosen's office. For a whole week peaceful preparations went along nicely.

Then one of the biggest ever rows broke loose. The noise Velva made might as well be the sack of a city and the rape of all its women. Bart had decided that he was not going to Florida. Not even to oblige her by driving the car. Not even for a weekend. He was going to Washington. The screaming row went on all day and late that evening. Bart left with two suitcases. He took his new sports car.

Shutting the doors could not keep out the dreadful sound of Velva's hysteria. Her mother and stepfather were heard pleading with her. Stella had to hold Carlo's trembling body for hours. If she let go, he crawled back, clinging frantically. Some time after midnight, Uncle Gil phoned a doctor to come in. Velva was given an injected sedative and a blessed peace fell on the house. The televisions were turned off and only the clicking of the everlasting cameras could be heard.

Velva had made herself ill. She lay in bed all the next day, moaning and breaking out into heart-stopping screeches. That night the doctor gave her another sedative.

Uncle Gil came to visit, as was his daily habit. The usual grandfatherly greeting with Carlo was not exchanged. He stood at the door, not coming over the threshold, and he spoke in a loud, dictatorial way that gave Stella the shivers.

"It has been decided that my niece-in-law, Velva, will travel by plane when she has recovered. Her health is low. Mr Bart is not available to drive the car. Ambert will take most of the luggage. I will take you and Carlo, although it was not on my agenda to go to Florida before Christmas. For the child's sake we will take the journey over several days. You will know what to bring, Nanny, for his comfort and for your own, of course."

His familiar footsteps echoed down the stairs. The up-and-over garage door thudded and his car drove away. Stella exhaled a long, slow breath. Whatever about the weekend in the Amish country (to which he had not since referred) he could not be accused of engineering this two-day trip. Or could he? Was he in league with Bart to give him time to go over the ground again in the persuasion of Stella to become permanent nanny? The prize for Bart was Gil's agreement to the divorce. But then, why was Gil's agreement necessary for another adult to do anything! They would lose the millions to Velva if they could not prove that taking Carlo from his Nanny was detrimental to the child. How would they prove a thing like that in court, wondered Stella.

Stella thought the whole situation was like the coloured box puzzle that Ross had sent from New York for Philip's children. No matter what way you turned the box, the blue or the black or the yellow or the red fell out of place. Yet one of Philip's small children had got it right with all the colours in line. I just don't have the knack with the Nathan box, Stella thought.

At last, the day came for the journey. Mrs and Mr Rosen stayed with Velva. In a week they would put her on the plane for Florida. They would set out for their visit to Atlanta when Gil had returned to the house in Larch Hill. Ambert and Alice were already on the road. Stella could not but feel thrilled to be off in the big comfortable car with Carlo happily strapped into his car seat in the back. He seemed to be very excited and happy too. Stella kept talking back to him, understanding his gurgled replies, and his oft-repeated mmummm.

Until they were out on the southbound highway, the bulky figure at the wheel was silent and preoccupied. Then gradually he moved over into the slower lane and Stella could almost feel the thaw, the loosening relaxation. She had made up her mind to ask no questions, to reveal no suspicions, to be simply a guest on a journey. She, too, relaxed.

"I am sure," he said in an ordinary, friendly way, "that you have brought all Carlo's meals for today?"

"All packed in the cooler. Enough for a week, if necessary."

Now he gave her the benefit of his special smile, "A week would be nice, Stella."

She wanted to say, don't flirt with me, Gil Nathan, but flirt suddenly seemed very out of date. She tried out several American expressions in her mind but none seemed to suit. She divided her smiles between him and Carlo.

"I think you will like this trip, Stella. There are several ways to go. Washington is worth a visit but not with Carlo in the car. I am going to branch off and let you see a bit of West Virginia. This is the time of the year, autumn, to see the trees. Tonight we will stop over in a lakeside motel I know. To-morrow we should make it through North Carolina. It is an excellent route and by the end of the day we will make Augusta, but it is a lot of driving."

"Yes," Stella said, "it is hard on you. I cannot help wondering if you would not have found it easier to put Carlo and me on a plane?"

"That was suggested by Mrs Rosen," he answered drily.

"I wonder how you responded to that. She is hard to refuse. I often do things for her, sometimes ironing her special blouses. She is so beautiful; her smile is enchanting."

"Is it?" he asked. "I suppose it is. She is the real southern belle. Maybe I was a bit enchanted once! A long time ago."

Maybe he was one of the five husbands, Stella thought, but I won't ask him. I don't want to know. I would be better engaged in keeping in touch with Carlo in the back seat. She turned around to find that Carlo had fallen asleep. Asleep, with his pudgy lower lip a little loose, with his chin, normally so determined, now like a tiny double chin, he looked remarkably like his Uncle Gil.

CHAPTER FOURTEEN

G il made detours so that Stella could see the trees in all their autumn colour. They stopped several times and Stella was able to keep Carlo comfortable and well fed. He had not a big appetite: often mealtimes were to him a waste of precious time when he could be climbing over the chairs and practising the trapeze act of getting unaided from one piece of furniture to another. This day, however, he was a model of correct behaviour. Stella wondered if that was because Uncle Gil's eyes were on him all the time.

"You manage him so well, Stella," observed Uncle Gil, "and see how he watches you."

"He has a wary eye on you, too!" Stella laughed.

"Do you think he is afraid of me?" Gil asked.

"You have never given him reason to be afraid of you, Gil," Stella answered. "An instinctive respect."

"Is that all?" Gil sounded wistful.

"Isn't that the best foundation?" Stella asked. "I think children take a long time—years—to realise the meaning of love for a parent, and longer for uncles and aunts," Stella added quickly. Gil began to say something but he changed his mind. Instead he asked Stella, "Do your children love you?"

Stella was not to be drawn on a personal opinion of her own family. "Parents, mothers more than fathers, are usually more concerned to give love, to do the best they can, rather than look for a return. The getting-on-with-the-rearing job becomes the important thing."

"You love little Carlo quite openly, Stella."

"I adore him," she answered. "He came into my life almost as a renewal of family love. I needed him. Unfortunately for this little mite, he needs me too. This is not family life, Gil. In family life, the children quite rightly take everything for granted."

"I wish it were family life, Stella." He was silent for a long time. It was a gloomy silence. Stella was careful to keep herself to herself, always conscious of Dave's rule of no nattering on long drives. Dave was never that far away from her mind. Dave was a good car driver until the latter years when he found it hard to pass his favourite pubs. That had made Stella nervous and less anxious to accompany him whenever he took off. Which was frequently, and more frequently, thought Stella. I should have gone with him, been a good companion, even drunk with him. But was there enough money for two? I know now there was not enough money. Maybe that was a reason for his not pressing me to go on his skites. Ah no, he preferred to be with men. He made no secret of that.

"Forgive my going a bit glum, Stella."

"It is all the driving, Gil. Is your neck stiff?" Now he was in good form again. "Stiff as hell, Stella! But it will keep until we get to the hotel. Would your gentle touch be available then?"

"Of course it would." Stella thought to herself that rubbing his back was only fair, after all. She suspected herself of rather liking the task, but she assured herself it meant very little, and his neck and shoulders must be hurting. She was a bit restless herself after a long day in a car. Luckily the motion of the car kept on sending Carlo into long dozy sleeps.

"I have never stayed in a motel," Stella said. "They are a new thing in Ireland. Well, not very new but new to me."

"I promised you a lake-side motel for to-night, didn't I? This particular one is known as the Garden of Allah."

Now Stella laughed gaily. "I remember being found reading a book with that title, *The Garden of Allah*, and being thumped on the head with the book for daring to read a grown-up book. An exotic love story of a monk and a lovely woman. Years later I saw the movie with Marlene Dietrich. The book was better but then I was younger. Tell me about the motel, Gil."

"You know," Gil said in his mischievous voice, "I will just leave you with the name of it now and watch your reaction later."

Stella's reaction was worth watching when at twilight they arrived at the lantern-lit Garden of Allah. She could scarcely breathe with trying to find words for the Sahara-like low white buildings on the edge of the lake. She kept saying, "Oh, Gil! Oh, Gil!" He was plainly delighted.

"Not quite in the same class at the Amish chalet?" he queried as they unloaded the car and Stella carried Carlo into the gleaming white tent-shaped bungalow assigned to them. The bungalows were built in quadrangles, and the central square of each quadrangle was filled with sand, palm-trees, oases. The quadrangles were not open to the sky, but they appeared to be, because on looking up one saw twinkling stars and a hazy moon. Stella gasped at this, "Gil, look! A sky!"

He was amused. "To-morrow morning you will look up and see small white clouds against a blue sky and somewhere reflected sunshine."

"I could spend a holiday here!" declared Stella.

"I don't think so," Gil smiled, "One night with these hordes of people would be enough for you."

There were families settling down in the sandy garden. The oases and little rivers under the palms and flowering creepers were doing double duty as swimming pools, as many of them as there were bungalows, so a family could commandeer its own pool.

"Could we play happy families with Carlo by that little river?" Stella asked. "He has slept so much on the journey it will be hard to get him to settle down."

"I think that's a swell idea." Gil looked very pleased. "While you get him ready, or whatever, I'll go up on the balcony and order dinner. They will bring it down to us, all ready to serve up. Hot or cold, Stella? How would chicken and Caesar salad appeal to you? They do that well here."

Stella was nodding enthusiastically. "And wine? White?" Stella liked white wine. Gil said he would bring a sherry for her, and he would have a whiskey.

"I feel pampered!" Stella called after him. He should remember, she thought, I am only a hired help. Oh, well, I am sure he does. A sherry would be nice right now.

When Gil came back, Stella said to him, "Will you look after Carlo while I shower and change? He just could get upset in a strange place. If he does, just carry him over near, and I'll sing out to him. Okay?"

While Stella was changing, Gil took his shower.

He commented on the fact that while there were two bedrooms, the shower arrangements were communal. He did not seem altogether displeased.

Stella was sure she would never forget the lovely feeling of togetherness as they sat under the palm trees in canvas chairs. Stella had put his little swim trunks on Carlo and he was ecstatically happy to splash in the shallow water, feeling for little pebbles and dropping them back into the pool. By some undetectable way, the water in the rivulets and pools constantly renewed itself, looking clear and fresh. Young attendants were touring around and around picking up any papers or plastic cartons that happened to be dropped. The coloured lanterns were everywhere under the trees and in the arched doorways. Stella and Gil joined in attending and amusing Carlo. Gil proved wonderfully adept.

"How is your stiff neck, Gil?" Stella asked.

"Still waiting," he laughed, "hopefully!"

"How did we forget?" Stella smiled at him.

"I just had to accept that a first view of the Garden of Allah overpowered your memory of me!"

Stella was very sincere in her answer. "Nothing could do that. You are very kind. When we get Carlo settled down, I will massage your back."

He will now turn on that smile that makes me keel over backwards, Stella thought. And he did.

Gil helped her with Carlo, although Stella had the impression he was standing by simply to admire both of them.

"How would you describe this little boy's face?" he asked Stella.

"Vivid is my word for his face," Stella answered. "He will break many a girl's heart later on!"

"That sounds very Irish!" Gil laughed at her and then he said, "I wonder now did my Irish nanny say that about me long ago?"

"I am sure she did," Stella said. "We Irish are always predicting the future. You seem to have good memories of that nanny, Gil." And she remembered he had called her, Stella, his nostalgia. "What was her name?"

"Her name was Rosie. Rosie Farrell. She left to get married when I was six and a half. I remember the exact day. My world ended that day. And for a whole year, or more, I hated her for leaving me. Then my father told me that Rosie had died at the birth of her first baby and that the baby died. My mother died in bringing me into the world. When my father told me, his eyes and his voice were full of tears. That was when I cried for the first time, not because of my mother, but because of Rosie and her baby. I had to hide upstairs to cry. My two older brothers were always teasing me about being Rosie's boy. I suppose they were jealous because I had someone to love and they had not. I did not know that then. I did not even know that I loved Rosie."

"Look, Gil, Carlo has dropped off to sleep. Would you like to lie down on the bed and I will rub your back."

He stretched out, face downward, on the bed. Stella lifted Carlo's crib to the far side of the room and she sat on the side of the bed. Gil's voice was so sad, so full of longing, she felt great sympathy for the lost little boy in him whose world had ended when he was six. Her mind quickly shied away from the sudden thought that she was the one who now stood in Rosie's shoes: for Gil, out of the distant past, and for Carlo in the uncertain present.

"If you loosen your shirt, Gil, I could push up your singlet and use some of this baby cream to massage more easily."

"Thank you, Stella."

Stella worked away on Gil's back and shoulders, loosening the muscles which were quite knotted. The cream helped and her hands felt soft against his skin. From where she sat she could see his eyes closed, and gradually his body relaxed.

"We should have done this when we first arrived," she said gently. "You must have been in agony when we were sitting out there at our oasis."

"I never enjoyed a 'sitting' so much in a long life," he murmured, slowly and happily.

"How is that now?" Stella asked at last.

"Wonderful, Stella, wonderful." He heaved himself up off the bed, pushing down his shirt. "I would like to fetch us some wine from the balcony."

"But the bar will be closed, surely?" said Stella. "It is nearly eleven o'clock."

"No, not in the Garden of Allah." People go on arriving all night and do just what we did when we arrived—that is a good reason you wouldn't want to spend your holiday here, Stella."

Stella stood at the door while Gil went up the moving staircase to the balcony. It was exactly as he had said. The stars were twinkling overhead, the lanterns were all lit under the trees and another few hundred people were still moving about admiring this American Sahara. A man, passing by the door, said he felt like a big oil sheikh and Stella smiled at the idea.

When they went inside with the wine and glasses, Stella said, "Have you noticed how soundproofed these little bungalows are? You would not hear a thing."

Gil poured out a glass of white wine for Stella and from his flask a whiskey for himself.

"Are you very tired, Stella?"

She looked at him over the rim of her glass. "Well," she drew the word out, "a little tired for discussions or maybe arguments. I do not want this lovely day to end in a wordy boxing-match."

He smiled at her. He knows damn well what that smile does to me, Stella thought. I wish he wouldn't.

"May I stay with you to-night, Stella?"

"Gil, I am going to be firm with you. Please let me have my say. If I were a woman on your level, I would surely fall into your arms. You are very attractive to me. No, I am not quite finished. I am the hired help. The Rosie of this establishment. To-morrow, I would feel used. You would feel degraded. And..."

"Yes," he said softly, "finish your say."

"And love-making is for young people. At my age, it is non-aesthetic!"

"I don't think Rosie knew that word." His voice was tender, tired, emotional.

Suddenly Stella was crying. "Oh, my God," she wept, "I hate women who cry." She was in Gil's arms and giving way to a passion of grief that swept away all resistance.

When Stella thought afterwards of that night, she realised that she had never known what making love was all about. With the brief exception of one misguided hour when she had flirtatiously sought an

innocent rebellious liberation with Dave's friend, she
had known only one man since she was eighteen
years of age. For Dave, a man's natural right was to
vent his lawful passion on his wife and only on his
wife. Dave was a very moral man, a trustworthy man.
He often said that he had had his chances; he could
not deny that. In his position, dealing with
generations of young women, passing them through
his hands as it were, he had certainly had his chances.
Offered to him, so to speak. The flattery of it! He
knew he was very good-looking; many of them had
fallen for his looks, so they told him. Dave had made
only one mistake, and that was with Stella. He never
used the word "mistake" and he gave the impression
of having to laugh later, at himself. Twenty eight
years of age! You would think he would have had
some common sense—"that most uncommon of
senses." He was fond of quoting Shaw. Dave was a
professional Shavian expert; he had published to prove
it. Shaw had ridiculed the weak human undignified
necessary mechanics of procreation and Dave liked
to think he emulated his literary hero's strictures.
Stella's sexual education began as Dave's pupil and
that was all the education she received on the subject
of sex.

Women, in Dave's view, were free to feed the
romantic side of their natures by reading, by going

occasionally to the theatre and very occasionally to the cinema. Romance appeared beautiful to women; Dave allowed that. Let them stay with airy-fairy romance. However, a woman who took pleasure in sex was no better than...(Dave avoided the word) and certainly no better than she ought to be. And as a mother of children, well...He did not have to go further. But of course he went further: Shaw would never have approved of the modern trend of using sex as a visible recreation, freely available. Copulation (Shaw and the Catholic Church were in agreement on this) was strictly for procreation not recreation. Mr George Bernard Shaw would not have approved of fore-play, by-play, or any other play. A quick in and out, and no nonsense, and you kept it moral that way. A wife should not get ideas below her station. Stella had long ago lost interest in what was called "that side of life." She remembered her mother's sister, Aunty Patty, had always been most discreet about "that side of life" in the grown-ups' private talks long ago. Stella had been regretfully relieved when Dave's manly passion turned permanently to golf, whiskey and the unsubtle male joke with his exclusively male companions. His later life was encompassed in the words: the "lads." The "lads" took care of everything.

Gil Nathan had invented the art of love-making. Even as Stella was clinging to a strong male body to assuage all the pent-up grief, she was becoming aware of that strength being turned to her comfort. Warm hands were enfolding her body almost as if she were a child again, as if she had found refuge in an unhurried embrace that had always been waiting to take her close, an embrace that was her right, a holding-in-love that was a primeval innocence. There was no lustful pressure to engender fear, no forcing to surrender. Stella entered into a dream-world in a time long before age was reckoned. Time had no future place in Gil Nathan's love-making. There was a stillness, no going forward, no tomorrow of recrimination. His love-making carried Stella back into a sunny woodland past, where two people came in search of peace and found it and held it—a peace that seemed interminable; a peace that was an answer to all questions.

At five o'clock in the morning, as was his custom, little Carlo woke. Stella prepared an orange drink for him in his bottle. Slowly and lovingly, she changed him and settled him down. Their eyes held each the eyes of the other until his eyelids began to flutter drowsily. In the background, Stella heard Gil going to the bathroom and returning to bed. She went to the bathroom. She washed her hands but she did not dare to look in the mirror. Now fully awake, she did not want to see what a fallen creature looked like. Is that what I am, Stella mused, a fallen creature? She went back into the room and looked down at the sleeping child. Then she stood beside the bed she had shared with Gil. He did not open his eyes. She whispered, "I'll go into the other bed now." But he was not asleep. He held out his arms, "Come back here at once, Stella Shane!"

For a second, Stella was aware of choice. Just for a moment, there was an alternative. Fallen creature be hanged, she thought. She went back into his arms.

"How long will the little fellow sleep?" Gil asked softly. "Until about ten," Stella whispered.

"Wonderful, wonderful, wonderful," murmured Gil.

CHAPTER FIFTEEN

They were on the road again by eleven o'clock. The Garden of Allah presented the self same busy picture when they were leaving as when they arrived, except for the blue sunny sky overhead instead of the twinkling stars. Stella had to be careful not to engage Gil's glance. She did not want to be the one looking for recognition. She found much to busy herself with in preparing Carlo's drinks and little meals of tinned food for the journey. Gil wanted to help with everything as if to identify with her. Stella wished she could be sure of his attitude towards her. There was an apprehension within, which asked her had she been imprudent?

When they had driven some miles in a kind of silence of which neither knew the exact meaning, Gil said, "I hope to make Augusta, across the Savannah River, by evening. It will be a lot of driving to-day but with less to-morrow. I know the long drive is tough on you and Carlo."

"Shall we make the usual stops for his changes?"

"Oh, of course. And for lunch and tea. I will phone

the house in Augusta to remind them that we are expecting to arrive in time for dinner."

"You know this house in Augusta, Gil?"

"Yes, Stella, very well. My wife was born in it and she was always devotedly attached to it. She and Fanna Rosen were friends in their youth, neighbours almost."

"Were they both southern belles, like you said about Mrs Rosen?"

He smiled, a little sad now at the memory of his dead wife. "Very different women. My wife was tall and slender. She had been very delicate in her girlhood, and perhaps she was never destined for old age. She was a brilliantly clever lawyer."

"Please accept my sympathy. Try not to be sad," and Stella lightly touched his hand on the steering wheel.

"I like how natural you are, Stella. Are all Irish people natural and kind like you?" He was changing the subject of Augusta just when Stella was about to ask who lived there now.

"I suppose it is never possible to generalise about a whole nation of people," Stella laughed. "But," she added, "as it is only a small nation on one small island, we would be all much the same, I suppose."

"How small a nation? How small an island?"

So Stella described her homeland as she saw it far away across the Atlantic, and her tone was a little bit lonely.

"In school, when we looked at a map of the world, Sister Clare used to say that Ireland could be easily submerged in one of those Great Lakes, Lake Huron, I think. A few hundred miles in length and much less in width, that is Ireland. Before the famine of the 1840s there were over eight million people in Ireland; now there are just over five million." Stella paused, longing to boast about Ireland but she knew it would sound silly. "I could not help thinking," she said, "that yesterday we had done the circuit of Ireland four times over!"

Gil laughed. "So that is what you are thinking! Calculating the miles! Well!"

"Not all the time!" Stella laughed softly. Now they were talking and laughing as old friends. Stella shared all the little jokes and stories with Carlo. The baby was the centre of their lives and he seemed to know it. However, her imagination was not so set at ease. How could a man who had loved her all night never refer to it the very first thing the next day? Maybe "loved" was not the right word? She pondered that while pleasantly acting out the nanny for her little charge. But it had felt like love. Even now, the feeling was of love given and received. What he had done to her had induced a tranquillity of emotion, even a stilling of suspicion. The fear that Gil Nathan would get her into his power to further his own aims for Carlo was not so keen a fear now. Her giving of a loving response had surely made equal their fragile relationship? She could convince herself of anything when she glanced at his hands on the steering wheel. He had beautiful hands. She had noted their beauty the very first day, when he drove her to Larch Hill. Stella was a "hands" person. She had always known that. Dave's hands were very beautiful. Stella had often gazed at Dave's hands holding a book, his long fingers meditatively curving a couple of pages. Come to think of it, Stella had admired everything about Dave: his lean body, his wavy hair. She wondered now why she had not told Dave of her admiration? What had held her back from pursuing Dave, from chasing away all those men and installing herself in their place?

"You are becoming abstracted, my dear Stella. We will take the next intersection and make a break for lunch. I could do with a comfort stop."

"Me, too," Stella smiled gratefully.

After lunch, Stella harnessed Carlo into his car sleeper. If it was going to be a long, long drive, the little fellow could not be expected to sit in his car seat, his head nodding forward as he grew sleepy. He had eaten well and he fell off asleep almost at once.

"There are several pairs of sun-glasses in the

dashboard, Stella. We will be driving far south this afternoon. You may find the sun more oppressive than it has been so far."

"You are wonderfully thoughtful," Stella told him. She found a pair of sun-specs to fit her, rather glamorous feminine specs. She wondered whose they were. Gil selected a pair that fitted over his long-distance glasses. He settled into the driving seat, holding the fitted glasses in his hands. Then he turned around to face her.

"Take off the specs for just a moment, Stella. I want to kiss you." His kiss was very sweet and very satisfying. It was not a kiss of mere friendship. Stella persuaded herself it was a kiss of promise. Nevertheless, as the miles rolled away and the overhead signs predicted the familiar name of Chattanooga and soon afterwards the Blue Ridge Mountains, Stella still had not the hardiness required to question him about Augusta. His dead wife's home. Was it now his? Who lived there? She supposed she would just have to wait and see but she wished Gil would guess at her natural curiosity. Her instinct told her not to question him about the house in Augusta in the easy way she had said, "Tell me about the Garden of Allah." And look what happened there! Say nothing intimate, Stella warned herself. Act the nanny even if in your heart you are longing to become the lover. It was now hard to remember to tell herself that Gil Nathan laid traps for unwary Irish simpletons. Suspicion seemed to have been laid to rest.

They stopped at a small-town park for some tea. Stella spread a rug on the grass under the trees. She changed the little boy and gave him a little freedom on the grass while Gil got out the flask of iced tea. Carlo was now of the tea-party. To his delight he was allowed help himself to a biscuit.

"Gil, you are very happy to have this time with Carlo?"

"You will never know the joy I have been given to have him with me," he said.

"When we are in Florida," Stella told him, "he will miss your daily call."

"Do you think he will have forgotten me by the Christmas holiday, Stella?" Gil was anxious.

"Hard to tell! I remember once, when Ross was two years old, I was in the nursing home, to have Sybil, and Ross screamed when he saw me returning home. He ran off and hid. I was very upset."

"Good grief!" Gil said. "And that was probably only a couple of weeks!"

"More like a week!" Stella smiled. "But maybe I had changed—the big roundy figure gone. And I had had my hair cut and re-styled and, I think, coloured much brighter. I think I wanted to look like a new woman! I must have forgotten to think of the effect on a two-year-old baby."

"Only two years between them? That was quick, wasn't it?" he asked.

"The Irish way," Stella smiled at him. "If a married lady is not having a baby, she is having a miscarriage." Stella laughed at his astonished face. "But cheer up, Gil, that was long ago. Even in Ireland, they have heard of birth control."

"And did you have miscarriages, Stella?"

"Now, that's a loaded question, Gil Nathan. To answer truthfully, or to answer untruthfully, would give you an impression of my married life that might very well be false."

"In court, Stella, you would have to say 'yes' or 'no.'"

"Oh, are we in court again, Gil?"

"Stella, tell me. Did you have miscarriages? I mean natural miscarriages. I am not talking about abortion."

"There is no legal abortion in Ireland, Gil. It is sad that unfortunate Irish women have to cross the Irish Sea for that facility."

"You mean, go to England? Did you go to England, Stella?"

"No, Gil. I was married at eighteen because I was pregnant. I told you that already. No one told me there was such a thing as the possibility of abortion:

it was simply unheard of at that time."

"And the miscarriages?"

"There were a few," Stella said reluctantly. "I think because I was approaching the menopause."

Gil took her in his arms and drew her down on the rug. "You turn my heart over," he said very, very tenderly.

"Now you make me want to rub your stiff shoulders, Gil Nathan. Roll over there."

He submitted gladly to this. Carlo sat staring at this performance. It struck him as funny. He wanted to join in; so he rubbed Gil's legs. Gil's eyes were open, crinkled in that way he had of being mischievous. "Maybe this is the best part of all this trip! All this massage! Could there be a higher heaven?"

When they were settled back into the car for the last part of the journey, Gil asked the question again. "Could there be a higher heaven, Stella?"

It took a bit of courage to give Gil Nathan a straight answer. Stella was a bit afraid of overstepping and she had not lost her awe of the feeling of power which was his aura. At last, she answered in a small clear voice, "I think I have known one...recently."

"I am happy with that." He was all geniality as he started the engine. "So on we go to a higher heaven!" Stella wondered if he realised the implications she could take out of that airy statement. She had got to the stage when thinking was no longer an option. Maybe it was the result of time spent confined in a car, mixed with the sense of double identity: Carlo's nanny and Gil's...what? That was the point of obscurity and confusion in her mind. What was she to Gil? No use in trying to figure it out. Stella gave up.

"Tell me when we are coming to the Savannah River, Gil. I always make a special wish when crossing over a great river for the first time."

"You have missed a few wishes to-day," he teased. "Didn't you notice the bridges over rivers?"

"Yes, some," Stella answered, "but you see, I never heard of them. 'Savannah' is like a word from Fenimore Cooper, part of literature, part of history."

"It is a good thing Velva cannot hear her very literate hired-help. She would re-gather her forces for the attack of the International Kidnap Gang! Have you missed all those cameras and phones and televisions? What would Velva have thought if she saw you walking Carlo through that little park earlier to-day?"

"I never know what she is going to think about anything," Stella answered, adding to herself, "and I don't much care."

"Would you be up to a spot of kidnapping, Stella?" and his tone was as light as a falling leaf.

Stella was half turned to make sure Carlo was at ease in the back. Her body was caught in a rigid grip of sudden fear. Almost as if her brain had been struck by forked lightning and split open to receive a warning. The lulled sense of being at ease with a friend ceased abruptly. The lightning flash laid bare the whole purpose behind all this gorgeous romantic cosiness. He had cast her in the role of an elderly kidnapper, acting for this gang whose name was Gil Nathan. Stella felt silly but also very unsure of herself.

With an effort of will she straightened her back and sat bolt upright in the car seat. She had no voice with which to answer the question. Obviously he had not looked for an answer but merely dropped the suggestion into her head. Stella tried to look at his profile for some indication. Her eyes saw nothing. He was intent on the road. He had assumed, she supposed, that she was half-asleep, receptive to a murmured word from a man to whom she had become wholly susceptible. You can bet he knew that too!

Well, now I am wide awake, said Stella to herself, and I'll stay that way. God! The damned cheek of him. But wasn't I the right fool to think I was charming the pants off this guy. (Where do I hear these phrases? Hazel, I suppose.) Kidnapping! And who, I wonder, would take the rap if the kidnapping plot fell to pieces? Not Mr Big, you can be sure! Stella knew that the silly phrases tumbling about in her head were an indication of her anger. It was always like that with her. Anger was a childish reaction at times when she should be setting her thoughts in logical order. She sat very still and made an effort to empty her mind.

"Not too far now to the Savannah. Better get your wishes lined up. Please put in a wish for me, Stella." The lingering note of his voice on "Stella" did strange melting things to the emotion she was determined to build into obstinacy.

"Are you awake?" he asked.

"Oh, yes. Oh, yes. I am thinking about my wishes. Deciding for myself."

"What put that hard edge on your voice?" He took one hand from the wheel and laid it for a second on her skirt. "You all right?"

"Getting a little tired, I think."

"Another ten minutes, or so," he promised.

They went over the Savannah on a huge double loop, into the city of Augusta, out again and back on a highway by the great river. At last, they turned off the road and entered a long avenue lined with autumn foliage. The immense house was like a stock building from an old film. It had an overhanging portico on pillars. Gil Nathan drove around to the back and pulled up the car. A black couple came out into a glass porch to welcome him. He made rapid introductions and went into the house. There he was very much the lord and master and the couple accepted his instructions. Almost, Stella was thinking, as if they were well-treated slaves in a bygone era. And Stella was at once struck by the thought that that was her position too. Hired help in Philadelphia, nanny-slave in this far south place. Gil Nathan probably saw himself as a master with feudal rights. Stella did not have time to examine this unwelcome idea. With Carlo in her arms, she followed the black woman up a massive staircase, and the man joined the procession carrying Carlo's crib and an assortment of Carlo's blankets.

"What is your name, please?" Stella asked the woman, who seemed a person anxious to help.

"I am Hessy," she answered, "and my man is Daniel." Daniel went downstairs to get more baggage. Gil Nathan had gone straight to the phone, and his voice at its most dictatorial carried up the stairs.

"I am the nanny," Stella said, "if you like to call me that." She put Carlo down and he began to explore. "I suppose I had better shut the door or he'll be off down into the hall!"

"That's the age, Mis Shane," Hessy smiled and sniffed at one go. It was a habit she had.

"Have you a family, Hessy?"

"Seven we have. They all growed up and living all over—some married, Mis Shane."

"Don't any of them live here with you?" This was the question Stella had wanted to ask for the last hundred miles: who lives here?

"We here in the garden house, just him and me. We look after the big house, and the garden. Mostly just cut the grass."

"You are er, like er, the caretakers, Hessy?"

"Oh, no, Mis Shane. Mr Nathan, he pays us. We always been here."

Now Gil came into the room. "Hessy will look after you, Nanny," he said in his decisive way. "What about Carlo? There is hot water, is there Hessy?"

"Oh, yes, Mr Nathan. All done as you instruct on the telephone. What time dinner, Mr Nathan?"

"What does Nanny say? When will Carlo be ready for bed?"

Stella was afraid to catch his eye for fear she would giggle. He was like a man in a polite parlour drama; so she joined him there.

"I will give him his bath, sir, and let him have a good romp after his supper. He should settle down in about an hour and a half, sir."

Gil looked at her in surprise. He was not conscious, evidently, of playing the actor. "Very well, Nanny, I will come to take you down to dinner at eight."

"Thank you, sir," Stella said obsequiously. He asked, "Is this room warm enough? Or cool enough?" Hessy indicated the plug for the electric fire and Stella nodded.

When they had gone, Stella took a quick tour of the enormous room with its enormous bed. There were flowers on one bedside table, and a tray of sherry with glasses on the other. There was a bathroom *en suite*. It was all very ornate and rich. Stella did not feel elated. She felt put in her place. She had not come from a poor background; she had never been deprived. Until the day of the bank manager's interview she had never given much thought to money. There were always bills for Dave to grouse about but somehow they were paid. The house in Larch Hill was wealthy, ostentatious even, super comfortable in the "all-modern-conveniences" style. But this! This mansion was the place of a dream world. A woman here would dress in the feminine silks of the turn of the century. Stella looked in the wardrobes. They were empty now, but a delicate perfume was present within their mirrored doors. Her own luggage for Florida was already gone with Alice and Ambert. She had a fresh blouse and a cotton skirt in her travel bag. They would have to do. She had wondered, despite her new suspicions, if she would be asked, or allowed, to rub Gil's shoulder muscles. He had not come back.

Stella had plenty to do for Carlo, who was in marvellous form: so many new pieces of furniture to inspect and climb over and under and walk around, which he was now doing easily. Sometimes, just lately, Stella had found herself thinking that while she was well able to handle a baby, a little boy of such energy could prove too much. A young mum, she thought, that is what he needs. She had thought that from the beginning and this evening she was convinced of it. She got into the big bath with him when he had soaked her so much that it made no difference

When it came to settling down, he was still in hilarious humour, not a bit tired. Stella dressed and used a bit of make-up, and then she sat at the mirror brushing her hair. She read a story for Carlo from the little book she had brought. Finally she cradled him in her arms and paced up and down, singing in a low murmuring voice. Stella could always remember tunes but never all the words. Now it was an old country-and-western song that came to her. Up and down, up and down. "Have I told you lately that I love you? Well, darling, I'm telling you now. Have I told you lately that I miss you? Well, darling, I'm telling you now..." over and over and over, her voice sinking to a whisper as she saw his dark lashes giving up the attempt to stay open. Once he dropped off, he was good for a sound eight hours, although he might wake momentarily for a drink or a change around four am.

When she turned from lowering the little boy carefully into his crib, Gil Nathan was standing at the door watching her. The position of his body and his head betokened a deep thoughtfulness. Before he could speak, Stella said lightly, neatly putting herself in the correct niche for nannies, "Used Rosie Farrell sing you to sleep?"

He seemed surprised. "I hope she did," he answered. "I bet Carlo loves it." He draped a net over the crib, securing it at each corner. "Against the mosquito fly," he said. "Although Carlo is fairly secure from stings if the windows are kept closed. In very hot weather, there is air conditioning. Come, Stella."

CHAPTER SIXTEEN

Walking down the staircase, Stella could not help remarking that the whole house was like a film set in an old movie. "It is magnificent!" she exclaimed. "So huge! How did people live in such enormous places. Like ancient Romans!"

Gil smiled at her, but a little grimly. "They lived very nicely with a hundred niggers to shoulder the endless toil. The old couple downstairs are past it. It is nearly a year since I have been here and I can see the deterioration. I should sell. The Rosens sold their place years ago. It was hers—it was her family place. Even bigger than this. More land. And even more dilapidated—Fanna never wasted money on repairs."

Hessy and Daniel were waiting to serve the dinner. There was a big dining-table and many heavy chairs. A small round table was set for them. There were blue lights strung around the room. "They are for mosquitoes—hopefully," Gil told Stella. "They crash against them and expire."

They sat at the table. "We will serve ourselves, Hessy," he said. "You secured the windows, Daniel?

Then I think you pair may take the night off, if you wish." He passed some banknotes to the woman. "Get over here at about nine o'clock in the morning. I will make a ten o'clock start. Goodnight, Hessy. Goodnight, Daniel."

When Hessy and Daniel had gone, the business-like manner dropped away from Gil. He was all solicitude for Stella's comfort. Pouring her wine, helping her from each dish, he made a point of touching her lightly and very tenderly with every act of courtesy. Watch it, Stella, she warned herself—this is a very crafty guy. While she was lullaby-ing Carlo to sleep, the decision had been forming at the back of her mind to have it out with him. I may have been a fallen creature once but, like the time we were in the Amish country, I can show him who has strength of character. But sure maybe that was a once-off because I was crying. Maybe he intended only to comfort me. Never again, Stella resolved firmly, but she could not believe he would have the insensitivity to make love to her in the home, maybe the bedroom, of his dead wife. Oh, never! He was not that kind of man. The cheap afternoon lover who had an hour or two to cavort in a husband's bed? Stella did not know any woman who had allowed such a thing but she had read about it often in women's magazines. Now she was accepting food from him, tasting nibbles of this and bitefuls of that to see if the flavours blended to her liking, to her surprise even taking a small piece of chicken into her mouth from the tines of his fork on his recommendation. Stella realised that love-making had begun. She was being coaxed into the mood for it. She strove mightily to keep her mind on rectitude. Yet so close and constant were his little acts of offering pleasure that her thoughts spun out of sequence. This man was invading her imagination like a vortex, whirling away *her* resolve to question *him* on his intentions, dissipating the words she had conjured up to question his involvement in his schemes for her, an innocent bystander. He was intent on bending her to his will to do an act in which she did not want any part and of which she was terrified. The words kidnapper, kidnapped, false imprisonment, flashed on and off in her mind but refused to be let fly out around this dining table.

"This is a lovely dinner, Gil. Thank you." Stella's words sounded weak, far off, not at all those that were on the tip of her tongue. He poured more wine for her, touching her bare arm as he leaned across.

"I like it when your eyes go moody, Stella. I imagine I have found favour?"

If only you knew, she thought, but she heard herself saying, "Only sophisticated women know how to dispense favours. Ordinary women just get caught up on a wheel—sometimes by accident."

"Was last night an accident, Stella? I thought it was a favour?"

"Oh, Gil, you are just trying to make me feel good. What happened should never have happened."

"Why never?"

"Because—oh, you know why. I should have high principles. Look, because you are you, I have respect for you, I am in awe of you, I am a little afraid of you—and I have never been with a man in that way. Could you forget it happened?"

"Of course not!"

"Please—I am so recently a widow—all that held-back anxiety—please!"

"Recently a widow is a fact, Stella, but so long without having a sex relationship is a mystery." His question was measured, in his legal style.

"I never said—I mean how would you know—that is to say—how could you know that I—"

"Do not be distressed, Stella." He stood up, "Come, I want to show you the library."

They walked arm-in-arm out of the room and along a gallery filled with paintings. The library was exactly that, a book-lined room. There were side tables, cushion-filled sofa-beds and an electric log fire. More old-style Hollywood movies, was Stella's impression. Who could believe that such a room was for real?

"I never liked this room," Gil Nathan said. "I find it oppressive. But this is the room in which we are going to have our talk, Stella."

What a moment he chooses! Stella was full of the slight abandon that comes with a little too much wine. Dave had always told her she had no head for wine, that she should stop at one glass. Come to think of it, he told her all of those things at every party they ever went to. What was it Dave used to say? Oh, yes—"Stella has lost the run of herself." She just stopped herself in the nick of time from thinking: Dave can go to hell!

Now she was comfortably ensconced among the sofa cushions, almost within the circle of Gil Nathan's right arm. Magically more wine had appeared on a side table. She had often wondered what a real "wine session" would be like. Stella believed drink ruined a woman's skin, she seldom finished a glass. She took the glass of wine from Gil, and placed it on the table.

"Are we going to have a 'wine session'? Or should I keep a clear head? Gil Nathan, just listen to my muzzy voice!"

"A couple of questions and answers and then you will tell me what a 'wine session' is."

Stella tried to chase her weak thoughts back into line. That was another phrase from the past, "meeting your Waterloo." Why was to-night made up of phrases and not one coherent code or purpose? The hell with it. She picked up the wine glass. Drunk or sober I can only stay in America one year. One year! She tried rehearsing that mentally.

"Stella, have you thought of my proposition?"

So Stella said very carefully, enunciating the words, "Gil, could you please tell me your plan once more so that I am quite clear. And please, please don't treat me to that seductive smile or I'll faint." Stella had never fainted.

"Very simply then: I want to get you and the baby into an apartment to yourselves in Philadelphia."

"But Gil, he is not our baby." She tried to smile.

"If he were, would you agree to co-operate with me?" he asked.

Stella stared at him. He was in deadly earnest.

"Gil, you are going to steal Carlo?" Was steal worse or better than kidnap? She sipped more wine.

"No, that would be illegal. I believe I could have him made a ward of court."

"You mean, if they divorce?"

"Yes. Not if. When. And you are perfect for Carlo. And you love him. You cannot deny that."

'But you see, I have a family back in Ireland. I could not stay here for ever," Stella was pleading.

"Stella, all I ask is a couple of years—an assurance for the court that Carlo will be in the right care."

Stella was not really of much importance. A nanny for Carlo was all that was important.

"But I am not a legal landed immigrant," she said.

"I have someone working on that, back in my office," Gil answered firmly.

Stella plucked up her courage. "Mr Nathan, you brought me here for a year. That was my commitment."

Now Gil Nathan turned on all the charm. "And you have succeeded beyond my wildest hope. You have been the answer to prayer, and I am not a man who prays, so somewhere out there beyond that far horizon there must be a power that directs angels to help poor mortal men."

Even Stella, sipping wine, thought he was going a bit beyond the beyonds. What should she say? All this talk about angels when what he had at heart was little Carlo's millions.

"Stella, I caught this opportunity of watching you with Carlo. I could have sent you on the plane, rather than come in the car. I wanted to see for myself the relationship between you and Carlo. It is all I could possibly want. It must continue."

So that was what this gorgeous car trip was all about. And while he was vetting the nanny, he was making his spare time profitable. Rather tipsily, Stella asked, "Killing two birds with the one stone?" Phrases abounded although she longed for some clever, original formula to confound him.

"Stella?" His surprise seemed genuine.

"Do you mean 'Rosie?'" asked Stella. "Where does Stella come into all this parable of good behaviour?" Now she really had lost the run of herself.

"Shall I take you up to bed, dear? It has been a long day."

"I suppose you had better do that," she murmured, knowing that what she wanted to say was: are you coming too? But she didn't say that. She was well brought up, she remembered, even if she felt a bit high. Educated by an elite order of nuns. She had high principles, hadn't she? Tonight she didn't feel like weeping so she couldn't throw herself on his sympathy. And as well as all that, this was his dead wife's house. Dead wives and dead husbands always came back in the dark of night, green ghosts trailing muddy robes. Stella was aware of her guilt from the Garden of Allah. Perhaps Dave in his nether world would know her guilt and accuse her in the strange dark of this enormous house.

On the stairs Stella said, "Could we sit down for a moment, I must be tired, I was confusing this house with my house, which is silly because this house is like a museum. I just must be tired, I think." She linked her arm in Gil's arm. It was comforting.

"Here is your room, Stella, and there is Carlo's crib over in the corner. Now, how are you? Yes, lie down on your bed. You'll feel better."

Stella held out her hand to him. "Don't go for a minute, Gil, just give me a minute to sober up. I get crazy ideas about ghosts. Please stay for a minute, and then I'll be all right. I am a bit muzzy. Dave always said I should never drink more than one glass of wine."

"Do you still think of Dave's presence in your life?" She shook her head, her voice slurred and only half-awake. "I should, but I forget to. I feel guilty about forgetting and then I get afraid. Especially at night."

"Come, Stella," he murmured tenderly, "why don't I put you to bed. You are tired, poor darling." He slipped the blouse off her shoulders, and unzipped her skirt. The underwear was minimal. He drew the duvet over her. "I will stay until you fall asleep."

Stella made a last effort to control the situation. "What about high principles, Gil Nathan? Why don't you sack me for not being morally correct?" Her voice was a mere whisper, her reasoning dim and distant. Maybe there would never be another night in a man's arms...and what had she to lose that she had not already lost...Dave was lost for ever. Home seemed so far away...Dave's study...Dave's desk and his literature notes that she loved to read. Lines from Yeats's poetry drifted across her mind: "God loves us for our worth,/ But what care I that long for a man's love, /And I a mere shade at last, /Transparent like the wind, /I think that I may find a faithful love, a faithful love."

Gil's arms were holding her in the duvet. Perversely she wanted to ask for his love-making before sleep carried her away. Drowsily she wished he would make an offering of love words. Was this offering in his voice, repeating her name over and over, Stella, Stella? The search for meaning lasted only for moments and then the warmth of his embrace became an oblivion. Sleep came and went. There were spaces when she joyously recognised that he was still there, moments when it seemed his arms had almost lost her, moments when she was drawn back to safety and shelter. In the morning, he was gone. If only wonderful dreams could last for ever, Stella thought.

She was lifting up Carlo when Gil came back into the room. "Thank you," she said. There was happiness in knowing that Gil had told her more by his absence than she could have wished. She was rewarded by his special smile, the mischievous crinkling of the eyes so like little Carlo's. "I shall go down and make coffee for us and bring it up when I have showered," he said. "We have lots of time."

"Oh, good!" Stella smiled. "Carlo and I will shower

together."

"Lucky Carlo!" Gil called back to her.

She found coherent thought impossible holding a chuckling child under a shower. Wet babies demand full attention. Stella forced her mind off the feeling of pure happiness, a feeling she had never before experienced. She had Carlo dressed and had put him to explore the room on his unsteady little feet when Gil came with the coffee. Stella had not got beyond a wrap-around towel.

Gil put the tray down very carefully on the table. Then he turned to Stella.

"No, no, no, Gil—please don't." He had removed the towel and was studying her naked body. "Oh, that's not fair! Please!"

"Is it non-aesthetic?"

"It certainly is." She crushed herself against him rather than endure his quizzical smile.

He held her closely. "You are sweet and appealing. Totally aesthetic. Stella, this is the last time we will be together alone. I shall be returning to Philadelphia on the night flight. I am banking on Bart's absence from Boca Raton to hold the marriage together until Christmas. In January, Velva returns to her office. You have three months, at least, to consolidate your hold on Carlo. Look at me, Stella. Do you trust me? Do you believe me?"

She wanted to ask him why he had said that Carlo was his son. How could she trust him when he had told that lie? But she was standing naked in his arms, and Carlo was essaying a dangerous climb. This was not the moment. She grabbed the towel from him, and hastily wrapping it about her, she retrieved Carlo from a tottering chair.

"Gil, keep an eye on Carlo for me, just while I get dressed. Yes, pour out some coffee. Thank you. Please put a little coffee in Carlo's bottle, yes, a little sugar, a little milk, not too hot. Oh, Gil, please! Look the other way for a moment. Look, watch Carlo!"

Gil's very correct manner was reserved for the breakfast with Hessy and Daniel. Carlo now was in tremendous form. He had got completely used to the travelling life. Gil was very amused when Stella said, "Carlo, you would have made a great little tinker!"

In the car on the highway Stella had to tell Gil about the travelling people of Ireland, their horses and their caravans. Gil knew the word "tinker" but only as a verb. When Stella told him that long ago, the tinkers (or travelling people, as they preferred to call themselves) used to repair pots and kettles. Gil decided that was how they got their name. "Unskilled tinsmiths, they must have been," he said. Stella had gone silent.

"Are you thinking of Ireland, Stella?"

"In a way," Stella said. "There are times you remind me of my husband, Dave, and of my father sometimes."

"In what way, Stella?"

"I think it is the way you use words, and you like ferreting out meanings and reasons. My father was a teacher of English and French and, as you know, Dave was a professor of English. I suppose their interest rubbed off on me. With you, I suppose it is your legal training?"

"I guess so. Do I remind you of Dave in any other way?" He took his hand from the wheel and placed it over her hand. "Do I, Stella?"

She glanced sideways at him. His eyes were on the road, and he was smiling. Sure of himself, as ever, Stella thought, and he has a right to be.

"Absolutely not," she said. And then she added, "You keep on using my name—Dave always said 'my dear.'"

"Deeply interesting." He was using his court-room voice again. "And which usage does the defendant prefer?"

"Oh! Senior Counsel's—every time."

CHAPTER SEVENTEEN

In the week following Gil Nathan's return to Philadelphia, Stella had scarcely a moment to herself. Alice and Ambert kept a close eye on her every movement. They had made out a detailed map of the house and the grounds and had added a timetable of immense importance to account for every minute of Stella's day. She was amused to notice that twelve minutes were allowed for her shower but no minutes at all during the day for a visit to the toilet. The absolute fatuity of the timetable became apparent when she found it also applied to Carlo. They had made a spy-hole into her bedroom over which Stella promptly stuck the gummed end of an envelope. The cameras were in place in every room and clicked away. Stella left the map and the timetable in the sunniest part of the bedroom where the brilliant light would surely tan it and curl up its corners. When this had happened, by the end of the week, she brought the faded papers downstairs and left them in the laundry.

She began the second week with a feeling of being in control and of being able to ignore the tortuous plotting of Ambert and Alice. Day after day the weather was flawlessly bright and sunny. There was a swimming pool where she and Carlo spent much time. He loved this and never tired of bobbing up and down. His inflated ankle-bands and wrist-bands ensured his safety but Stella stayed always close to him in the pool. From the house-deck she could see the distant sea through the palm trees. There was no question of her getting her day off until Velva and the Rosens came. The peace of being without Velva's voice was remarkable. Towards the end of the second week a large envelope came in the post from Philadelphia. Inside were a collection of letters and cards for Stella, some of them many weeks old. On Gil Nathan's impressive office paper there was a typed message to say that this post was at Larch Hill and had been overlooked. Stella found herself searching the big envelope for a personal message from him. Surely there would be a few lines in his own writing? There was nothing. She put aside the disappointment and spread out the letters into some sort of date-arrangement, taking the earlier ones first. They were all from the family, except one which was from her bank. The money she had sent from Philadelphia and the widow's pension which was being paid in had all been receipted to her name, and they had given her a new account number. There was one query. They could pay the insurance on the house but the house should be occupied to make the insurance valid. Stella would write and tell them to pay anyway. There were two letters from Philip, predictable and reasonably concerned. A very cheery letter from Hazel announced her intention to come and visit her mother during the Christmas break from college. Would the Nathans give her a room? Stella doubted if Velva would be the soul of hospitality. There were half a dozen cards from Ross thanking her for her letters and promising to write fully when he could find a space on his cluttered desk. Stella smiled. At least he had sent cards.

There were three large cream envelopes which Stella recognised as Alec Mackay's. Three? The dates were spaced over several months. Why did Velva hold back the post? Oh, well, all of these rotten things: forgotten post, cameras recording every knee-jerk, maps, timetables, beady eyes eternally watching, the whole sickening lot would give her the courage to say No! No! No! the next time she laid eyes on Gil Nathan. He just might have added one little line for her personal perusal. She searched again. Well, he didn't, did he? She went back to the three cream envelopes. The earliest one was very brief:

Dear Stella,
Just another line to hope that you are well and
happy in America. Sybil has not been too good
ever since Dave's death. I am trying to persuade
her to see a doctor or a psychiatrist. Perhaps a
word from you would help. I should be grateful.
Sincerely yours,
Alec

Sybil was no Velva but she had a certain way of
focusing attention on herself. Evidently that was what
she was doing now. Stella opened the second letter,
dated three weeks after the first:

Dear Stella,
Having no reply from you, I managed to get
your phone number from Ross in New York.
The lady of your house (I presume) said the
nanny does not receive phone calls. So another
letter: I am worried about Sybil. Would you
write an affectionate letter to her, please. I am
unable to cope.
Sincerely,
Alec

Stella quickly realised that Alec must have coped
for months before he put pen to paper. Writing must

have been the last resort of desperation. The reality of Sybil suddenly flared up in Stella's mind. She opened the third letter, wondering if he would stop writing the name Sybil, and say lovingly, "my wife":

Dear Stella,

I have concluded that the "nanny" is not allowed receive post. I feel sure you would have come to my aid. Sybil left the house and for a week I could not find her. I feared the worst— as she had threatened it. She is staying now with mutual friends but she will not see me. I have to come to New York on business at the end of November. May I come and see you? I have, of course, very little hope that you will receive this letter but if you do, please write or, better still, phone. I feel I have failed miserably with Sybil.

Sincerely,
Alec

Stella never allowed herself to ponder on her own problems while taking care of Carlo. She felt he would know, with childish instinct, that she was abstracted. She believed in the old maxim of a day's work for a day's pay. Carlo was a full-time job from early morning until eight o'clock at night. She dare not let her thoughts wander. And when he had finally settled for the night, she felt like doing the same. Oh, to be young again with so young a child, was her constant prayer.

She finally decided to write down her problems and difficulties. Written down, she could assess them. Otherwise her mind was in chaos.

To write letters had been easy. She used to post them on her day off in Philadelphia, getting stamps from a stamp machine. Could she entrust letters to Alice and Ambert? Or to the friendly Filipino woman who worked in the kitchen? A big question.

To phone Alec Mackay was impossible because of the time difference. His day was her night. The phones in the house were bound to be tapped or taped or whatever.

Her mind on the subject of Gil Nathan was greatly troubled. She longed to rid herself of the guilt of the two nights she had spent with him. More than *that* guilt was the insidious guilt of suspecting that if he had said something she would feel less guilty. Something like what? Like telling her he loved her? What a hope! He had pleasured himself at her expense. Now that is a good old-fashioned expression, thought Stella to herself. Wasn't I brought up not to take pleasure in it? And I did too, didn't I? Tremendous pleasure in a tremendous mortal sin. If I got a day off (with someone suitable to mind Carlo), I could go to confession. The Filipino woman told me she is a Catholic. She would know where the church is—she might even know the times of confession.

It occurred to her that the three letters about trouble at home with her daughter would be a good reason for going home to Ireland. She could send them to Gil Nathan. Then immediately, as always happened, she remembered Carlo's big dark eyes fixed on hers in a kind of dumb seeking for security. That thought was now followed by the fact that in the last twenty years, Sybil's greatest joy in life was to disobey and obstruct her mother. Until Dave lay dead in his coffin, Stella had never known the nature of Sybil's love for her father. She had kissed the dead lips many times with impassioned fervour, her tears had rained down on Dave's dead body almost soaking the Capuchin shroud in which he was laid-out. At the graveside, as the coffin was being lowered, she had called out most heartrendingly, "Daddy! Daddy! Daddy!" Stella had despised herself for thinking such a blatant show of grief to be unseemly but she had meant to go and comfort her daughter after the funeral. The demands of showing courtesy and hospitality to the scores of mourners had come between them and Stella could not remember seeing Sybil afterwards.

Stella composed a letter to Alec in affectionate terms. She had always been fond of him since he came to Dave's undergraduate evenings more than thirty years ago. Dave had been very proud of the headlong success Alec had made of his college career, proud when he went into business and prouder again when Alec set up his own business. Thirty years ago in Ireland the title of entrepreneur was a very new idea. To Stella, the marriage was a total surprise but to Dave it was a triumph. Now, in the letter, Stella counselled patience. She told him of her own delayed shock. How, only now, could she think of Dave without tears? She offered her loving sympathy in his dilemma. Everything would sort itself out. And yes, of course, she would be glad to see him when he came to the States—if he got as far as Florida where she expected to be until after Christmas. His letters would probably reach her in Florida as the person left in charge in Larch Hill was more obliging in sending on post than the person previously. He should continue to use the Larch Hill address rather than the Florida address as the unobliging person was expected in Florida very soon. Stella read the letter over. Alec had always been very bright: he would be well able to read between the lines and size up the situation.

Having the letter ready to post gave her relief of mind. She put it away in a safe place—a sort of hiding place where she kept her savings book. Nothing was ever totally concealable in this household.

It was not the misalliance of her daughter and Alec that occupied her sleepy night thoughts. It was Gil Nathan. Stella was truly shocked at her need for him. She wished fervently that he had never awakened her to this fantasy life. Even if she purged her guilt in confession, she knew well she had no "firm purpose of amendment!" Would she not do it all again—if the chance came her way? She upbraided herself for allowing herself to be used, and misused, in some sort of power play for ends of which she could not, and should not, be a part.

And all the time, as day succeeded day, she was drawing closer and closer to a little child who was not her child. She took a joy, never before experienced, in his almost hourly advances: another word learned, another activity, longer toddling walks; and all the time his great big dark eyes growing more expressive with each new adventure. Most of all, he was inexpressibly full of lively affection. Stella had a deep feeling of bonding. She tried to ignore the growing dread she felt at the prospect of Velva's return.

CHAPTER EIGHTEEN

It was a very chastened Velva who came to Boca Raton a few weeks later. If she knew of the process of turning over a new leaf, then that is what she had done. She spoke civilly to Nanny of her plans for the winter. Stella was surprised and pleased—it did not occur to her to remember that Velva was devious.

"You will accompany me and my son to parenting classes, Nanny. Uncle Ambert has enrolled our names. Three days a week. From nine am to midday. The afternoons are too hot. I will meditate and siesta."

Stella hoped that her eyes had not become like saucers. "Yes, Ma'am," she said dutifully.

"On two mornings, we are enrolled for transcendental meditation, and yoga exercises."

Stella wondered if Carlo would be up to meditation. This new Velva was something else again.

"When my mother returns, her masseuse will come in every night to prepare me for sleep."

"Yes, Ma'am," Stella said, since a reply seemed called for.

"I am giving consideration to what you can do to

help me, Nanny. I'll be talking to you."

Stella swore inwardly. The royal family in Buckingham Palace could not be more full of themselves than these Nathans. And that includes you, Gil, she added. Classes in parenting? That's a new one! Parenting a child you never ever hold in your arms—not even now when you haven't seen him for three weeks. In fact, you look at him without seeing him. He can now walk, dammit. And almost string the words together. But have you, his parent, listened? Not to mention fussed and praised? Parenting? That's a good one all right.

When the ever-beautiful Fanna Rosen (without her sleek but silent husband) returned, the new life began in earnest. There was no more early splashing about in the swimming-pool. Uncle Ambert had the car at the door at eight forty-five, and Stella had to be there with her little charge all spruced-up and ready to learn. Velva then emerged carrying the class books, all six of them filled with instructions on how to be the best mother in the world and (presumably) rear the best baby. From the sun-deck, Mrs Rosen waved delicately, but encouragingly, at her quiet daughter as the car drove off.

There were six other ladies in the parenting class which was held in a room of the Lutheran church. The instructress was a great Amazon of a woman who looked as if she could command silence on a battlefield, but who, nevertheless, was unable to quite control the progeny of the seven assembled ladies, not all of whom had brought a nanny. When the little kids saw each other, they were naturally filled with curiosity and tried to get at each other. Carlo had brought with him his favourite teddy bear. When a tiny girl tried to take it from him, he flew into Stella's arms to hide his teddy. The tiny girl began to roar and bawl.

"Make him give it to her, woman," snapped the Amazon. Stella held Carlo tighter. It was his bear, so it was. The little girl bawled louder and some of the other babies took up the howling. Velva would be aghast that her child had started it and disgraced her. Carlo, safe against Stella's bosom, arched his eyebrows with disdain. Stella expected Velva to castigate her publicly but Velva did not seem to have the energy. Saving it for later, thought Stella as she watched Velva staring into space.

"Open your books, ladies: *Loving All Our Children.* Thank you. We will leave aside the first chapter which you will all have read in preparation and turn to page twenty. Thank you. We are going to talk this morning about the fair and equal and impartial treatment of each child in the family."

And how would it be, thought Stella, if there is

only the one child in the family? And does this massive big lady not know that each child is different, even if you had a dozen, and draws out of each parent a different response to his need? Same mother, same father, same home, same school, same teachers, same relatives, same friends, and each child turns into a different man or woman at the end of it all. What more can you do than love them, even when that love is rejected? I had better listen, Stella admonished herself, I might learn something. Her eye was caught by Velva's attitude. Velva was listening, or she appeared to be. Her fingers turned the leaves of the book when others turned their leaves. When some of the others were trying to hold their babies and pay attention, Velva, sitting unencumbered, gave all the appearance of being absorbed in the lesson. Yet there was a listlessness in the stillness of her body. To Stella, who had always been wary of Velva's pitched intensity, there seemed now to be a vacant stare in her eyes.

Stella reminded herself that her job was to keep Carlo in order. He was not used to being cordoned into a little circle. His nature, physical and mental, was that of an explorer. His eye was on chairs piled up against the wall, obviously to make room for the class circle, and Stella knew that each time he struggled to get toddling, he wanted to toddle over to that lovely pyramid of chairs and climb to the top. He eyed Stella speculatively and questioningly and she tried to give the hands-off sign. When she whispered into his ear, the Amazon lady called for silence, not just Stella's silence but that of the others as well. The idiocy of it for kids! Stella was very thankful when the coffee-break came. All the ladies were then told to change their children's disposables and to-morrow they would swop around and change each other's children. The Amazon lady made this sound like a delightful promise. Velva went to a window and began to smoke a cigarette. However, she had to extinguish it. It was unsocial, she was told. It amazed Stella that Velva silently submitted to this. The big lady walked around, commenting on the way the ladies changed their children. She considered some of them were inept, and meekly they accepted her criticisms.

After the break, Carlo snuggled into Stella's arms and fell asleep. Velva did not seem to notice. His little body was warm which made Stella feel that she too could doze off but she did not dare. She forced her mind onto the thought that the Parenting classes (this insane and stupid form of torture) would go on until Christmas. She longed to close her eyes and dream of home. It would be getting towards winter now in Ireland. The leaves would be off the trees but there would be plenty of green around. She pictured her garden overgrown and weedy. Then she stopped herself thinking. She shifted Carlo into a more comfortable position and fixed her eyes on the big woman who was now drawing diagrams on a blackboard. Apparently, from treating each child fairly, the class had now moved back in time to finding out how the child got into the womb in the first place. Grown-up Americans, Stella thought, were weird. Hadn't these ladies learned all this in biology class in school, quite apart from their personal experiences? It took a lot of resolution for Stella to keep her eyes open.

Mrs Rosen did not think it strictly necessary for Nanny and Carlo to go to the transcendental meditation classes, she said, but Velva needed them as adjuncts.

"We must all give Velva moral support," the beautiful woman smiled beautifully. "She has been through a great ordeal." She did not say what kind of ordeal and Stella was left with the problem of guessing whether Velva had been given electric shock treatment, or was it that the divorce had been put in train finally and for ever. Stella hoped it was the former since that did not involve her personally. Not, she told herself, that Gil Nathan was going to be let involve her. Certainly not. It was best to distance herself from the time she had spent with him. Best but not easy.

Carlo was quite unable to stay still and silent during the meditation classes. He and Stella were accustomed to a non-stop dialogue of delightful but meaningless gobbledegook. When he had been silenced several times, he burst into wailing noises and turned his large reproachful eyes on Stella. She guessed he was thinking of the splashy fun in the pool and why were they here and not there? Why, indeed? Finally, Stella was allowed take Carlo into another room which proved to be securely locked when Stella tried the door out into the yard. The spark of rebellion this kindled in Stella gave her the courage to speak to Velva. "I was wondering, Mrs Nathan, when will I be able to have a day off?"

Velva was too apathetic to answer; a heavy sigh was all she could manage. Stella watched for a chance to ask Mrs Rosen the same question, and here she got an answer.

"But Nanny, surely life is all a holiday to you? You have the pool and the garden."

"I should like my day off, as arranged."

"Ah, that was in Philadelphia. Here we are, and you are, on holiday."

Here, Stella thought, I am an indentured slave. Worse, a prisoner. "Well," she began, but Mrs Rosen interrupted, snapping her fingers as if to ward off a mosquito.

"Besides," she said in her rich southern drawl, "we are under orders from Carlo's Uncle Gil, that you are not to go into the shopping area. There is to be no sightseeing for you."

Stella's eyes opened wide in amazement.

"Why?" she asked, but Mrs Rosen had an un-hurried, unflurried, graceful way of moving out of hearing. You would think she was on damned castors, swore Stella furiously. Carlo's Uncle Gil? He was puppet-master here as well as everywhere else. And I was beginning to think I had fallen in love with him. Couldn't get him out of my head. The sooner I get back to Ireland the better. How in heaven's name did I land among this lot? But, as ever, there was little Carlo calling for her attention. "Coming, sweetie," she called back.

Sometimes Stella wondered if time had a different value in America. Was the sky so enormous that the sun took much longer to cross it? In Ireland the days flew by, time simply whirled away. She knew that was silly because there were twenty-four hours from dawn to dawn even here. The weeks went very slowly. The parenting classes became an obsession with Velva although no one would ever be able to tell if she listened or simply sat in a silence that might be penitential. Or, Stella wondered, if it was boredom why did Velva go on? During the meditation classes, Stella sat in the locked room trying to keep Carlo amused. In the afternoon Velva had her siesta. Stella would have enjoyed a siesta also but at least there was the pool which kept Carlo happy. By nine o'clock at night, when the little boy was asleep at last, Stella was ready to fall into bed. Oh to be thirty years younger, she thought a thousand times.

Then, at nine o'clock one night, there was a tap on her door. It was Alice. "There is a phone-call for you." Stella picked up the phone in her room. "No," Alice said, "you must take the call in the den."

Stella did not argue. There was no point. Marie Antoinette on her way to the guillotine, she followed the grim-faced Alice down the stairs. With Alice, it was usual for Stella to summon up whatever bit of humour was to be found in any situation. The equally axe-faced Ambert was seated by the phone, holding the receiver. When Stella took it, the instrument was tacky from his damp hands. Stella put it down. Taking a couple of Kleenex tissues from the table-holder, she wiped the receiver thoroughly. This would not endear her to Ambert who spoke instantly. "Keep it brief."

Buzz off, Stella said in her own mind, adding aloud, "Stella Shane here."

"Mum! Oh my God, have I had a time getting to you! Who is that creep on the phone? He asked me was I a close relative. You all right, Mum?"

Hazel's voice was so Irish, so lilting, so fond. Stella could only nod. "Mum, you still there? You all right?"

"Hazel, where are you? Have you bad news?"

"Mum, I am in New York but I have been in Philadelphia." Stella could see the rigidity of Ambert and Alice. They were both holding books but she was sure their ears were listening. Stella moved across the room with the phone.

"Darling," she said softly, "would you come closer to the phone and talk in a very low voice. Why are you in New York?"

"First tell me you are all right?"

"Yes, I am," Stella answered, "only counting the days to be home. Now begin again."

"I am here because the mother of one of my students was murdered in her apartment in New York. A girl named Louise Komsky, a real nice kid, very bright. I was deputed to get her home. She is in the care of an aunt and uncle now."

Stella glanced at the sitting pair. "I would like to comment, Hazel, commiserate, but I will not. Trust me, and continue."

"Right, Mum. I took a train to Philadelphia. Hired a cab to go out to your address in Larch Hill although I knew from an earlier letter that you expected to be in Florida—all I wanted was your phone number. I had rung the Larch Hill number but only got an answering machine."

"And how did you get this phone number, Hazel?"

"Well, when the cab pulled up at the house in Larch Hill there was a young man about to drive off in a nifty sports car. I presumed he was a friend as you had said in the letter that all the family except the old uncle would be in Florida."

"Hazel, I know who you are talking about but keep your voice down. Trust me." Mister Bart and his nifty sports car!

"Okay, Mum, so you know. He dismissed the cab and he drove me back to New York. He is good fun. He is here now. He insists on taking me out to dinner, and the old uncle is coming along later to have coffee with us. He is coming from Philadelphia and I think we are going to a concert. We like the same music."

A concert, dinner, coffee, and Hazel back on the plane to-morrow. That sounded safe enough. Quite a long drive from Philadelphia to New York—should have given them plenty of time to discover other things they liked! But Hazel was not Bart's type. She was an extrovert, open-air, call-of-the-wild-waves sort of a girl. Nothing of the seductive siren about Hazel. Not Bart's type at all—thank the Lord!

"Tell me about things at home," Stella asked.

"Oh, yes, well! Alec told me he has written to you

several times but no reply. He is having problems with Sybil. You know her! Never easy to figure out what is eating her at any time. She is the only one to grieve for Dad—the rest of us are heartless. Poor old Alec is having a tough time—she goes off for days at a time and he doesn't always take the time to chase after her. She resents his total preoccupation with his business. I don't make a point of seeing her, although Alec has asked me to help. It would be useless. And my thesis is still hanging fire."

"What about her work?"

"I think she has taken a sabbatical. She spends a lot of time in the graveyard—and I think she sleeps in your bedroom. I know she got the key of the house from Philip. He thinks she'll get over it and you're not to worry. I was in touch with Ross—he is in terrific form. He has a new love-affair. You know Ross and the women."

"It's wonderful listening to you, darling. You have cheered me up enormously."

"Were you feeling down, Mum?"

"Oh, just a bit, but I'll be home soon."

"I hope so. I miss you, Mum."

When Stella put the phone down, she hurried back to her room before any sound could disturb Hazel's warm Irish voice in her head. Hazel was so normal, so practical. Hazel would never do the stupid, senseless things that her mother had done. Like falling for Gil Nathan. Like sleeping with him. Stella wished with all her heart and mind that she had not done that. What had possessed her, a woman of her years, to act like a cheap tart. It did not matter how heavenly it was at the time, it was the act of a cheap woman, a woman without honour, without principles. It took Stella a couple of hours of tossing around in bed, unable to sleep, before she tumbled to the fact that her underlying emotion was jealousy because at this moment Gil Nathan was drinking coffee with pretty Hazel and Stella was nowhere in his mind. So much for all my intentions to repent, my firm purpose of amendment! I had to come all this way to find out what an empty-headed hypocrite I am. The sooner the better for me to get out of here and start living all alone like a proper widow. Only another few months. They cannot hold me.

Then Carlo woke up for his usual reassuring change and a drink of orange juice from his bottle. Stella took him up and hugged him. He giggled delightedly. "You are a little rascal, aren't you! Somehow, things must be made to go right for you. No, no, settle down now. That's my lamb."

There were some nights when she could not sleep at all, so restless was the compulsion forbidding her to dwell on the thought of Gil Nathan.

CHAPTER NINETEEN

When Stella was a little girl, her mother insisted she must have riding lessons. Perhaps she was not a natural horsewoman or perhaps she had a poor instructor but the lessons were a weekly agony. Her pony, and there was a choice of several, always stopped and shied at even a tuft of grass. It seemed cruel to force the pony on. It became easier to plead sick on the day of the riding lesson. After a while, Stella's mother dropped the idea. Sometimes, Stella wondered if her own habit of compromise was formed when she was six years of age.

There were so many things in the Nathan household in Boca Raton against which Stella wanted to protest, even rebel. There was a definite erosion of the hired help's civil rights: she was not permitted a day off, even a few hours off; a chance to catch up on her religion; the facility to post a letter, or get to a hairdresser. There was the city of Miami somewhere out there, which Stella would like to see. A whole-day coach tour could surely be arranged? Worst of all, there was a chronic shortage of books to read. Didn't the Nathans ever think that the nanny's mind needed nourishment, even if her body survived on their ready-to-microwave packets? Stella longed for home, the bookshelves, the deep chairs beside the fire, the autumn chrysanthemums in the garden of which she had been so proud. She did not protest. Her mind had caught the idea so long ago of shying away from obstacles that each day she invented for herself a new compromise. The blank wall of indifference which surrounded her stiffened her pride. And there was always Carlo to protect from the possibility of loud arguments.

Nevertheless, the brief phone call from Hazel had become a bench-mark in her life. Stella liked the full-stop sound of dates: BC or AD, and even BT which meant Before Television, she now thought of the time "before Hazel's phone-call" as a time-warp into which she had drifted and become a zombie. Hazel's call had re-created Stella's "real" life: the life of Hazel's flat in Dublin; the troubled marriage of Alec; the fact that her genial and accessible son, Ross, lived so many miles up the road in New York. Things she was in danger of forgetting. Hazel's phone call had re-established the further-back life when Dave was her everyday husband. At home in Ireland, she would be an everyday widow, and the name "Nanny" would be wiped off, forgotten. Another few months, Stella kept on thinking, another few months. She could take on Velva and the Rosens and the loathsome Ambert for another few months without protest, with constant compromise. Peace at all costs, if only for little Carlo's precious happiness.

There was another aspect to the time-warp into which she had been trapped before Hazel's call. That was the strange play between herself and Gil Nathan. In some book of Dave's, Stella had read Saint Paul's words, written from prison where he was incarcerated in chains. "Self-indulgence is the enemy of freedom." She pondered on those words each time the recurring fantasy of Gil's love-making came to her. She forced herself to consider the meaning of Saint Paul's words, not merely the spiritual meaning, but the very practical application to her own existence. Self-indulgence had sold her into a sort of slavery. She had put a yoke on herself, a chain as real as the chains binding Paul in prison, a heavy chain which could drag her into a betrayal of her own best principles. She should have adhered to the standard of self-denial she had set in the Amish chalet. What happened in between that night and the Garden of Allah? Loneliness? Was that sufficient vindication? And the man's increasing attraction! That, too.

Stella had never questioned her fall for Dave, when she stayed back in his study after the other students had left his tutorial. She had not been conscious in any way of lusting for Dave. She had only wanted to ask a question about some poet or other. She and her friends, Rita and Angela, all agreed that Dave must be the handsomest, most attractive thing on earth. Angela said she personally could faint, dead away, when she met their gorgeous professor on the stairs. They all three went into shock when he stopped, on meeting them on Front Square, and passed a comment on the weather. Into shock they went and had to restore each other into fits of giggles by drinking many coffees in the buttery. When Dave drew her into a most intimate embrace and they rolled over each other on the floor of his study in college, Stella had accepted that was how such matters went. When her mother discovered that Stella was pregnant and her father asked Dave to come to the house, Stella never thought for a second that she had sold her freedom for five minutes of self-indulgence. She did not know those words then. She was a stupid kid. But she knew them now: self-indulgence is the enemy of freedom.

Christmas was coming and with it, Gil Nathan to holiday in Roca Raton. The great important thing, Stella told herself, is to remember the price of freedom. She must be free of all obligations to the Nathans. She must keep remembering the sound of Hazel's breezy voice on the phone: it was the sound of home, the sound of normality. Stella had a life waiting for her in another country. Just another few months to bear up.

In late November, Alec Mackay arrived at the house in Boca Raton and was stopped at the security gate. To the security man he said he had come with papers for Mrs Nathan from Mr Gil Nathan. The security man phoned this to the house. At the front door Alec said he had come from Mr Gil Nathan with papers for Mrs Shane. Mrs Rosen realised at once that he was not from Philadelphia. She detained him while she phoned Mr Gil Nathan to check this story. Stella watched and listened from the slightly-opened nursery door, marvelling that Alec Mackay had lifted the siege—for that is what it amounted to, so security conscious were the Rosens against these legendary kidnappers. Stella even wondered if Ambert would be called upon to frisk Alec. Apparently, Gil Nathan gave his approval on the telephone. Was he amused, or amazed? Stella could not remember if, in talking to Gil, she had actually used the name Alec Mackay. No doubt the name was on her dossier along with everything else about her.

"I shall be taking Mrs Shane out," said Alec to Mrs Rosen. "So please call her."

Stella could see only the back of Fanna Rosen's

head but she could easily imagine the enchanting, fascinating smile with which Mrs Rosen delivered the words: "Ah, I am afraid that is impossible. Nanny has her duties here."

Stella took Carlo up in her arms and walked the short flight of steps to the hall.

"Alec, how lovely to see you! Mrs Rosen, Alec Mackay is my son-in-law."

Stella kissed Carlo. "Now you be a good little boy until Nanny comes back. I won't be too long. Have a nice nap!"

She placed the surprised little boy into the even more surprised arms of his maternal grandmother and, without another word, she led Alec through the front door and into his hired car.

"Drive," Stella told him. "Don't hesitate."

When they got beyond the security gate, they were both smiling. "Shock tactics for that lady, huh?" questioned Alec.

"You got it!" said Stella, affecting a Yankee accent, and then they were laughing in a kind of relief.

They passed the Lutheran church in which the parenting classes were held. "I have not been any further than this," Stella said. "So I hope you know the way?"

"The motorway is just ahead. I have booked into a place and I am good with maps, so could I pull over for just a few minutes to sort ourselves out."

"All right, but I hope you are going to buy me a meal. I have been starving for months."

When the car was stopped on the verge, they hugged each other warmly.

"Stella, I cannot tell you how much I have missed you. Were you not able to write?"

"I wrote but since I came here I have never been allowed out, even to post a letter."

"Good God! Why?"

"I'll tell you all that kidnapping stuff later. Just tell me, please, how you got this address, and also is there some sad reason why you have come such a distance—hardly just to see me?"

Alec hugged her again. "We'll talk about the reason later and I would have come anyway. But I got all the gen from Hazel."

Stella was surprised. "I thought she was given the phone number, mainly because she had gone to so much trouble trying to locate me in Philadelphia. She would have drawn a blank there, only she bumped into Bart, the husband of Velva, whose little boy I mind."

"That's the guy, Bart," Alec said. "Hazel struck up a friendship with him. He drove her to New York and they met his Uncle and they went to dinner. Seemingly, the young man and Hazel got on so well—

he gave her all the gen about getting to you down here—and what name to use to get past the security man."

"But that night they went to dinner, did Hazel know you were coming to the States?"

"No, but this Bart is on the phone to her a lot. They seem to get on very well. She was telling me this; so I primed her to find out this address."

Stella's heart sank. Bart! Of all the men in the world, Bart was not a man to associate with Hazel.

"I hope Hazel doesn't get mixed up with him," Stella said.

"Don't sound so despondent! Hazel has put a good few fellows through her hands."

"Has she?" Stella was surprised, but come to think of it, Hazel had lived a very independent life since her first year in college.

"She sure has!" Alec laughed. "I should know—I was one of them! Lovers for a while, then friends. No doubt, Bart can look out for himself! Hazel has plenty of men friends to her credit!"

"She sounds awful!" Stella smiled at him.

"Hazel is the best in the world," he said. "Now let's talk about you. I hardly recognised you when you walked into the hall."

"Why on earth?"

"Well, you know, you looked young enough to

own that little kid!"

"Silly—you know my age."

"And you are very slim and very tanned and you've done something to your hair?"

"It's months since I've been to a hairdresser. The hair got so long and bushy, I had to put it up in a kind of a roll."

"It suits you," he said admiringly.

"Alec, how about that lunch or dinner or whatever? Then I will be fit to ask a hundred questions."

CHAPTER TWENTY

They found a cafe along the sea front. The food was probably much the same as that which came from the frozen packets to which Stella had become accustomed. However, the service was efficient, the fare nicely presented and the place reasonably quiet.

"I really am hungry, Alec. I won't say a word until I have eaten everything on this plate."

Impulsively he touched her hand on the table. "God, Stella, you'll never know how much I've missed you."

"And I you," she answered, "more than I can say."

When the meal got to the coffee stage, Stella was ready to hear why and how her daughter had failed this nice, kind, uncomplicated man.

"So tell me, Alec, why do *you* think that you are not settling down happily."

It sounded banal but after all she was his mother-in-law.

"Why do *I* think?" he repeated. He lifted his eyes and gazed at Stella. "You know, here with you, I stop thinking. Please don't be angry if I say that being with you is enough. Look what *you* are doing. Why did you not tell me what you were going to do when Dave died? There was no need for you to do this."

"Don't let your sympathy for me take precedence over your own problem, Alec. Talk to me about it. Has all this odd behaviour—Hazel mentioned it and you said in your letters—has it to do with her being pregnant?"

"Pregnant?" He was astonished. "We never got to the first stage of consummation. There was never a First Night!"

Stella was distressed for him. "I thought she was unable to overcome her grief for her Dad's death. But you were married nearly a year before Dave died."

"Yes," Alec said heavily, "and Dave's death finished any hope we had. In that year, Dave was counselling her how to cope with sex."

"Did you permit that?" Stella felt a sense of disgust. "I don't think I understand."

Stella was struck by the disloyal thought that her late husband knew damn all about sexual congress. Was he instructing his daughter in the Shaw method, the quick in-and-out, rather like a seagull in flight, method. Oh my God, Stella thought, what's got into me? I never ever questioned Dave's love-making long ago. Never until the Garden of Allah. Never until Gil. Wasn't I content with Dave? No, not content.

Nothing. Mere acceptance. He was Dave and there was never anyone else.

"Why didn't you exert your will on Sybil? Put a stop to these talks?"

"I did not know. I did not know what was going on until Dave was dead. I am sorry, Stella, but all that is part of the problem. Did you not notice that I stayed away in that year, the year of Dave's retirement?"

"Yes, I did. After you were married, you did not come to the house. I missed you." She looked very directly at him. "Did you think I knew about these so-called counselling sessions?"

He answered wearily, "Only now do I know that the nature of these endless talks was not known to anyone. I was hurt because you knew they spent hours together of which I was no part. She never allowed me to come with her, although you and I and Dave had always been so close before the wedding. I was sore because you did not send her packing back to the man she had insisted on marrying."

"Alec, why did she insist?"

"Please do not be hurt by anything I tell you now," and Alec's eyes were fond and regretful. "If I had known then what I knew later, I would not have married her."

"Why, what is wrong with her?"

"There is nothing wrong with her. Nothing physically, and nothing mentally wrong with her. One could attribute the lowest emotions: jealousy, possessiveness—or sensitive emotions: emotional immaturity, insecurity. Or," he sighed very heavily, "perhaps she suffers from too much love for one person alone. I understand that suffering all too well."

Stella chose to ignore his hinted plea for compassion.

"What do you mean by this confusion of emotions?"

"Now, Stella, please do not be hurt...please...Dave told her that...that his life...was over."

Into Stella's memory flashed the word "expected." Dave's death had been expected. And Sybil was the one who knew. Sybil. All those hours and days they had spent alone together, Dave and Sybil, expecting Dave's death. Dave had bypassed his wife; he had placed his confidence in his best-beloved, his daughter...a confidence of extreme secrecy, the forewarning of his death. Yes, he counselled her to marry Alec. Dave would make sure that his Sybil would have a strong wealthy man to take her father's place. Alec would be the substitute for Dave—not for his bereaved wife but for his bereaved daughter. And the sex counselling? That was not Dave's style: the long talks would be about Dave, his unachieved ambitions, his failure to publish more. Sybil would have lain on his knees, across his chest, his hands fondling his hair, adoring him with her eyes. She did just that at the age of twenty-eight as openly as she had done it at eight years of age. And Dave, who prided himself on being a completely moral man, had always lapped-up the adoration. His interest in sex began and ended in self-adulation. Suddenly, Stella remembered the frantic rolling on the carpet in Dave's rooms in college. That had happened only once. And on that episode, a lifetime had been constructed.

"No," she said slowly, "I am not hurt that I was the one left out. I took my life for granted. I was a woman, dutiful and fond but of no perception. Dave could not have borne my reaction to his secret. Only now do I know what he wanted of me. Initiation had never happened between us. He took what was his due from the only one who offered it to him."

"Are you trying to tell me something?" Alec's tone of voice was bitter.

A strange thought came unbidden to Stella. Sybil may even have been saving her virginity for Dave. She looked at Alec with deep-felt sympathy. She really liked him but it did not seem they would ever know a mutual response.

"In the year after your marriage, they did (as you have said) absorb every moment of their time alone and together. Sybil may have hoped, since she was then safely married to you, that her father might exercise a feudal right. Apparently, they had left it too late."

"Stella, what an extraordinary thing to say!"

"Alec, you know very well that since Sybil was three years of age, I have had no rapport of any sort with her. She obeyed Dave's rule in every detail, so I did not even get to correct her, lecture her, slap her. I think I tried to love her but that effort dried itself up eventually. You have always known all that. You know as much about her as I do."

He still wanted Stella to console him. "I got so angry because she spent so much time with you, and I was excluded."

"Never by me," Stella said. "She and Dave always, always, spent many hours in each other's company. The year of your marriage was not out of the ordinary. It was not in my power to send her packing home to her husband—had I ever thought of doing so. I accepted what had always been."

"Sybil was always very angry when I told her that I missed seeing you every day, Stella."

"Naturally she was. Why say such a thing?"

"She always knew my feelings for you. I never concealed them. You are my ideal of what a woman should be."

Poor Alec! If he only knew what a right little trollop his dear Stella has become. And quite ready to fall more if she cannot bear in mind those necessary words about self-indulgence.

"Alec, may I ask you (and please do not misjudge me) didn't you make love, even a little, with Sybil before you asked her to marry you?"

"No, she wouldn't permit such a thing. I tried. I thought that would all change when we had sworn the vows at the altar, that on the honeymoon she would let go. A whole year of refusal." He mumbled on about the honeymoon...touring in the Orient...the lavish expenditure...

It was clear to Stella that when Sybil knew her beloved father would be no more, she had made sure to close the gap through which Alec could walk to take Stella (his ideal woman) to wife. And Dave had connived at that. That should hurt. And if I had my chance with Alec, would I have taken it? She remembered the bank manager's face, and she knew she would. She wondered, though. She would have missed out on the fantastical dream she now entertained. She had gone to bed with the man who invented love-making.

"But you made love with Hazel, you said. Didn't you?"

"Oh, yes—in a sort of a way! When Hazel was in

the humour, she would make a play for a bit of hugger-mugger. And it was good. I have always been mad about Hazel, you know that. I asked her to marry me a few years ago but she said she wasn't interested in marriage."

Stella was silent in a kind of trance. Could she believe this stuff she was hearing? And the stuff she was thinking?

The one she thought of as *her* friend—in *her* house—with *her* daughters? She could not credit this "carry-on"—if that was the right word.

On the other hand, would Alec believe *his* ears if she herself were to start that line of talk about Gil Nathan and the nanny? But it must be all over now. Never a word from him. Stella addressed herself severely: be pious, be brave. Brave had a better sound.

"Don't let's talk any more about Hazel or Sybil," she said. "Tell me about yourself in the big world. How are all your business ventures?"

"Booming," he said in the same weary voice. "Dave's death had the same effect on me that it had on everyone else. No one there to provoke or propitiate."

Stella thought about that. When did she break loose from the need to provoke or propitiate or even invoke? Was she contemptibly fickle? After all the years of being married to him, how could she survive now?

"You miss Dave most fearfully?" Alec asked.

"I guess I have so many crises of will every day," she answered slowly, "that I cannot stop to look backward. These Nathans are difficult and hard to kowtow to. If it were not that I have fallen so much in love with the little boy, Carlo, I would go home tomorrow."

"Come home with me, Stella. Why not today?"

"I'll admit this is a golden opportunity to fly, down-face them and not even go back to pack my clothes. But there are several reasons why I will not do that. I said a year, and I'll stay the year. Then there is Carlo. His future is so uncertain."

And there is Gil Nathan. Of course, Stella assured herself, she had broken out of that net. No one could force her; no one could subjugate her will to take little Carlo in an act of kidnapping. No one. And hadn't Gil acknowledged the illegality of that? So that was that.

"The Nathans," Stella told Alec, "live in daily fear that Carlo will be kidnapped. You read in the papers every day about rich children being kidnapped and held to ransom. It seems to be an everyday occurrence in this America. Even ordinary poor children are kidnapped or murdered or abused. Never seen again. No note or phone call. Just disappear. You see their little faces and names on sugar bags and milk cartons—their parents begging for their return."

Alec was struck dumb by this outpouring. He was horrified into silence for a few moments. "But Stella, why have you to be a part of all this awful worry? If you insist on working, why not some other job? At home, in Ireland?"

"Maybe I came here in a state of shock. I don't know, I never cried for Dave until a couple of months ago." And that was a memorable night, she thought. "I was imagining Dave at home in the garden or sitting in the old glasshouse cleaning his golf clubs. Then one night, I realised he was gone for ever, and I cried."

"Poor Stella. And you were all alone in your grief with no one to comfort you. Oh God, if I had only waited another year. I knew the writing was on the wall for Dave. And I have not been able to comfort his daughter either. At least, let me try with you. Please, Stella!"

Stella let him put his arm around her shoulder. He had always been so friendly, so easy to share confidences with, so comforting in his affection.

"Thank you for coming to see me, darling. I really have missed you. And thank you for taking me out. I think we had better head back to the house. I doubt if they will invite you in."

He did not start the car. "Do I imagine it, Stella, or have you gone a bit cool towards me? I was sure I would have your sympathy, and we could...talk?"

And take you to my bosom, Stella thought, and make up for the lack of ardour in my daughter?

"You know you have all my sympathy and devotion, my poor Alec. But let's face it. You are a married man and I am your unfortunate mother-in-law who happens to have to get back to her employment."

"I never think of you as a mother-in-law and you make me very angry with this employment thing." He sounded angry. "You know perfectly well that I can make you an allowance at home."

Would I be tax-deductible? Stella wondered. God! An allowance! It sounds niggardly but I suppose he means well.

"Look," Stella said emphatically, "no one asked me to come here and it is only for one year. You did not know I am of an independent disposition? Philip wanted to help, and I refused. Now, shall we go back?"

Still, he did not start the car. "I thought I could take you away for a few days? I have booked into a decent Spanish place in Coral Gables. I think you would like it, Stella."

Now Stella could imagine Carlo's dark eyes, his small vivid face. "Look," she said again, "I am here to mind a child who will be waiting for me right now to put him to bed. So let's go."

He started the car. "I am disappointed," he said. "I came a long way."

"I know," Stella said contritely, "and I am sorry for the way things have turned out. But I will be home soon and we will work something out. I promise." God knows the Nathan house was not inviting or welcoming. Stella could not understand why she was so anxious to fly back to it. Carlo? Always Carlo. But that wasn't all. "Hugger-mugger" seemed so lacking in style.

When the car pulled up at the door and Stella turned to give Alec a quick kiss before jumping out, he caught her arm. "Sybil is looking for an annulment; she talks of entering a convent." He reversed the car and drove away.

Stella wished he had not told her that. There was a tinge of madness about it. It made her feel she had a duty to go home and take care of Sybil. A duty as a mother? Alec had said in a letter that Sybil resented Stella's taking-off for America. Sybil had a habit of resentment. There would be no use trying to turn her from annulment or any other flight of fancy that came into her head.

Walking slowly up the steps to the nursery, she could hear Carlo's chirrup. It was the little sound he made to attract her attention. Quite obviously, he was all alone up there and trying hard to be brave and good. She ran up the last flight of steps. There he was, sitting in the middle of the room, a very small boy waiting in hope for Nanny to come and rescue him.

In a moment, they were kissing and hugging. His eyes were asking where had she been. His eyes were telling her of his joy that she had returned.

It was only when Carlo had been bathed and read to and loved and reassured and had fallen off to sleep, that Stella admitted to herself that she had been tempted. She stood at the nursery window and gazed away to the place where she imagined the wide ocean stretched thousands of miles to Ireland. She could so easily have gone with Alec. She had only to say the word. She could so easily take him from Sybil. But why deprive the nuns of getting a clever new recruit? Stella almost smiled to think of the mayhem Sybil could create in a convent. If I had never come here, she thought, but I did and now I could never settle for a lesser way of loving. Even though, she warned herself, I'm not sure if it is all in my own mind. And in no one else's? Even though!

CHAPTER TWENTY-ONE

Velva's interest in going to the parenting classes
flagged in the early weeks of December. There
were days when she did not emerge from her room.
Stella and Carlo passed the sunny hours in and out
of the pool. When the mosquitoes came out in the
late afternoon they had to stay in behind the screens.
There were not only mosquitoes but many other sorts
of winged insects and peculiar lizard-like little
creatures. Stella was constantly saying to the little
boy, "Watch out for the creepy-crawlies." Carlo found
this a funny word, hard to pronounce, so he was
always telling Nanny, "Looka kleepa klawla," and
she never failed to oblige with much laughter. Each
day they grew closer and closer to each other. Stella
knew this was inevitable. There was no way she could
fend him off to make him self-absorbed. In his second
and third year that might be possible. Now he was
still very much a baby, needing lots of cuddles and
care. He was unaware of Velva as an important figure
in his life. Velva seldom glanced at him and she
enquired for his well-being even less often. She and

her mother went out to dinner every night, presumably with the friends with whom Fanna Rosen had long phone conversations during the day. Fanna Rosen's beauty routine continued every morning, as in Larch Hill, with the arrival of the beauty van and the masseur. She grew more beautiful each day, Stella thought. The lustre of her hair was unbelievable. She was wearing fashions ever more becoming since the operation to reduce the size of her bosom. Stella, always eavesdropping since no one ever told her anything, gathered there would be a further reduction in the New Year. Mother and daughter were in constant conspiratorial conversation. Occasionally Velva was weeping, but not hysterically now. The battle with the transcendental meditation was lost after the first few weeks.

Stella had a hard time, from the first day in Larch Hill, in trying to like Velva. Slowly now in Boca Raton, and despite herself, she grew sympathetic. Velva was two people, the adult who was clever technically and the child who had never been weaned emotionally. Stella began to see the similarities between her own daughter and Velva. Until now, Stella had simply taken it for granted that Sybil was a daddy's girl. Stella had never given thought to the meshing of emotions in the hearts and minds of Dave and his daughter.

Stella's sympathy was all the stronger for Velva as she grew to know the circumstances of her young life. Not that anyone in the household ever took Stella into a confidential breakdown of family history but rather, Stella thought, if you become part of a family, you become part of the background. In Larch Hill, Stella had spoken when spoken to. In Boca Raton, she ventured the odd remark, and was often enlightened by the response.

"It is lacking in intelligence the way Carlo will not take an interest in television," Velva said. "He should be able to watch the *Children's Hour* now."

Stella bridled at the idea that Carlo was lacking in intelligence. "He is a very clever little boy, Ma'am."

"Perhaps you are spoiling him. He never wants to sit still. My mother finds that unmannerly."

Like a peasant from the Third World, I suppose, Stella thought. I'll answer her, for once.

"Maybe there are children of a year old who like to sit still. Carlo likes to be active: climbing, investigating, actually playing with his toys in a way that is advanced enough for a two or three year old."

"My mother calls that hyperactivity. She has remarked on it to her psychiatrist and the indications are that it should be curbed or it will get out of hand. My mother suggests therapy."

"I am not an expert, of course," Stella said

diffidently, "but about television, Carlo needs the attention that is focused on the TV set to be, even a little, re-directed on him."

Velva was smoking, almost chain-smoking. The cigarettes had not much actual smoke: they gave off a sweetish smell. Stella knew nothing of drugs beyond what she read in the newspapers. She wondered if the cigarettes were the cause of Velva's dopey lassitude or even the cause of her willingness to talk to the hired-help? To hear her talk was a new experience.

Velva gazed abstractedly at Carlo, now piling the cushions from one chair onto another. "I do not remember a time when I was not watching television," she said. "I lived with my father until I was twelve. He was dying most of that time with a complication of diseases. When I was not in school, I stayed in his room and watched television or he used the sjambok."

Not knowing the meaning of sjambok, which sounded like a spittoon, Stella said, "I am sorry. That is very sad. Your poor mother! You must have loved your father, sitting with him so patiently."

Velva drew on the cigarette. "My Mother left him when I was a year old. He was..." She paused for a long time, gazing at nothing. Her eyes seemed coiled inward as if reviewing her words. "Yes," she said languidly, "he was a vile and hateful man."

When Stella reflected on the implications of this

conversation and the few other short conversations that Velva permitted, she could excuse many of Velva's faults. She remembered that Gil Nathan had said that Velva got Bart into bed when they were fourteen years of age. Twelve of those fourteen years had been spent watching television in company with a vile and hateful man. Who could blame the little girl for rushing into the warm and cheerful embrace of young Bart? Stella had liked Bart in Larch Hill. He was a playboy, if one were to take seriously all Velva's screamed allegations in their hysterical rows. To an Irishwoman, a playboy husband was not all that terrible. So long as he managed to find his way home eventually.

Stella felt sure that in the beginning, when poor little Velva had needed a loving attachment, Bart had supplied much consolation. Bart was still handsome, still rich and very attractive to women. Velva would never let him go.

There were just two snags in Stella's musings. Bart's attitude to little Carlo was almost as devoid of love as was his attitude now to Velva. And the other major snag was the lie Gil Nathan had told when he said Carlo was his son. Why did he lie when his main concern was not, so far as Stella could reason, his paternity of Carlo but Carlo's millions? Was it possible that Gil had seen Velva as Stella had seen her lately, weak and defenceless, clinging to an emotional life if only with her beautiful mother? Had Gil been capable of lifting Velva up and giving her something to live for? Was that how Carlo came into being? It was sad that the wonderful solution to misery had not turned out the way Gil must have intended. Did Velva care at all for the child?

Stella, in her thinking, was never sure if she were making up the fairy tale because it *might* be real. Or inventing stories to console herself for being unable to accept that Gil Nathan had used *her* simply because he was a man and she was a female incapable of resisting. Stella was a disappointment to herself but she was high on promise. He would see a valiant-for-virtue Stella at Christmas.

Actually Stella detected a flaw in this idea of girding herself into a Joan of Arc resolution. At Christmas, she would surely revert to Nanny and he to Uncle Gil. It was best to think in those terms all the time and to remember Saint Paul's words.

Stella kept her mind on the care of little Carlo. And that was a task she found enthralling. Never was there so delightful, and rewarding, a child. Each day he seemed to make spectacular advances, learning to do so many things for himself, picking up little tunes, making marks with a pencil on papers which he passed to her to read as if the papers were letters. He chuckled with delight when she studied these marks with close attention, pursing her lips and nodding in agreement. His Uncle Gil, if he did nothing else, would marvel at Carlo's progress. On the other hand, and this thought made Stella apprehensive, was it in her own best interests to have made too good a job of her nannyship? Well, that was an impasse over which she could not have control. Carlo was the real little hero in all this affair. He was the priority. Going home to Ireland, to her home in the woodland, to her friendly neighbours, to her garden, to having Philip and Mída over for dinner—all dreams which would have to go "on hold" until she knew what Christmas was going to bring.

She knew that, to the Nathans, Christmas did not mean the crib, the holly and ivy, the Christmas tree. It might not even mean peace. There might be no celebration, not even the commercial act of giving presents. Nevertheless, each day was bringing Christmas nearer.

"Do you think," she asked Velva, "that I could get to a shop to buy a Christmas present for Carlo?"

"Why?" Velva said, dully. Her eyes were devoid of colour or interest.

"It is in my tradition. I would like to," Stella answered.

"There is a Toys-R-Us in the Downtown Mall,"

Stella continued. "Maria in the kitchen told me," she said.

Velva turned away. "I will see if there is time."

That was about as much as Stella could expect. Carlo had so many toys it would be difficult to get something different. Stella hoped for something on which he could make music: a toy piano or xylophone.

Then, on the twenty-first of December when Stella drew back the curtains in the nursery, she saw Bart's sports car in the drive. When she took Carlo out to the pool, Bart was floating lazily in the sunshine, a man without a care in the world. "Hello there, junior!" he called out. Carlo loved company. The moment Stella clipped on his wrist and ankle inflators, he tumbled into the pool. He was quite fearless in the water. He could paddle and float on his back, all the time gurgling and shouting with enjoyment. Stella had a busy time tracking him. She, too, enjoyed the pool. Bart quickly invented a game with the big beach ball. Carlo had no bother responding to this. Bart was quite obviously very impressed. The fun continued until Stella insisted on a break. "More later," she promised. "Now it is time for your Checkos." The cereal was the meal he liked best, so at last she got him towelled and into his shorts, toddling off happily with nanny, waving to Bart, promising (in his own lingo) to come back and play more ball. "Sure! We'll have lots of fun!" Bart called after them in a big brother kind of way.

Stella remembered that in Larch Hill Bart said Carlo should call him Papa (or was it Poppa)? The child had two fathers, she thought drily. When, in an hour, they returned to the pool, there was no sign of Bart, although his sports car was still on the drive. Stella found herself murmuring to little Carlo, "Curiouser and curiouser: your Daddy and Uncle Gil were not due for another two days, and then they were to come by plane, if my inquisitive ears picked up the right message."

As the day wore on, Stella became aware that a family conference was in progress: Bart, Velva and Mrs Rosen, but not Mr Rosen. Stella had not seen him around for a week or perhaps more. This was not unusual; very often he was in conference with architects in other cities and in other countries. The beautiful Fanna did not always accompany him.

There were no raised voices in the family room; so the subject under discussion remained a mystery. Stella built up hopes that a reconciliation was taking place. Velva and Bart would come back together, and together they would look after their little boy. If they would only give little Carlo a look-in, as it were, they would realise the treasure they had produced.

She watched the little boy now, drifting off to sleep; his long eyelashes were fluttering in the attempt to hold out on oblivion. He so loved each minute of every day. "I'll miss you, sweetie," she whispered, "but you will have a real Mum and Dad—young with you, able to keep up with you. You won't be a little fellow for always. The years slip away so fast. You will be a teenager and then a young man. What career will you choose? A musician, maybe?" His eyelashes were still now, spread out on his tanned cheeks. His lower lip had loosened, as it did when sleep came. His determined little chin softened. This was always the moment he looked so like his Uncle Gil.

There was a tap on the nursery door, and Bart's voice with "May I come in, Nanny?"

"Ah," Stella said softly, "you have just missed him. Out like a light, just five seconds ago."

Bart stood looking down at the sleeping baby. "He seems a happy little chap!"

"He is," Stella smiled, "and the best little guy in the world." She was folding Carlo's little garments.

"May we talk for a moment?" Bart said, "or would we wake him?"

"I don't think he would wake," Stella said. "We can keep our voices low."

"You are very like Hazel," he said. "Even your voices are the same. Soft Irish voices."

Sounds a bit sentimental, Stella thought. Well, as Alec informed me, Hazel is well able to look after herself. "Yes?" she said with a slight interrogation.

"I wondered," he said, and he gave her his most charming smile, "if you have any message you would like to send to Hazel. I am going to Ireland over Christmas."

"Oh, a holiday?" Stella tried to hold back the gasp of surprise.

"I hope that too," he repeated the smile. "Actually, I am standing-in for Uncle Gil—a handing over of legal papers in connection with the setting-up of one of these multinational companies for which he handles the legal work."

"In Ireland?"

"Yes, in Ireland. Not in Dublin. A place in the south-east of the country, I understand. Knockalee is the name of the place. Do you know it?"

"Knock signifies a hill in Ireland—from the Irish word *cnoc*. There are dozens of Knocks in every county. I don't remember all of them. Why doesn't your Uncle Gil go himself, Mister Bart?"

"He prefers to come here for a bit of sunshine, I suppose. So, a message for Hazel? She is going to be my courier."

It is weird the things they are able to plan without putting a tooth in it. "You see, Mister Bart, we exchange presents at Christmas and that is what I would like to send but I haven't been into any shopping place since we came down here."

"What about your day off, Nanny?"

"Not down here," she answered, "and I understand, by order of your Uncle Gil."

"Oh, yes, he mentioned that. He doesn't trust this place. But he intends to take Carlo and you to Disney World at Christmas."

Oh, does he now? Stella vowed to herself that dear Uncle Gil would get his answer.

"That would be a nice change," she said. "And no, unfortunately I have no present to send. So nothing beyond telling Hazel that I send my love and I will see her soon."

Bart looked puzzled. "How is that?" he asked. "You are staying after the divorce goes through? Aren't you, Mrs Shane?"

"Divorce? When will that be?"

"Double divorce, really!" And it was no trouble at all for him to smile again, which Stella admitted to herself, made him look very handsome. "Oh," he added, "they didn't tell you the dates? Mine and Velva's is set for the third of February. Hopefully there will be no delay. And Mr and Mrs Rosen are in court on the ninth. Pretty straightforward, I think. You look surprised? Didn't you know that Theo Rosen had gone off with a friend of his partner? Now, it may have been the partner's wife, or was it the partner's first wife? Anyway that is the situation. I must go. I am taking the MG over to Miami and going up to New York on the night flight. First stop to-morrow will be the Emerald Isle." He smiled his incredible smile once more. "I shall give your love to Hazel and I shall get Christmas flowers to give her from you. How about that?"

And he was gone. Stella collapsed into the rocking-chair. I hate women who cry, she told herself, and I won't cry just because they take me for granted, push me around. I will not cry no matter how much I want to go home. And neither will I give in. They can figure their own way out.

She wondered what all the quiet talk downstairs had been about. No screaming invective at Bart's departure. She had never known this family to talk quietly before. In Philadelphia, they were like forces of nature: avalanches, volcanoes. And not a sound from Alice and Ambert? Their previous roles had always been to busy themselves on the staircase, half-opening doors, tiptoeing into the erupting room with trays of coffee.

To hell with the whole lot of them. Stella determined to be as crafty as they were. She would keep her own counsel and act for herself when the moment came. Give *them* the shock treatment! Then she started remembering the pathetic ugliness of Velva's first twelve years. Winning the custody of Carlo out of this divorce would surely make up to Velva, if not for losing Bart, at least for that ghastly childhood.

CHAPTER TWENTY-TWO

Early the next morning Stella was surprised to have a visit in the nursery from Velva. She looked pale and thin. She had not bothered to put on the eyelashes, nor comb the hair. There was no one around to impress, Stella supposed.

"You wanted to go to a toyshop? Have the kid ready at ten o'clock."

"Yes, Ma'am."

"You have money, have you?"

"Enough, Ma'am."

Nobody had mentioned money since they arrived in Florida, and it was pointless to ask for it since there was no way of either spending it or sending it. Stella marked the weeks on the calendar. She would ask at Christmas. Gil Nathan had said he was the one who employed her. It was a wonder he wouldn't post on her wages. But don't worry: Gil Nathan would get his comeuppance in due course. Stella could work up fiery vindictiveness at the very thought of Gil Nathan. She could—until she saw Carlo's little face and then every bit of maternal tenderness within her took her heart and emptied it of all ill-feeling.

She strapped Carlo very carefully into his car carrier and took her place beside him, fastening her seat-belt and pulling it tight. She had asked for the stroller to be put in the boot of the car, so that Carlo could be wheeled around the toyshop. The Toys-R-Us in the big shopping mall north of Boca Raton was the original and biggest of a chain of such shops. The Filipino woman who worked in the kitchen had told this to Stella and she was telling it now to Carlo. They had not been in the car since the classes had stopped. The little boy's eyes glowed with the anticipation of an adventure. Stella sat contentedly beside him. It really was a change to get away from the house, comfortable as it was. She told him they would go in the pool when they came back.

Velva got into the car. She had put on her make-up. In a trouser suit she seemed almost too thin. Ambert took his place at the wheel and very sedately they moved off. This was the road down to the seashore on which Stella had come with Alec. When the road curved away from the shore, the massed buildings of the shopping mall could be seen on the horizon. There were some boutique-type shops along the way, fashion, jewellery, magazines.

"Pull over at Ricardo for a moment," Velva said to Ambert. She gave him some money. "Pick up my

Tell-Tale magazine. They always keep it for me." She lit a cigarette and tucked the ends of her silk scarf into her jacket.

Ambert left the engine running. He took a couple of minutes to get onto the sidewalk. He is like a tortoise, Stella thought. It was the last coherent thought she had. Velva slipped into the driver's seat, moved smoothly into the traffic, beginning to go much faster than Ambert had. Out on the eight-lane highway she went up to the maximum, passing the mall without a glance.

It took Stella a couple of minutes to realise that Velva was out of control of common sense, of any sense, the way she was zipping past other cars, almost grazing them.

The highway settled into a high open road without any sign of habitation. Stella was at a loss what to think, what to do, what to say. She was conscious that this was the sort of American countryside which frightened her ever since that wilderness film. It was an intensely hot day; the cooling system did not seem to be working. She could see the drops of perspiration at the edge of Carlo's curls. The driver could control the opening of the windows or doors. During the first hour, Stella was hoping that Velva would suddenly change her mind and stop. In another hour, she realised that short of a crash (which must be the intention) there was no way of stopping the mad driver. Calling to her had no effect. Stella had brought an orange drink for Carlo but it was in the cooler in the trunk.

"Carlo is very thirsty!" she called again, very loudly, leaning forward but afraid to loosen her seat-belt at this speed. There was no reply from Velva. "He will get dehydrated. I have orange juice in the cooler!" On they flew, off the highway onto another road at a right-hand bend. Now the road began to have a downward slope. Now it was a two-lane gravelled road, with neither lane very wide. When they met huge sand-trucks, Stella squeezed shut her eyes in sheer terror. After many miles, the car veered off onto a narrow track, going through many rocky tunnels, and always descending. The track fell away from Stella's petrified eyes, revealing the blue ocean through tumbled rocks on cliff-edges. The car skidded onto an escarpment of stones and Velva pulled up. She shut off the engine and lit a cigarette. With deliberation, she drew a gun out of her purse-bag. She turned in her seat, her face expressionless.

She said, "Get out, and take the kid with you."

"Why?" Stella had to force the word out. She had never seen a gun so close up.

"I am going to shoot both of you." Velva appeared calm; her dead eyes gave the impression of being logical and reasonable. "And we would not like blood all over the car, would we?"

"Why?" repeated Stella. "Why?"

"You always asked too many stupid questions. Just get the hell out! Now!"

"I won't," said Stella.

Velva touched the door lever. All the car doors sprang open. "Get out, now. I will not have your blood in the car nor his," and she pointed the gun at Carlo. He was looking from one to the other. When the car stopped, Nanny always lifted him out. He waited, his eyes full of questions.

"I won't get out," Stella said. "Put that thing away."

Velva pointed the gun out of an open door. She barely pressed on it and a shot reverberated like thunder across the open space.

"So it is real, isn't it," rapped Velva. "You are making me angry. Get out."

It was impossible for Stella to think. In a dim, confused way she knew not to lunge forward or that thing would go off in her face. And not to lift Carlo out. It would be easy for Velva to roll their bodies over the edge of the cliff. She urged herself to talk, but what to say to a mad woman?

"Why?" Stella said again, not fully aware that she had said the word before.

"Why what? I have got my settlement without

the kid. That is why. Bought off. I have got it. It is in my mother's bank."

"So, please, Mrs Nathan, please let us go," Stella heard her own voice, shaky, pleading. "Please, please."

Velva seemed to laugh. "But that is the best part. Gil Nathan wants the kid and you. That shit is not going to get either of you—the fucker can't buy everything."

"You are Carlo's mother," Stella pleaded desperately. "Please, poor little Carlo!"

"Don't act the stupid! Everyone knows it was Gil Nathan's fucking semen. He was the almighty shit with the big ideas!" She gripped the revolver tighter. "There are five shots left...three for you and two for him. Get out! Get out! Lift him out!"

"Mrs Nathan, *I'll* go with you and Carlo. I will stay and look after him for you. You can keep the settlement and the baby." Stella was struggling to make sense.

"I don't want him," Velva retorted. "He is Gil Nathan's bastard. And I don't want any kid. I never did. Get the flaming hell out and take him with you— I hate him."

Velva flicked the cigarette out on to the stones. Now she gripped the gun with both hands, rock steady, no panic.

Stella had had a few seconds to get a grip on herself

and to release her seat-belt. She turned fully away, her two arms around Carlo in his car-seat, her back presented to Velva's gun.

"You will have to take us this way!" Stella, who never raised her voice, was shouting, "Go ahead!" From long tradition, an Act of Contrition was forming on Stella's lips. "O my God, I am heartily sorry..." The shots rang out, Stella felt the pain ripping through her shoulder. In an instantaneous reflex movement, her arm flung itself backwards striking Velva across the face and knocking the gun out onto the stones. Stella was over the back of the seat, struggling with Velva. Carlo began to howl loudly. The two women clung together in a fury of desperation. Trying to retrieve the gun, they half-tumbled, half-stumbled out onto the stones. They were unable to hit each other with any force, so entangled were they. Velva got her teeth into Stella's hand and Stella gripped her good hand into Velva's red hair. Neither would let go, although the blood from Stella's shoulder was streaming over Velva's face. They thrashed around on the stones, each trying to force the other into subjection, each tearing at the other's clothes, each trying to push the other's arms upwards. Although Stella was the heavier, fitter woman, she was rapidly losing the use of one arm. With an energy that was sheer mania, she sat on Velva's chest and tore the silk scarf from the woman's neck, trying it around and around her ankles. Moving up across Velva's face she tethered Velva's wrists with her own belt. To get Velva into the trunk of the car was almost too much for her but she managed. At the last second, she pulled the cooler out, then banged down the cover.

Trying to keep the bloody hand away from the child's bottle, she gave him the drink, half-stuffing it into his howling mouth. "I'm sorry, lamb, I'm sorry." She kissed his head, wondering vaguely was he hurt, so scattered was the blood. The keys were still in the ignition. With extreme trepidation she started the car and pressed the lever to secure the doors. In the background, she could hear the other woman screaming.

Turning the car on the narrow ledge was a piece of driving virtuosity that Stella would never have attempted in a calm frame of mind. She was partly conscious that though her shoulder was pouring blood she could not feel any pain. Every nerve in her body was concentrated on steering the car away from the cliff edge. She could not take in the screams of Velva nor the gulping sobs of Carlo. The noises were there but Stella was a steel image in a steep, steel world of revolving wheels. One steering twitch would send them all crashing. A bird flying suddenly into the wind-screen was like a knife between her eyes. Slowly,

slowly, slowly, it seemed like hours before she regained the double track and more hours to the approach of the highway. The fingers of one hand were going numb; it was agony to grip the wheel. No speed, no speed, just keep going.

At the highway there were many cars, some with the flashing revolving lights and loud sirens of police. Stella stopped and shut off the engine. In a brilliant haze, she saw Cousin Ambert. Stella forced her bloody fingers to the door lever. She made an attempt to step out with dignity but pitched forward onto the road in a dead faint.

CHAPTER TWENTY-THREE

At the end of a long narrow corridor there was a small moving creature. Stella walked slowly down towards this little thing. She could almost see its eyes. She walked more slowly until she stopped. The corridor was longer than she had thought. She began to walk again. The eyes were further away. She stopped again. She walked again. The corridor was endless. It was very tiring to walk and walk and never get nearer. If I only knew its name. If I only had a voice. In this place you do not speak. You are not allowed speak. Just walk. Walk. Walk.

It was three days before Stella recovered partial consciousness. She became aware of a strange bed, a strange room, strange voices. She longed to look but her eyes would not open, the effort was too much. She drifted back to walking the endless narrow corridor. Who was the small huddled creature at the far end? Who?

At intervals she could make sense of the talking voices. Were they talking of that tiny mite on the corridor?

"But how long?"

"Profound shock takes its own course."

"Has everything been done that could be done?"

"She is as comfortable as is possible under the circumstances. She lost a lot of blood."

"But I want to know…"

"Allow me to interrupt you. Any discussion will have to take place in my office. There is no guarantee that the patient may not be upset by voices. It is too soon to judge."

"But I want to stay. I must be here when…"

"No. Absolutely not. Nurse, no visitors."

In the silence, Stella drifted away to pace the corridor. She began to recognise that the corridor was part of a dream. The struggle to get back to the time before the dream was uphill work. Begin at the beginning, her instinct told her. This is not my bed but this is my body. If I had the energy I could flex my toes. Where is the energy? Am I hurting? I do not feel pain; yet there is not an absence of pain. Does this mean a numbness? Too many questions to answer. Too tired now.

When Stella came fully back to a recognition of where she was, and why she was there, it was the middle of the fifth night. There was a dim light a few feet away and a young woman was sitting in an upright chair. She had been reading because a book was face down on a table beside her. Stella tried out her voice. It was a whisper. "Are you awake?"

The nurse came instantly to the bedside. "I will turn up the light a little," she said. She laid her fingers gently across Stella's eyes. "Now take it easy, a chink at a time. Let me hold your hand in mine. Do not say anything at all for a few minutes."

Stella knew who was crouching in a miserable little bundle at the end of the narrow corridor. The names rose up like an antiphon in her throat, two voices calling to each other: Carlo, Nanny, Carlo, Nanny.

"Where is Carlo?" she asked, or rather croaked.

"The little boy is safe and well. Do not worry."

"Where is Carlo?" Stella repeated urgently, her voice a loud rasp in its effort to speak out. "Where?" The nurse made soothing noises. "Now, now. Do not get upset. I assure you he is okay. With his uncle, I think."

"The wicked Uncle Ambert?" Stella clutched at the nurse's hand. "Uncle Ambert?" Through a brilliant haze of light flashing behind her eyes, Stella could see the flattened nose and frog-like jaw of Uncle Ambert, the hooded beady eyes.

"Uncle Ambert got Carlo?"

"Calm down, Mrs Shane; the little boy is safe. He is here in the hospital. They have taken a suite. He and the little boy. And, I understand, your daughter is helping out since a few days."

"You aren't making this up to keep me quiet, are you?" Stella croaked plaintively.

"Why should you say that?" asked the nurse.

"Because, you see, I do not have a daughter in America." Stella's voice sank away to a sad murmur.

"You do now," smiled the nurse. "And you will see her in the morning. Now it is three am. I am going to give you a little shot so you will sleep for the rest of the night."

Stella would have preferred to lie awake and review all the issues and questions in her recovered state of consciousness. In hospital, one submits. Within minutes she was asleep. She slept for eight hours.

In full daylight, Stella saw the beautiful bouquets of flowers in her room. Somebody is treating me like a queen, she thought. The nurse of the night before, the one who had evaded the answers, had gone. Stella began again with the day nurse. "Where is Carlo?" she asked, her voice coming now a little easier.

"I think you will be allowed visitors to-day," the nurse said, "later on when your physician has given the word. Shall we spruce up a little now? Your shoulder is in splints so be careful with your movements." A soft, familiar accent?

Now fully conscious, Stella could locate the

numbness in her shoulder and arm. She had not been aware of the bandages until now. "Do I look a sight?" she enquired.

The pretty nurse laughed. "You do indeed," she said, "a sight for the gods!"

"You are Irish!" Stella was delighted, "I am too!"

"I know," the nurse said, "it is on your file. We are from neighbouring counties. I am from Kildare. Carmel Condon."

"And I am from Meath. Stella Shane."

The girl laughed again softly. "In here we must stick to the formalities. They are very strict on us."

"You are very pretty, Carmel." Stella was feeling so much more at ease. "But I'll be good."

Stella remembered the doctor's voice as part of her dream. Now he was a lot milder. Probably relieved, Stella thought, to see she had survived.

"You have a strong constitution, Mrs Shane. You gave us quite a fright."

Nothing to what I gave myself was Stella's reaction to that, as through her mind flashed the car drive from the cliff.

"Have you been able to recall your ordeal?" he enquired.

"More or less, doctor. Where is Carlo, please?"

"Do you think you could take a five-minute visit with him?" he asked.

"Here?" said Stella in surprise. "Wouldn't that frighten him? I have seen my face in a mirror when the nurse was washing me."

"Yes, your face is badly bruised on one side but if we wait until you look perfect, the little boy will suffer more."

"You mean he is missing me? Is he crying?"

"He was crying. We think he is cried out. He is apathetic. Deserted."

This was heart-breaking. "So will you have him brought here?"

"Actually," and the Doctor smiled, "your daughter is wheeling him in a stroller up and down on the landing." He went to the door. "Hi there! You may come in."

Stella and Carlo stared at each other. She could not find a voice, so pathetic was his usually so vivid little face. She could not lean towards him because of her stricken shoulder. She did not even notice who had wheeled in the stroller. At last, she made a painful effort to smile and murmur his name: "Carlo. Carlo."

His response was instant: "Mummmm Mummm!" And he held up his arms.

"Let him sit up here by me," Stella pleaded, brokenly, "here on my good side. Oh, Hazel! I am sorry! Hazel! Hazel!"

Carlo snuggled in against Stella as he had done

from the very first day in Larch Hill. His dark eyes filled with light. As if he knew not to hurt, he put his little hand very gently into Stella's hand.

"Mumm Mummm Mummmm." He had his own special way of prolonging the m sound like a croon. Stella murmured to him all the little endearment words that were special between them. When Hazel bent to kiss her mother, Carlo raised his cheek for a kiss as if to apologise for not being friendly to Hazel up to then. Stella made a tremendous effort to control her voice and her tears.

"Hazel, why are you here? Lovely and all as it is to see you? I thought you were giving Mister Bart the Grand Tour of the Emerald Isle—or did I dream that too?"

"Mum, the whole family are here. We thought you were a goner! I could kiss you forty times for coming back to life for us—only I am afraid to hurt your shoulder!"

"I did get down from the ledge, didn't I?" Stella asked, tremulously. "I didn't plunge the car into an abyss, did I?" Was it a dream, she wondered, a black nightmare of hatred.

"Oh my God, Mum, we have all been out to see the place. It was a miracle! Ross said he would not take a car up there for a million!"

"Neither would I!" rejoined Stella "—now that I

think of it!" And she tried to smile.

Hazel said, "We are only allowed to visit one at a time. Philip and Ross and Alec are waiting. Who will come next? And only for a few minutes."

"And Sybil?" asked Stella, seeing as how they thought she was a goner. "Did she come?"

"I'll let Alec tell you about his wife. Shall I take Carlo?" The little lad sensed the meaning of his name, and he tensed in against Stella.

"Ah, no! Carlo may stay." She pressed her good fingers against his black curls. "My little lamb! Let Philip come, then Ross, then Alec. And then you come back for this little treasure." No one had mentioned Velva. Were they waiting for her to ask?

It was almost worth shipwreck to see the affection in Philip's face. Since before Mída came into his life, he had never been so expansively fond and concerned. "You know I never wanted you to come here, Mother. I hope you will let me take care of you now. Why, in God's name, didn't you write and tell me you had landed into a nest of lunatics? That woman was as high on drugs as it is possible to get! Why on earth did you get in that car with her? And taking a child?"

Stella thought of Velva with pity. Not just smoking some harmless stuff to dull her senses but high on drugs? Velva never had a chance. Would they judge her very harshly?

"Philip, what is a sjambok?"

"There you go, Mother! Off on some streak of your own. Do please listen to me—what is a what?"

"A sjambok. What is it?"

"I have an idea it is a hide whip or a lash. What put that in your head? Now, listen to me for a moment. When you are better, I will come out here and fix everything up…"

Stella waited until Philip had laid out his plans. She contented herself with saying what she always had said to Philip: "Yes, darling. Of course, darling. Oh, yes, of course."

"There is a top-sergeant nurse out in the corridor," he said, "with a stop-watch. I shall be back to-night, Mother, so do please give my plans your best consideration."

"Of course, darling."

Ross was, as always, so typically Ross. He made light of the adventure his mother had had. "Move up to New York, old Mother Courage," he said in the debonair way he talked as if, in fact, he could hand her New York on a plate. "Doss in with me until you have recovered." Now he addressed himself to the little boy. "A bit of a mud-larker, that's what you are. Is this the famous Carlo?"

Philip had not even noticed the little boy. Carlo was always responsive to anyone who took notice of him. He allowed himself to be set down on the floor by Ross. He toddled around the room followed by Ross who had always loved very small children. Stella wondered fondly why Ross did not settle down and have a few children of his own. Too many adoring females around him. He was just too attractive to too many.

"Would he let me carry him around outside?" asked Ross. "Would you, kiddo Carlo?"

Carlo looked at Stella, a big question in his dark eyes. "Mumm Mummmm?"

Stella nodded. "Back again soon?" Carlo gave her a big grin with all six teeth. Ross hoisted Carlo up on his shoulders and ducked out through the door. "We will go and see the glamorous nurses," he said. Stella knew Hazel would co-operate and no harm would come to Carlo.

Alec was the most upset of her visitors. He knelt beside the high hospital bed and kissed Stella's good hand. The other arm was bandaged to the fingertips. "Oh God, Stella, what a mess I have made of my life. If only I had waited. I could have looked after you. I never knew Dave had left you so badly off. I never loved anyone but you. God, Stella, I would give anything to save you from this place. I should have seen how it was that day I saw you. I should have taken you away that day despite your resistance. God, if only I had realised!"

He buried his face in the quilt. Stella thought he had started too many sentences with "I." It did not leave much room for a response. She patted his head.

He looked up at her. "I love you, Stella. I have always. I will always."

How many more "I's" will he think up? She patted some more.

"I am taking you away from here just as soon as they let you up. I am sure in a week or two you will be convalescent. I could take you on a cruise, Stella. Bermuda? The Caribbean? I'll see these people never impose on you again. Stella, I'm crazy about you."

She just could not summon up the energy to give him the mother-in-law new-husband spiel. Why had Sybil not come? Under the circumstances? Alec was still talking.

"I am leaving to-night. This is not what I want to do but I am unsure about Sybil. No, I do not want to add to your upset. Not now. I will be back as soon as possible and I will take you away for a long holiday. What about the cruise I suggested? Or California? Would you like that?"

Stella was beginning to feel very tired now. Her eyes were closing. She tried to be a good visitable person but she was losing interest. Was it possible, she thought sleepily, that Alec bored her. But why?

She needed a friend and he had always been kind and good, and her special friend. Hadn't he? Wasn't he still?

"Stella! Stella! That sister is tapping on the door. Stella!" But Stella had dropped off asleep.

CHAPTER TWENTY-FOUR

Ross and Hazel brought Carlo back in the late evening to say goodnight.

"Your timing was very good, Mum!" Ross told her. "The Christmas holidays!"

Carlo snuggled beside Stella. "Isn't he an angel?" she asked them.

"We are only to stay, and let Carlo stay, for the bare ten minutes," Hazel said.

"But I am grand now." Stella tried to sound in good voice. "Apart from this arm and a general stiffness. See how good my voice is?"

"Sure you're one of the Seven Wonders, Mum!" Ross laughed at her, and then he said very seriously, "But you were out cold for half a week."

"They called it shock," Hazel said, "but I thought we had lost you."

Hazel was walking around the room with Carlo in her arms, and the little boy was loving every minute of it.

"Is there a long, narrow corridor out beyond that door?" Stella asked. "Is this where I was brought when

I was unconscious?"

"I shouldn't think so," Ross replied. "This is a short wide corridor of private rooms. You are number 12! Why the interest in the corridor?"

"Is there a corridor where people are admitted? Say, in an ambulance?" she asked.

"That is at the side entrance. Casualty, I think. Yes, that is a narrow all-glass place. Mum, why? What's the problem?"

"Oh, just something I was puzzled about. I'll tell you some time." Stella tried to smile at them although her face was stiff and very sore. "Have I still got teeth, Hazel?"

Very gently, Hazel prised Stella's lips a little apart. "You have, Mum, the same nice teeth you always had. You will be able to brush them when the swelling goes down. Your face is still very purple and patchy but even since I saw you on the first day, it's a bit less angry looking. You know, you had to have seven stitches on the side of your head where you pitched onto the road when you stopped the car."

"They thought at first you had a fractured skull," added Ross.

Isn't it funny, Stella thought, how no one has asked me exactly what happened? They seem to know the whole story. And no one has said a word about Velva. I couldn't have killed her, could I? Choked her? Why does no one fill me in? They assume I am not fully conscious, perhaps? But I am. And I want to know. Not knowing is maiming me worse than this shoulder.

"Mum, our time is up. Get Carlo to come with us. I will stay with him. Don't worry."

Why has his grandmother not fetched him away? So many questions made Stella frustrated.

Carlo made no fuss at all when Hazel took him up. It occurred to Stella that very probably Hazel looked rather like Nanny, before the poor lady in the bed got bashed up. In fact, Carlo may have been happily thinking that he now had two nannies, a young pretty one and a faded model. Like he has two fathers, Stella mused wryly—but I am not going to think about that yet.

In a day or two when Philip came, he told her that he had talked to the doctors. "You are on the mend, Mother. It will be some weeks, they said, before they will allow you out of bed. I am flying out early to-morrow. However, I will be in constant touch. Just as soon as they give the word, I will take you home. Mída is most concerned about you, Mother. We should have insisted. You should have said how strapped for cash you were."

"How do you know that? How does Alec know?"

"He didn't even know what you were doing until

you were gone, Mother. Then he went into the bank—or maybe his secretary did all that. He is a director of that bank, as you know."

"That was all Dave's own private business." But Stella's voice was not determined. Maybe they *were* right and she had brought this ghastly trouble on herself with her silly ideas of independence. She had certainly given her family an awful lot of worry and expense.

When Philip was at the door, having made all his last minute speeches, she croaked after him.

"Philip!"

"Yes, Mother."

"I am sorry. I have put you all to so much expense—air fares and everything."

"Oh," he sounded very surprised, "I haven't put my hand in my pocket, and neither have the others. Mr Nathan has arranged everything. I can't even buy a drink. There is a bar in the suite like a Grade A hotel. Meals appear by magic. Proper order too! After all, it is all their fault, that is, apart from the fact that you came here!"

"Philip, thank you and thank the others for the beautiful flowers. All these bouquets!"

"Not guilty, Mother! They were all here—and more besides on the landing outside. We arrived like Irish emigrants with our little offers of Duty Free!"

Peasants from the Third World! And that made Stella wonder again about Velva. Thinking made her sleepy. When the nurse who had the soft Irish voice came on duty, Stella was awake again.

"Hello, Carmel Condon!" The voice was still a croaky voice.

"Ah! We are getting better, are we! I have a message for you, but first your temperature and a few other arrangements for your comfort." The pretty nurse worked away very efficiently. She had brought a cup with a small spout on it. She filled this with mouthwash several times and held Stella's head while she endeavoured to rinse the mouthwash out of her dry mouth.

"That feels a lot better," Stella said.

"It will be a while before you graduate beyond sucking on a straw," the nurse told her, "so twice a day there will be some intravenous feeding. Do not look alarmed. I assure you they know what they are doing."

When Stella was bathed and changed, Nurse Carmel was smiling at her. "Now the message! I am to say that it is entirely up to you—how you are and how you feel. Would you receive a visit from Mr Gil Nathan?"

Stella paused for a few minutes. "I should have to think about that," she said slowly. "Could I try to collect my thoughts?"

"May I tell him that you are giving the matter some consideration?"

"I guess so." Stella's thoughts were scattered in so many directions. Would he steady me, she wondered. My mind and my imagination and my emotions are all like a bare waste place with hundreds of birds circling around picking up a scrap here, a scrap there. Hundreds of birds pecking and sometimes colliding in mid-air. When I am awake and listening to my visiting family, I am seeing their faces but their minds are hidden. They use visitor-speak. When I drop off asleep, I am all the time walking into space.

She watched the nurse using the telephone, and coming back to her bed. "He will ring at nine o'clock tonight for your decision," the girl said.

"Will I still be awake then?"

"Rest now. Look, I am reading Jane Austen's *Emma*. I will read aloud to you for a while." Stella re-read Jane Austen every year.

"That would be perfect," Stella said and she closed her eyes, the better to let no distraction come between her and the soft, rolling accent of County Kildare.

"*...there had been an interesting mixture of wounded affection and genuine delicacy in their behaviour; but she had believed them to be well-meaning, worthy people before; and what difference did this make in the evils of* *the connection? It was folly to be disturbed by it. Of course, he must be sorry to lose her...ambition, as well as love, had probably been mortified...so easily pleased—so little discerning—what signified her praise...distressing for the moment..."*

The pretty nurse was speaking to her. "Mrs Shane? Mrs Shane! Mr Nathan is on the phone for your answer. It is nine o'clock."

"Oh, yes! Oh, yes!" Stella came out of a dream. "Yes, of course." She heard the nurse's voice on the phone. "You may come. Yes, she said so!"

"Could you please give me a cold drink?" Stella asked. The nurse selected a straw and placed it between Stella's lips. "This is spring water," she said. "Is it cold enough?" The girl took up her book and went to the door. "I am right out here if you want me," she said.

Then Gil Nathan came. Unable to turn her head, Stella closed her eyes. Her voice, she knew, would desert her. His footsteps stopped a little way from her bed. Stella felt he was looking at her: the immobile head, the purpled face, the bandaged arm, the tousled hair. Now, she would hear at last the truth of what had happened. Carlo was safe but had Velva been killed? Stella was fully aware of the murderous hatred she had felt for Velva when the gun was levelled at her and at Carlo. The liquid hatred had surged up into her throat. Everything, whatever everything was, that happened after Velva fired the gun out of the door, was cloaked in a black seething mess. She waited now as condemned prisoners must wait for the hangman. Fearful in every nerve. Had she killed Velva on the stones? Had the screaming stopped in the trunk of the car?

"Stella, can you ever forgive me? To see you like this is—is—Stella, are you in terrible pain? Is everything being done to relieve the pain? Please, please, forgive me. I beg you, I implore you..." It seemed he could not go on, his voice was blocked with emotion.

Stella's eyelids were weighted on her eyes. It took an enormous effort to look at him. He was the same Gil. A big man, silvery hair receding. She liked his voice. She tried out her own voice before she could speak. "Velva?"

"Velva?" He repeated in some surprise. "She is in a detoxification unit."

A great wall of tension within Stella gave way in an enormous heaving sigh of relief. "I was beginning to think I had killed her," she whispered. "I wanted to. She had a gun. I never saw a gun so close. If I could have got the gun from her, I would have shot her before she could shoot Carlo."

Now Gil was beside the bed. He held her hand. His grip was warm and firm. Comforting.

"The police found the gun on the cliff. Her fingerprints were on it, only hers. No others. Stella, please forgive me. Please say you will forgive me."

"Was it your fault?"

"Yes. After weeks and weeks of secret planning, I showed my hand. I sent Bart to buy her off. My money. His divorce."

"Your child?" Stella asked generously.

"I suppose that too was a mistake. Another mistake of many. I thought I was almighty. Although, at the time, I was participating in a mystery or a miracle. It was for the family, to save the marriage. I believe in the grace and power of a little child. Bart and I went together to the clinic. He had evaded twice. At the last minute, he disappeared again. I stood in his place. Money will even beget a life."

"Carlo is a miracle, a perfectly wonderful miracle," Stella whispered. "Never regret him."

He smiled in gratitude. "Some day will you forgive my part in what you have been forced to go through?"

"I am not good at holding grudges," Stella tried to reassure him. "But this America is not for me."

Nurse Condon came into the room. "Your time is up, Mr Nathan. Doctor is coming on his night visit."

"Just another few minutes, Nurse?"

"No, Mr Nathan. Mrs Shane is far from being in a state to have any visitors, in my opinion." She had a very deft way of getting between the bed and the visitor and shooing him towards the door.

"Sleep well, Stella."

"She will," said Nurse Condon.

"Gil!" Stella forced out a croaky whisper, and he looked back from the door. "The flowers are lovely."

CHAPTER TWENTY-FIVE

There were not many days left now for Ross and Hazel to visit. Their Christmas break was nearly over. As Stella grew stronger, they were in and out of her room frequently, always with Carlo. "I know how you feel about little Carlo," Hazel told Stella. "He gets right into your heart, doesn't he." Carlo was thrilled to have two nannies. He looked from one face to the other with proprietorial love. He kissed Hazel with unabashed ardour but he was very gentle with Stella. In his own mysterious way, he reserved his "Mummmm" for Stella, which made her heart contract with pride, and yet saddened her because she thought of Velva.

Stella was curious to know the details of what had happened to her, to Velva, to Ambert, to Fanna Rosen. She was very curious but asking the right questions took more energy than she had. At last, she managed a question for Hazel that might fill in part of the story. Ross had taken Carlo out on what he called a perambulation. Stella thought vaguely about the possibility of kidnappers but she felt Ross would laugh at her. Ross was tall and strong, not a nanny well into the fifties.

"Hazel, did Bart ever get to the Emerald Isle?" His name for Ireland.

"Of course he did, Mum. I met him in Shannon. I had the car. We drove to Jury's in Cork. He had plans for the five days of Christmas. The first night in Jury's was great fun. We were having breakfast— a late breakfast, of course—when the phone call came from his Uncle Gil. We both came back on the same plane. We had to come through Heathrow..." Hazel's voice broke. "It was no longer fun. *His* wife and *my* mother. I never cried before. I wouldn't let him comfort me. The last thing I remember saying was telling him to go to hell."

"And did he?"

"Maybe. He is in the clinic in Miami with his wife. He has rung me but I don't take the calls." Stella let it go at that.

Although she was not prepared to admit it to herself, the best part of every day was Gil Nathan's visit at nine. Each night, she had almost enough energy stored up to tell him that she had pondered on the words of Saint Paul, "Self-indulgence is the enemy of freedom." Each night, he did not seem to give her the opportunity. He was concerned only for her daily improvement. He sat by the bedside holding her good hand firmly in his. He did not refer to their past nor to their future nor to the problem of who, now, would look after Carlo. She had said, on Gil's first night visit, that America was not for her. To that remark he had not subsequently responded. While he sat there, she seemed to draw strength and contentment from him. His visits did her good.

Then Ross had to return to New York.

"Hazel has been wonderful with Carlo," Gil said. "She is leaving us to-morrow."

"Do you like Hazel?" Stella asked, her voice now almost back to its original soft brogue.

"How could I not?" he said. "When I look at her, I see the girl with whom her father fell in love."

Stella was pleased. "Do you suppose, with this face, I could blush?"

He held her hand even more warmly; he said, "I remember asking you if you were considered very beautiful when you were a young woman. I know now you were."

When he said precious things like that, Stella felt it would be making cheap to ask questions to satisfy her curiosity. Besides, when he went away, his voice echoing in her ears, "Sleep well, Stella," it was happiness enough to be dreamlike, basking in his pretty compliments.

Hazel had a busy day on her last day. Gil had lined

up four girls for her to interview. He had, in the week before, had their family backgrounds thoroughly investigated. He had given Hazel a list of likely questions and she was to ask any other questions she wished. On her judgment, a girl was selected.

"My God!" Hazel said to her mother, "He is heavy! You would think I was recruiting them for MI5 or the CIA or whatever. Assistant nursemaid is the job specification. She will never actually be allowed take Carlo outside the building! Mum, I feel very bad about leaving you. You have a long way to go yet. I want to know if this is all your idea. This business of Carlo being left with you in here while the assistant takes a breather."

Stella tried to smile. Nothing had been discussed with her but what else could Gil do? Carlo, too, had had a shock. When Hazel was gone, he was going to need plenty of reassurance.

"Hazel, just tell me one thing. Is there any mention of Carlo's Grandmother, Mrs Rosen? Is she also at the clinic with Velva, do you think?"

"Trouble is," Hazel answered, "not knowing the set-up, I am quite at sea. Gil has his office in the suite. He has brought down a secretary from Philadelphia— nice person, Miss Knowles, very formal. They spend a lot of the time faxing stuff to his office and he uses the phone in there in the office—it all sounds very legal what I can hear of it. There is another phone in the suite, in fact there is an extension beside every bed, and on a couple of occasions, I heard him talking to someone called Fanna. By the voice of him, I wouldn't say she is his favourite person. His voice would crack thick ice!"

"Do you like him?" Stella asked.

"Well, yes, personally. But when he is ordering or demanding or whatever, he can get very high. Heavy is what I would call him. But nice when he remembers to be!"

"Has it been arranged," Stella asked, "who will take Carlo overnight when you have gone? The assistant nursemaid?"

"I gather not. His things are being moved into Gil's room for night time. He says he understands what to do when Carlo wakes. The first time I saw Gil (the night we got here) I thought he was as old as the hills, about a hundred and ninety at least! But I saw his passport yesterday—he is only fifty eight. I was showing my new passport, the new EEC passport; no nice green hard cover nowadays."

Stella missed Hazel very much when she had gone. Maybe it was her lovely, candid smile or the funny way she tossed off remarks or the odd tender look of affection she bestowed on everyone around her. Now, Stella's thoughts of Ireland and home were piercingly sad. For a day or two, she did not make improvement, she lost interest. Then, one afternoon, Gil came carrying a piteous-faced Carlo. "Mum Mummm Mumm." The little boy made his crooning name for Stella.

Gil put him down beside Stella. "He is like a tiny whip-poor-will with that love-call," he said, smiling, hoping to see Stella's eyes light up. "May we sit with you for a little while? Ah, he knows his place! See how he knows!"

"Little nestler!" Stella whispered. The small face gradually took on its accustomed vivid look: glistening lips, sparkling eyes, a rosy glow on his tanned cheeks. He slipped his hand into Stella's hand. He was content.

"That is how I feel when I am with you, Stella," Gil said softly.

All the things I want to say, Stella thought, all the resolutions I made to resist him...and all I ever do is surrender my will to this man. He does not need to use Carlo as a weapon. It goes without saying that Carlo must be taken care of. But I am being used. Even now with my physical resistance at its lowest ebb, he is prepared to use me. If he would only commit himself a bit further than flowery compliments. Oh, no. No. No. I don't want him. I want to be my own mistress at home in my own house in Ireland. Free to come and go as I please. All the easy passing-the-time things I used to do. Go shopping. Play bridge. Meet my friends. Go to the theatre with Hazel.

She found she had put her good arm around Carlo. "We used to read his little books together," she said, "and he used to write letters to me." Carlo sparkled up at her. He knew he was in high favour again.

"Stella, could we make plans for the immediate future. With your approval."

Hah, thought Stella, your plans will be made whether or which. Approval how are you!

"Speak," Stella looked at him. "I will listen." Only don't whatever you do, give me that smile. It destroys me.

As it turned out, Gil did not smile. Only Stella thought she knew him better, she would have said he was apprehensive. In her view, apprehension was not a facet of his character at any time. He said, "If you feel well enough to be moved from here in a couple of weeks—very carefully moved, of course, would you consider returning to Philadelphia? I should mention the weather there is very cold at present. Snow and ice."

"To Larch Hill as before?"

"No." Gil's voice was stern. "Nothing is as before. To an apartment in the centre city. There is every comfort and convenience, of course. I would take up my previous apartment in the same block."

"Alice and Ambert?" asked Stella.

"Certainly not. That was Fanna Rosen's idea. Ambert should have known. But there will be security. There has to be. I have it here for you and Carlo."

"To what would I be committed?"

"To stay until the divorce goes through. Not in court now in February as previously dated, because of Bart's wife's condition. I am fighting for a hearing before the recess."

"Months and months!" Stella said sadly, rebellious yet knowing that it was inevitable. Carlo's future must be safeguarded. She was trapped.

"While you are here, I have arranged for a special nurse. Until you are on your feet again. You like Nurse Condon, don't you? What do you think of the new nursemaid?"

He had it all arranged! "She is good. Carlo likes her."

Gil now addressed Carlo. "And you? So long as Mum Mum is in your sights, you are happy?" Carlo rewarded this with his little chuckle. "Yes," Gil said, "me, too!"

"Stella, your Hazel was kind enough to tell me that I am a very bossy man. I do not mean to be. Be patient with me. There are difficulties I have not spoken of."

Stella closed her eyes rather than stare at him.

And she told *me* you were heavy. And *I* think you are egocentric.

"Actually," she said, "there are really very few decisions for me to make until, as you say, I am on my feet again. In full fettle, I might have put up a fight." She tried to smile, but smiles were not yet so easy. "I suppose I will get better?" she added hopefully.

"Completely," he said. "There is no doubt at all about that. Now, Carlo, we have tired your Mum Mum, so we will retire to our own quarters, where your maid servant awaits you."

With Carlo in his arms, he asked, "May I come back for my nine o'clock visit?"

CHAPTER TWENTY-SIX

Each day Stella warned herself to be wary, very wary of this still-growing friendship with Gil Nathan. There were times when he could not come during the day because his legal work kept him in his office in the suite. Stella began to be able to manage Carlo a little better. But a little and often became the rule. Much as she loved him, he tired her. She was not yet allowed out of bed. Another two weeks passed.

One afternoon Gil came without Carlo. He looked somewhat worn and worried. His greeting had become a kiss, an increasingly fervent kiss.

"How are you to-day?" he asked.

"Great!" Stella said. "I think they will let me up soon—maybe to-morrow!"

He looked at her very fondly. "Your lovely face is almost back to normal. Almost! Are you still in pain, Stella?"

"Not worth talking about!" she said gaily.

"I wonder, then, if I may put a couple of questions to you? Do you wish to engage a lawyer?"

This was unexpected. "Am I in trouble with the

law?" she asked.

"I could explain the legality of the position to you. The trouble is I do not wish to influence you unduly. It would be better to have an independent lawyer present when we talk. Your son-in-law has been on the phone a number of times. To put it mildly, he is very concerned."

"You mean Alec? What has he got to do with what happened!"

"He has appointed himself your adviser, Stella, and he is advising Philip and Ross on your behalf. It is right and proper that they should look after you." His voice was warm and sympathetic but Stella was quite suddenly, and irrationally, afraid that Gil was disengaging himself from her side of the case—if it was a legal case they were talking about! She fell silent. She wished she felt strong and free and independent. She hated lying there a helpless victim of do-gooders. This was a moment when a flood of tears would relieve her perplexity. She was damned if she was going to cry without knowing what she was crying for.

"So, shall I engage a lawyer on your behalf, Stella?"

She summoned up a hard-edged tone and she said, "Do exactly what you think you should do. Circumstances seem to have put me in a cleft stick. I have no idea what I need a lawyer for; I gave no one *carte blanche* to speak for me. Equally I have no idea why I do not need a lawyer." She had better shut her mouth, the tears were threatening.

"You need a lawyer if you decide to press charges against Velva. Not only against Velva but (according to Alec Mackay's advice) against the Nathan family. Alec Mackay talks in terms of substantial damages."

Stella conned this over. Alec Mackay had an almighty cheek! Without as much as a by-your-leave! And yet, in all honesty, hadn't she led Alec Mackay into the belief that he was her champion? Hadn't she let Alec Mackay's shadow fall between her and Dave— practically all of her married life? Even though she had not committed adultery, she had adulterated the substance of fidelity. She had always had a special friend in Alec, thus making a lightweight issue of Dave's friendship with both of them. Carelessly, thoughtlessly, her need for Dave had been eroded by her own actions.

"Talk to me, Stella. What do you think?"

She heaved a very heavy sigh. "Is it possible to arrive at my age without knowing myself?" she asked him, sadly.

"Oneself is not easy to know. One seldom has the courage to explore. Perhaps one is instinctively afraid to find nothing beneath the surface."

"Maybe there is nothing." Stella felt desolate.

"May I say that is not true of you. I have glimpsed

depths beyond depths in your love of Carlo. You, who came as a stranger from another world."

"Carlo brought his own love with him into this world," Stella said very gently. "Love in abundance. I have been very conscious in the last few weeks that Carlo is also Velva's baby. And even before the last few weeks, my sympathy had gone out to Velva. She had it very tough."

"Ah, Stella, Velva knows how to get to people. That is how I used to feel about her—when she was young—when she and Bart were lovers in the beginning. Her frailty, her need."

They were silent. Their thoughts were trying to commune. There was a reluctance to put the thoughts into words. Stella hoped they were drawing nearer, each to the other, in an understanding that did not depend on physical satisfaction. She looked at him through half-closed eyelashes. Physical satisfaction was nice too. I must be getting better, Stella thought.

"I will not be here to-morrow," Gil said. "I am taking the night flight to Philadelphia. Your son-in-law, Alec, will be in my office there. He may have engaged a lawyer for you. There will be a consultation."

Stella's mind was a blank astonishment. Gil had been testing her out for reaction! He could have said all that when he first came into the room.

"You are a lawyer first, last and all the time, aren't you?" she said quietly.

He considered that. "Yes," he said.

"And after that a financier?" Stella said.

"Very definitely," he answered. "I am very conscious of the early struggles of my family. Do you find it wrong that I reverence wealth and that I will plan as far ahead as is possible in this life to safeguard the family? Do you think of me as some sort of craven miser? Counting my coins in a cellar. Do you, Stella?"

She looked at the flowers. So many flowers since the first night she had recovered consciousness. "Of course I could not think of you as mean, Gil. Never mean. Just, I puzzle over who or what is next to be sacrificed, so that Carlo's millions will be saved."

Gil stood up. He paced around the room. Then he stood at the end of her bed. He was a big and very stern man.

"You are a captive in this bed, unaware of events. I have forbidden anyone to bring newspapers into this room. There is a security guard outside your door for every one of the twenty-four hours. It is only now that you are beginning to wonder what is going on out there. I enjoined on your family to keep discussion to the minimum. In your state of absolute shock, you could absorb only their affection. I have gathered from your son-in-law that his affection for you is very deep and long standing. I have gathered that if he had not married your daughter a year ago, he would on your husband's death, and I use his words, have claimed your hand."

Stella placed her fingers on his lips. "Please, may I interrupt you? Are we playing the court game again?"

"Speak but keep it brief. I have a plane to catch." He could be infuriatingly intimidating.

"Right!" Stella said. "One sentence. Alec has been a lifelong friend, since Dave brought him to the house as a prizewinning graduate. A lifelong friend. I have never, never for a single moment, had a relationship a shade warmer than friendship. Not with him. Not with any other man in Ireland."

Now Gil smiled. Stella had to turn her head away. That smile is my undoing, she thought, and actually I hate him. Big buck-cat lawyer! Full of himself!

"I may be gone several days," Gil said. "There are many difficulties. Please go on making progress. Get strong. Sleep well, Stella!" He went away.

He makes me mad, mad, mad. I am being left to think things out for myself. What things? What did he mean when he said he did not want to influence me? Doesn't he know damn well that he has me in the hollow of his hand. And I hate him, she assured herself. When Nurse Condon came that night, Stella had a temperature, a headache and she was unable to sleep.

"No visitors to-morrow," the pretty nurse said.

"Carlo?"

"For three minutes at a time. Three minutes! Although by all accounts, little Carlo is your best behaved visitor."

Gil Nathan had left on Monday. He came back late on Friday night. Nurse Condon attended to Stella in the early morning before going off duty.

"You had a visitor last night. Mr Nathan," she said. "A peep from the door was all that I permitted. You were sleeping soundly. There were four men in the suite last night. I caught a glimpse of them on the stairs."

"I do really feel much, much stronger to-day, Carmel." They had become good friends.

"Yes," Nurse Condon agreed. "I can see that. No more setbacks, now! This morning, after Doctor's visit, Sister and your day nurse are going to allow you up for a few hours. You will be able to receive your visitors from this big armchair."

"Could I use a bit of make-up?" Stella asked.

"Do you have any?" The nurse opened the bureau drawers. "Several bottles of perfume and some silk scarves and some handkerchiefs in boxes. No make-up."

Several bottles of perfume? If the gift giver had

been Hazel or Ross or Philip—or Alec for that matter—
they would have fussed over it and referred to it.
They always did—one thank-you was never enough.
No, not the family. The gift-giver was Gil, she felt
sure of that. And all the flowers!

"Before I retire for siesta, I'll slip back with some
eye make-up and a couple of lipsticks. Which perfume
would you like!"

"Is there Chanel or Nina Ricci?"

"Both, in fact. Try the Nina Ricci."

"Carmel, don't forget the eye make-up."

"Of course I won't! As soon as breakfast is over, I'll
do the eyes for you. One hand is not much use for
make-up! Although, I think the bandages are coming
off on Monday."

"I wondered lately," Stella said, "what happened
to my handbag. We were on our way for me to buy a
Christmas present for Carlo. I had money and my
little savings book."

Carmel smiled back from the door. "Your life is
one Christmas less! You were out for the count over
the festive season!"

"But the handbag?"

"Probably still with the police!"

I am very slow, was Stella's thought. The police!
The newspapers! And of course, the proud Nathan
name! Is it possible that I got a worse crack on the

head than they thought?

How many weeks ago was Christmas? Only now is one idea able to follow another in some sort of sequence. Maybe I was *never* very bright. It was not a good idea to leave home the way I did. That was done in a state of shock. And now I am emerging from another state of shock—with a bust-up shoulder added to it. Maybe what Gil Nathan said is right: my menfolk should be looking after me. She thought about that.

The deepest part of Stella was her independence. All her life, she had appeared to be part of a family circle. An only child. A much-loved daughter. A young woman seduced. A mother at eighteen years of age and three times more before she was twenty-six. That all looked like dependence but the antidote was all the time establishing itself. The minute she was on her own, she rebelled. Why did an unkind providence set her down in *another* family circle to become again dependent? Oh yes, you are, Stella Shane! Don't deny it. You are dependent for the breath you draw on Gil's smile. It devastates you. Be more of a woman— resist! He is out for himself. He wants to keep Carlo— and he is not a bit abashed to keep the millions. He just wants the right person to look after Carlo. When Carlo gets beyond needing a nanny, Stella Shane will be put on the next plane—bag and baggage.

Meanwhile, of course, she has other uses!

The trouble was that Stella could not bear to entertain cynical thoughts. A rebel yes but also a trusting person. Life would not be worth living if you had to look twice at every thought, twice at every action, twice at everyone in sight. And, Stella added wryly, twice at every shilling.

Carmel Condon came back when Stella was settled into the big armchair. From some unknown source, pretty night attire had been produced. A bed jacket of sheerest chiffon completed the effect.

"You look very nice," Carmel said. "Now just the littlest touch on your eyelashes and the smallest trace of lipstick. Shall I bring a mirror? Wait, I will draw your hair back. Next week perhaps we will shampoo. Brushing has helped."

Carlo came for his little visit with the nursemaid, Joanne. He was walking very steadily now and he was adding words to words every day. Quite obviously, he thought Mum Mum was gorgeous. He snuffled at the perfume on her throat very appreciatively. He could not sit as close to her as he had been able to sit on the bed but he did his best so snuggle at her knees. When Stella looked at her face and his little brown hands, her heart filled with love so she could scarcely speak.

CHAPTER TWENTY-SEVEN

A couple of extra chairs were brought to Stella's room. The day-nurse, a nice but rather silent woman, busied herself in re-arranging flowers in vases and in placing a table more centrally in the room.

Gil Nathan and Alec Mackay arrived together. Gil's manner was formal and distant. Alec made a display of fuss and care and a show of what Stella considered a rather overweening affection. They were soon followed by two other men, who took up separate positions on entering the room. One gravitated to Gil, the other to Alec.

"Stella," said Alec Mackay, "allow me to introduce Mr Justin Brady, our solicitor."

Gil said, "Mrs Shane, meet Richard Sond, a junior partner in my firm. More accustomed to this type of law than I am."

"Won't you all sit down?" Stella said.

Alec pulled his chair close to Stella's as if in a protective attitude. "Our man will speak first," he said, "since we are on the offensive."

Stella was surprised but she said nothing.

Justin Brady opened his brief-case and placed his papers on the table. He looked a pleasant young man, Stella thought.

"Mainly what we have here are statements made to the police by witnesses. So far, you have not been allowed, Mrs Shane, or perhaps not been able, to make a statement. It would be necessary for you to do so before we initiate proceedings."

"You see, Stella," began Alec Mackay in a kind of hectoring voice, "we must..."

Stella stopped him with a gesture. "Alec, you found it necessary to bring a spokesman although you could have come as a friend to explain what you are up to. I will, for my part, confine my remarks to your spokesman."

"But Stella..."

"Alec, I am in full possession of my senses. I insist on speaking for myself." Thunderstruck would describe Alec's expression.

"Yes, Mr Brady?"

"Mrs Shane, I am empowered to take a preliminary statement from you now." He had a tape recorder on the table beside his papers.

"A statement about what?" Stella asked.

"About the events leading up to the assault on your person, Mrs Shane, on 22 December, last year."

"And what would you do with my hazy account

of that event?"

"Mrs Shane, you are the person to press charges—it must be done formally and sworn—and then we will proceed."

"And what do you say, Mr Sond?" Stella asked. Her voice was soft, courteous and almost uninvolved.

"I am here to accept all charges that may be levelled. Those are my instructions." He, too, looked like a nice young man, maybe not as handsome as Mr Brady.

"I see," Stella said.

A silence fell on the room. After a moment, Alec Mackay started drumming his fingers on the edge of the table beside her armchair.

Stella bore it for a few moments, then she said, "Please, Alec." He stopped at once. He crossed and uncrossed his legs as if with impatience. Stella took a quietly perverse delight in his annoyance. But wasn't he always my friend? Didn't he say to me, "I wanted to bring you pleasure, never pain"? Something like that.

"I am sorry, Alec, but this isn't easy."

"Stella!" he burst out. "When I think of the way these people treated you, I..." But she interrupted him. "You don't know the half of it, Alec Mackay. There are two sides to every story." Her voice was very low. "Please say no more. Let me speak."

Stella had to draw a deep breath.

"You have all gone to a lot of trouble. I have no doubt you have all done what is best and legal to the highest standards. I must tell you now that I cannot pay any of the expenses incurred in your coming here."

Stella paused. She took another deep breath. "My coming to Philadelphia involved a promise to look after my little charge for one year. Beyond that, I am not under an obligation to anyone. I came of my own free will. In the same way, I will go. What happened in between is entirely my own business. That is all."

"Stella! Don't be crazy! You must take out an injunction against the Nathans! An indictment! You must press criminal charges! You could have been killed! You damned nearly were! You have to press charges!"

Stella's voice was very gentle but acid with reproof. "Alec, may we talk later—about other things? This is over."

Alec looked as if she had struck him.

Justin Brady asked, "Do you say you do not wish this matter to go further? Perhaps you wish for time to reconsider? It is very unusual to refuse to press charges in a criminal case, Mrs Shane."

In the same compassionate voice Stella asked, "May

we say this debate is over? Be assured I have considered deeply all aspects of my position. There will be no charges."

Stella closed her eyes. She was terrified that tears would betray her own uncertainty. She knew Alec was still sitting near; she could hear him breathing; the other three had gone. By Alec's silence, she judged the extent of his anger. When she was sure the threat of tears was under control, she looked at him.

"Why, Stella? Why? You are the one who suffered. You could take them for everything they have got. You need the money. Why?"

"I do not even wish to talk about charges." She spaced out the words evenly. "Not now. Not ever."

"I do not understand you," he said.

That makes two of us, Stella thought.

"What will I say to Philip?" he asked.

"Philip will survive." She took his hand in hers.

Suddenly Alec's face lost its clenched jaws. "Have I lost you, Stella?"

She smiled at him. "We will always be friends, Alec, always. I know why you rode out on your white charger to fight for me. You have been my Sir Galahad since you were twenty. Now it is finished and it should have been finished years and years ago."

"I am left with nothing," he said very sadly.

"No," Stella said earnestly, "you are left with a

person to fight for, a person who is part of me and part of Dave. She is a person worth fighting for, a person who will make you fight for her. All that passionate energy you were prepared to use on my behalf, use it for her. Winning her will be very rewarding."

"Stella, you know..." She put her fingers on her lips. "Alec, think of what I have just said and then act on it. Please go back to Ireland. I am so tired now that I shall start saying the wrong things. Please."

Stella heard him close the door but the sound brought no relief to the muddled jumble of uncertainties in her head.

Stella fell asleep in the armchair. She did not wake until Carlo was brought into her room by Joanne for his goodnight visit.

Stella asked for tea and biscuits. Carlo loved this idea whenever it happened. Stella wondered if he remembered the little alfresco meals they had enjoyed on that two-day trip all those months ago.

"When I am better, sweetie, we will have a picnic and play splashing in the pool."

"Kleepa Klawla?" he asked, very importantly.

"Oh, you are such a clever little boy!"

Stella did not expect to see Gil again that day. She had not the faintest idea if he would approve of her reception and dismissal of the legal team. She had ceased to work out the ins and outs of the whole business. She knew she had followed her own independent instinct and she knew that was the only way she could be personally satisfied. If Gil Nathan thought she was a fool because she had not (what was that expression?) taken him to the cleaners— well, too bad. So far as Stella was concerned, he could think whatever he liked to think. She assured herself it was of no further interest.

When Gil came at nine o'clock, the twinkle was back in his eyes. This time he did not content himself with a kiss: he put his arm a little around her shoulder and he held her for a long time. Stella was not sure if this was affection or gratitude. Would she ever be sure? "Where are your henchmen?" she asked.

"I put them on the 8.30 plane." He was smiling broadly. "Stella, that was a real Rosie Farrell-one you gave Alec Mackay!"

"How?" she asked and thinking wistfully, am I still Rosie Farrell?

"Listening to you, I was suddenly transported across fifty years and I could hear Rosie saying, 'I'll put a flea in that fellow's ear!'"

"Poor Alec! He was always kind to me. Will he forgive me for telling him off in front of other men? It was cruel. Will he ever forgive me?"

"Of course he will. When he makes a success of

his marriage. Isn't that what you want him to do?"

"He will have his work cut out." Stella felt sad for Alec. Sybil was so contrary. He would have to fight hard. She hoped he had the guts for it.

Gil was saying, "I echoed Mackay in one thing he said: 'You could have been killed.'"

"And then he and the others could have gone to town on the litigation! I would not be there to stop them!"

"Stella, let me say that I..."

"No," Stella said decisively, "I don't want to hear what you are going to say. I am sick and tired of the whole thing. No more, please."

"But Stella, I..."

"I am only counting the days until I am free from this bed, this splint, these bandages. When that happens, I will forget whatever happened ever happened. I will then start making plans to return to my own country, my own home, my own position in society."

"You do not mean this!"

"Yes, I mean it."

"And Carlo?"

"You found a suitable woman to look after Carlo. You can find another. There must be hundreds."

"Stella, look at me." So you can smile at me, Gil, isn't that it? Poor susceptible Stella!

"Mr Nathan, please ring for the nurse. This armchair is tiring. I will be going back into bed now."

When he had gone, Stella felt no victory. I guess I had to stand up for myself sooner or later, she mused. Let him go back now to being the great dictator. The lord of all he surveys. The hell with him!

CHAPTER TWENTY-EIGHT

Now Stella improved rapidly. Carlo and young Joanne (with whom he had quickly established a little master-slave relationship) were able to spend more time in Stella's room. Joanne could now take time off and Carlo was happy to have Stella read to him. No one was at hand to use the name "Nanny," and Carlo had long since called her Mum Mum, as if it were a fact. She tried out "Stella" on him but he would have none of that. His characteristics were becoming apparent; obstinacy was one of them. It was always a logical obstinacy, not to be confounded with a lack of charm. He was never rough, never naughty in the accepted sense of the word. He was, however, still a very small child and it was easy enough to find ways around him, to circumvent his more ambitious aims. Stella found his company more pleasurable as she grew stronger. Into her mind and into her emotions came the daily thought: how will I ever leave him?

"He will not come and still I wait; He whistles at another gate. The world is calling, I must go. How shall I know he did not pass barefooted in the shining grass?"

Barefoot on grass. A lovely picture. Ah, Carlo, Carlo! I love your small brown feet and your hands. But, little love, how can I give up the hold on my longing dream of home? This America is your country. I don't belong here.

Her short conversations with Gil Nathan were now confined to the plans for moving back to Philadelphia. She did not ask about Velva or Bart and he did not volunteer any information. She listened, with very few comments, to his descriptions of the centre-city apartments.

"Directly behind the cathedral, Stella. You liked going to Mass there, didn't you? I remember you mentioned Cardinal Kroll. I am giving you and Carlo the penthouse apartment. I will take the one directly below. I shall try not to be too close a neighbour. I would, however, be able to baby-sit, if you would allow that?" Stella wondered with whom she would be going out at night and under what circumstances she would be requiring a baby-sitter.

"Is a penthouse apartment safe for such an adventurous little boy? He climbs everything."

"But I doubt if he could climb a fourteen foot high

wire fence on which climbing roses have been trained for the last half-century."

"Is that where he would have to play?"

"It is where I played," Gil said, "and my brothers. It is a big patio-ed area. There are shrubs in boxes, flowery things."

So we are going into his world, Stella thought. She could expect to revert to the nanny role when he brought them back to his own place. She would be a very small cog in his big legal world. Her imagination ran riot on the pictures of Gil Nathan in Philadelphia. No doubt he would have his millionaire clients to catered dinners in the flat below the penthouse. She would hear the music and the muted conversation drifting up through the climbing roses. There would be women. Would she glimpse them in their fabulous evening gowns? Women with their wealthy husbands. Naturally Gil would have a woman to partner him. No doubt a very beautiful and clever woman. So practised a lover must have had a great many experiences of women.

Stella had to take a grip on what she suspected might be frustration or even jealousy. She assured herself repeatedly that just as soon as she was in full fettle (a phrase she used often because it had a hearty sound), yes, in full fettle, she would make short work of all his long-term plans for her continued service to the Nathans. He had already mentioned a playschool for Carlo which was run by the Quakers. A homely little school, he said, very near the apartments. There's another thing, thought Stella. I have never lived in a high-rise block. Didn't I read somewhere that such apartments are hard on the nerves? Now I am trying to make up silly excuses. No, I will not make any plans of any sort until I am in full fettle. And actually, Stella, you could try being a bit more agreeable. The poor man looks very downcast at times. But, all the same, playschool? That would be years ahead!

The move was made at the end of February when, Gil said, "Spring could not be far ahead. Isn't that a quotation?"

"You have it skewways," Stella told him, being pleasant for once. "If Winter comes, can Spring be far behind?" She noticed his smile. Harden the heart, Stella. You have begun to weaken. It was hard not to weaken. Gil was amazingly concerned for her comfort. Although she told him repeatedly that she felt fine, he nevertheless insisted on monitoring her every move. Joanne would go with them to Philadelphia and, if she liked being there, she would stay until June. This was her year before college and she was glad to earn the money. However, she described herself as a home-bird and she was not sure of how she would feel away from her family.

"Beginning the end of March," Gil suggested, "you could have a weekend home each month—March, April, May? I'll provide the ticket."

"Who would help Mrs Shane with Carlo?" Joanne wanted to know. She had grown very fond of the little boy.

"I would," Gil said turning to Stella. "Would that be permitted?"

"Oh, thank you, sir!" Joanne was delighted.

This time the plane journey was merely a matter of hours. The two-day journey down to Florida, way back in September, was fresh and green in Stella's memory. Six months ago, Carlo had been in need of both their care. Now he was a robust little boy, his hand firmly clasped in Joanne's hand; refusing to be lifted up the steps; settling himself into the plane seat; learning how to lock and unlock his seat-belt; put up and down the table; accepting pencils and drawing-book from the stewardess; beaming around out of his dark eyes under the fringe of black curls. Stella suddenly realised that she and Gil were staring, wide-eyed, at Carlo as if they were besotted grandparents. Hard not to weaken!

And even harder when Gil showed her into the penthouse apartment. Stella almost gasped at the beauty of it. The furniture was turn-of-the-century, solid, comfortable. The landscape paintings drew the eyes into vistas of lake and mountain. The chairs by the fireplace were warmly inviting. There were books everywhere. The windows looked outwards into sky and rolling clouds, downwards to the Benjamin Franklin Parkway and indeed onto the city of Philadelphia. Joanne was showing Carlo the big patio beyond the glass screens.

Gil flicked a switch. The fireplace had an arrangement of glowing logs and small spiky flames.

"It has to be artificial," he apologised. "We are too high to drag up coal or logs and they used to make too much dust." Stella was gazing out at the view. He came and stood beside her. His tone of voice was very anxious. "Do you like it here?" he asked.

She turned to him. He was a big man. She had to lift her head back to meet his eyes. She placed her hands each side of his face and she drew down his head for a kiss. His arms went around her in an immediate response.

Stella drew back after a second. "I love it, Gil. When I came through the door into this room, something said, 'Welcome.'"

"You will be contented here, Stella?"

"Just tell me one thing," she asked. "Is the ghost of Rosie Farrell in the kitchen?"

He shook his head. "Ah, no. We bought this block of apartments when I was eight years old. Before that, we lived near Elfreth's Alley in two old houses which my grandfather had renovated."

Stella said, "There is just one last question—something I want settled in my mind, so I can forget about it. Be patient with me. I come from a very ordinary background and, apart from a few short months in college in Dublin, I have always lived in a rural, untouched area—even the shops are several miles away."

She paused and looked up at him.

"What is the question, Stella?"

"Can we now dispense with security guards?"

"We cannot. I am sorry. Would that this were rural Ireland but it is not. The security here is not the security in Larch Hill—the nuisance value of which I did not understand, all those cameras and Fanna's Uncle Ambert. I know more now than I did then. The security guards are and will always be, on my landing below this level. You will not be troubled with their close presence. Nevertheless, if you wish to go out to take Carlo shopping for example, you will be accompanied. Discreetly. It would be best for you to make definite arrangements—certain days, certain hours."

Stella was silent. The idea of being a prisoner was repugnant to her.

"Is that too much to ask?" he pleaded.

"No," she answered slowly but with determination, "I will respect your rules—while I live here."

It pleased her to put in the little proviso. She knew he recognised that. There was, nonetheless, a partnership established. A sort of an equation.

"I, for my part," he said, "wish you to keep in constant touch with your family. The phone is there for you to use. In this bureau there is notepaper and a copious supply of stamps. I give you my word I never knew that attempts were made to keep you unposted."

"But you knew I was never allowed out in Boca Raton? They said that was your order."

"I can only ask you to believe that my concern there was as much for your safety as for Carlo's. A very strange place, that coastline."

"When I lived in Larch Hill, I came freely down to Philadelphia every Sunday, didn't I? You got a ticket to the Free Library for me. I went to the museums. I posted letters—not very many because I got scarcely any in return. But I walked around as I pleased."

"Stella, that was never so. I had a detective shadowing you always."

"But you trusted me?"

"The shadow was for your own safety—not for any other reason."

At that moment in her life, Stella longed for Ireland

as never before. Oh God, she thought, what madness possessed me to get myself into this trap.

"Stella," Gil said, "just bear with me and with all that is so unfamiliar to you—just until these divorces are through. Please!"

Nobody can live at fever pitch all the time. Things settle down. Routines get established. Days develop meaning. Habits are formed and habit is what makes living tolerable. So it was with Stella and Carlo and pretty Joanne and after a week or two, with Gil also.

Almost always, Gil came to say goodnight to Carlo. He stayed a few moments only at that time. He returned a half-hour after nine. He left again at fifteen minutes to eleven. The hour and a quarter became very precious to both of them. It was a serial in their lives, each night a taking-up of the night before. They did not kiss on meeting, nor on parting. They were not courting. Tacitly they were giving each other time.

One night, smilingly and very gently, Stella said to him, "We are like two novices in an enclosed order."

"I see it a little differently," he said and his voice too was mild. "I am a man who has put himself on probation."

"Will we need a novice master? Or a probation officer?" asked Stella.

"I think we will know, ourselves," he answered.

When Joanne went back to Boca Raton for her

weekends, Gil spent more time in the penthouse. The little tasks that Joanne usually did were done by Gil. Turning up the beds, stacking the dishwasher, attending to Carlo's laundry in the wash-and-dry machine. Stella wondered if he would offer to stay the night. She had fortified herself with a remembrance of St Paul's words: self-indulgence is the enemy of freedom. She needn't have bothered. Gil invariably went off to his apartment on the dot of ten forty-five. Stella was left with the thought that she had damn-all freedom anyway. Nor was she discontented with this thought. Life, as she was living it, had many compensations. Now that she could talk to the family at any time, she was happy enough to leave them to get on with their own lives. She had been able, with a few letters, to get the bank in her home village to take care of any money due to her on the social welfare widows' pension. Philip had set Stella's house for one year to a visiting American professor. It was a minimal rent but the house would be lived in. And, Stella thought, Sybil could not use it to escape her husband. Ross was, typically, into and out of enough torrid love-affairs to fill what time he had left over from a very upward career. Stella phoned him every week for the sheer fun of hearing his laughter. Hazel was, as ever, her own person happily living her own life and working towards her geography doctorate. Of

Alec and his "present" wife, to use Philip's phrase, there was nothing new. Alec was beavering away and, Philip supposed, Sybil was still up to her tricks. The rest of the family had never taken daddy's girl too much to heart.

Then one evening, Gil had news. Bart's divorce hearing had been set for 30 May and the Rosens' for 10 June. Mrs Rosen and Velva were in Larch Hill. Bart had rooms in a hotel.

"There are a few things which must be done," Gil said. "I will make them as few as possible. Fanna's case for Velva to retain custody of Carlo has been considerably weakened by Velva's drug taking and her attack on you."

"Should I have taken out charges against her?"

"My instinct was the same as yours," he answered, "but not for the reasons Alec Mackay gave—that you were entitled to monetary recompense. You are and you may trust me on that issue. But it was a case that could have dragged through the courts for years. You would have been separated immediately from Carlo. The rights and wrongs were never in question; the point is rather the weight of legal counsel."

"But you? Surely you...?"

"Yes, I am big in Philadelphia but the Rosen money could get advice as big as mine. And legal quibbles can be prolonged for a lifetime."

"So what are the things that must be done?" Stella's voice was very apprehensive. All this easy time was too tranquil to last, she thought.

"I regret this but you must make a formal statement of every incident of that fateful day. Do you remember it?"

"Oh yes," Stella told him, "now I remember it very well—and with a sense of astonishment at my own part in it."

"Poor Stella! You have suffered so much pain. May I suggest that you write down the event as if you were writing a letter to—perhaps Hazel? Holding nothing back? Then you will be prepared to make the statement on oath."

"I hate the idea of publicity," she said.

"Your statement will be made public only as a last resort. It will be the ace in my sleeve, if they try to take Carlo. I do not think they will. I had sent Bart to Boca Raton with an offer, his divorce and my custody of Carlo in return for a sum of money. That was accepted. I have the documentation signed. It is my second ace."

Stella remembered that Velva had sneered at her, the gun held steadily, the queer crazed eyes; "Everyone knows it was his semen. He can't buy everything."

"Then there is very little doubt? They will not oppose, not contest, the divorce of Bart and Velva?

Why are you afraid?" Stella asked.

"They have engaged excellent counsel. They are after Carlo (his inheritance has not been forgotten) or they are after more money. In my view, they have had enough. Nevertheless, that could be a haggle. And there is always one other thing." His face was grievously, almost hopelessly, downcast.

"Yes?" Stella prompted.

"There is always a feeling, no more than a feeling in the law, that in the end a mother has the first and last right to a child. There have been notorious cases of child abuse where a father was awarded custody."

"Is this where I come in?" Stella asked faintly.

"Will you do this for me and for Carlo? Will you allow the Children's Protective Custody people to have an interview here with you and Carlo? Almost informally. To allow them to see you together, your so special relationship with him?"

"And would I have to go into court?"

"Only in the very last analysis would I permit that. Only if all else fails," he promised.

"I have to trust you. What option have I now? When this is over, I trust you..."

"You can trust me. I give you my word."

"I mean trust you," Stella said, "to release me at the end of my year?"

"Would that, too, be an option?" he asked.

"Gil Nathan, how do we turn every conversation into this court of law game? Lawyer and client! Afterwards, I never can remember if you take me as seriously as I take you."

"Stella, just give me until the divorce is over."

"What will Bart do with his freedom?" Stella wondered. His trip to the Emerald Isle had been sadly and quickly cut short.

"Our conversations have been brief and confined to legalities but I gather he is in love," Gil answered.

Stella laughed with relief. "So what's new? For the ninety-ninth time?"

Gil was very serious. "Bart has had innumerable (well, many!) attractive girl escapades. Or should one say, affairs? He never has been and he has never claimed to be, in love. In love for Bart is new."

"Good heavens!" Stella was surprised. Gil saw big differences? Escapades? Affairs? Wouldn't another affair be just a love-affair?

Gil was watching her puzzled face. She caught his eye. She smiled at him, a friendly smile.

"You are thinking, Gil, that it is time I grew up, aren't you? Your face is assessing my mind."

CHAPTER TWENTY-NINE

I t took Stella hours and many attempts, before she managed to set down a clear, coherent account of the happening with Velva. She had shied away from talking of it to Gil. She thought the entire puzzling incident was now over, forgotten, safely in the past. She had healed. Her shoulder was a bit stiff occasionally but less as time went on. Her thick hair had grown back over the stitches in her head. She always promised herself a complete new hairstyle when the wound ceased to be sensitive. She paused now, the pen in her hand. Gil was watching her. "Problems, Stella? I wish I could help—but I must not make suggestions about the account."

"Oh," she smiled, "I am just being silly. I was thinking about a new hairstyle!"

"Is the head still very sore, where you fell on the road?"

"Just a bit tender. I'll make an appointment soon with a hairdresser."

"And what will you have done?"

"Chopped off!" Stella laughed. "Don't look so

anxious, Gil! I am not too serious."

"May I say I like the soft coil on the nape of your neck? It becomes you."

She wondered did she now look like Rosie Farrell? Did she bring his mind back fifty years? Because that is how this coil made her look, old fashioned! What's that old song?

> "Nor did she wear a chignon, I'll have ye all to
> know,
> And I met her in the garden where the praties
> grow."

"Sing some more," Gil said. "You always sing for Carlo."

"I am nearly finished," Stella said, "but I am not a bit happy about it." She was looking down at the writing critically. "It seems as if I am making myself out to be the heroine in a story."

"You were the heroine," he stated firmly.

"But heroines are brave," she said. "I had no feeling of bravery. Inside me, I was in a funk."

He smiled at the word. "You have written the facts very modestly. Let others be the judge."

Stella thought now for a moment. "I think I felt nothing only the effort it took, the strained effort."

"If I were not a man on probation, I would try to

show a more heartfelt gratitude to you. Please take my word for it. To-morrow I shall bring you flowers."

"Oh Gil, not more flowers! Look around you. So many flowers. Nothing more for now, I beg of you."

The following week, the account which Stella had written was sworn in a solicitor's office.

In the last week of April, two women officers and one male officer came from the Children's Court Protective Custody. Stella pretended to herself that they were merely nice people come for tea. Gil was not present. The tea ceremony was Carlo's special delight. It was an occasion when he was allowed eat biscuits and drink a little tea. He loved to play host, inviting everyone to "tate anuddah." Stella thought it meant "taste another," but Joanne insisted it meant "take another." He was a little boy who loved company. There was never any fear that he would "make strange." He shook hands on being introduced and liked to think he was passing on the introduction by presenting each "shake-hands" to Mum Mum. His smile was always charming and now he had nice teeth for smiling. His glossy black curls were greatly admired. Stella knew he could be obstinate. There were certain things that did not appeal to him at all. One was cigarette smoke. Sometimes Stella wondered if he associated cigarettes with Velva and therefore with that fearful fight in the car, when for days on end afterwards, he was without a familiar presence. Luckily none of the custody people took out cigarettes. The tea party was accounted a great success.

Time had moved into the month of May. Carlo had taken full possession of the patio. He carried out his toys, arranging them, setting up little avenues of space as if he had a plan, a design in mind. Quite often he carried out his plate and spooned the food into his mouth neatly and solemnly. He observed the great interest Stella took in the changing colours of the sky, how she loved to watch the sunset, how she always commented, on a rainy day, "We will have no beautiful sunset to-day." It was comical to watch him planting his feet sturdily and pointing to a fluffy cloud to attract Stella's attention.

Each night she had some little tale to tell of Carlo's adventures.

"When I was about ten years old," Gil said, "out on that patio my father set up a telescope for us to watch the sky at night. When all this present tension is over I will have a search for the telescope. There is a big storage space in the basement where all sorts of things got dumped—bicycles, surfboards, boys' books, crates of baseball bats. Endless rubbish."

"It sounds very promising for Carlo! He will surely be an explorer—he investigates everything. Not always just his toys—the little weighing scales in the kitchen is his present fascination."

Stella caught Gil's watchful speculative glance when she chatted enthusiastically about Carlo. It was not hard to guess what he was thinking. How long would Stella's loving enthusiasm last when the result of the divorce was known? Would she stay or would she go? The question of her commitment to one year was pushed firmly to the back of her mind. For now, Carlo was her special charge.

Then, one week before the divorce hearing, Gil came home in the middle of the afternoon. He looked dazed, deflated and very tired. Stella had never seen him like this, like a man who had had a physical attack. He almost staggered through the door and into a chair. "What is it, Gil?" Should she call a doctor? She stood beside the chair. She chafed his hands anxiously. "Some whiskey?"

"Yes, please. I am not going back to the office today." He swallowed the first whiskey in one rush. He sat nursing the second. "Where is Carlo? Is he asleep?"

"No, he is playing on the patio. Joanne is with him. He will not miss me for a while."

Stella looked at Gil, slumped and tired and sad. Yes, he was dictatorial and dogmatic and, at times he was (like Carlo) very obstinate. Yes, she had heard his stylish, imperious manner to herself in Larch Hill and to all kinds of people from doctors to security guards. Yes, to-day he was looking older and he was slightly overweight. And yes, she insisted to herself, she longed to be free of him, to be her own person again. Wasn't she sure now that he had used his wiles on her to get her under his influence? And wasn't she sure that he guessed all the time at her vulnerability? Then her eyes travelled down to his hands, brown and shapely. I am going to regret this, Stella thought. But what the hell!

"Gil, I have been dreading that I should have to make my statement publicly—in a court. But, if it is a help, then I will. You can depend on that."

He covered his face with his hands. She could barely hear his voice. "Yes, it would be a help but I could not ask you to do that. You have no idea what the divorce court is like. Raving reporters. A witness in the divorce court is at the mercy of prosecuting counsel—treated as a criminal—a perjuring criminal. Merciless cross-examination. When custody is in question, both sides are prepared for a bull-fight. No, Stella—not you. Your gentle nature has taken enough abuse from the Nathans."

Stella knelt down beside his chair. She took his hands from his face. "Look at me, Gil. I am only Stella who stands in Rosie Farrell's shoes. Wouldn't Rosie Farrell have gone into the witness box for you?"

He put his arms around her. Against her hair, she

could hear his muttered "No, no, no!"

"Gil, please tell me what is worse since yesterday. Yesterday, you were calm and hopeful." She disengaged herself from his arms and sat opposite to him. She had placed the whiskey on the small table beside his chair. He took a little more. "Will you have some?" he invited, courteous as always. "Later," she said softly, "and please tell me."

"Stella, do you remember saying to me that I had power? Do you remember? You said you were in awe of me?" Stella nodded. The awe had not gone away.

"You are going to be sadly disillusioned—if you are not already. I think you know that I tried to act as an all-powerful deity when I was told of the miracle of in-vitro fertilisation. For a long, long time, Velva had all my sympathy. I know a lot about her early childhood. I was convinced that a child of her own was the answer and certain of it when the marriage counsellor advised a baby as a solution. I was inclined to blame Bart for the marital discord (easily attracted to a pretty face)—although I thought also that Velva's mood-swings must be hard to take. In fact, I really knew nothing of what was going on in the marriage and Bart did not enlighten me. My emission of seed at the fertility clinic was done in his name, which is the same as mine. We are both Gilbart Nathan. It was the work of four minutes to beget a life. How wonderful, how marvellous, how truly miraculous, if there had also been passionate pleasure in it!"

"Gil, I think I have said this before: never regret Carlo. He is a wonderful little boy."

"I realise every time I see him, how much he owes to you. From the moment you came into Larch Hill."

"Gil, he owes nothing to anyone. He is his own little miracle. He has reserves of strength. Look how he snapped back after my...er...accident. He is very obstinate in the way you are obstinate. In sleep, he looks as you must have looked at that age. I do not try to form his character. That is fully formed; it came with him; it speaks for itself. All I have ever done is to love him and that has been easy. I notice each day *you* come here that he draws *your* love into himself. I notice you feeling the pull."

"Stella, that frightens me. I notice that too. I feel it sweetly but is it not wrong to go overboard in loving a child? Sort of spoiling?"

"At our age, we cannot help it. We have mellowed. We depend on loving them to win their respect and with respect comes reciprocation. I believe Carlo is unspoilable. You will never have to anticipate trouble from him."

There was nothing said for a while. What he had told her before her praise of Carlo must be a preamble to a newer problem. At last, he said very wearily,

"There is much worse to come."

Stella judged that he had said enough for the moment. He was a man badly in need of rest.

"I am going to call in Carlo and Joanne for afternoon tea. Carlo will cheer you up—you'll see. Afterwards you should go away and sleep. Come back later on tonight if you want to talk more. Joanne likes to watch Spanish TV in her own room."

Stella went to the screen doors onto the patio, which was now colourful with late Spring blossoming.

"We have a visitor for tea and biscuits!" she called out.

Gil could not but be refreshed, and delighted, to see Carlo acting out his favourite role of host-of-the-tea-ceremony. In his passing of the biscuits he was very much the head waiter: "tate anaddah." He had a toy camera, bought for him by Joanne who quite simply adored him. With the manner of a little professional, summoning Joanne as his film crew, he went about the business of taking pictures of his guest, grouping him with Stella and the flowers, instructing them to "say fleas, fleas!"

When Gil came back late that night, he looked a little better. "I lay on my bed. Then I lay in the bath. Then I lay on the bed again."

"For a layabout," Stella smiled, "you don't look too bad."

But she could hear the deeply serious note was still in his voice. When he had settled into the chair that had become his usual chair and the whiskey was ready to hand, he began to talk. "I know it is like a scene from a film, in your memory, that you stepped out of the car which you had driven down from the cliff, you pitched forward and passed out. I know your last memory is of Ambert in the midst of police and (what you did not know) a gang of reporters and photographers already on the spot. If you had not lost consciousness, which mercifully you did, you would have seen handcuffs on Ambert very soon after."

"But, but, it was Velva who tricked Ambert into getting out of the car!"

"It was Ambert's car. The car itself was under suspicion. Apparently it had been under police surveillance for weeks. It was already being searched, there on the road, while an ambulance was called for you and Velva and poor little Carlo."

"Searched for what? There were no packages in the car. It was empty. We never did any shopping!"

"They searched for drugs. The car was torn asunder for drugs, which were found in considerable quantities. Heroin and other stuff. Worth an untold amount of money."

"Ambert! Ambert's car!" It was incredible. Stella

had regarded Ambert as she would regard an ancient odious toad half-buried in slime. "Ambert!"

"Ambert is what they call a 'trafficker.' *And* Velva. *And* Fanna Rosen if she has not covered her tracks. Her husband got out some months ago. Out of her life or out of drugs? Who knows?"

"I cannot take this in," Stella said. Surely Gil, who knew everything, who organised everything, who had his fingers on everyone's cash-book, surely he must have known what was going on? Or Bart must have known?

Gil said, "When I gave instructions that you and Carlo were never to be allowed out in Boca Raton because of the danger of kidnapping, you or Carlo, the security men at the gate were my men. When Fanna Rosen phoned me that a man (who was Alec Mackay) had passed the security check, to call for you at the house, I forbid her to let you out of the house but to allow you talk in the house with your son-in-law. Apparently you got out so fast that she had not re-checked with me nor with the gate security. You were watched by the police that day. All unknown to Fanna Rosen (or to the others involved) the net was closing-in on the house. That day, you personally (nor Mackay) did not do anything to arouse suspicion. The car was a hired car, rented out by the police themselves—for reasons of their own. You returned to the house. In Mackay's absence from his hotel in Coral Gables, his room was searched. He left the next morning. There are many circumstances, in my experience, in which that hired car could have been riddled with bullets."

He saw Stella's stricken face. "You are shocked and incredulous, my poor darling. This is America. Quite often the police have to fire first. The questions come long afterwards—if everyone is not defunct. The Florida coast is a drug dealer's paradise—and much else that is dangerous—all covered with hibiscus and bougainvillaea."

Stella said, very slowly because understanding was slow in coming, "Your orders were that I was not to leave the grounds at any time. Twice I disobeyed you. Did I bring all this trouble on you?"

"Or rather did I bring it on you!" he asserted warmly. "Your head, your shoulder, your pain. I was the one who knew nothing—although instinct warned me against Florida. Power! Wisdom! Legal omniscience! You have a right to be disillusioned." He smiled a little. "To lose your awe of me."

"The awe is still there," Stella said, "but it is being crowded out by bewilderment. Up until this moment, I thought we were talking of Velva's murderous designs on Carlo, on me too. I thought Velva was gone crazy from those weird cigarettes. That day, that night! When did you come on the scene? When did you know what had happened?"

He answered her, "I arrived just after ten that night. The news broke on TV at 4.30. The evening papers had the headlines."

"And where were we before you came?"

"Carlo was taken back to the house. He was alone most of the time. When I got to him, he was bloated with tears but he let me hold him—for minutes only! I went before that (assuming Carlo was in good hands—an ill-founded assumption) but I went to the police. Stella, you were on a stretcher in the police ward-room. When I saw you, you were covered in blood, you were ice-cold, rigid, a dead woman. Your hair was matted with blood. Your face was almost unrecognisable. I was sure I had lost you. I was sure your eyes would never open again. Almost a *week* before you were out of danger."

Stella stared at him. His distress was moving and strange.

"And Velva? And her Uncle Ambert?"

"She was unhurt. They were being questioned by the police. She is out on bail for the divorce hearing."

"Gil, when you say you had lost me, do you mean Carlo had lost me—you thought?"

"No, I mean I thought I had lost you. Lost you for me. My own loss was selfishly uppermost when I saw you that night almost beaten to death. You know, I think you must know, that I had begun to hope I had a chance with you after the night in Augusta."

"Not after the night in the Garden of Allah?" Stella kept her voice light. It would be so easy to give in to him. They were closer at this moment than she had ever imagined.

"In the Garden of Allah," he said very seriously, "you were in tears for a lost love, a dead husband, the passing of a way of life. You were a woman in need of a shoulder to cry on and I think you had held back the tears for a long time. Perhaps since long before your husband's death."

"That may be true," Stella said and she did not tell him that in the Garden of Allah she had come to realise the delights of sexual love for the first time in her life. Sexual release? No, sexual love. In her tradition, there had to be love.

"You remember, don't you Stella, that in Augusta you came to me of your own desire. You returned my love-making freely and with joy. I was not a substitute in Augusta. I was your reality, as you are mine." Augusta, to Stella, had been a dream-sequence but there was no need to tell him that.

"Two different tenses there?" Stella queried, still lightly.

"Because I am aware you do not trust me," he

answered.

"How do you know I do not trust you?" She wondered what had she said to reveal her secret distrust both of herself and of him.

"I get the sceptical look," he smiled a little, "the left eyebrow raised, or the thoughtful-through-the-lashes-look."

"Is that why you put yourself on probation?" Stella asked.

"Yes," he answered simply. "It is to encourage your trust."

Stella decided to change the subject. To-night there were undoubtedly more urgent things to discuss than their mutual desire. A subject, Stella hoped, for a different night.

"May I ask you something? You see, in Ireland there is no law for divorce, so I was never surrounded by case histories. It has seemed to me, when I was living in Larch Hill (with divorce available for all) that a lot of heartbreak all round could have been avoided if Velva and Bart had sundered years ago. May I ask why you moved heaven and earth rather than let them divorce?"

He smiled again the smile that moved her so. "This calls for another whiskey. Please join me this time? Good. This is how I see it, Stella. Marriage is a tough assignment. To make it work, two people need a tough commitment. I do not handle divorce cases now. A totally different department of my office. I worked in the divorce court for twenty years. I became thoroughly and completely disillusioned with divorce. If the same two people employed the energy and the money they use in getting rid of each other, to come together instead, as they did on the first day they met, there would be very few divorces. The same two people, made up of the same sensibilities, after divorcing enter into new commitments—very often with new partners for whom they do not even feel the pristine glory of their earlier loves."

"Oh but Gil, there must be cases where a couple are tied together in heartbreak. Perhaps the Romeo and Juliet love of Bart and Velva was much too young for wisdom?"

"Yes, that is so. On the other hand, the younger the couple the better the chance for wisdom to grow, always provided the need for wisdom is agreed, recognised. Long ago, in the divorce court, I witnessed much soul-searching, much tragedy. Not today. I became totally disillusioned. Now, divorce is a law like any other law. Divorce did strange things in my own life."

"Bart and Velva always seemed oddly at variance," Stella said.

"I began to see that in the last few years. Even so,

even so, I was reluctant to encourage Bart into the divorce court. Work at it, work at it, I said to him repeatedly. Divorce, I told him, proves nothing except your own inability to cope. His working at it was the reason he did not reveal to me that Velva was on drugs. That was repulsive to him but I believe he made repeated efforts to rescue her."

Stella remembered the crazy nights in the Jacuzzi in Larch Hill. The naked Velva fawning on the half-inebriated G-string-wearing Bart, she smoking, he drinking, the struggles over what she called her paradise pills, his leaving in the middle of the night and staying away for days, she screaming her head off. Was Uncle Gil locked away in his sanctum above the upper circle, listening to Beethoven on those nights? Or did Velva choose the nights when Uncle Gil was out of the country (as he often was then) to put on those exhibitions reminiscent of some ancient orgy?

"As you said, you really didn't know much about their private lives, did you?" And yet their fights had gone on for years. Didn't the coloured woman, Leola, say that?

"I thought I knew it all," he answered sadly. "Life itself has changed in style. I told you, Stella, I went to that clinic to save Bart from divorce. To put his marriage on a firm footing. A firm footing with a drug addict!" He snapped his fingers. He said again, "So much for my power and your awe! So much for my almighty insight and my legal wisdom!"

"If Bart did not tell you, how could you know?" Stella did not want to see him so harsh, so hard on himself.

"When Velva's mother moved into the house, I began to know what I had done in bringing Carlo into Velva's life. Before you came, Stella, I had realised that to them Carlo was not a helpless baby in need of care. He was a money magnet."

That is a good phrase, Stella thought. That is exactly what I thought Carlo was to you, Gil Nathan. When did I realise you cherish him for his own sake and because he is yours? Perhaps that, too, began in the Garden of Allah?

"Gil, asking questions, I interrupted the story of which my unconscious state knew nothing. Are you too tired to finish?"

"There is not a great deal more to tell. By the time I got to the police, it became a matter of pulling rank and throwing my weight around to get you released into my custody and into the hospital. You were under suspicion. The police had the theory of gang-warfare, two women fighting over the spoils. There was, as I think I told you, only one set of prints on the gun. They took her prints when they charged her and the match was made. Your tying her up, tied-in with their theory."

"Were you questioned, Gil?"

"Grilled," he said.

"You know my questions may sound silly but you are always patient. If Velva, who is Carlo's mother after all, is under suspicion of this serious charge, wouldn't that automatically bar her from taking custody of Carlo?"

"The entire matter of the drug-trafficking is *sub-judice*. It cannot be quoted in the divorce court. That would be illegal. It is another fact that gave me to-day's setback. And there is yet another."

He paused for a long time. He glanced at Stella a couple of times. He took a small amount of the whiskey.

"In the end, we may have to rely on your sworn testimony and trust to luck that it does not occur to any judge to ask if you are illegal. I will only allow your testimony against Velva to be used as a last resort. Do you trust me in this, Stella?"

"I trust you," Stella said, "and I must add, as I told you, I am standing in Rosie Farrell's shoes."

"We will deal with Rosie when this is over," he said. "You recall, in your testimony on oath, that Velva told you that Gil Nathan thought he could buy everything with the money which she had lodged in her mother's bank. She called it her settlement, you said. I have in her handwriting her agreement to give Bart his divorce and to forgo the custody of Carlo, in return for the cash settlement."

"Doesn't that make sure certain—my oath and her signature?" asked Stella.

"Absolutely, if the bank had cashed the cheque. Apparently the money I offered, considerable as it is, does not compare with Carlo's millions, if they win custody. Without the cashed cheque, I have a piece of paper only. To-day my cheque, intact, was returned to the bank from which it was issued."

So that was what happened to-day. So all he has is my testimony against Velva, thought Stella. "And Friday is the day? Shall I be in court on that day?"

"Yes, at ten. I will have you escorted."

"And Carlo?"

"I regret he must be with you. So will Velva and Bart be in court. And probably her mother."

"And you?"

"If my counsel calls me. In the very last resort I will claim paternity. That involves me in the birth certificate forgery, despite the identical names. I could go to jail for that. A sad end to a legal career. Ah! I see your face, Stella. Now you have the enormity of it all."

Anxiety kept Stella awake far into the night. Almost

on the edge of sleep, almost, almost, the phone rang. It was Hazel.

"Sorry, Mum. I know it's the middle of your night but I just hoped you might be lying awake."

"I'm awake now, darling. You haven't bad news, I hope? Are you all all right over there?"

"It's about the divorce, Mum. I had a call from Bart. He was in despair!"

Now Stella was wide awake with the certainty that sleep was gone for the night.

"Mum! Are you there? What does Gil say?"

"Gil? Well, he's a lawyer of course. First, last and all the time." And after that, what? A financier! A lover?

"Is he hopeful? Bart says Velva is in dire trouble with the police but she refused to be bought off. Bart says Gil is going to double the offer first thing in the morning rather than drag you into court."

"Honestly, Hazel, you are way ahead of me. I do not know whether hope or despair is the word. Who knows?" Hazel could look after herself—or could she? Bart? I mean, look at his record with women!

"Hazel, I only worry about little Carlo."

"Mum, you know damn well we are all in this together—all of us. Sink or swim. I'll ring Friday night. Bye!"

"Wait, Hazel! Won't Bart ring you with whatever

the result is?"

"No. I told him not to ring me again. I want to know the result and then I want to think about it. You will tell me—not Bart. I hate snap reactions. Bye! Love you!"

CHAPTER THIRTY

The divorce hearing was set for the last Friday in May. It was Joanne's free weekend. She was driven out to the airport by one of Gil's security men on Thursday night. The girl was going to talk it over with her family whether she would return for a further month or two before college.

"You can do with her help, Stella, can't you?" Gil asked. "And you like her?"

"I am very fond of her and she is very good with Carlo. But actually, *having* her around leaves me with too much free time. As he is getting a little bigger and a little older, I want to start lessons with him..." Then she added hastily "...that is, if I am still here."

"Oh Stella—just for a second my poor old heart leaped as high as this building."

"Gil, you are never serious! Let us concentrate on tomorrow. Do I wear a suit or a dress—and be warned, it won't be glamorous stuff anyway."

"First of all, I am *very* serious—be clear about that. Yes, tomorrow? An outfit you had last summer always looked well. A kind of two-piece with a white silky shirt that came out over the lapels. Greenish kind of colour, wasn't it?"

"*That* thing!" Stella was very chuffed that he remembered something she had worn. "I always wore that on Sundays. You used drive me to Ambler Station on my day off. Imagine your remembering that!"

"I remember a lot!" He smiled so nicely she had to turn away.

"If you think it suitable, then I'll wear it."

"Bring a change for Carlo. It could be a long day."

Stella was apprehensive about Carlo. "It is necessary, is it, that Carlo be there? I should perhaps have asked Joanne to wait until next weekend. Would he be scared, I wonder?"

"Not nearly so scared as you may be, Stella dear. And yes, it is necessary. I will see to it, although I shall not be *in* court, that he is seated beside you."

"You won't *be* there?" Real fear started up inside her. She had, subconsciously, banked on glimpsing him in the court. There was comfort in the bulk of him, even when he was bossy and domineering.

"In the event that my counsel calls me, I assure you I will not be too far away."

"I thought you would be there all day to-morrow," she said forlornly. "I wish to-morrow were over."

When they said goodnight, they wished each other a good sleep. Stella never felt more wide awake. She delayed in the bathroom. She delayed looking for a book to read. She delayed at the dressing-table, brushing her hair. She delayed the task of examining the suit and the silk blouse. She sat on the side of her bed for a long time before trying to settle down to sleep. At last, she gave up. She walked out to the patio and stood looking down at the never-sleeping city. Through the tangled foliage she noticed a light in the apartment below. Gil was either working or reading. Perhaps he could not sleep either. Again she began the delaying tactics: walking to the phone and out again to see if his light was still on. Back again to the phone, out again to the patio.

When she dialled, she did not know what to say beyond "Gil, it's Stella." His response was immediate, "You are frightened? Afraid of to-morrow? You want to talk some more?"

"Please," Stella said in a small voice, not at all sure what she wanted. I should say no to myself. What were those words about self-indulgence? The words I was going to use as a staff?

Gil had his own key for the penthouse apartment. Within minutes he was in the bedroom. He too was ready for bed, in pyjamas and robe. She was still sitting on the side of her bed, holding the phone, talking sense to herself. Then she was in his arms. She feared that the words he might say could very well lead to self-indulgence. That was not what Stella thought she was longing for. She was limp and silent in his embrace, embarrassed at having called him.

"You are terrified of something, Stella. Can you put it into words? Is it the court appearance?"

"That too," she said.

"Seeing Velva—your potential murderer?"

"And that." Stella sighed an enormous heartfelt sigh.

"Losing Carlo if Velva wins? Talk it out. Put words on it."

"Everything about this divorce court and everyone in it, all alien and scaring. This America is not for me. And Gil, the urgency of you and of the way you make me feel in return—that is not really me. What I want from life is so much simpler. I am not me when I am thrusting, pagan-like, at things to which I have no claim. I shy away. I take refuge in thoughts and inward comments that are so ordinary, so banal, you would never comprehend. I think I look sophisticated enough, grown old enough, to be self-sufficient but I am not."

He held her tenderly. "I know. I know. I have often read your thoughts. Years and years of the law have not left me much cloak for others' thoughts. They come across in the glance and the half-glance. Your thoughts have often scoffed at me."

"Is scoff the word?" she asked, half wondering.

"I am afraid so. Your inward castigating of what I see as my sincere hopes and aims has been hard to take."

"Oh Gil, I never meant to hurt you! It is myself I have to curb. On myself I have to put strictures of pride. Because I want to give so much, I am fearful of being used."

He turned her face towards him. "You want me to say I love you. You want it in words?"

She hid her face against his shoulder. She whispered because she was unsure. It was all a gamble. She would not be the one to throw the last dice and perhaps be refused.

"Stella, we are in the same boat. Neither have *you* said you love *me*. Look at you! You could have any man. There is beauty in your every movement. And more than that, you are infinitely appealing. You never said you loved me. Not in Augusta when we both let passion rip as if we were young again. And not here when we are alone for several hours each night. Not even a chaste goodnight kiss."

Now Stella did not hide her face. She was wide eyed with a bewildering question. "In my tradition, it is the man who speaks of love."

"The Irish way, is it. I know nothing of Irish courtship. Is it the men or the women who are called the indomitable Irishry? Do they do as we did in the Garden of Allah before, or after, the man uses the word 'love'? That night was all-revealing, Stella. That night I waited for the word love in return for the pleasure I gave. But I wouldn't call it my tradition. I wouldn't call it the American way. It was us. Uniquely us. And I waited because you are the giver. I am nothing a woman like you would want. Since you were nearly murdered, since you were reduced to a state near to death, defending with your life *my* child, I have waited for the word 'love' because that *was* love, that bloody fight with Velva. I am only second in the queue. Carlo comes first. I must go on waiting."

My God, Stella thought, no wonder he is a great lawyer! He could argue the birds out of the bushes! I would never be a match for him. He twists me around his little finger.

"All the same," she said, "it would make me proud to hear you say it. Are you afraid I will sprout wings and fly off across the patio?"

"Back to Ireland, for ever and ever. Amen," he added.

She slipped out of his arms and moved fully into the big double bed. "I like this bed very much," she said. "It is the most beautiful bed I have ever seen. And so comfortable! Like to try it?"

He lay down beside her. "I have never slept here,"

he said very gently, "but I and my two brothers were conceived in this bed. It came with us from Elfreth's Alley. If I were to say to you, Stella, that I would give my life to conceive a child with you to-night in this bed, would you believe I love you?"

She came very close to him and whispered, "Even though we cannot do exactly that, if I said, shall we go through the motions, would you believe I love you?"

"We love each other, my dearest. I know for me, it happened at the airport in Philly. You were standing by two suitcases, innocently and nervously—a woman thrown on the world's mercy. Someone had warned you to clutch your handbag and not to talk to strangers. I looked at you; so appealing were you that you gave me back my earliest and indeed my only love. You have become my beloved nostalgia."

"I have been jealous of Rosie Farrell, Gil. But she was not your only love. You told me you loved dearly your lost wife."

"I also told you that she died of inoperable cancer. That is true but she was not married to me when she died. She had divorced me for another man. Strangely I did not mourn the divorce—pride, I suppose—but I mourned her death. That stupid divorce was all so useless—it killed her. I loved her but I was intimidated by her. Her health was desperately poor and her pain, to me, was aggressive. I loved her but not, I came to know, with the dependent love I would offer a wife. I did not want a wife who was a competitor, brainy and often brainier than I. That part of her was unattractive to me in a wife, although it was the attraction in our legal life. I wanted a wife with whom I could be at rest."

"Poor Gil!" The murmur seemed to satisfy him. He rested, as Carlo often did, against her warmth. They drifted off to sleep. Perhaps they dreamed. Some time in the night, they went drowsily under the duvet, not letting go of each others' hands, one of them stretching a free hand to put out the light and settling back to rest again.

At daybreak Stella woke. Carlo was often awake with first light. He always called out to her from his room when he heard Stella's radio-alarm. This morning there was no sound from him. The comfortable weight of Gil's big body beside her was thoroughly satisfying. She eased around to look at him. He was awake.

"Hello!" he said softly.

"We slept!" she told him and he smiled.

"I am awake for one minute and you have just woken up. I like that!" Stella liked that, too.

"I hope you remember," he said, "that you invited me last night?"

Stella touched his face with her free hand; the other hand was still in his clasp. "Shall I say the offer still holds good?"

"And shall I say that I appreciate the offer? And that the offer is declined? Last night, when you invited me to try the comfort of this bed, you inflicted a very hard decision on me. You will never know how hard it was to refuse—maybe the hardest thing I ever did."

Stella had trust enough now to know that he was not playing on her emotions. He had reasons and in his lawyer-like way he would reveal them. She smiled very lovingly at him. "I await your honour's worship! The court game, so?"

"To-day will be your day of decision," he said; "to quote an old friend, your day of 'To be or not to be.' The decision on *my* future rests in your hands. And perhaps your decision rests on the result in the court. I could be wrong but I am not going to influence you by accepting your offer of the next half-hour."

I would have liked it though, Stella thought. I may never get the chance again. Afterwards I could do penance.

"Moreover," and this was the Gil Nathan Esquire voice, "the quick snatch before breakfast would never be my way."

Stella gazed up at the ceiling. The snatch before breakfast? The seagull in flight?

"Love-making in my book begins in the late afternoon," he described it for her. "A lazy processing passage of time. Perhaps a visit to a jeweller, certainly a giving of pleasure. Flowers must be involved—roses are best—or freesias in quantity. Wine—bourbon too—a leisurely dinner somewhere exotic. A stoking of desire. A woman should take her turn at seduction— a very occasional turn but essential. A man needs seduction, just as a woman needs words of love."

He released her hand. He threw back the cover. He was out of the bed and on his feet. "Before I give myself ideas, I am going to get ready for today. I will ring you, Stella, before I leave for the office."

Four young attorneys from Gil's office escorted Stella and Carlo into the divorce court. She had never before been in a court anywhere. She had expected something overpoweringly magnificent, a legal *palladio*. She looked for tiered benches of judges in sumptuous red attire. There was none of that. The divorce court was plain and moderately large, three-quarters full of people, noisy with cameras and reporters. Stella and Carlo were seated in a second row from the front, behind their lawyers who were in their turn behind an enormous table on which they piled their books and papers.

After a while, Bart came in and took the seat behind Stella. Carlo, although ready to smile at everyone, had no particular recognition for Bart. He had not seen the piano-playing friend from Larch Hill, or the man met briefly in the pool at Boca Raton, for long enough to remember him.

Then Velva and her mother and their lawyers seated themselves on the other side, level with Stella, perhaps twenty-five feet away. Velva looked much better than when Stella had seen her in Boca Raton. Perhaps her mother's beauty van had given her the treatment. She was in full make-up; long lashes, hair flicked red, carmined lips and cheeks. She was very slight and gave an impression of such precious fragility that Stella's heart almost turned over with pity and caused her to think that she herself must look like Bessie Buttermilk compared with Velva.

Mrs Fanna Rosen, in russet colours, looked (if it were possible) more stupendously beautiful than before—and younger. The handsome, blond man in his middle forties who joined them would be Fanna's son from Georgia, whom Stella remembered coming overnight to Larch Hill with equally handsome friends.

Now everyone stood up. The judge took his place in a high-canopied chair on a raised dais. He knocked on his table for quiet. There were a few minutes of silence. Then the low conversation and the shuffling of feet and the rustling of papers began again. There appeared to be about twenty lawyers, or solicitors, or legal clerks—both men and women—who went with their sheaves of papers up to the judge's desk and back to their places. Up again and back again. Conferring together and apart, with the Judge. Stella glanced sideways at Bart. He had closed his eyes. He may have dropped off to sleep, Stella thought. Carlo was all liveliness at first but he was penned in and that was never easy for him. Stella was sure that quite suddenly, in a clear voice, he would call out "Mum Mum toyla fleas!" To her surprise, he did something he had not done for many weeks, he climbed onto her lap and went fast asleep.

What happens now, Stella wondered, if I am called to the witness stand? Could I hand him to Bart? Will Velva rush over and grab him from me? Acute anxiety manifested itself as a dryness in her throat.

They had come to the court at ten am. It was almost one o'clock when an adjournment was called. O heavens! Stella thought, it has not even begun yet! The young lawyers who had brought her in, now brought her out. Carlo was heavy but she carried him. On the corridor, Gil was waiting. "These men will bring you and Carlo home now. You will not be required until Monday morning. I am sorry, Mrs Shane, but that is how it goes."

Gil could be so cold in the public eye! He had not

thought of giving her a clue as to how the case was progressing, if indeed any progress at all had been made, which seemed unlikely from what Stella could observe.

When Gil came to visit late that night, she asked him to explain why all the lawyers walked up and down to the judge all day—or the half of the day that she was there. He told her:

"That was his submission of evidence. In divorce cases, each side gets to assess the strength of the other side. The judge has before him copies of every file from which the attorneys will work. He has the documentation. Your testimony is part of that. Also all of the medical certificates pertaining to your injuries. The police case of the arrival of Ambert's car down the cliff with Velva tied up inside. The gun. Your complete collapse on the road. Carlo's state of near-catalepsy from fright and fear."

"You never used that word about Carlo before now!" Stella remembered vividly the nightmare of the endless corridor; the bundle with two eyes, dwindling ever further away. She must have had a split second of consciousness when they brought Carlo to the hospital as she was being wheeled in. She would like to ask, to find out but there was no point. She could see Gil was upset to remember. His voice was full of grief.

"We would have lost Carlo, I am sure of it but for Hazel. When she and Bart got to us, she gave herself over to Carlo, to bringing him around. It was her face, her lovely face. She is so like you, Stella. Her voice is the same as yours."

"I meant to mention that Hazel was on the phone. She said you were offering a further settlement?"

"Bart told her. I did offer. It was refused. They are going to fight to the end for Carlo."

And his millions, Stella thought sadly. Poor little chap to be the victim of his mother's and grandmother's greed.

"The rumour has got around," Gil said, "that Rosen is fighting alimony. He is not meeting her pre-divorce demands. By the time the Rosen divorce gets to court, the drugs case will be out in the open and Fanna may be in jail. I gather there are no wealthy suitors waiting her pleasure in the wings—her first time ever to draw a blank."

"You fancied her yourself at one time?"

"Did I admit that?" He laughed. "Yes, I did. I was about twenty. In Harvard. She came there to visit the girl I afterwards married—they were friends from the South—I think I told you that?"

"Fanna Rosen is the most beautiful woman I have ever seen," Stella said very solemnly.

"Well," he smiled at her, "Fanna Rosen would

never compare for beauty with a woman I have seen! As well as which, Fanna has all the natural proclivities of a killer shark!"

The phone rang. "That could be Hazel," Stella said. "Will you please speak to her since I really haven't a clue?"

She heard his voice talking to Hazel.

She liked the sound of his voice, deeply friendly, yet measured. She watched his brown hands, one on the phone, the other holding the flex. She studied the half-moons at the base of each perfect curved nail.

"You heard me telling her I was hopeful?" he said. "She sends her love to you. She will ring on Monday. No news until then."

Stella forbore to ask to which exact question of Hazel's he was hopeful of the outcome.

"I wonder why it is so important to her? Hazel has always lived her own life, telling very little to anyone."

"Perhaps," Gil said with the old note of mischief in his voice, "perhaps she thinks you will be on the next plane home?"

"Hardly the next!" Stella teased and watched him smile.

"I thought last night was the last night of my probation. Here is yet another. Walk me to the door, Stella. I have a whole week-end to endure. To-morrow

I must work. Do you think we three could drive out on Sunday?"

At the door they stood, each knowing the other's reluctance to part.

"You know, it is a strange thing," he told her, "but ever since you have come into my life, I seem to come on things that are Irish, sometimes a legal point, sometimes a literary reference. The other day, in my favourite book shop I picked up a very old book, some poetry by Jonathan Swift and a verse caught my eye. I bought the book and I have memorised the verse—for you."

"Tell me, Gil. I adore Jonathan Swift's strange life story. I have been in his cathedral many times. Tell me."

Gil took her hands and held them.

"Thou Stella wert no longer young
When first for thee my harp was strung...
In all the habitudes of life
The friend, the mistress, and the wife...
Variety we still pursue
In pleasure seek for something new...
But his pursuits are at an end
Whom Stella chooses for a friend."

Stella was deeply moved. She lifted her face for his

kiss.

"Am I your friend, Stella?" His kiss was tender, his look was very fond as he closed the door.

CHAPTER THIRTY-ONE

Saturday was a very long day. Gil rang very briefly around midday to say that, quite unexpectedly, there were people to be interviewed. He was working at home with the attorneys and a couple of secretaries. He would try to ring later to keep her informed. Stella judged, by the icicles in his voice, that there were other people near his phone. If he wanted to talk privately, he would have gone to his bedroom phone. He did not do that because he did not want to say too much to her. By giving her the icicle voice he was, in fact, making a public announcement that something had come up. Stella hoped she had good reason to analyse the situation this way. She hoped she was beginning to understand his character.

Devoting herself to Carlo was always the best way to make time pass quickly. He was very entertaining and very enterprising. In a gobbledegook language, of which he was sure Mum Mum understood every word, he explained all the workings of his toys. Gil had given him a toy tape-recorder and half a dozen tapes for his birthday. He knew exactly how to put the tapes in and now he knew all the music to sing along. "Old MacDonald had a Farm"; "Yankee Doodle Dandy"; "East Side, West Side" were his three special tapes and he recognised the names on each. He had a favourite among the little stories Stella told him: "The Three Pigs." She named them Alfie, Bertie and Charlie. He watched her mouth for every word, forming with his lips the sounds she made. He could almost say: "He huffed and he puffed, he huffed and he puffed..." and Stella would finish for him: "till he blew the house down"—when he would clap triumphantly. Sometimes when he was listening to her storytelling, he would gradually curl up on the big chair and fall fast asleep for a couple of hours. She used to try lifting him into his cot when that happened but he always woke up if she did this and having missed his cat-nap, he could be quite cross. Being cross never lasted long, he was easily distracted. Now, if he fell asleep, she let him be in the chair, covering him with a shawl. She read then whatever her current book was. There were so many books in the apartment, she had endless choice.

This long day, when Carlo fell asleep, Stella did not take up her book. She sat very still, dreaming of home and the long-ago days when her children were little, like Carlo now. Philip was always obedient and careful and possessive of his toys. Ross was a rapscallion, up to every mischief, climbing trees and falling out of them, falling into the lake and nearly being drowned. Sybil? A strange little girl, condescending and aloof to everyone but Dave. There was no doubt she adored her daddy. Little Hazel, who was plain enough when she was three or four and blossomed into a beauty when she was fifteen, managed somehow to be happy and contented when no one took much notice of her. Although Alec did. Alec always made a fuss of little Hazel. Stella wondered why she did not observe more in those days. She realised now that she had just taken each day as it came, expecting no more and no less than what was offered. And what am I doing now, Stella wondered. Trying to measure up to Gil Nathan. He'll discover how ordinary I am and not for all the Carlos in the world will he…will he what? But he said we love each other! He said we are in the same boat. Face up to the big question, you dolt of a Stella! If Velva and Mrs Rosen win Carlo, what use are you to Gil Nathan? Carlo is his son and that is the important thing to him. The only important fact in his life. And if he wins Carlo, do you then automatically go back to the role of Nanny—what you came to this America for, anyway. Nanny—nothing more. You, Stella, despite his blandishments and your craven submission to them, you are still full of distrust.

Stella's pride rebelled. She had said a year. One year—and that year was about over. Give up her home and her beloved country for strangers? No. Never.

Carlo stirred in his sleep and murmured her name, Mum Mum Mum Mum. He was a beautiful child—a model for a great oil-painting. His shining curls were pressed against the velvet cushion, his long dark lashes fanlike on his flushed cheeks, his stubborn chin softened and relaxed. His little hands were going to be exactly like Gil's hands; now they were spread open as if pleading. Stella knelt down and gazed closely at him. Trapped, she thought. Trapped until he is grown beyond needing me. Even if Velva wins him, I can see myself begging to go with him, to take care of him. Stupid Stella, persuading yourself that you are the only one in the world for Carlo.

Carlo was always ready for bed about seven-thirty. He loved his splash in the bath and having been towelled dry to run around his bedroom before the sleeping suit was zipped on. Stella sat and watched him, a naked little boy in perfect proportion. His skin all over was the pale coffee colour of Gil's skin and his hands the same brown. Every night she remembered the night prayers of her own children when they were very little:

Now I lay me down to sleep,
I beg of God my soul to keep.
And if I die before I wake
I beg of God my soul to take.

A bit scary come to think of it, thought Stella. She
did not say prayers for Carlo to learn because she had
no idea what form of religion, if any, would be chosen
for him. She herself had not been to Mass since her
last free Sunday in Philadelphia. Security was a queer
thing in this America! Neither had she been in a
supermarket. The phone supplied everything and the
security men brought the orders to the apartment.
She wondered would she rather be poor—and free to
come and go? She would think about that some other
time.

For Carlo, about to sleep, she always said the same
little speech, counting his fingers: this little fellow
went to market; this little fellow stayed at home; this
little fellow got bread and jam; and this little fellow
got none; and this little fellow said: "Who loves ya,
baby?" And sleepily he always murmured, "Mum
Mum Mum," as the eyelashes flickered shut.

At ten o'clock, the phone rang. Stella rushed across
the room. It was Joanne.

"Is that you, Stella?"

"Oh, it is you, Joanne. Yes, Stella here."

"Just for a minute your voice sounded different—like breathless. Are you okay?"

"Fine; and how are you, Joanne?"

"I'm great. How is Carlo? Does he miss me?"

"Of course he does! I am sure he does! Are you coming up on Sunday night?"

"Well, that's the thing I'm ringing about. Stella, my Mother could use my help here in the motel in July and August but I could come back for June—if that would suit you?"

"Of course, Joanne. Whatever you decide. Will we see you Sunday night, then?"

"Well, that's the other thing, Stella. Would it be okay if I came up on Tuesday night? It's my Mum and Dad's twenty-fifth wedding anniversary on Monday and there's a family celebration."

"Joanne, how lovely! Come on Wednesday night. That will give you time to recover! And having you here for June will be just fine!"

"Thank you, Stella. Will you give Carlo a hug and a kiss for me? *I* miss *him* all the time. And Stella, could I say how great it has been to get to know you. You are a terrific human being."

"May I return the compliment Joanne—and thank you."

"Bye, Stella! Have a nice night!"

Now Stella smiled to herself. I hope so, Joanne. A

nice night would be just what I need.

She walked around the apartment, touched things here and there, admired the flowers, re-aligned some books. She walked in and out of the bedroom, willing the phone to ring. She looked at her face in the mirror but briefly. Stella had no great concept of her own looks. Another glance would not take ten years off the face. She was much too old, far too old, nearly decrepit, to have notions of falling in love. For heaven's sake, she told herself, stop fantasising. But he said we love each other. He said, "We love each other, darling." I didn't imagine it. He did say it. Why doesn't he ring? At my age, you would think I would have a bit of sense. Or indeed, Stella, you would think you would be faithful to Dave's memory. Widows used to have statutory periods of mourning—years! In some countries, she chided herself, widows wear black for the rest of their lives. You really should feel some shame instead of taking out your night-dresses to see which could possibly be reckoned seductive. What's the matter with you—perfume at this hour of the night! "We love each other, dearest." He must have meant it.

At eleven twenty, Gil phoned. She knew at once that he was very tired but it was not his way to begin with himself. "How was to-day, Stella? Are you all right? Did you and Carlo enjoy the sun on the patio?

I looked from the window a few times and I saw the colours of your clothes through the leaves—you were wearing blue?"

"You are very tired, Gil—even your voice."

"Jacked, my darling—but not down and out."

"Hopeful?"

"Guardedly. I will ring in the morning around about eleven. I want you and Carlo to come down here at one. After that, we may be in the clear."

"When you ring in the morning, you will tell me a little more, Gil?"

"Yes," he said. "Sleep well, Stella."

"I'll try," she answered. "You too. Goodnight."

"Goodnight, sweetheart."

She hugged the precious word, folding her arms across her bosom and saying the word like a child who believes in magic: sweetheart sweetheart sweetheart until she fell asleep.

Promptly at eleven, Gil was on the phone. "Did you sleep, Stella?"

"After a while, I managed to get off. Did you?"

"Like the proverbial log! I am having breakfast now—coffee and a bagel. The overnight security man gets these bagels fresh every morning from some bakery nearby. They are good."

"And you sound a lot better!"

"I have a couple of people for you to meet, Stella.

I am expecting my colleagues shortly—and I hope not to keep them too long. If you and Carlo, of course, come down here at one, we should be able to wrap everything up by two. Would you like the three of us to go somewhere nice to eat? Out to the coast or out Valley Forge way—do you remember the Place? I know an antique shop in the King of Prussia—you might see something you would fancy?"

"Wherever you decide," she said, betraying her delight in the gladness of her voice. If she were to take this phone message the way she wanted to take it, he was indicating that love-making began in a leisurely afternoon. She reminded herself, in a rapid descent to solid earth, that very probably this interview at one o'clock was the final deciding factor. The King of Prussia? She supposed it was a shopping mall but somehow, the name added to the romance. I am in it now up to the neck, Stella thought— romance if you wouldn't be minding! I sound like Rosie Farrell must have sounded!

She and Carlo stepped into the elevator and rode the one floor down to Gil's apartment. The two security men were on the landing and one opened the door into Gil's vestibule. She knew the two men very well now because they were the same two who brought delivered goods to the penthouse. Gil had requested that she not get on name terms with them—

and that applied to Carlo also. A nod and a smile could be exchanged, no more. Stella obeyed this injunction. It was a little difficult to stem Carlo's outgoing friendliness. Luckily, he was still small enough to follow her example in most things. Later on, she hoped he would model his manners on Gil, whom he now called Lunka Gil.

To Stella's amazement, the first person she saw in the crowded room was the big woman from Boca Raton who ran the parenting classes. Near her was the benignly smiling elderly man whom Stella remembered from the couple of occasions they had attended the transcendental meditation classes. Carlo took one look at the big lady and dived for cover into Stella's long full skirt. There was no doubt in anyone's mind but that Carlo saw an unpleasant association here. Holding the little boy securely with one hand, Stella offered the other hand to the lady and then to the elderly man.

Gil was wearing his heavy tinted glasses so it was difficult to guess at his expression. With a wave of his hand, he made a perfunctory introduction. "You have all met Mrs Shane in court yesterday. You are all aware of why she is here. Once again, gentlemen, I will ask you to bear in mind that we are not going to court to try for attempted murder. Mrs Shane has not chosen to press that charge. You are going into a divorce court. Your client, Gilbart Nathan, is filing suit for divorce against his wife on the grounds of character deterioration and unfitness to be the mother of his child. You are all clear that I do not want excessive vilification, or defamation, of Mrs Velva Nathan's character. You are clear on that?"

There was a general nodding of heads. Then one young man raised a pen in hand tentatively. "Sir?"

"Yes, Mr Prestly?"

"Wouldn't the proof we have of attempted murder be enough to prove a woman is not a fit wife?"

"Not at all, Mr Prestly. We would have been through such a case in a different court if we were bent on introducing it in divorce."

He looked around and continued: "I said no excessive vilification. On Monday, Mrs Velva Nathan will be cross-examined on the attempts she made to improve her character, namely she joined a parenting class: *How to be a Good Parent*. Any judge will be impressed with that. I have brought Mrs Leverson from Florida to make her own honest comments on Mrs Velva Nathan's interest in those classes. You have heard what she has to say. You will make your rebuttals against Mrs Velva Nathan's good intentions very succinct. Remember—even in the simple matter of changing her child's diaper, she left that to Mrs Shane. She never held her child. She never took part in the shared experiences of the other mothers. She smoked her cigarettes, although each time she was asked not to smoke. Mrs Leverson has told you that it was her opinion the child gave his total affection to his nanny, whom he called Mum Mum. The Filipino woman who worked in the house, who does not know Mrs Leverson, formed the same opinions as Mrs Leverson. I mention that although you may not call her, although she is a very intelligent woman. Mrs Leverson is an acknowledged expert on the subject of parenting. She is also a very gifted observer of human behaviour. She has many books to her credit. She is an excellent person under questioning. Use her."

Under the pretext of attending to Carlo, Stella bent her head into his curls. Weird, she thought, Americans are weird. What I might have learned from this big lady if I had only paid attention!

"As to transcendental meditation and the beneficial effect it might have had on the character of Mrs Velva Nathan had she pursued the course for any length of time, she gave up after three sessions. If you ask her the mantra word which was chosen for her, she will not remember it. Mr Ingolls"—and here Gil bowed solemnly to the elderly man—"had the mantra recorded in his register. This is a simple trip-up question—remember our judge on Monday is a simple man, a man who believes in human goodness. Do not confuse him. But bear in mind he has a weakness for a pretty face. When he should be listening, he will be noting the batting eyelashes of the lady who is resisting divorce. Always remember, gentlemen, in the divorce court it is enough to prove a witness is lying. Any questions, gentlemen?"

This time Mr Prestly kept his hand down. Stella would have liked to ask, "Isn't it all a bit simple?" but she was learning. She could feel the sting of the whipping tongue on Mr Prestly.

"May I apologise for bringing you in on Sunday. Make your own arrangements about expenses. I would buy lunch in the Club but unfortunately I have a prior lunch engagement. Thank you, gentlemen."

Courteously, he escorted them to the door. "See you in court, Monday," they said to each other the way other people say "Goodbye." Gil was particularly charming to Mrs Leverson and Mr Ingolls. Maybe that was part of the act? Weird to think, Stella mused, that those two unlikely people were to sway the balance in a woman's life. One of the balances, anyway. Poor Velva was facing a sea of trouble.

CHAPTER THIRTY-TWO

C arlo was still snug on Stella's knee. He did not stir until Gil had closed the door.

"Toyla, Lunka Gil!"

When they came back from the bathroom, Stella said, "Would it be all right with you if he dropped that 'Lunka'?"

Gil held out his arms and without hesitation, she went into them. "Do you think," he asked tentatively, "that it would take long for you to teach him to say 'Daddy Gil'?"

"Are you as sure as that?" Stella asked in wonder.

Gil drew an envelope from his desk. "I have this. It came last night. An agreement to relinquish Carlo. The divorce is certain anyway."

"Are they giving up Carlo in return for all the money you offered them?"

"No, they blew that. Two offers. Two refusals. They are giving up Carlo in return for my undertaking to get them off the drugs charge—off the hook, so to speak."

"And can you do that?" This was power indeed.

"Oh, I think so," he said casually. "From the moment the drugs story broke, I have had them worked over. Not only can I get them off, small fry as they are, although they don't know that but I can haul in the big fish. I should have seen what was happening months ago but since Carlo's birth I have been obsessed by the fear of losing him to some damned kidnap gang and the Rosens fed my fear to obscure their own activities. They were genuinely afraid also but for different reasons. I was blind."

Stella walked over to the window from where she could see the penthouse foliage fence. I could never be part of this life, she thought. I seem to think of him the way a child thinks of the man in the moon, mysterious and unknown and millions of miles away. I am so amazed at Gil's life. Is he not afraid of so much power that he can know people are guilty of crime and yet fight to get them off the punishment?

She turned to Gil. "I would feel so much safer at home in Ireland...in my own garden in the grasslands of County Meath. Sometimes when I am lonely and fearful of this unknown America, a special place keeps coming into my mind, a particular spot up on the Navan Road. Beyond the Dublin hills, I see the Wicklow mountains. I know those mountains are a good way away but in Ireland no place is very far. Here I am always a lone figure in an enormous space.

Those mauvy, misty mountains of my mind's memory comfort my thoughts. They are gentle. There are no peaks of love or fear, no high-rises of hope and despair."

She fell silent, almost embarrassed by her long speech. She was looking again up at the penthouse foliage and telling herself she would go home as soon as possible. She could make plans now in this freer place. At least the phone was available.

Gil was standing behind her. "Thinking again, Stella? Taking refuge in your thoughts? Are you condemning me in those thoughts?" He turned her around to him. "Ah, now I see it in your face. I am a wrongdoer and you are going to run away?"

Carlo had found a colourful magazine and he was turning the pages the way Stella did: holding the corner up at an angle between thumb and forefinger. Tears came into her eyes. I love that child. God, what kind of a trap am I in? I want to go. I want to stay. No, be honest, you want to be persuaded to stay.

"Stella, you promised me today. Yes, you did. You said, 'Wherever you decide,' remember? I want us to go out to the Place for lunch. We will go by Germantown and stop at the King of Prussia. No, it is not an ordinary shopping mall, more like a German market square. All sorts of little shops, food and fashion and antiques. You would like it. Come on,

Stella, you can't refuse me. I have been working so hard for weeks—even all day yesterday, Saturday. No good lawyer should work on Saturday! Ah, you are smiling. I need to relax and you relax me. You promised. And Carlo would love it. And the sun is shining. Carlo has not been out since we came here to Philly. I have a car-seat for him in the trunk of my car."

She looked up at him. She remembered that look in his eyes. Tired, tender, emotional. Just for today, she thought and then I will make plans.

So they went in the big comfortable car. Vaguely Stella was aware of a security man. She had not got used to their perpetual presence but she no longer questioned the necessity.

In the King of Prussia, Gil insisted she walk around the antiques shop. "Take your time," he said. He took Carlo strolling along the line of stall-like shops. The open pride with which he displayed Carlo was a joy to watch.

"You haven't chosen anything, Stella," he accused, "and we are getting hungry, aren't we, Carlo?"

"Ess, Lunka Gil."

Gil asked for a tray of rings from the locked glass case. He hovered over the tray. He picked out a fabulous ring of diamonds and rubies. The price of it made Stella feel her knees go shaky. She pretended to be gazing at a picture of flowers.

"Stella," Gil's voice was very serious, "if this ring exactly fits your finger, I will regard it as a lucky omen. That old angel beyond the far horizon will be looking out for me again."

"Oh Gil, I couldn't...I couldn't...I..."

He slipped the ring on the third finger of her left hand. "See," he said calmly, "a perfect fit." He tilted her face with his finger-tips. "Does that deserve a kiss?" The kiss was wonderfully sweet. "That was one of my extra specials," he told her, smiling. Then he lifted up Carlo and they each kissed the little boy. In a stage whisper Gil said to Carlo, "You are now reduced to third party in protocol, so watch out for the correct pecking order." Gil held Carlo in his arms while he handed his card to the antique dealer.

"I am not good with children," he confessed as they got into the car. "I was having heart failure in case Carlo would knock over that Chinese urn-thing—probably Ming Dynasty, the fellow would claim!"

"And that would be another enormous sum of money," said Stella who could not take her eyes from her ring, so richly sparkling.

"The money is nothing," Gil said, "but breaking something five hundred years old would really hurt me."

The day was so beautifully warm that their lunch

was served outdoors, half-hidden in a small arbour. This was just right for Carlo who liked, at home, to take his plate out to the patio. He had a solemn concentrated way of eating, never slopping and considering each bite.

"I often meant to congratulate you, Stella, on the good manners you have given Carlo."

"As I told you, Gil," Stella smiled, "Carlo is his own creation. I wonder were you also?"

"May I mention Rosie Farrell and arouse your jealousy? It is immensely flattering to my ego that you should feel jealous. I am reminded of Rosie, not by anything you ever say to me but by your loving treatment of Carlo, your disavowal of any credit for him and quite often by the things I do myself. She used to say, 'You are a proper little bossy-boots, Master Gil!' So perhaps I too, was my own creation."

"There is one thing I should like to say, Gil—and it is about Carlo. At the moment he is not listening to us. Now you are his father all the way and now I am the one who looks after him, may I (in all humility) make one small rule?"

"Don't turn timid on me," Gil said. "I am with you all the time, a hundred per cent."

"Thank you. Just one thing; when the three of us are together, like now, not to talk of Carlo, not to comment on him, not to recount his funny sayings, anecdotes, incidents. We take all that as natural, for granted. When we three are in each others' company, we talk to him, to each other about anything else but never, never about him."

"We must never discuss him in front of him?"

"'Tis your honour has the gift of the short sentences," she smiled. "Myself the gift of the gab!"

They laughed together. "I'll keep the rule!" Gil promised, hand on heart. "But you will save all the stories of his uniqueness for my private ear."

On the way home, they were passing again the King of Prussia. "The flower shop is open," Gil said. "I'll pull in. To-day is the day for roses."

When they were back in Philadelphia, weaving through the streets to the Benjamin Franklin Parkway and around the fountain to the apartment block, Gil said, "I know where I would take you to-night if we had Joanne to baby-sit—the Four Seasons. The food is fairly decent there."

"I can cook," Stella said. "It won't take long."

"Not to-night. You give Carlo whatever he wants and get him off to bed. I will have dinner sent in—leave it to me."

Stella was amused at how quickly he had taken command. He just did not see himself as bossy but certainly as boss.

"I must shower and change," he said. "It has been

a long day. Are you tired?"

"What would make me tired?" smiled Stella. "You are the one who has worked and driven." She touched his arm in gratitude.

When he had delivered them into the penthouse and gone away, Stella sat in her favourite place and examined her ring. Never had she thought to own anything so extravagantly beautiful. She had not thanked him sufficiently. Would she be given the chance? She hoped so. Did this magnificent ring on her engagement finger mean what such a ring was meant to mean? Or was it a rich gift preparatory to Gil's love-making? No more than that?

And what more do I want, Stella questioned herself? Let me now think of home and the far-off hills to the south and to the north and the paths to the old castle through the woods. Let me think with fond remorse of Dave's grave at the end of my garden where I should go daily to pray like a proper mourning widow. How long since I prayed for you, Dave? Let me think of living near my family, of laughing aloud with Hazel who is always so light-hearted. Let me think of freedom. Free from the burdens of wealth, free from security men, free to go out and leave the door unlocked. But then, there was the other side. Let me remember how I was prepared to give up the car and be dependent on neighbours. Or being without electricity, lighting candles and boiling an old black kettle on twigs gathered in the woods. And living on coddle. I bet Rosie Farrell would know what coddle is. And managing to live alone in the dark nights coming up to Christmas. And growing old and older and older without the comfort of loving.

"Carlo!" she called to the little boy on the patio. "Carlo!"

He rushed in as he always did when she called, rushed straight into her arms and up on her lap. "Mum Mum?"

"Look at this beautiful ring, Carlo." She turned it slightly so the diamonds shot out blue-and-pink-and-green twinkles into the evening sunshine. "This is a magic ring, baby, a ring with magic powers."

Magic came into a lot of Stella's stories. Carlo settled back. "Stoly?"

"Long long ago," she told him, "there was a little boy like you. A little boy who was you, curly hair and brown eyes and brown hands—just like your hands. He had a Mum Mum who came to look after him, just like you have a Mum Mum and she came from a place called Ireland. You know that place; I have told you about it many times." Carlo nodded emphatically. "And this little boy loved his Mum Mum from that place very much, very much. Sadly, she went away and he never saw her again but he never forgot her. He stored up all his love for her for years and years—umpteen years which is an awful lot of years. And you know what? All the store of love turned into gold and diamonds and rubies. The love turned into a magic ring, a lovely, gorgeous ring of love. He waited and waited to give this magic ring of love to one special person. He wasn't a little boy any more but in a way he was. You often have to wait for a special person to give a special gift. You see, magic of this sort only happens once. You have to be sure, very sure."

Carlo touched the ring very carefully. "Wing a Lunka Gil?" He had not forgotten the shop in the King of Prussia.

"Yes, baby, he gave it to me. Do you think he gave it to the right person?"

The little boy snuggled closer. "Mo stoly?"

"I think," Stella said, "when you have had your bath, we will go back to Alfie, Bertie and Charlie."

"Puffin'! Huffin'! Puffin'!" Carlo chuckled.

Gil came at nine o'clock. He brought champagne. He looked like a man ready for a game of tennis: white trousers, white open-neck shirt. "Ah!" he said immediately, "you are wearing the poppy flower skirt and the black blouse! The night you pretended to be the elegant Lady Shane from Ireland!"

"So you are in the mood for mischief, are you?

Mocking the humble hired help!" Stella pirouetted on her high heels, swirling the skirt.

He smiled at her. "I hope you like champagne," he said, pouring it into glasses. "It makes me dizzy. I usually have to lie down."

"Immediately?" enquired Stella. "Or after dinner?"

"Which time would the plaintiff prefer?"

"The plaintiff may have to take counsel on this timing."

"The plaintiff must state reasons for need of counsel." And Gil knew he was giving her the smile from which she always turned away but she did not now.

"The plaintiff finds herself in two minds," she said.

"The defendant is shocked! Two minds quite obviously means, before *and* after!"

The court battle could not be resolved just then. The dinner, accompanied by one of the security men, arrived, and was wheeled in.

For a few minutes there was a fuss of transferring to the dining room where Stella had set the table. She had arranged some of the roses as a centre-piece and there were candles to be lit.

When they were alone and ready to eat, Stella said, "Would you like to go in and say goodnight to your son?" Gil's gratitude shone in his eyes. "Thank you, Stella. Thank you for everything. Is he still awake?"

"No," Stella smiled, "he fell asleep very quickly after such an exciting outing. He is exquisitely beautiful when he is asleep."

"Will you come with me?" Gil asked.

They stood beside the cot, looking down at the little boy. Stella whispered, "Now can you see the exact resemblance?"

Gil took her in his arms. "I owe so much to you, Stella. One by one, you make good for me all my mistakes. I love you, sweetheart."

Chalk it up, Stella, you had to wait a long time for that. "Shall I tell you something?" she asked.

"Tell me," he said.

"I think I am going to love you, too, Gil Nathan."

They laughed and talked all through dinner. Never afterwards could they recall what they had said or what they had eaten. Eventually Gil piled all the dishes back on the trolley and wheeled it out to the elevator. He rang through to the security men who would know what to do. Then they drank brandy and coffee sitting in the summerhouse on the patio.

"I am glad we are alone to-night," he said.

"Yes," Stella agreed, "it is good to be alone."

"Stella, is my probation over? Do you trust me?"

She wanted to say a lot of things but she put out her hand to him and said nothing. Let him make love to me to-night. To-morrow I'll do penance in sackcloth and ashes.

"I was so proud of you this morning when you walked into the apartment downstairs. You look so innocent always. I wanted to shout out: look at her! Look at her! I love this woman!"

He stood up and took her hand. They wandered through the rooms into the bedroom. The luxurious room full of lovely things was not remotely like the Garden of Allah, yet, entering the bedroom, Stella's body was calling out for the same experience she had then.

"Gil, I never knew what desire was before the Garden of Allah. Please hold me as you did that night."

"Take this gradually, Stella my darling. It has been a long time since that night. Let me caress you and talk to you for a little while."

He used his hands as only he knew how and as he used them, she could see them—his so shapely, so beautifully coloured hands, so curved his nails.

"I am not sure what I love most," she told him, "your hands or your smile."

"The very look of you turns my heart over," he said tenderly. "Your innocence is so apparent in your eyes that I want to be with you all the time to keep anyone from telling you this is a bad old world. You and Carlo fit together; the appeal is identical for me."

"Maybe," Stella murmured, "maybe, after all, it is your voice I love most."

"Good, because there are things I want to tell you before I start loving you."

"You have started," she whispered.

"Oh, no, my darling, the night has not begun yet. I want to tell you that since the first time I heard you singing Carlo to sleep in Larch Hill, I have thought of you as the mother of my child."

"It worries me a little bit," she answered softly and now her hands were learning from his hands, "that you should see me as the mother, while you are the real father and very quickly as Carlo gets older, he will know we are not—that we are a besotted old pair living together from year to year."

"Are you turning me down?" he asked in great affected incredulity, his eyebrows raised. "I took note of the time. I thought we were engaged to each other since 3.15 pm today. You are wearing my ring?" He ran one hand smoothly down the length of her back. "Are you not promised to me?"

She said, "You never asked me to marry you."

"Ah! I forgot! The Irish need words for everything!"

"Say it, Gil Nathan or I shall never forgive you." Gil was smiling down at her. "Only I have you here, you would turn away and think your thoughts, wouldn't you? Three weeks ago, I applied for a marriage licence in City Hall. I have it in my desk."

She lay back on the pillows and gazed at him. "You knew I was wanting you? You knew?"

The mischievous gleam was in his eyes. "Of course!"

"Oh my God, if you only knew the trauma and drama I have been going through!"

Gil sighed mightily. "If you only knew what a man on probation goes through trying not to even touch the hand of a woman he is ravenous for. In the beginning you were not fully recovered and that helped. The last four weeks have been endless. The night I lay beside you on this bed—almost afraid to breathe—well, I hope you never go through such torture! I slept a little but it was a very long night!"

Stella's heart stirred. She had never told him but there were long nights when she was afraid to fall asleep. There were haunted nights full of fear when the graveyard at the end of her garden at home could come as close as the climbing roses on the patio. There were nights full of loneliness when the ghostly apparition of Dave stared into her terrified eyes, pleading silently for fidelity. Death demanded undying fidelity. That was the Irish way. The desolate widow. She had promised Dave she would go back in a year, hadn't she? And visit his grave every day and get money for Masses to be said for the repose of his immortal soul.

Poor Dave! Poor lost love, the year is gone. Did you think I had forgotten? She drew away from Gil's embrace and her body shuddered with grief for her lack of purpose. In losing sight of the need for her prayers to rescue her husband's soul from Purgatory, was she lost to her own tradition, maybe lost to the salvation of her own soul? Tomorrow she would do penance. Tomorrow she would remember who she was. Sackcloth and ashes tomorrow. Tomorrow, Dave, tomorrow.

Gil drew her back to him, gently and very closely. He had magic powers and Stella loved magic. He was compelling time to stand still in a rejection of fear, in a total surrender to his loving. He was conjuring her fine resolutions into golden autumn leaves drifting on a faraway country road in Ireland. Her elusive thoughts were spiralling downward into the possessive tenderness of his murmuring voice: "Stella, Stella, Stella."